Things We Never Say

Sheila O'Flanagan
Things We Never Say

headline
review

First published in 2013
by HEADLINE REVIEW
An imprint of HEADLINE PUBLISHING GROUP

1

Cataloguing in Publication Data is
available from the British Library

ISBN 978 0 7553 7843 2 (Hardback)
ISBN 978 0 7553 7844 9 (Trade paperback)

Typeset in ITC Galliard by Palimpsest Book Production Limited,
Falkirk, Stirlingshire

Printed and bound in Great Britain by Clays Ltd, St Ives plc

Headline's policy is to use papers that are natural, renewable and
recyclable products and made from wood grown in sustainable
forests. The logging and manufacturing processes are expected
to conform to the environmental regulations of the country of origin.

HEADLINE PUBLISHING GROUP
An Hachette UK Company
338 Euston Road
London NW1 3BH

www.headline.co.uk
www.hachette.co.uk

Acknowledgements

A reader once said to me that it must be hard coming up with so many ideas for books. Truthfully, the ideas are easy, it's doing justice to them in the final book that's hard! The concept behind *Things We Never Say* has been rattling around in my head for a long time but eventually I felt I'd found the right characters to bring it to life. I hope I've done justice to their stories.

I was – as always – helped along the way by some wonderful people:

My agent, Carole Blake
My editor, Marion Donaldson
The fantastic team at Hachette/Headline in so many countries.
The publishers and translators around the world who work so hard on my behalf.

Even after all these books my family and friends are great cheer-leaders and supporters and I thank all of them, especially my mum, Patricia, for staying with me on the journey.

Big thank you to Colm for spotting the deliberate mistakes!

A special thanks to Paula Duffy for the legal help on Wills (I know now why I never became a lawyer!). Any errors in law are entirely my own.

Thanks to Alison Riordan for giving me the benefit of her knowledge and experience of medical emergencies.

Thanks also to the booksellers and librarians who have supported me for so long.

Most of all, thanks to all my readers, new and old, especially those of you who've got in touch with me through my website, Facebook or Twitter. It's always lovely to hear from you. I hope you enjoy this one!

PART 1

THE PAST

Chapter 1

Tipperary, Ireland: 55 years ago

Dilly was terrified but she was trying her hardest not to show it. She wanted to appear strong no matter how she felt inside. It was important not to give in. So she kept her eyes tightly closed, shutting out her surroundings and trying to imagine that she was somewhere else. In the meadow behind the farm, perhaps, with the smell of the newly mown hay on the breeze and the heat of the sun on her back. The meadow was a good place to be. But then, anything was better than here.

'Look at me when I'm talking to you.'

The words were icy cold and Dilly didn't have to open her eyes to see the face of the woman she'd secretly nicknamed Fury. It was already fixed in her mind. Long and narrow. Lips clamped into a thin, angry line. Eyes flinty grey behind steel-rimmed glasses which rested on a sharp nose. The nose was red with anger, the same anger that made the cheeks almost white. Dilly could count on one hand the number of times she'd seen that face not looking angry. And even then it never looked particularly happy. Dilly couldn't understand why. Surely the woman should be happy? She'd chosen her life, hadn't she? Unlike Dilly, who hadn't exactly chosen hers.

'I said look at me.'

This time Dilly allowed her eyes to open slowly. The face was

3

as she'd expected, although the mouth was even thinner than usual and the cheeks whiter than ever.

'Where did you think you were going?'

I was leaving, thought Dilly. Running away. It was a stupid idea, of course, because there was nowhere for her to run to. But even nowhere would be better than here. Wouldn't it? She didn't say the words out loud. Fury didn't really want her to speak. She knew that already.

'I do my best.' There was a despairing tone to the woman's voice. If anyone else had heard it, it would have seemed as though her patience had been tested to its very limits. As though she genuinely had tried and tried without success. As though Dilly had worn her down.

'Wouldn't you agree that I do my best?'

This time an answer was expected. Dilly tried, but although she formed the words, her mouth was too dry to speak.

'Cat got your tongue?'

Dilly said nothing.

'What am I going to do with you?' The voice was still despairing but there was an undercurrent of hardness. 'What will make you understand that there are rules and you have broken them?'

Dilly knew there were rules. Over the last few months her life had been framed by them. But they weren't her rules, and she didn't want to live by them. She wanted a different life altogether. She wanted freedom. To go wherever she chose. To be the person she'd dreamed of being. She wanted to walk outside the walls that surrounded the big granite building and to keep on walking until she reached the sea. Then she wanted to get on a boat. She didn't care where it was going. And after that – well, maybe she'd keep on moving. There was no reason for her to stay after all.

'Stand up.'

Dilly hadn't realised that she was on her knees. How strange, she thought, that I didn't know that. That I didn't realise she was towering over me because I was on the floor. My mind must be going.

'Quickly.'

But Dilly couldn't move quickly. She used the arm of the big chair to haul herself to her feet. Then she fumbled at the thread-bare band that held her golden hair back from her face, adjusting it so that there wasn't a single strand out of place.

'Still vain, I see.' Now the voice was scornful. 'A bit late for that, don't you think?'

That was a difficult question to answer. Dilly didn't think she was vain, but she was perfectly aware that she was beautiful. People said it to her all the time, although not in a way that was designed to make her feel good about it. Usually they were pointing out that looks like hers were bound to get her into trouble one day. There weren't that many golden-haired, blue-eyed girls in the Midlands. Certainly not many who had a slender body on top of endlessly long, elegant legs. Edel Mullins, her best friend, said that she was just like Marilyn Monroe. She was wrong about that; Dilly didn't have Marilyn's curves. But she did have a way of walking, and a way of peeping from beneath her hair, that was as sensual and voluptuous as anything Marilyn could manage. She wondered if Marilyn's looks ever got her into trouble. Because they'd been right about that.

'I'd like to say I'm disappointed in you, but then I didn't hold out great hopes from the start.'

Dilly maintained her silence.

'Being lenient with you was a mistake.'

Lenient? She nearly laughed out loud.

'You need to be taught a lesson.'

Dilly's eyes widened in alarm.

'Yes, you do.' The woman reached out and took her by the arm. 'It's time for you to find out once and for all that you're nobody special around here.'

'Please.' The word escaped from her involuntarily. She didn't want to plead. Pleading only made things worse.

5

'Too late for that.'

No. This time she didn't speak out loud but she thought it anyway as she realised that the older woman was unbuckling the thick leather belt around her waist. No.

The white cheeks were pink now. Flushed with anticipation. Dilly caught her breath as the faintest flicker of a smile touched the woman's lips.

'You bitch.' A spark of resistance suddenly flamed within Dilly as she found her voice properly. 'You spiteful, evil, dried-out old bitch.'

She heard the gasp as she turned and ran as fast as she could. But it wasn't fast enough. She was only halfway along the corridor when she felt the *thwack* of the belt across her shoulders and she fell to the ground.

Chapter 2

Dublin, Ireland: 10 years ago

It wasn't fair, thought Fred, as he stood beside the priest, the cool easterly wind tugging at the few remaining strands of his grey hair. It simply wasn't. After all the hard years he'd put in, all the tough times that had gone before, he'd thought that he and Ros had deserved to take it easy together. He'd made the money, after all, from the sale of the company, and he'd made plans for it. Plans for them. He'd spent a long time deciding on new places to go, new things to see.

In his seventy-one years he and Ros had only been abroad a handful of times, mostly to Spain or the Canary Islands because she liked lying on the beach and he liked cheap drink, and both of them enjoyed the buzz of the resorts where everyone spoke English and there was always a fry-up for breakfast. The holiday he'd been planning until recently was a round-the-world cruise. He'd reckoned it would be a way of experiencing new things without any risk. He didn't mind risk. But not the kind of risks you could run in foreign countries where you didn't know the customs or the language, and where you'd be clearly marked out as a tourist and therefore fair game to be ripped off.

Fred didn't like being ripped off. He'd based his whole life on being shrewd and careful. As a result, after more than forty years of building his business from a yard at their home in East Wall to a thriving enterprise with locations around the city, the offer to buy him out had finally come. Fred dealt in security systems – mainly car and household alarms – and the ambitious company that had taken over CallRite had paid a high price for his loyal customer base. Old enough for a pension, and with Ros's pleas for him to give up control in favour of their eldest son, Donald, ringing in his ears, Fred had finally decided to cash in and live the good life. He'd been anxious about retiring because despite Donald's belief in his own entrepreneurial skills, Fred didn't rate him that highly and he didn't want to see the company he'd built up sink beneath the weight of his son's lack of smarts. But the buyout meant that he didn't have to worry. Donald was carrying on the family tradition by remaining as sales director, while the new company's management would build on what Fred's hard graft had accomplished.

The first thing he did after his retirement was to buy a spacious split-level seventies-style home in a spectacular location at the summit of Howth Hill. Growing up, he'd seen split-level houses on American TV shows and they'd always seemed the height of glamour to him. He'd never dreamed that he'd be able to afford one in one of Dublin's most exclusive suburbs.

Stepping over the threshold of Furze Hill was a validation of everything he'd ever done. He knew that his children had been shocked by its purchase at his age. But Fred didn't care. He could afford it now and it was better late than never to have a crack at living the dream. Besides, being in your seventies wasn't old any more. And Ros was only sixty, with plenty of spring in her step. They were entitled to know that the home they now owned had a lounge which was bigger than the entire downstairs floor space of their East Wall house. Fred loved sitting in it and seeing (almost literally, because of its panoramic views) how far he'd come.

He took out a large white hanky and blew his nose. He could feel the eyes of his children turn towards him. They wouldn't think he was crying, of course, because they knew that Fred wasn't a man for crying, even at the funeral of his wife, when it was practically mandatory.

It was hard for Fred to believe that she'd gone. She'd always been a strong person. She'd been the one to keep things going in the bad times, when money was scarce, when Fred was struggling to find customers. She was the one who'd held it together for the children, making sure that when they went to school they had all the right books and the right uniforms, even though it had been a struggle. She was the one who'd put food on the table, kept the house warm, remembered birthdays and anniversaries. She'd picked him up when he was down, forgiven him when he'd strayed and comforted him when he'd had tests for chest pains a few years back which had scared the living daylights out of him.

And yet it was Ros who – at a time when she should have been enjoying life – was being buried that morning. Ros had been an almost daily Mass-goer, but Fred couldn't help thinking that whatever God she prayed to had pulled a damn sneaky trick in taking her before she'd ever had the opportunity to sit at the captain's table on the *Seascape Splendour* and know that she deserved to be there as much as anyone else.

The priest had finished praying and was looking at Fred. He hesitated for a moment, and then picked up a handful of dry clay to throw on to the coffin, which had been lowered into the open grave. He followed the clay with a red rose. He'd felt it was expected of him to have the flower, even though roses hadn't been his wife's favourites. But tulips were out of season, and besides, chucking one into the grave probably would've looked silly.

'Come on, Dad.' His daughter-in-law, Deirdre, took him by the arm and he winced. He never liked being called Dad by her. He wasn't her father. In fairness, he didn't know how he'd prefer her to address him, but Dad wasn't the right word. He hadn't been a particularly good father to his children, he knew, so it seemed wrong that someone else would want to use the title for him.

However, he said nothing to Deirdre and allowed her to lead him across the graveyard to the black Daimler that was waiting. A nice car, thought Fred professionally. Great suspension. Very smooth. He got inside. A few minutes later his two sons and his daughter got in beside them. Nobody said a word as the car pulled away out of the cemetery. They'd never been good at communication, and today, Fred knew, wasn't the day that things would suddenly change.

The mourners had been asked back to Donald and Deirdre's house in Clontarf, where she'd arranged to have soup and sandwiches waiting for them. Fred had been happy to allow her to organise the refreshments because he hadn't wanted anyone back at Furze Hill. Not without Ros. He sat on a chair in the corner and listened while people talked about his late wife and said how wonderful she'd been. They were right, of course. She had been wonderful, and Fred suddenly wished that he'd bothered to tell her when she was alive how much he'd appreciated her and loved her. She'd probably known anyway. He comforted himself with the thought. Ros had understood him. She'd married him for the man he was, not the man he should have been.

His three children were standing in a group. It was the first time they'd been together in almost ten years, because it was the first time Suzanne had been home in that long. Ros had blamed Fred for that, but he didn't blame himself. Suzanne had always been, and still was, difficult. The youngest of his three children, she'd caused far more trouble than Donald and Gareth. She was headstrong and opinionated, wouldn't listen to him, wouldn't live within the rules he laid down. Fred was a great believer in having rules and regulations, but Suzanne used to scoff at him as she broke them. Although in many ways she reminded him of himself, her stubbornness was a constant source of anger to him. He watched as she said something to Donald, who gestured dismissively. He wondered what they were talking about, what catching-up

10

they felt they had to do. Perhaps they were sharing stories about Ros. They'd all loved their mother, he was pretty sure about that. And equally sure that they'd loved her more than they loved him. She'd always been there for them. He hadn't.

There was a lot of emphasis put on 'being there' these days. But the truth was you couldn't be there every single time; sometimes you were too busy doing other things, important things, things that mattered. All this being there stuff was happy-clappy nonsense, Fred thought, not allowing his thoughts to travel that road. Lot of good his being there for them would have been if there hadn't been a roof over their heads

Suzanne glanced in his direction and for a moment the two of them looked at each other. He couldn't read her expression, but he was pretty sure there wasn't any forgiveness in it. He admired that in her. He admired the fact that she'd gone away, hadn't come back and still hated him. (Perhaps hate was too strong a word, but she certainly didn't love him.) If he was being strictly honest with himself, he was probably prouder of Suzanne than he was of the boys. She'd never compromised. Not for a single moment.

'I should probably talk to him.' Suzanne turned away from her father and back to her brothers.

'Be nice,' said Gareth. 'It was a shock for him.'

'And it wasn't for the rest of us?'

'You don't have to carry chips on both shoulders,' said Donald.

'It keeps me balanced.' Suzanne made a face and Donald laughed. It was the first time any of them had laughed since Ros's death.

'I've learned to live with mine,' said Gareth.

'You have chips?' Suzanne looked at him in surprise. 'What on earth about?'

'About how I was treated by him.'

'Huh?' As far as Suzanne remembered, the boys had got off far more lightly than her. Gareth surely had no reason to complain about how he'd been treated by Fred.

'He always thought I was gay, you know.'

'What?' She smiled as she looked around the room and saw Gareth's elegant French wife, Lisette, pregnant with their first child.

'Because I didn't like Gaelic football and pints of Guinness,' said Gareth. 'Because I chose to do a poncey degree – his term – instead of working with him. Because I read the broadsheets and not the tabloids.'

'Noah's Ark would've been way too socially inclusive for the likes of Dad,' remarked Suzanne.

'He does his best,' said Donald.

'So speaks the favourite,' Suzanne said.

'I'm not,' protested Donald.

'You did what he wanted and went into business with him. It would have been Fitzpatrick and Son if there'd been a family name on the company,' said Gareth.

'There were no other jobs at the time,' Donald pointed out.

'But you liked working for him, didn't you?' asked Suzanne.

'Are you mad?' Donald looked at her in disbelief. 'He was a total slave-driver. Always criticising me, always wanting things done differently.'

'Sounds familiar,' agreed Suzanne. 'But it must have worked out. Didn't the new crowd keep you on as a director?'

'Yes. But it's very different from the old days. It's all meetings and strategies and targets . . . the aul' fella is well out of it.'

'He did OK out of the sale, didn't he?' observed Suzanne. 'It made him richer than I'm sure he ever thought possible.'

'He blew a vast chunk on that bloody house.' Donald made a face. 'Such a waste.'

'He's entitled to spend it on himself if he wants,' said Gareth. 'It's not like any of us need his money.'

'How's Dad's own health?' Suzanne ignored the sudden look her brothers had exchanged.

'Do you care?' asked Donald.

Her tone was impatient. 'Of course I care.'

'He seems well enough.'

'All the same, without Mam, it's hard to know how long he'll keep going,' said Gareth.

'It is a mystery to me how well your father is.' Lisette, who'd joined them in time to hear Gareth's comment, made her own assessment of Fred's health. 'He eats all the wrong things, drinks too much and smokes.'

'I suppose we all need some vices.' Suzanne looked over at Fred, who was pouring a generous measure of Powers whiskey into a glass. 'Though he has more than his fair share.'

'He's not that bad,' said Donald.

Neither Suzanne nor Gareth responded, and Donald shrugged. 'He's getting on,' he said. 'You've got to make allowances.'

'Maybe.' Gareth didn't sound convinced.

'Hope he doesn't drink himself to death,' remarked Donald as Fred downed the whiskey in one gulp and poured himself another.

'You can't kill a bad thing,' Suzanne told him. 'Besides, he likes being a thorn in our sides.' She glanced towards Fred again, and her father, catching her look, raised his glass to her, a mocking expression on his face.

Suzanne turned away. She was glad she'd left. She was glad he didn't have power over her any more.

Chapter 3

San Francisco, California: 8 years ago

When the door to the art gallery in Geary Street opened, Abbey Andersen immediately switched her computer screen from the game of solitaire she was playing (and losing) to the generic one which carried the gallery's logo. But when she looked up and saw the person who'd walked in, her eyes widened in surprise.

'Pete,' she said. 'What on earth are you doing here?'

'Don't sound so pleased to see me.' Pete Caruso, a tall, balding man in his early fifties, walked past the paintings hanging on the walls without looking at them and sat on the edge of the enormous glass table that Abbey was using as a desk.

'You don't often drop by. And I'm *delighted* to see you,' she added hastily. 'As my father figure you're always welcome. But as a customer . . .' her eyes twinkled, 'you're way down the pecking order!'

'I am, am I?' Pete took a moment to study the art that he'd just ignored and then looked at her. 'Anything you recommend?'

'There's always this,' said Abbey as she stood up and reached behind her desk. She selected a framed painting which had been leaning against the wall. 'He's a new artist, going to be huge.'

Pete studied the painting. 'It's a blue dot on a pink background,' he said finally.

'Got it in one.'

'So why would I buy that?'

'Because you can look at it as a blue dot on a pink background,' said Abbey. 'Or you can interpret it as how one small thing can affect something much greater.'

'You're jerking my chain.' Pete scratched his head as he stared at the painting.

Abbey grinned. 'Slightly. But it's true that he's becoming more popular, and it's a good price.'

'How much?'

'A thousand dollars,' Abbey told him.

'That's a joke, right?'

'Not at all. And with the discount I can give you, it's yours for nine hundred.'

'I didn't come in here to buy a painting,' said Pete.

'But you will one day.'

'Maybe,' he said. 'Though not blue dots on pink backgrounds. You know me, honey, I like proper pictures.'

'Oh, Pete.' Abbey shook her head in mock despair. 'I'm doing my best to drag you into the twenty-first century, but you're not making it easy.'

'I know what I like,' said Pete stubbornly. 'Anyway, if I wanted abstract, I'd go for something with more bite. Speaking of bites,' he added. 'The real reason I dropped by was to ask you if you wanted to have lunch with me.'

Abbey looked disappointed. 'I'm sorry, Pete. I can't, I've got to work.'

'Isn't today your half-day?'

'It is,' said Abbey. 'From the gallery. But I'm due at the salon as soon as I finish up here.'

Pete frowned. 'I thought you were giving up that job.'

'And why would I do that?' asked Abbey. 'I like it and I make more money there than I ever could here. There aren't any tips at the gallery, you know.'

'Don't you get a nice bonus if you sell a painting?'

15

'Hmm. Theoretically. But I don't sell that many paintings. I'm only part-time, after all.'

'How much did you say that silly blue dot was?' Pete reached into his jacket and took his wallet out of his top pocket. He extracted an AmEx card and handed it to her.

Abbey smiled at him. 'That's sweet of you, Pete. But I can't let you buy a painting you don't want or like just so's I make some commission.'

'You were perfectly prepared to hard-sell it to me a few minutes ago,' protested Pete.

'That was when I thought you might buy it as an investment,' she said.

'Look at it as an investment in your future,' said Pete. 'And in my lunch.'

'A damn pricey lunch!' Abbey laughed. 'Honestly, I can't let you do this. And I can't bunk off no matter what. I have clients waiting for me at the salon. Why don't we meet later this evening?'

'I'm busy until around nine thirty. Is that too late for you?'

'Of course not,' said Abbey. 'We can grab a coffee.'

'Great.'

'Is there something wrong?' Abbey looked suddenly anxious. 'Some reason you want to see me?'

'I like chewing the fat with you,' said Pete. 'I always have.'

'You've got to give up that full-fat lifestyle,' she joked. 'Meet you at our usual.'

Pete nodded. 'See you later, honey.'

'See you later, Pete,' said Abbey.

She looked after him as he walked out the door. There was still an anxious expression in her eyes.

An hour later, she was at the much smaller table in the beauty salon where she worked three days a week. Unlike the gallery, which was edgy and modern, the salon on Valencia Street was warm and welcoming. Abbey always felt relaxed when she arrived there, and she enjoyed working with Charlene and Bella a lot more than she did with Nerissa, the manager of the gallery. She could have a laugh and a joke with the other two nail technicians, whereas with Nerissa she continually felt on her guard, as though the older woman was waiting for her to make a mistake. She knew that at twenty, she had a lot to learn. She wasn't stupid or overconfident. But she couldn't help thinking that the salon was a friendlier place to be, and she wondered if her heart was really in the world of art as she'd once believed.

'Hey, Abbey.' Charlene, five years older and the most experienced of them all, sat down in front of her and began to rearrange some of the bottles on the table.

'You leave my stuff alone, Mizz Taite,' said Abbey. 'I know you, you're trying to nick that bottle of Absolute Scarlet.'

'Totally not,' said Charlene. 'I've a bit of news for you.'

'Which is?' Abbey replaced the bottles of varnish in the order she preferred.

'I'm leaving.'

'What!' Abbey was surprised. She'd thought that Charlene enjoyed working at Mariposa as much as she did. The other girl had never said anything about wanting to leave.

'Tripp's got a job offer on the East Coast,' Charlene said. 'He asked me to go with him.'

'No way!' Abbey's expression was a mixture of delight and hesitation. 'You want to go? Well, sure you do. You're going!'

'It'll be fun,' said Charlene. 'Besides . . .' She extended her hand to show Abbey the small solitaire diamond on her engagement finger.

'Oh, wow!' exclaimed Abbey. 'You're properly engaged! That's wonderful. Congratulations.'

'Thank you,' said Charlene.

'Were you expecting this?' demanded Abbey. 'Did you plan it? Because you never said a word.'

'We talked,' admitted Charlene. 'But it was "one day in the

future" sort of talk. When he got the job offer, though, and wanted me to come, he said that he couldn't ask me to give up my job here without offering me something better. And then he produced the ring.'

'How cool.' Abbey sighed. 'He's such a romantic.'

'He is a bit,' agreed Charlene. 'And you know, even though I always wanted a circle of diamonds for my engagement ring, this is perfect.'

'It sure is,' said Abbey. 'I'm so happy for you.'

'I'm pretty damned happy myself,' agreed Charlene. 'Anyway, we're going for drinks tomorrow night to celebrate. You OK with that?'

'Sure am.'

'One other thing.' Charlene looked directly at her. 'This is an opportunity for you.'

'For me?'

'Nail work is one of the most popular things we do here. Right now, I'm the only full-time technician. Selina will want either you or Bella to take over. You're exceptional at this, Abbey. It should be you.'

Abbey glanced towards the table where Bella usually sat. She wasn't working this afternoon.

'Bella's as good as me,' she protested. 'Besides, nails are her full-time job. OK, she's only part-time here, but she works in that hotel salon too.'

'Thing is, she's not as good as you,' said Charlene. 'You've a talent for nails, Abbey. You know you do.'

'I'm not a nail person,' Abbey told her. 'I'm an art person. Admittedly the gallery can be a bit of a drag sometimes. But . . .'

'You say that all the time,' said Charlene. 'And you also say you prefer working here. So why not grab the chance?'

'Well, because . . .' Abbey looked thoughtful. Suddenly she didn't know what the *because* was. It wasn't the money. It wasn't the atmosphere. It wasn't that she didn't enjoy doing nails.

It's because Mom wouldn't approve, she thought suddenly. Nor would Pete. He's convinced that I'm destined for great things in the art world, and Mom believes that beauty is frivolous and silly.

'We'll see.' She smiled uncertainly at Charlene. 'Selina might prefer Bella.'

'You're the best,' said Charlene obstinately. 'And Selina always wants the best.'

'I must be the best,' said Abbey to Pete later that evening as they sat in their favourite coffee and doughnut place overlooking the bay. 'Because Selina offered me the job.'

She'd been surprised. She'd thought that Selina would turn the full-time post into a competition between her and Bella, a prize for them to fight over, but before the salon had closed for the evening, Selina had called her into her office and made her the offer. Abbey was glad that Charlene had given her a heads-up, because otherwise she would have been utterly speechless. As it was, she still told Selina that she needed to think it over. The salon owner's response was that she had forty-eight hours to make up her mind.

'You're not going to take it, though.' Pete wiped his sticky fingers on a napkin. 'You're not a nail woman.'

'Nail technician,' Abbey corrected him. 'And yes, I am.'

'Don't be ridiculous,' said Pete. 'You're an artist.'

'I studied art,' Abbey corrected him. 'Doesn't make me an artist. Not one little bit.'

'Abbey, sweetheart, you can't spend your day doing rich women's nails.'

'First of all, they're not rich women,' said Abbey. 'Everyone gets their nails done these days. It's big business and you should know that. Secondly, my appointment book is always full, so I can easily spend all day doing it.'

'That's not what I meant and you know it.' Pete's brow darkened. 'You're wasting your talent.'

'Oh, Pete, I wish I had the sort of talent you're talking about to waste,' said Abbey. 'I really do. But the truth is, I'm only a competent artist, and even if I was beyond brilliant, it doesn't guarantee I'd sell any paintings. You see way better people than me struggling.'

'You've got to have belief,' said Pete. 'What have I always told you?'

'I do have belief,' Abbey insisted. 'But I'm also realistic. Someone in my family has to be.'

Pete's expression softened as he looked at her.

'I'm sorry,' she said. 'I wasn't trying to get at you. You're one of the most realistic people I know. One of the best, too.'

'And I want the best for you,' said Pete.

'I know you do,' Abbey said. 'You've always only wanted the best. For me and for Mom too, even though we don't deserve you.'

'Hey, don't try to make me into the good guy,' Pete warned her. 'I'm not that great.'

'You are to me.' Abbey's voice wobbled. 'You've been . . . I couldn't ask for a more supportive person in my corner. And the thing is, you don't have to be. There's nothing keeping us together. No reason for you to care.'

'Now you're being silly,' said Pete. 'There's every reason for me to care. I've known you for the best part of seven years. I've watched you turn from a scrawny kid into a stunning woman . . .'

'Enough already.' She held up her hands. 'Stunning is pushing it.'

'You *are* stunning,' protested Pete.

'I work in a beauty salon, I know all about stunning,' said Abbey. 'The best we can say about me is that I deal well with what I've got.'

'You don't need to ramp it up like some girls,' said Pete. 'Bottom line is that you're both smart and pretty and you can do a lot with your life.'

'But what if I don't want to? What if all I want is to be happy?'

'There's more to life than being happy,' said Pete.

'So speaks a man whose life is his career,' teased Abbey. 'Seriously, Pete – isn't it all about happiness? Isn't that what I should have learned from Mom?'

'I don't think happiness is her motivating force either,' said Pete.

'That's probably true,' Abbey agreed. 'Thing is, I spend lots of my time hoping that she's happy with the choices she's made. Which I guess is silly of me.'

'We all want our nearest and dearest to be happy,' said Pete. 'And the constitution affirms our inalienable right to pursue it. It just seems to me that happiness is a by-product of other things. Of achievement mainly.'

'You're becoming quite the philosopher,' said Abbey. 'Why am I surrounded by people who look for the meaning of life when all I care about is making the rent?'

Pete smiled. 'You care about a lot more than that.'

'Hmm,' said Abbey. 'You'd be surprised. Anyway, whether we're happy or not, the important thing is that we're getting there. Which I think I will with this whole nail business.'

'If that's what you want, you've got to go for it,' said Pete.

'I've two days to make a decision,' Abbey said. 'I won't rush into it. Then if it all goes pear-shaped, I can only blame myself.'

'Fair enough,' said Pete.

They sat in silence for a moment while Abbey idly stirred her coffee. Then she looked questioningly at Pete.

'D'you think she'll stick it out?' she asked.

'Your mom?'

'Who else?'

'I don't know,' replied Pete. 'She seems pretty determined so far.'

'When you came into the gallery, I thought for a nanosecond that you were going to say that she'd called you. That she was coming home.'

Pete looked at her sympathetically. 'Sorry.'

'Oh well.' Abbey sighed. 'I suppose that's a good thing really. But I can't help wondering what happens if she changes her mind.'

'She'll leave,' said Pete.

'I can't imagine it would be easy to just up sticks like that,' Abbey said. 'But even if it is, even if they say "so long, nice to know you", how will she feel about that? And how could she possibly cope after it?'

'Your mom is one of the best copers I know,' said Pete. 'How many other women would have travelled across Latin America with a small kid like she did? If she chooses to leave, she'll be fine. Besides, she'll always have those nursing skills. And if the worst comes to the worst – or the best comes to the best, depending on your point of view – we'll be here to support her.'

'We will?' Abbey looked at him enquiringly. 'I'm her daughter, Pete. I'll be here. But you – you don't have to hang around.'

Pete nodded. 'I care about her, so I will.'

'Not for ever, though,' said Abbey. 'Nobody waits for ever.'

'I guess I'll wait until I know that she's done the right thing.'

'Oh, Pete.' Abbey's eyes were full of tears as she looked at him. 'I do love you. And you've been more of a father to me than I deserve.'

'I love you too,' said Pete. 'How could I not?'

'That's good to know,' she said.

'Stop worrying,' said Pete. 'You can't change anything that's already happened, and the future is an open book.'

'Y'see.' Abbey sniffed. 'Philosopher Pete strikes again.'

'Practical Pete,' he amended. 'Anyhow, honey, sleep on the job offer, then do whatever you think is right.'

'I will,' said Abbey. She blew her nose and wiped her eyes. 'And thanks for understanding. Again. It was the same when I said that I didn't want to be a hotshot lawyer like you, and when I decided to study art even though you think the art world is full of pretentious fools. Sadly, though, same as I was never going to be a great lawyer, I'm never going to set the art world alight. And the thing is, I hate working in that damn gallery.' She stopped, surprised at herself. She hadn't thought that she hated the gallery, just that she preferred the salon. 'I do hate it,' she said slowly. 'Nerissa is a bitch and the art we show isn't my thing either.'

'You mean you don't like blue dots on pink backgrounds?' asked Pete.

'To be honest, I do like that one,' she confessed. 'But the others – you know how we show a lot of Francis Bacon type stuff. Visceral and sort of . . . disturbing. It's not very uplifting.'

'Y'see, you're like me,' said Pete. 'You like old-fashioned painting. Proper pictures.'

'I like modern art too,' she scolded him. 'But I like a painting to be a joyous thing. Something that you can look at and take pleasure from. Not something that makes you shudder and gives you nightmares no matter how brilliantly it's done.'

'So go to a different gallery,' said Pete.

'I'll think about it,' she promised. 'But in the meantime . . . well, I guess I really want to give the nails a try.'

'Pity you can't paint on nails,' said Pete. 'Then you could combine both.'

'But you can.' Abbey's eyes widened. 'You can create nail art too.'

'I don't see too many fingernails hanging in MoMA,' said Pete.

Abbey laughed. 'I wouldn't rule it out. Though that might be more Bacon than beauty.'

Pete laughed too. 'If anyone can conquer the world of nail art, I'm sure it's you,' he said. 'And I look forward to seeing your designs displayed in the window of the salon at least. Though I'm sure they'll be even better than that.'

'Perhaps,' said Abbey. She lifted her bag and opened it. 'Until then . . .' She took out a small canvas and handed it to him. 'I brought this for you.'

Pete unrolled it on the table in front of him. It was an A4-sized painting of Alcatraz, the Rock, looking grim and forbidding, almost totally wreathed in sea mist except for a single ray of sunlight that hit one of the walls.

'You must have enough of these for an exhibition of your own,' he remarked as he studied it.

'Don't you like it?'

'It's fantastic.' He looked up at her. 'Honestly. You get a real sense of despair and isolation and . . . and yet that piece of sunlight. I love it.'

'I thought it would look better in your office than the blue dot,' Abbey told him. 'It's more you, somehow.'

'And you're like the Rock too,' said Pete. 'Tough and unyielding, but with a ray of sunshine.'

'I'm so not tough or unyielding,' Abbey said with a smile. 'But I like the fact that it's always there. I like the fact that it's a permanent part of the city.'

'It'll crumble eventually,' said Pete. 'No matter how tough it is.'

'Maybe we all do,' murmured Abbey, as she took a bite out of the strawberry-iced doughnut that, because she was trying to lose a few pounds, she'd already promised herself she wasn't going to eat.

PART 2

THE PRESENT

Chapter 4

Suzanne Fitzpatrick pulled into the small car park in front of the hotel and stepped out of the bright red Mini. A blast of Mediterranean heat hit her and she felt beads of perspiration break out on her forehead. She fanned herself for a moment until she'd adjusted to the temperature, then looked around her.

The hotel, four storeys high, was like a thin ivory wafer. It was taller than it was wide, with art deco carvings across the width of the facade. There were small white balustraded balconies outside each full-length window on the first, second and third floors, although right now, faded green shutters covered the windows themselves. Suzanne could see that the paint was peeling from the balconies too. But, she thought as she turned around, the views from them would be fabulous.

It was fabulous at ground level already. From where she stood, she could look down over dark green pines to the turquoise Mediterranean sea below. Even with her oversized Carolina Herrera sunglasses shielding her eyes, she had to squint in the brilliance of the sunlight as it hit the water and shattered into a pool of diamond lights. It was impossible to put a price on that view, she thought. Although she was going to have to try.

She turned back to the hotel and walked up the tiled path towards the building itself. The glass doors were locked, so she made her way around it. To the side, facing south, was a medium-sized swimming pool, surrounded by dazzling white tiles. There

27

was a small puddle of water at the bottom of the deep end, as well as a scattering of seeds and some dried bougainvillea blossom from the nearby palm trees and flowering shrubs. A white plastic chair was on its side in the shallow end. Suzanne walked down the steps into the pool, took out the chair and placed it on the terrace.

Folding doors, all locked, led into what Suzanne assumed would be a bar and restaurant. She closed her eyes and imagined the terrace full of holidaymakers lying on sun-loungers, sitting at tables, drinking juices and beers and sangrias, soaking up the sun in idyllic surroundings. Or surroundings that would be idyllic when the palm trees and the bougainvillea were pruned, when the pool was cleaned and filled and when the doors of the hotel were opened again.

She glanced at her watch and retraced her steps to the front of the building. Just as she was thinking that he was late, a black SUV with the logo of the estate agent pulled into the car park, sending up a spray of gravel. The door opened and a man, younger than Suzanne had expected – somewhere in his twenties, she thought – got out.

'Sorry,' he said. 'I was delayed on the road.'

'No problem.' She extended her hand. 'Suzanne Fitzpatrick.'

'Jaime Roig. Delighted to meet you. So, you are interested in the Mirador Hotel?'

'Perhaps.'

'It's a wonderful opportunity.' Jaime began to talk about the hotel, telling her what she had already seen for herself, that it was in a fantastic position overlooking the sea, that it was full of character and charm, that it was crying out for someone to restore it to its former beauty and bring the tourists to this unspoilt area, a mere half an hour's drive away from the historic town of Girona.

Suzanne let him talk without interruption. Until it got to the question of money, there was very little he could say to influence

28

her. She continued to appraise the building and the gardens around it, moving into the shade of one of the palms as Jaime continued with his spiel.

'Would you like to go inside?' he asked eventually, and she nodded.

He took a bunch of keys from his pocket, selected one and opened the doors to the hotel. Suzanne pushed her sunglasses on to her head, stepped inside, and then stood still, waiting for her eyes to adjust to the darkness.

Jaime reached behind the door and switched on the electricity. A fluorescent tube spluttered a few times before it lit properly.

'I'll open the shutters.' Jaime moved to the windows of what Suzanne could now see was a spacious reception area. There was a leather-topped marble reception desk to one side, pigeon-holes and a row of silver keys on enormous fobs behind it. In the centre of the room was an expansive glass table. A few brocade seats were pushed against the wall. When the shutters were open and the daylight streamed in, Suzanne realised that a layer of dust covered the table and that the fabric on the seats was faded. But the floor was cool white polished marble, and the chandelier that hung from the ceiling was both ornate and elegant.

'There are thirty-six rooms in total,' said Jaime. 'Also a restaurant, a bar and a salon.'

'I'd like to see one of the rooms,' said Suzanne.

'Of course. Follow me.'

He walked past the reception desk and stopped in front of the lift. So did Suzanne, who exclaimed in delight.

Jaime looked pleased. 'You like it?'

Until now Suzanne had been able to keep her emotions under control, but she couldn't help herself.

'It's amazing,' she said.

It was an old-fashioned cage lift, with inner and outer grille doors that were manually opened and closed. The metal frame and doors were painted in gold and green and were decorated with the coats of arms of Spanish noble houses.

'Want to use it to go upstairs?'

'Is it working properly? Is it safe?'

Jaime grinned. 'I hope so.'

He pulled open the doors and she stepped inside. The wooden floor was worn, as were the brass buttons that identified each level. When Jaime stepped in beside her, he pressed 3 and the lift began to move slowly upwards. As it passed the other floors, Suzanne could see occasional abandoned items – a vacuum cleaner, a mop and (strangely) a guitar. She wondered about the people who had stayed and worked here, wondered what they were doing now.

The lift juddered to a halt and Jaime opened the doors again. 'This way.'

He selected another key from the ring and led her to a room at the end of the corridor, which he opened. She stepped inside. He was about to turn on the light, but she stopped him. She walked over to the window and opened the shutters instead.

This time the light was almost blinding. She dropped her sunglasses on to her nose, opened the window and stepped out on to the balcony.

The view, merely beautiful before, was breathtaking now. From her higher vantage point, Suzanne could see the beach, where a few people were lying on towels sunbathing, and further along, the coves and inlets that dotted the coastline. The green of the pine trees contrasted with the blues of the sky and the sea. It was perfect. There was no other word for it.

'*Impresionante, no?*' said Jaime.

'Absolutely,' she replied.

'When I was small, my mother used to take me here for ice cream,' he said.

She turned to look at him, her expression sceptical.

'No, really,' he assured her. 'It was one of our favourite places.

There are steps down to the beach. Not easy for elderly people, but for children, no problem.'

'Can older people or people with mobility problems access the beach from anywhere else?' Her tone was suddenly brisk.

'Yes. A little further from here,' he replied. 'Maybe, oh, less than half a kilometre. Five minutes' walk. There is a gentle slope down to the beach. In the summer there is a beach bar too. It's very nice.'

'I want to look at it,' she said.

'Sure. No problem.'

Suzanne couldn't help feeling that if she said she wanted to hire a boat, or paraglide or drive the hundred or so kilometres to Barcelona, Jaime Roig would say it was no problem. She knew that the hotel had been on the agency's books for over two years. They were keen to sell it. The question she had to ask herself was, was she keen to buy? And if she was, would the investors she'd already spoken to about a possible purchase agree that it was the right choice? Would they be able to raise the finance for it? And even if all those things panned out – the most important question of all – would she make a success of it? Would she be able to look her father in the eye and tell him that she was the best of them all?

It was late by the time she got back to the top-floor apartment she was currently renting in Girona, about forty minutes' drive from the Mirador Hotel. The building was old, with high ceilings and tiled floors, and every time Suzanne walked inside, she felt as though she were stepping back in time.

She let herself in and made herself an industrial-strength coffee, which she took on to her tiny balcony overlooking one of the narrow streets. She could hear voices and laughter drifting from the square and the occasional snatch of music from a nearby café-bar. The laughter and the music would go on for a few hours yet. The town was still in holiday mode, buzzing and warm. It had been a long, hot summer and some people were counting the days until the cooler weather returned. But Suzanne never found the heat oppressive. She liked how it seeped into her bones, into her body, filling her with a sense of well-being. A sense of belonging. She felt that more here, in Catalunya, than anywhere else in the world. And she'd travelled to a lot of places. Most of her working life had been in Europe and the Americas, Asia and Africa, always in hotels, from the day she landed her first job as a receptionist in a small family-run hotel in London, to her role as a senior manager in a global chain, to her current position as the manager of a boutique hotel in Girona itself.

In the early years, she'd been seduced by the idea of working for a chain. By the glamour of executive hotels where the fittings and the standards were exactly the same, no matter where in the world you were. But after her marriage to Calvin, a senior VP in the same chain, had gone horribly wrong and had impacted badly on her career, she'd opted for a change of scenery and pace, a change which had ultimately ended up with her taking over the running of one of Girona's most charming hotels.

At first she'd thought of it as a comedown. She'd been angry and upset at how Calvin had been able to continue in his role at the chain whereas she had suddenly become an embarrassment. Admittedly walking into a board meeting and dumping the entire contents of a Waterford crystal vase over his head hadn't done much for her reputation, but he'd bloody well deserved it. He'd cheated on her and lied about cheating and his goddam colleagues knew it. Nevertheless, publicly emptying dirty water and half-dead flowers over your husband's head, when he was a member of the board and more senior to you, wasn't the way to get on in business. Suzanne knew that. She knew that they had decided there and then that she was unreliable and flaky even though she was one of the best people who'd ever worked for them, and . . .

She took a deep breath and banished the memory. That was all in the past. Her ill-fated marriage, which she'd rushed into less than a year after her mother's death, was long over. She hadn't seen or heard from Calvin Schwartz since their divorce, although she knew, from insider gossip, that he was still in the States and that he was seeing someone else (although not, it turned out, the woman with whom he'd had the affair). Anyway, nothing for her to care about there. Nothing to get upset about. Except that she couldn't help the occasional rush of anger she felt whenever she thought about him and his betrayal.

But things had turned out for the best. As they so often did. She'd left the chain and got another job and eventually moved to Girona and started working in the boutique hotel, and she'd suddenly realised that this, for her, was what running a hotel was all about. Meeting real people rather than businessmen (the majority were still male) who were simply in town for a meeting or a conference which could have been in any other city in any other country, staying in a big hotel because they felt safer in the security blanket of a chain where everything would always be the same.

Being in charge of El Boganto had been a revelation to her and she'd enjoyed every single minute. But now she wanted more. She wanted to be the owner, not the manager. She wanted to be able to make the long-term strategic decisions. She wanted to give it a go herself. She knew that she'd never be able to do it all entirely on her own, so she'd built up a network of contacts in the region's hospitality industry. She knew that they'd been impressed with her credentials – and impressed by the fact that El Boganto's occupancy rate had soared under her management. As a result, she'd sounded them out about potential opportunities and the response had been heartening. But whether it would be as positive when she actually had a deal on the table would be another matter altogether.

She knew that the Mirador would be a massive undertaking. She knew that she'd have to pitch it perfectly. She also knew that – even with the consortium that she and Petra, her financial adviser, had put together – it might be difficult to get the financing she

33

needed. But she had a strong track record (if you excluded the emptying of Waterford crystal vases over the heads of board members) and she knew what she was doing. She'd seen other hotels over the past few weeks. The Mirador was the only one that had excited her.

She opened the folder that Jaime had given her and spread the brochures out in front of her. This hotel had a certain something about it. Had the potential to be wonderful. The fact that its potential hadn't been realised in the past didn't make it a bad bet for the future. From what she'd learned, the previous owners had borrowed heavily at the top of the market to take it over, but business had slumped and they hadn't been able to keep it going. Suzanne thought they'd got their business model all wrong. And that they'd got the feeling of the hotel all wrong too. The Mirador wasn't the sort of place that should ever have had plastic chairs around its swimming pool. It should be an exclusive hotel, playing up to its wonderfully evocative decor and the unparalleled beauty of its location. It should be a byword for elegance and style, the kind of place for which visitors would pay a premium. And it could be. She knew it could.

Tomorrow she would ask Petra to arrange a meeting with the two female investors she knew were interested in buying a hotel with her. She shivered with excitement. This was possible. It really was. She'd make it work.

Which would definitely be one in the eye for her father.

It was a long time since she'd allowed herself to be riled by thoughts of Fred. It was funny, she thought: no matter how much you got over things that happened to you, you never forgot how people made you feel. Fred had always made her feel stupid and worthless. Not, she thought, because he believed she was stupid, and maybe not even because he thought her worthless, but her father was a relic from a different age, with views about women that had long since been consigned to the dustbin of history. All the time she was growing up, he had somehow managed to hang on to the idea that what women wanted (regard-less of any assertions to the contrary) was to get married, have children and settle down to a life of domestic bliss. He also seemed to think that he should have a say in who his only daughter settled down with. Additionally – and this was the most irritating, infuriating, insane thing of all – he seemed to think that she shouldn't see any other men until she met the one he approved of.

Her mother, Ros, said that Fred was being protective. Particularly protective, she would add, because Suzanne was his youngest child, a precious late arrival so long after Gareth. Suzanne, however, thought he was being controlling and freaky. Bullying, even, she told Ros sometimes, giving her grief if she'd gone out without saying where she was going, no matter who she was with. She was smothered by Fred and frustrated by the way he tried to rule her life. She hadn't realised until years ago, when she'd gone home for Ros's funeral, just how much he'd influenced all of them. But however difficult it had been for Don and Gareth, it had been a thousand times worse for her.

Having a father like Fred had isolated Suzanne. She found it hard to socialise with other girls of her age who had normal parents, not overbearing like her father and subservient like Ros. She envied her school friends their apparent freedom and swore that when she was old enough she'd be walking out of the house and never coming back.

The walkout happened sooner than she'd originally planned. She was seventeen and had gone to the first party she'd ever attended that wasn't for small girls in lacy socks, and where the drinks weren't orange squash and red lemonade. The party had been thrown by the older sister of a classmate and everyone was invited. Suzanne was determined that she wasn't going to be the only one not to go. She was tired of being left out, tired of being different. So she made her plans, thankful that on the evening in question Fred was working late at his car-alarm business, while

Ros was also out because the party coincided with her bingo night, her one social activity.

Of course she knew that eventually her parents would wonder where she was, but she didn't care. She was going to have a night of total freedom and tomorrow could look after itself.

The party was fun, and she was pleased when one of her class-mates called her Sexy Suzy, remarking that the short dress she was wearing showed off her long legs. Suzanne sipped cheap red wine and basked in the compliments, even though she was well aware that the guys at the party would probably compliment any woman if they thought she was good for a bit of fun later. (Her opinion of the opposite sex was entirely influenced by her father and brothers, and by Ros too, who frequently warned her darkly that boys were *only after one thing*.)

However, Danny Murphy certainly didn't seem like that. She'd got talking to him halfway through the evening, and he'd chatted with her about a wide range of subjects without once indulging in any kind of inappropriate behaviour (which, if she was truly honest, was a little bit disappointing). Later, he offered to drive her home. Suzanne thought that being in a car with him might lead to some of the inappropriate behaviour she'd been hoping for, and so she accepted.

It was the unaccustomed drinking of red wine that had dulled the usual alarm bells in her head. But the alarm bells weren't to do with any activity she might have got up to with Danny, they were about her overprotective father. Danny had no sooner pulled to a halt outside the house when Fred had catapulted himself into the street and was dragging the passenger door open. He hauled Suzanne out of the car, told her to get inside and yelled at Danny to keep his filthy hands off his daughter. Danny hadn't waited around. He'd put the car into gear and gunned it down the street. Meanwhile, Fred frogmarched Suzanne into the kitchen, ranting on at her about sneaking out of the house, letting herself down and being cheap and tarty – and drunk.

'I'm not,' she wailed. 'I was invited to a party and I went. I'm entitled to have a life, you know.'

But Fred didn't see it like that. He told her she was grounded, which made her shake her head and say that she wasn't a child and couldn't be treated like one and that he'd embarrassed – no, mortified – her in front of Danny Murphy, who was a nice guy but who'd never want to see her again. He was a bullying old git, she raged, before Fred told her not to be cheeky, that she was still a child to him and that her behaviour that night had been completely unacceptable. Suzanne had looked at her mother in despair, because Ros had been sitting in her armchair while all this was going on, not saying a word. But when her mother did open her mouth, it was only to say that Fred was concerned for Suzanne's welfare and he knew what he was doing.

Lying in bed later, Suzanne knew that she'd had enough. Her father was a tyrant and her mother downtrodden. If she stayed, she'd begin to think it was a normal way of life. She had to get out. And so she made her plans. A month later, on another evening when both her parents were out, Suzanne walked out of the house with a backpack and all the money she had. She went straight to the ferry port and got on a boat to England. She swore that she was never coming back.

It had probably been easier to lose yourself in the crowd back in the eighties than it was today, Suzanne thought. It was harder now to avoid being tracked down, because of mobile phones and Laser cards and CCTV all over the place. But over twenty years ago, even though she knew her parents would have been looking for her, nobody found her. She called Donald from London, asking him to tell Ros and Fred that she was alive and well and not to worry about her. Donald had begged her to come home. He said that she was being selfish and that of course everyone was worried about her. But she said that she was tired of being worried about, that she needed to stand on her own two feet and that it would be a long time before she set foot in Ireland again.

When she did eventually return, for Ros's funeral, she realised that there was nothing to keep in her home town. And nobody she wanted to come back to either. So the day after her mother had been buried, she left again and hadn't even thought about returning since.

Chapter 5

There were a million places Lisette would have preferred to be other than standing in the kitchen of her father-in-law's house on a beautiful Saturday morning. But because Fred had fallen and sprained his wrist quite badly a couple of days earlier, he needed someone to call by and help out, and she was the obvious choice. She supposed they were lucky he hadn't broken the wrist. Or his hip, which would have been a damn sight worse. The way Lisette saw it, if Fred's hip had gone, that would've been the end of him. Eighty-one-year-olds didn't recover well from broken hips, although Fred might have been an exception; he was strong as a bull, despite the fact that he'd had a heart bypass five years previously. All the same, thought Lisette, he'd never fallen before. Maybe he was finally on the slippery slope to infirmity.

She unpacked the groceries she'd brought and began to put them away. Fred, sitting at the kitchen table, watched her.

'I probably could've done it myself,' he said. 'I'm not helpless, you know.'

Lisette bit back the retort that it was because he'd been trying to reach something from a high shelf that he'd lost his footing and hurt himself in the first place. And that anyone would be helpless with their arm in a sling.

'It was an accident,' Fred continued. 'Could've happened to a bishop.'

Lisette looked puzzled. Sometimes her father-in-law's expressions defeated her, even though she'd been living in Ireland for nearly twenty-five years and knew most of them. What had accidents and bishops got to do with each other? She gave her Gallic shrug and continued to put the shopping away.

'I should've bought my stuff online,' added Fred. 'Saved you the journey here.'

'It's no trouble,' Lisette told him. 'I had to go to the super-market myself this morning. And we only live five minutes away.'

'Lucky me,' said Fred.

Lisette glanced around at him. She thought she'd detected a touch of sarcasm in her father-in-law's voice, but she wasn't certain. She put the last items in the cupboard (three pouches of microwave rice, a culinary travesty in her opinion) and then asked him if he'd like a cup of tea.

'If you're having one yourself,' he replied.

She didn't really want tea, but despite his comment she felt obliged to have one with him, so she filled the kettle and, when it had boiled, poured the water over the tea bags in their individual mugs. When she was at home, Lisette made weak loose-leaf tea in a pretty ceramic pot, enjoying the ritual, but Fred liked his brew as strong as it could possibly be, so two cups and two tea bags was the only option.

'There's Jaffa Cakes in the biscuit barrel,' he told her.

Lisette said nothing. She opened the fridge and took out a carton of milk, telling herself that if Fred liked microwave rice or wanted to eat those disgusting biscuits, or if he liked his tea to resemble tar and stocked his fridge only with EasiSingles, full-fat milk and bottles of Guinness, that was entirely his business.

'So how's things with you?' asked Fred after she'd placed the mug of tea and a plate of biscuits in front of him. 'Did you enjoy your holiday? Are you glad to be home?' He winked as he said this, and she knew it was because he was perfectly aware that she was always a little depressed when she and Gareth returned from their annual six weeks in their holiday home near the picturesque town of La Rochelle.

'The holiday was perfect, as always,' she replied. 'And I suppose I can't complain too much because the weather has – naturally – been lovely since we got back.'

Summer had arrived in Dublin with the end of August and the beginning of the new school term, when Lisette and Gareth, both teachers, returned to work.

'It was always lovely in September when I was a boy,' said Fred. 'Though, funny, all the summers I remember as a kid were warm too. They couldn't have been, I suppose, but I don't ever recall being stuck indoors because of cold or rain.' He gazed unseeingly in front of him and Lisette knew that he was lost in those memories. He did that more and more these days, though in fairness to him, a good deal less than her own *maman*, who was ten years younger but frequently waxed lyrical about her idyllic childhood in Nantes.

She continued to listen as he began talking again, but was suddenly distracted by the heavy cream-coloured piece of paper she saw poking out from the folder on the table in front of him. Half the page was hidden, but on the visible half she could see the letters '. . . ament' in bold scripted type. Lisette instantly knew what it was. Another version of Fred's last will and testament.

She felt her body tense. That bloody will! Fred was forever changing it and then dropping hints to his sons about what decisions he'd made about his legacy. Lisette had told him ages ago that the best thing to do was to divide it up equally between his three children (even though she wasn't convinced that Suzanne, who couldn't be bothered to visit and never enquired about her father, deserved anything). Fred, however, always tapped the side of his nose and said he knew what he was doing, which infuriated both Gareth, her husband, and Donald, who believed that he had a special place in his father's heart since he was the one who'd gone into business with him. But *he* hadn't provided a male heir,

41

Lisette thought, which to an old-fashioned man like Fred was still important. Lisette knew that Fred liked the idea of someone carrying on the Fitzpatrick name, and right now the only person who could do that was her son, Jerome. This surely meant, she thought, that Fred would favour them when he was drawing up his will.

She said this once to Gareth, who agreed with her in principle, but also reckoned Fred was simply toying with them whenever he talked about it. Her husband was probably right, thought Lisette. Making wills was a common enough pastime among the older generation. Her own grandmother had updated hers every six months until she died at the age of 102 (having outlived two daughters who'd long hoped to get their hands on her extensive jewellery collection). She hoped that Fred wouldn't live that long. The truth was, no matter how her father-in-law was dividing up his estate, both she and Gareth could do right now with whatever assets he might be leaving them.

Fred probably knew that too. Every so often he would make remarks to her about the plummeting value of their property portfolio, and murmur that she and Gareth might have been better off concentrating on teaching. Lisette never said that it was thanks to Fred himself that they'd got involved in property, and never wished out loud (though she often did in private) that they'd had more sense. As well as their beautiful home, Thorngrove, at the bottom of the hill, their investment properties (a house in Artane and an apartment in Swords) and Papillon, their house in France, were currently a noose around their necks. But that noose would certainly be loosened as soon as Fred's house and money were available.

Whenever thoughts of Fred's net worth entered her head, she found them difficult to dislodge. Her eyes kept being drawn towards the folder containing the will, even though Fred was still talking about his life as a young boy.

'Of course it wasn't always idyllic back then.' He put his mug down on the table with a thump, startling her. 'There were some bad times. Some terrible things, right up to very recent days.'

Lisette looked at him enquiringly. 'What on earth are you talking about?'

'Abuse,' said Fred. 'Exploitation of vulnerable young girls. The Magdalene laundries, for example.'

'What?' This time she was astonished. Although the stories of the unmarried pregnant girls who ended up in the so-called laundries, kept away from their families and treated disgracefully, had made headline news and created a national scandal, Lisette didn't think it was something that would have interested Fred very much. Her father-in-law was a typical unreconstructed man.

'There was another programme on about it last night,' said Fred. 'It was terrible what happened to them.'

'I didn't see the programme,' Lisette told him. 'But you're right, of course, it was dreadful.'

'They deserved better,' Fred said. 'Better than what they got from the state back then and better than the so-called compensation that some of them received afterwards. Not that most of them got anything.'

'It's a disgrace,' she agreed, thinking that Fred had got a bee in his bonnet about the subject. That was typical of him, though. There was always something. Traffic jams, greedy politicians, reality TV shows, poor infrastructure – all of these things made him hot under the collar from time to time. However, he rarely cared about any issues relating to women.

'I suppose times have changed for the better,' said Fred. 'But, you know, there's still stuff going on. Abuse of kiddies, for example. Violence in the family. Women having to run away and not having anywhere to run to.'

'Indeed,' said Lisette.

'And this government doesn't give them enough help,' continued Fred. 'They've cut funding to lots of very worthwhile projects.'

Lisette found it hard to believe that the old man had suddenly unearthed a social conscience. As far as she could remember, this was the first time he'd ever expressed outrage about anything other than high taxes and poor services.

'There should be more funds for people who help those women,' said Fred. 'It's something we should all think about.'

Lisette caught her breath. Fred couldn't possibly be referring to himself, could he? Was he thinking of leaving money to some kind of women's organisation? Or – an even worse thought suddenly struck her – he couldn't want them to turn Furze Hill into some kind of refuge? The thought horrified her.

'Not that I'll have to worry about what goes on for much longer,' said Fred as he took another Jaffa Cake. 'I don't have many years left.'

'Of course you have,' said Lisette, hoping that he had enough to get rid of any madcap ideas that were swilling around in his brain. 'You're as fit as a fiddle. I know you're probably upset about your wrist, but it will be better in no time.'

'I hope so,' said Fred. 'But you've got to remember I've had a heart bypass, and I'm getting on . . .'

Lisette looked at him curiously. Up to a few minutes ago, he'd been saying that he was perfectly able to manage even with a sprained wrist; now he was worrying about getting old. Concerns about his age were uncharacteristic of Fred, who still seemed to think that he was capable of doing things he'd done in his prime.

'We're all getting on,' said Lisette.

'True,' he agreed. 'Though you're luckier than most of us, because you've always looked a bit on the older side.'

Lisette said nothing. From the moment they'd first met, Fred had teased her (not always kindly) about being his younger son's granny girlfriend. This had nothing to do with their respective ages – in fact she was three years younger than Gareth – but was because of the colour of her hair, which was completely grey, and had been ever since her early twenties. When she'd seen the first silver strand appear, shortly after her twenty-second birthday, her heart had sunk. But she'd been lucky to ultimately turn the almost white-grey of her mother and grandmother, which, in the neat bobbed style she wore, looked sophisticated rather than ageing and which suited her pale skin. She hadn't succumbed to the tyranny of colouring it, and when she met Gareth Fitzpatrick, he told her that she had the loveliest hair he'd ever seen. But Gareth's father had asked her if she wasn't baby-snatching, despite the fact that he knew she was younger than his son.

'Are you coming to Zoey's birthday party?' Lisette wasn't in the mood for Fred's sniping today.

'There's someone who'll always look younger than her age,' he said.

'Indeed.'

'Of course she married Donald for money, more fool her,' added Fred. 'I don't see how any girl can possibly imagine that a divorced man of fifty would have lots of spare cash lying around.'

'Donald's still a good catch,' said Lisette.

Fred snorted. 'Not half as good as he thinks he is. As I'm sure she'll find out.'

Lisette wondered what Fred meant by that. Not half as clever? Or not half as well-off? She took a deep breath and released it slowly. Seeing the damn will had made her think of things she didn't want to think about right now.

'Anyway, are you coming to the party?' she asked again.

'I don't know,' said Fred. 'I'm a bit long in the tooth for thirtieth birthdays, don't you think? But then so's Donald!' He laughed, and the laugh turned into a cough. Lisette watched him anxiously until he regained his breath. 'I should give up the aul' fags,' said Fred. 'But when you're eighty-one, there isn't a great deal of point, is there?'

'Possibly not,' agreed Lisette. She stood up. 'I'd better get going.'

'Thanks for dropping by,' said Fred. 'Though I suppose it's in your interests, isn't it? Keeping an eye on me?'

'I don't know what you're talking about,' said Lisette.

'Come on, now.' He winked at her. 'I won't be around for ever, will I?'

'Fred, you gave money to the lads when you sold the business. I don't think any of them are expecting much when you . . . when . . .'

He gave her a twisted smile as he coughed again. 'Don't play games with me,' he said. 'I know what my boys are like. I know how they think. I know how you all think.'

'You're being silly.' Lisette hoped that she wasn't blushing. 'They love you. So do I. So does Suzanne.'

'Huh.' At the mention of his daughter's name, a shadow crossed Fred's face. 'She never loved me. She never will.'

Lisette didn't argue with him. She'd only spoken to Suzanne on a handful of occasions and she had a feeling that Fred might be right about that.

'Go on away with you.' He looked at her crankily. 'I've things to be doing this afternoon.'

'All right then. If there's anything you need, give me a call.'

'I don't need anything,' said Fred. 'Just to be left alone.'

Lisette sighed. There were days when she wondered why she bothered. The old man was an ungrateful sod. In reality, she didn't blame Suzanne for not wanting to come home.

The drive to her own house, in its less prestigious location at the bottom of Howth Hill, took about five minutes, time she used to worry that Fred might be drawing up a new will while he was in pain from his wrist and clearly under the influence of whatever TV programme he'd seen. She desperately hoped that he wasn't going to do something stupid, like leave it all to charity. That wasn't anything she'd worried about before, because Fred was the last man in the world to give money to random charities. Or so she'd always thought. His musings on the past treatment of unmarried mothers was an unusual and unwelcome departure from his normal views that social welfare only encouraged scroungers and that people should look after themselves and not expect the state to do it for them. Lisette wouldn't have been surprised if Fred's view on the whole Magdalene laundry situation was that the girls had got themselves into a mess by getting pregnant in the first place and that it wasn't up to anyone else to look after them. She found it hard to believe that he'd actually been moved by the TV documentary, regardless of what he said.

He'll probably have forgotten it all by next week, she told herself as she opened the gates to her driveway with the remote control. That was one of the small mercies of his age. New pet hates and new enthusiasms alike were short-lived.

Gareth was nowhere to be seen as she walked through the house and out to the sunny back garden, although their children, Jerome and Fleur, were outside, playing with the family's cocker spaniel, Chien.

'Where's your father?' asked Lisette, automatically picking up abandoned toys and putting them into the large plastic container that was in the garden specifically to keep it neat and tidy.

'He's upstairs working.' Fleur didn't look up from the game she was playing. 'He told us to stay out of his hair.'

'I see,' said Lisette. 'I'll go and talk to him.'

'He'll want you to stay out of his hair too,' Fleur told her. 'He said he was very busy.'

'It's OK,' said Lisette.

She went back indoors and climbed the stairs to the smallest of the five bedrooms, which had been allocated to Gareth as a study. Not that he needed a study any more than she did, but he liked to have it. Whereas she corrected her students' homework at the kitchen table in the afternoons, Gareth preferred to retreat upstairs. He said it was because it was easier to look at the boys' projects there than in the kitchen, but Lisette knew the real reason was because he wanted to have a place of his own in the house. It made him feel important. And she knew that, of the three

Fitzpatrick siblings, Gareth was the one who most needed to feel important.

'Hello.' She poked her head around the door.

Gareth looked up from the computer and, seeing her, immediately minimised the screen he'd been looking at. He pushed his slightly too long hair out of his eyes.

'Hi,' he said. 'How's Dad?'

'Not doing too badly. Insisted he could've gone shopping himself.'

Gareth gave her a look of disbelief.

'Yes, well, you know what he's like. Anyhow, I put everything away and left a ready-meal for him for tonight.' She made a face. 'You know how I feel about them, but he insisted he wanted a steak and kidney pie, so I bought one for him.'

'My heroine,' said Gareth.

'So why are you closeted away up here?' Lisette sat on the edge of his desk and crossed her legs. (Her legs were the thing about herself that she liked the most. They were slim and graceful, almost as good as they'd been when she'd first met her husband.)

'Things to do.'

'I thought you were going to cut the grass.'

'I will,' said Gareth. 'The forecast for tomorrow is good too.'

Lisette got up from the desk and walked behind him. Because he'd minimised the browser, the only thing she could see on the computer screen was the desktop picture. It had been taken a few weeks earlier, in their garden in La Rochelle. She was standing in the middle of the lawn, the children either side of her. They were all beaming at the camera.

Her legs were very visible in that photo too, because she'd been wearing a cropped top and shorts. Not something she would have worn outside the confines of their house – Lisette had very firm views about women over the age of forty baring too much flesh – but she noted with satisfaction that she looked good. Her body was trim, her face almost without wrinkles, thanks to the scrupulous regime of skincare she adhered to. Looking at the photo, she could almost have been mistaken for an older sister, except for the grey hair.

'Tomorrow is fine,' she said, not wanting to argue with him about the grass even though he'd been promising to cut it for the past week, and a week of dry, sunny weather practically constituted a heatwave in Ireland. 'Your dad was doing another will.'

'Not again.' Gareth turned from the computer, an irritated expression on his face. 'What's in it this time?'

'I've no idea. I saw it sticking out from under a folder. I thought that maybe he'd put it there simply so that I'd come back and mention it to you and you'd go hurtling up there to find out what he was at.'

'No point,' said Gareth. 'You know what he's like.'

'We all do.'

'It's so childish.' Gareth shook his head. 'He thinks he can keep us in line by holding the damn will over us like some kind of big bribe.'

'It works,' said Lisette. 'At least as far as you and Donald are concerned.'

'That's unfair!' exclaimed Gareth. 'We look after him because he's our dad, not because we're hoping for something.'

'I know, I know,' said Lisette quickly. 'I wasn't trying to imply that you didn't do enough – we all do.'

'But we're entitled to be remembered by him. We've put up with enough over the years, haven't we? All of us.'

'Of course,' she agreed. 'Anyway, today he was going on about abused women and Magdalene laundries.'

'What?' Gareth stared at her.

'He said the state didn't do enough for them and that they deserved better. I thought that maybe he was implying he was going to leave money to some kind of women's charity.'

'You've got that all wrong,' said Gareth. 'Dad might leave money to a vintage car club or something like that, but he'd never leave any to a women's charity.'

'That's what I would've thought,' agreed Lisette. 'All the same . . .'

'He'd even leave it to Suzanne before a women's charity.' Gareth suddenly looked doubtful. 'Well . . . maybe he would.'

'I know he should probably divide everything equally between you all, but she's never here and she's never offered to help.'

'True,' said Gareth.

'Though even with the dodgy wrist and that shocking cough and the whole bypass thing, I can't help feeling he'll go on for ever. And . . . it's not like I want him to die on us, but . . . well, we could do with the money, couldn't we?'

'Maybe I'll hit him over the head,' muttered Gareth. 'Finish him off.'

'Gar! Not even as a joke.' Lisette looked shocked.

'Who said I was joking.' Gareth glanced at his computer screen.

Lisette said nothing. She looked at the computer screen too.

'So what are you working on?' she asked.

'Huh?'

'On a beautiful day like today. When you should be out in the garden – even if you're not cutting the grass – you are in here hunched over the computer. What were you looking at before I came in?'

'Nothing.' Gareth tried to keep his expression guilt-free.

She leaned across him and maximised the screen again.

'An estate agent? In France?' Her words were sharp.

'Research.' His tone was dismissive.

'On what?'

'Prices. You know.'

'But why would we want to know about prices in France?' she asked, her eyes scanning the page. 'Near La Rochelle?'

'I wondered how much Papillon was worth,' he confessed finally. 'Why?'

'We need to know how valuable our assets are.'

'You're not thinking of selling it, are you?' She sounded suddenly horrified. 'Not Papillon.'

'Look, Lisette, I wanted to know, that's all. Just in case.'

'We are *not* selling Papillon.' Her voice was firm and ice-cool. 'No matter what. It is our home.'

'This is our home.'

'No,' she said. 'This is where we live. It's an entirely different thing.'

She walked out of the room and banged the door behind her. She knew that if she stayed, she'd only say something she'd regret.

Chapter 6

Zoey Fitzpatrick liked the Dundrum Town Centre mall. Being on the opposite side of the city to her home, it wasn't her closest or even most convenient shopping centre, but it had the biggest range of shops of any in Dublin. Zoey was hoping to find the right dress for her upcoming thirtieth birthday party. She'd trawled the entire length of Grafton Street without success, not even finding anything she liked in the exclusive designer rooms of the Brown Thomas department store. She was beginning to panic ever so slightly about the dress. She wanted it to be absolutely perfect.

'It's not like I won't pay for the ideal one,' she told her mother, Lesley, as she drummed her fingers on the tabletop in the café where they were having coffee before beginning their search. 'But so far none of them have been exactly right. It's my big night. I can't have people outshining me.'

'You'd outshine anyone, babes, even in a sack,' said Lesley. She pushed the sunglasses she'd been wearing on to the top of her head. Lesley often wore sunglasses indoors to hide her occasionally puffy eyes, but this time it had been the sun coming through the glass roof that had made her keep them on while having coffee. Now it had disappeared behind a cloud and she couldn't see her daughter properly.

'I hope so,' said Zoey. 'I want to look fabulous.'

'You always look fabulous.' Anthea, her best friend, who'd also joined them for the shopping expedition, spoke with conviction.

52

'Ah, thanks, hon.'

Zoey knew her friend was telling the truth, so there was no point in false modesty on her part. Always dressing for the occasion and looking her best was very important to her. Today's outfit was perfect for Saturday shopping. She was wearing her favourite Armani jeans and a baby-pink Juicy Couture tracksuit top over a simple white T-shirt. Her face was flawlessly made up, highlighting her dewy complexion, her exceptional cheekbones and her brilliant blue eyes. (The only let-down, Zoey always felt, was her lips, which were thinner than she would have liked, despite her regular use of plumping balms and lippy.) Her perfectly coloured brunette hair (with its highlighted extensions) fell around her shoulders in a cascade of GHD curls, and, like her mother, she had pushed the big sunglasses she habitually wore on to the top of her head.

'So let's stop drinking coffee and nattering and get shopping,' said Anthea.

Zoey was glad she'd asked both her mother and her friend to help her in her search for the party dress. There wasn't the same buzz in trying on loads of different outfits if nobody was with her to give an opinion (she didn't trust the salespeople in shops, ever since the day one sales assistant had told her she looked great in a totally unforgiving style that had, without doubt, made her bum look enormous). But she trusted Lesley and Anthea implicitly and she enjoyed having girlie shopping days with them.

They left the coffee shop and walked out on to the concourse. Zoey felt the surge of adrenalin rush through her, as it always did before she went shopping. It was one of her favourite occupations and she knew she was good at it. Since marrying Donald, it had been something she'd been able to indulge in to a much greater extent than ever before, although in recent months he'd been looking at her credit card bills with a certain amount of shock and making comments about having to cut back a little.

'Cut back?' she'd said on the morning he'd (literally) gasped when he'd opened the bill. 'Why?'

'Because you're spending the equivalent of a medium-sized mortgage on clothes and shoes every month!' he exclaimed. 'How could you possibly need all this stuff?'

'To look gorgeous,' she told him as she got up from the breakfast table and put her arms around him, engulfing him in a scented cloud of J'Adore.

'You always look gorgeous,' he said.

'Because I make an effort.'

'You look gorgeous now,' he said, 'and you're only wearing pyjamas.'

Zoey decided not to tell him that the pyjamas were La Perla and had cost nearly as much as his last suit.

'You don't begrudge me clothes, do you?' she asked, allowing her gleaming hair to brush against his face and swinging her legs over him so that she was sitting on his lap.

'Of course not.' For the first time in their married life he didn't respond to her move. 'It's just that – well, you hardly need any more, do you?'

'It's not a question of needing.' She kissed him on the nose. 'It's a question of having.'

'Having?'

'Being prepared,' she amended. 'For every eventuality.'

'We don't have that many eventualities you need to be prepared for,' said Donald.

'No?' She put her arms behind his neck and kissed him on the lips this time. 'What about the night you brought your managing director to the house for a drink? That's cocktail glam. Or the day we met your friends for lunch at the yacht club? Smart casual but not too casual. Or the night we went to dinner in the flashy restaurant? Sophisticated. Or the day we did the charity walk? Sports casual.'

'I know you need different things for those events,' conceded Donald. 'But there's not that many of them.'

'What about when I go out with my friends?' she asked. 'I have

54

to look good. I have to let them know that in marrying Donald Fitzpatrick I made the right choice.'

'Of course you made the right choice,' he said. 'I love you.'

'And I love you too,' she said as she nuzzled his ear. 'I want you to think you made the right choice too. I want you to be proud of me when you see me beside all those other women.'

'Oh, I'm proud of you all right.' Donald gave in to the allure of her body. 'How could I not be?'

'How could you not,' she agreed as she set to work to help him forget about the credit card bill and remember why it was that he'd fallen for her in the first place.

Zoey had met Donald at a low ebb in his life. He was going through a bad time personally and professionally, and (as he said at the time) the sharp pain in his tooth was the final straw. She was the receptionist in the dental surgery but she'd never seen him before. He confessed, as he cradled his jaw in his hand, that he hadn't been for his yearly check-up in, well, three years, so it was probably his own fault. Zoey, however, gave him a sympathetic look and told him that nobody ever did what they were meant to when it came to their teeth but she'd find out if Mr Johnson could see him straight away.

'I reckon you have an abscess,' she said.

Afterwards, Donald told her that she'd been like an angel, fussing over him, comforting him, calming him. He hated the dentist, always had, hated the noise of the drill and the helpless feeling as he lay back in the chair; hated too the way the dental nurses and receptionists always made him feel like a naughty schoolboy for not looking after his teeth properly.

'In fact you hate everything about it,' she said as she keyed in the details of his follow-up appointment. (She'd been right, it was an abscess.)

'Except you,' he said.

A week after he'd had his check-up, he'd phoned her and asked her on a date. She'd been surprised and then doubtful because he was way older than her, but she wasn't seeing anyone herself at the time (having dumped her most recent boyfriend for being a total bore) and she reckoned that it might be a nice night out.

Donald had taken her for a meal at a top city restaurant, followed by a drink in a quiet bar – although she'd nearly bailed out before the drink because he'd mentioned his ex-wife, Deirdre (afterwards often referred to by Zoey as Disgruntled Deirdre), and his two daughters, both in their late teens, who were placing enormous demands on him. The demands were for money, in the case of all three, who seemed to regard the bank of Donald as pretty limitless; and for his time, at least as far as Deirdre was concerned. Donald's soon-to-be-ex-wife hadn't seemed to grasp the concept that their impending divorce meant getting out of each other's lives, and would ring him up whenever she had a minor problem, which she expected him to solve for her immediately.

Zoey wasn't keen on going out with a man with a money-grabbing ex and teenage daughters, but Donald was good company and far more mature than the guys she normally dated – well, he *was* more mature, she reminded herself; he was in his forties after all! Nevertheless, she enjoyed being with someone who was confident, who wore nice clothes (she was fed up with guys who thought ripped jeans and a rugby shirt was actually dressed up) and, above all, who treated her well. If Donald said he'd call, he called, and if he said he'd meet her somewhere at seven, he was there at seven. Zoey liked that. It made her feel special.

By their third date, she'd decided that his age and his previous marriage didn't matter. They got on well together and he was fun to be with. Besides, all of his credit cards were platinum, he drove a top-of-the-range BMW and he was living in a penthouse apartment in the city centre while his divorce from Deirdre was being negotiated. Zoey couldn't help thinking that she could do a lot worse than Donald Fitzpatrick; that she'd done a lot worse than him in the past, and that she deserved the good times he was giving her now.

They'd married shortly after his divorce came through. Zoey had suffered doubts before their wedding, thinking that Disgruntled Deirdre had somehow managed to get far more out of the deal than Donald had expected or wanted, and worrying that his first wife and children would be a constant drain on their resources; but, as her mother pointed out, the Fitzpatrick family seemed to be very well off and Donald's father lived in a gorgeous house on Howth Hill, so one way or another Donald was probably a good bet. Besides, Lesley had added, he's a nice enough guy and not at all bad for someone pushing fifty. She'd chortled at her own comment, which made Zoey poke her in the ribs and tell her not to be a cougar, and to keep her hands off her fiancé.

Zoey had smothered her doubts because she loved Donald, although she had to admit that it wasn't exactly the sort of hot passion she'd had for some of her previous boyfriends. But those experiences had only made her realise that hot passion eventually faded, and she was satisfied that even if Donald wasn't the most inventive man between the sheets, he was thoughtful and considerate. Most importantly, he loved her, and she knew that she loved being loved by him too.

She wasn't entirely sure how the rest of his family felt about her. She knew that his father, Fred, thought she was attractive, because at their engagement party she'd overhead him speaking to his other son, Gareth, and saying that Donald had certainly applied a very different set of criteria to the second Mrs Fitzpatrick compared with the first, and that he'd upped the ante in the beauty stakes, which was no bad thing, the girl was a stunner. That had made her smile. She liked being thought of as a stunner.

Gareth's response to his father had been non-committal, and although he was always perfectly courteous to her, Zoey couldn't help feeling that he didn't rate her as highly as he did his brother's former wife. Gareth's own wife Lisette was a bitch, though, with her haughty air and her way of looking at people as though they were beneath her. When they'd been introduced, Lisette had pecked her on both cheeks and said 'enchanted' in a way that Zoey thought meant the exact opposite.

There was a sister, too, Suzanne, who hadn't come to the wedding despite being invited. Suzanne had sent a brief note with her regret card, saying that she was on business in the States and couldn't come but wishing them every happiness. Donald had been annoyed at the card and muttered that Suzanne still carried chips on both shoulders, that there was nothing stopping her from coming, she was just a hotel employee after all.

Zoey had hoped she'd get on with Sorcha and Karen, Donald's daughters, but she thought they were bitchy and self-centred and she hated how they only ever seemed to phone their father whenever they wanted something. Which, with both of them, was usually money. Zoey understood perfectly that girls of nearly twenty and eighteen needed cash, but she felt that they could be out there earning it themselves instead of sponging off their father, a habit they'd clearly inherited from Deirdre, who rang at least once a week complaining about something or other.

All in all, Zoey found that being Donald's second wife wasn't quite as easy as she'd expected, and she reckoned that an unquestioning payment of her credit card bills was the least he could do to compensate her for the fact that she had to put up with a lot of shit from other people with the Fitzpatrick name.

Another concern for Zoey – although it was for the future and not right now – was what would happen when they had a child of their own. She didn't want her own precious baby playing second fiddle to the spoilt princesses Sorcha and Karen. She hadn't discussed children with Donald yet. She wasn't ready to give up on her social life and ruin her figure, nor was she sure that Donald was ready to start putting his second family ahead of his first.

Eventually, however, she hoped he'd disentangle himself from Disgruntled Deirdre and her grasping children. Just as she hoped he'd inherit a big chunk of his father's estate. Zoey knew that Fred was a shrewd man; she reckoned he was far cannier than his sons. (She always took Donald's assertion that he himself was a smart businessman with a liberal pinch of salt. A smart businessman wouldn't have allowed himself to be shafted by someone like Deirdre.) She was aware that Lisette and Gareth were also hoping to cash in on Fred's eventual demise, which was why she made sure that she called to Furze Hill every couple of weeks to see how he was. She always dropped in after she'd been for one of her many beauty treatments, and wore a low-cut top or a figure-hugging dress, which she knew Fred liked. It didn't bother her that the old man ogled her. The way Zoey saw it, he didn't have much time left and he might as well look because he was never going to get the opportunity to do anything about it. From her perspective, the time spent parading her assets in front of her father-in-law was an investment in her future.

She was hoping that it might result in him leaving the house to her and Donald. Zoey reckoned that they deserved Furze Hill. Donald was the eldest, after all, and he'd had to hand over his lovely Clontarf home to Deirdre. Gareth and Lisette's house, Thorngrove, was huge. Suzanne lived abroad. So surely nobody could object to her and Donald getting Fred's house? She could see herself having breakfast on the sun-drenched patio overlooking the sea (though it would have to be renovated first; at the moment the flagstones were cracked and uneven and a potential death trap. Mr Fitzpatrick was lucky that he hadn't yet tripped over one and done worse things to himself than spraining his wrist). Furze Hill would be a big step up from their current home, and Zoey reckoned that Donald was entitled to it. After all, he'd been the son who'd stuck with the family business; surely he merited extra compensation for helping in its success?

However, despite the fact that her father-in-law was in his eighties, and had cheated death a few times already, Zoey wasn't banking on Fred doing the decent thing and checking out just yet. Which meant that she still had to keep as much money as possible out of the claws of Disgruntled Deirdre and available to spend on herself, no matter how jumpy Donald got over the bills.

He hadn't been too keen on the idea of a birthday party either, until she'd pointed out to him that it would be another occasion where he could provoke envy from his friends at having the most beautiful wife in the room. Zoey knew that the wives in Donald's set couldn't hold a candle to her, because most them were now relying on Botox, collagen and light-diffusing creams to look their best, whereas she still had the youthful, dewy complexion that they could only dream about. It was a boost to Donald's ego to know that he was with Zoey, and she wanted to make sure it stayed boosted. Which meant looking her very best in front of all of his friends.

She knew she'd find the dress to help her do just that. And the right shoes, underwear, jewellery too . . . Zoey smiled to herself. She loved shopping. It was one thing in life that she knew she was really good at. And it was important that her husband was able to allow her to keep doing it.

Chapter 7

After his daughter-in-law had left (he'd been grateful for the shopping and for the bit of company, but he was still glad when she'd gone), Fred went into the living room, with its panoramic views of the sea. But he wasn't interested in the views today. He opened the web browser on his computer and clicked on his search history. He wanted to go back to some of the pages he'd been looking at earlier.

Fred was comfortable with computers. He'd always been at the forefront of new technology, which was why he'd done so well in the car alarm and security business. He thought machines were a lot easier to understand than people, and far more predictable.

He loved being able to find things out at the click of a button, but it annoyed him how easily he was distracted from the pages he'd set out to look at. Clicking links dragged him off into areas where he didn't need to be but which intrigued him all the same. He understood why it was called surfing – that was exactly what he felt happened to him every time he was pulled from page to page in an undertow of irrelevant information – but it irritated him all the same.

He opened the last item he'd been looking at and then realised that it was the image of an old newspaper and not the page he wanted. He'd originally searched for it out of curiosity, but events from the year he was born didn't interest him very much. Fifty-five years ago, though, that was a different story. Fifty-five years ago mattered a good deal to Fred. Despite the proliferation of information on the internet, however, none of it was relevant to what he wanted to find out. The truth was, Fred thought to himself as he clicked on another futile link, he needed a professional to do the work for him. In his younger days he might have been able to track down the people he wanted to track down, but as it was . . . He grunted in disgust and rubbed his injured wrist. He hated being eighty-one. He hated that he couldn't depend on his once virile body to behave as he wanted it to behave. In his youth he'd jeered at doddery old gits who took half an hour to cross the road. These days he was a doddery old git himself and he only crossed the road at pedestrian lights. Old externally, of course. Internally he was the same person he'd always been.

Although that wasn't strictly true. He leaned back in his chair and stared at the keyboard. He was a very different Fred Fitzpatrick from the twenty-five-year-old Fred. Or the forty-five-year-old Fred. Or even the sixty-five-year-old Fred. The last few years were the ones that had changed him. And now he was a softer and less driven Fred. Maybe even a regretful Fred.

He hated having regrets, that was the thing. He never used to regret anything. He didn't regret for a second all the time and energy he'd poured into his business over the years, even though he knew of lots of people who said that they wished they'd spent more time with their families. He thought he'd spent exactly the right amount of time with his. He didn't regret spending the money he'd made on buying a statement house in one of Dublin's most affluent areas. He didn't care that he was rattling around in it on his own, or that most of his neighbours were – in his eyes – pretentious tossers. (He didn't regret not getting to know them either. Assholes, the lot of them.) He didn't regret his marriage to Ros, or even the affairs that had peppered it. These things happened. There was nothing he could do about it. He didn't regret how he'd brought up his children, because in the end, they'd learned to stand on their own two feet. He'd had a reason for everything he'd done, at home, at work, socially. He'd lived a full life, a happy life, and if there was one thing he'd learned during it, it was that there was no point in regrets.

But damn it, he couldn't help regretting Dilly. He couldn't believe that he kept thinking of her now, her pretty heart-shaped face infiltrating his dreams and reminding him that he'd once loved her. He didn't want to have to chalk Dilly up as a regret. But he couldn't help it. He'd have to do something about it.

He couldn't have said or done anything when Ros was alive. That would have rocked the foundations of their marriage in a way that his occasional affairs never had. Ros knew nothing of Dilly and he'd seen no point in telling her. His wife had been an understanding, supportive woman (her friends called her a saint, but of course she bloody wasn't; she just knew that she wouldn't do any better than him), but she wouldn't have been supportive about Dilly. He knew that.

Funny how he hadn't thought of Dilly in years, yet now, when there were times he couldn't remember what he'd gone into a room for, he could recall everything about her. Her peaches-and-cream complexion, her soft blue eyes, her mane of golden hair and her luscious, desirable body. When he thought of Dilly, he felt young again, he felt like the carefree Fred he'd been in the days before he'd had to worry about a wife and a family and a business that had been twenty-four-seven before anyone had ever used the expression. Sometimes he wondered how his life would have turned out if he'd treated her better. If he would have been a better person himself. If he wouldn't have anything at all to regret.

He grunted. He was being stupid now. Stupid and maudlin and acting like an old man. The past was a different country. He knew that. And as for the present . . . despite his physical infirmities, he was still a powerful man. He allowed himself a moment of satisfaction with the power that he knew he had. He'd seen it reflected in Lisette's eyes when she'd caught sight of the will. He'd meant for her to see it. He liked to remind her that he was still very much a part of the family.

Not that they should need any of his money now, of course. They had jobs of their own, houses of their own, lives of their own. Nevertheless, everyone had gone through hard times over the last few years, and he knew that they weren't as comfortably off as they might have expected to be by now. But perhaps that was their own fault too. Perhaps the knowledge that he was there in the background had made them take the wrong kind of risks.

One way or another, though, they still had expectations. They needed to tailor those expectations, thought Fred. He'd been generous to them before, and that generosity wasn't boundless. Besides, he now had other interests, other obligations to think about.

He'd call Alex Shannon in the morning and chat to him about it. His solicitor knew him well and would be able to advise him on the best way to go about things. Fred had a lot of faith in Alex. Even so, maybe it wouldn't work out. If it didn't, well, he'd rethink his future plans. But if it did, he'd have important decisions to make. It was unfinished business, after all. And Fred didn't like unfinished business hanging over him.

PART 3

THE DISCLOSURE

Chapter 8

Abbey Andersen worked late on Fridays, which was always one of the salon's busiest days. Today had been even busier than most for her – in addition to her regular manicures and extensions, the list of clients wanting nail art was growing all the time. Her last appointment had been identical twin sisters who were throwing a birthday bash and had asked for matching party nails with lots of bling and glitter. The girls were excited about the party and chatted throughout their time with her, commenting enthusiastically on the design she'd devised for them and telling her that she should set up her own website with pictures of all her work. Because, said one, they'd never seen nail art as funky and original as hers, and it was a shame not to share it with everyone.

She told them that there were plenty of samples of her stuff on the Mariposa site, but if they were OK with it, she'd add their nail work too. The girls agreed happily, gave her a generous tip and told her that they looked forward to seeing it there. Then they headed off, still chattering and giggling. Abbey smiled as they went. She got a tremendous buzz from seeing clients leave the salon happy, and the Benson twins had been fun to work with. They weren't the first people to have suggested to her that she set up a site either, she reflected as she sent the photo to Selina to add to the gallery. Her own friends had said it to her too. The last time she'd seen Pete, he'd told her that she should leave Mariposa and set up on her own, but then Pete was big into people being entrepreneurial and working for themselves. She usually dismissed all of these suggestions. She was happy to be part of the team at the salon. She was in her comfort zone. Besides, she saw too many stressed-out women trying to fit a little bit of pampering into an over-full day to want to take on stress of her own by working for herself.

She was tired but content as she changed from her heels into her trainers and began the ten-minute walk from the salon on Powell to the apartment she shared on O'Farrell with her boyfriend, Cobey. Selina had opened two more Mariposa salons since Abbey first started working full-time with her, and the Powell Street branch was now the flagship salon. The interior was bright and airy, with the salon's signature butterfly motif etched into the frosted-glass doors, and each of the treatment rooms named after a particular species. Although it was constantly busy, the atmosphere was one of complete tranquillity, which made it very popular with people who worked in the city.

I'm so lucky, thought Abbey, as she admired a chic (but totally unaffordable) jacket in the Saks window display before continuing down the street. I have a job that makes me happy, I work with a great team and my clients are lovely too. I have a cool boyfriend and a nice apartment and I think I've finally got to a place in my life where I know what I'm doing. I also have opportunities ahead of me, because even if I don't want to strike out on my own, the nail business is booming now. More and more people are wanting to express themselves with their nails. And they're right. Great nails are uplifting.

Back in the day, when she'd been studying art, Abbey's mom had declared that great art was spiritually uplifting. Did the fact that she herself was now saying the same thing about nails mean that nail art was every bit as spiritual as oils on canvas? Abbey wondered. Perhaps the next time she saw her mom she'd raise that question with her. Although she already knew what the answer would be. Nevertheless . . . Abbey adjusted her bag on her shoulder and picked up the pace as she neared the apartment. She'd made the right decision in abandoning the gallery for the salon. No question.

She keyed in the code to the entrance door and then walked up the stairs to the first-floor apartment. She still got an extra thrill every time she let herself in. She loved living with Cobey, a tall, lanky tour guide she'd met at a party six months earlier. They'd clicked straight away, the first time that had ever happened to her with a boyfriend. It usually took her time to allow someone into her life, and even then she liked to keep a certain distance between them. Which was why, according to Vanessa and Solí, her closest friends, she'd never had a long-term relationship. Abbey thought her friends were overanalysing when they talked about commitment. She was perfectly able to commit. It was about finding the right person to commit to, being confident that they felt the same way, being sure that you weren't giving too much of yourself away.

From the get-go she'd been confident with Cobey. And so, when after only three weeks he'd asked if she wanted to move in with him, she'd surprised everyone who knew her by saying yes. Moving in with him made her feel as though she'd finally grown up. She wasn't sure that her mom – when she eventually got around to telling her – would entirely agree, but given that she wasn't a major part of Abbey's life any more, it didn't really matter what she thought. The important thing was that she herself was happy. She hummed under her breath as she unlocked the apartment door. It was impossible not to be happy with Cobey in her life.

The moment she opened the door to the apartment, she knew something was different. Nothing seemed out of place, yet as she walked into the living room, she looked around warily, as though someone else might be there.

Then she saw the pink Post-it note stuck to the enormous larder fridge that took up most of the tiny galley kitchen. Abbey dropped her bag on the sofa and walked over to it. She read it where it was, still attached to the fridge, and then she tore it from the fridge door and read it again.

Babes, Cobey had written in his looping script. *I've got a job on a cruise liner. Easier for me to do it this way. I'm not good on good-byes. Was fun. Cx*

She turned the note over, wondering if she was missing something. Cobey hadn't said anything to her about applying for a job on a cruise liner. He hadn't even said that he was thinking about leaving the tour company where he worked. He was supposed to be setting up a tourist business of his own! She'd helped him design a website, for heaven's sake. So what the hell . . . She read the note again with increasing disbelief. He was having a laugh. He had to be.

Holding the note in her shaking hand, she walked into the bedroom. The bed was still unmade (on Fridays Cobey left the apartment later than her), and his half-empty bottle of water was on the shelf on his side. The magazine he'd been reading the previous night was beside it. She picked it up, replaced it, then opened the wardrobe doors. She stared at the empty hangers, then closed her eyes, waited a moment and looked again. The hangers were still empty. The shelves were still bare. All Cobey's clothes were gone. She reread the note one more time. She felt sick. And she still didn't quite believe it.

She sat on the edge of the bed and took out her cell phone. She scrolled to Cobey's number and dialled it.

'Hi, this is Cobey. I'll get back to you.'

She'd always teased him about his voicemail message. It was too short and too abrupt, she told him. But he pointed out that it got the job done.

'Cobey,' she said, trying hard to keep her voice steady. 'What the hell is going on? Where is this job? For how long? When . . . when are you coming back?' Although even as she spoke, her eyes were drawn back to his words. He wasn't good on goodbyes. And the note sounded pretty final to her.

Despite the fact that she knew she was wasting her time, she got up and searched the apartment for anything he might have left behind. Anything that would give her a clue as to why he'd walked out without talking to her first. Because regardless of the fact that he'd got a new job and wanted to leave, breaking up with her by Post-it note was unreal. Cowardly. Cruel. She hadn't thought he was that sort of person. She'd trusted him. Loved him.

And now she'd been abandoned by him.

I specialise in that, she thought as she stared unseeingly from the living-room window. I specialise in people walking out and never coming back. Why? What's the matter with me that the people I love do that? She leaned her head against the window. And she started to cry.

Later that evening, after leaving another two messages on his voicemail, she opened the Facebook app on her iPad and clicked on Cobey's page. As she looked at his public profile, she realised that he had de-friended her. She felt a hot rage well up to go along with her misery. The man who had told her over and over that he loved her, the man she'd trusted and believed in, had dumped and de-friended her.

She clicked on 'Message' and began to type.

I got your horrible note. What's it all about? Why didn't you say anything before now? Why didn't you talk to me? I deserve that much at least! Call me. Or message me. She hesitated for a moment, and then added, **Please. I love you. I thought you loved me.**

After hitting send, she sat in front of the TV with the iPad on her lap, constantly refreshing the page in case she missed his reply. By two in the morning, she realised that there wasn't going to be one. By seven thirty, ten minutes before she had to get up for work, she finally fell asleep.

She got through the next few days on autopilot, glad that she had to work through the weekend but unable, even moments after finishing a client's nails, to remember anything about the job she'd just done. Normally when they talked to her she listened attentively – half the job, she often told herself, was being a confidante for the ladies who came to see her. She reckoned she knew more about their lives than they ever realised. She'd never really understood before how it was that some of her clients opened up so much to her, especially those to whom she was a virtual stranger. She'd listened to stories of infidelity and jealousy, of love and betrayal, of highs and of lows, and she'd stored them all away while telling herself that she was too sensible a person to let these things happen to her. But I'm not, she thought now as she applied a coat of red shellac to a businesswoman who was making an important presentation that afternoon and who wanted to look assured and commanding. I moved in with a guy and he dumped me. I'm exactly the same as every other woman who's been let down. Even worse than lots of them, because he dumped me by sticking a goddam pink note to the fridge! Every time she thought of it, she felt a knot of miserable fury ball up in her stomach.

Selina, who'd spotted Abbey's pale face and red-rimmed eyes the moment she'd walked into the salon that Monday morning, had asked her if everything was all right, and Abbey had replied that she was a bit tired but that she was fine. Even as she'd said it, she'd realised that she was trotting out the same sort of excuses her friends came up with after a break-up, and she knew that Selina would immediately realise what had happened. But she couldn't bring herself to tell her yet. She still wasn't able to say it out loud.

She left early, her head thumping with one of the migraines that she occasionally suffered from, and let herself into the apartment. She opened the mail box and saw a letter addressed to Cobey inside. She brought it upstairs, unsure of whether she should open it or not. Then she told herself that he was the one that had walked out and he was the one that hadn't left a forwarding address and that she was entitled to look at his post. Vaguely, at the back of her headache-throbbing mind, she recalled that opening someone else's mail was a federal offence. But breaking someone's heart should be an offence too, she thought, and perhaps the letter would give her some idea as to which cruise line Cobey was working for and where he'd actually gone.

But the letter, when she unfolded it, was nothing to do with Cobey's career. It was a reminder from the landlord of a notice to quit, in which he was also demanding three months' overdue rent plus penalties. Abbey looked at it in horror. It wasn't possible that Cobey owed rental money. She gave him her share of it every month. The apartment, though not outrageous by the city's standards, wasn't cheap, and Abbey couldn't have afforded it on her own, but Cobey had been living by himself before she'd turned up and . . . and . . . She squeezed her eyes shut and wished her head would stop pounding. He'd been relaxed about the rental money, not to worry, he had it under control. But when she'd insisted, he'd put his arm around her and told her that they were good together, that they'd always be good together, that he loved her.

She gritted her teeth at the memory. And then the other memory came to her. The memory of handing him the extra money to pay off his credit card bill so that he could go to the bank with a clean credit history to get a loan for additional website development. She'd asked Vanessa, who worked in a bank, to set up a meeting for him with a local account executive, and he'd been so delighted that he'd taken her for a moonlight boat ride around the bay. The meeting had gone well, he said. Things had been set in motion. Soon Cobey Tours would be a reality.

How did getting a job on a cruise liner fit in with the great plans he'd had for his own business? With spending evenings messing around on his laptop 'setting things up', as he'd put it? With borrowing money from her? How did all those things fit in with him deciding to walk out on her without paying the rent, for which she'd already given him money every month?

She exhaled slowly. They didn't. The only thing all those things fitted in with was him taking her for a fool. Which she had been. No question.

She looked at the landlord's letter again. She wasn't sure what she was supposed to do. When she'd moved into the apartment, Cobey hadn't bothered updating the lease to include her. But now . . . She swallowed hard. What if she was liable for the rent he hadn't paid? What if she owed . . . she looked at the letter again . . . what if she owed nearly three months plus penalties? That would wipe out the rest of her savings – the savings she'd already raided to help him out! She caught her breath and her head hurt more than ever.

She couldn't do anything today, she felt too ill. But tomorrow she would try to contact his other friends, see if they knew what was going on.

Her phone rang and her heart leapt. But the caller display showed it was Solí. Abbey didn't have the strength to talk to Solí right now, and so, like the call she'd received from Vanessa the previous night, she let it go to voicemail while she lay down on the sofa and closed her eyes.

The following evening, finally feeling able to talk about it, Abbey rang both Solí and Vanessa and told them that Cobey had left her. She also told them about the notice to quit, but couldn't bring herself to confess to having lent him money. Both girls immediately called around to the apartment, bringing flowers and chocolates and giving her lots of sympathetic hugs.

'I can't believe it.' Solí's dark curls danced around her face as she shook her head in anger. 'I thought he was a nice guy! Post-it note? That's crap!'

Abbey bit her lip as Vanessa put her arms around her and told her that he wasn't worth her tears.

'I'm not crying,' she protested weakly, even as an unwanted tear trickled down her cheek. She hated the idea that Cobey had pierced her defences enough to make her cry. 'At least, I'm crying, but only because I'm so angry with him.'

'You've got to move on,' said Vanessa.

'I know. But first . . . I want to see Mike. Maybe he knows where Cobey has gone.'

'Is that a good idea?' Solí looked doubtful. 'Mike is his best friend. He's not going to be on your side.'

'I don't care,' said Abbey. 'I've got to see him.'

Vanessa and Solí exchanged glances, but Abbey was utterly determined so they said they'd go with her.

'Thanks,' said Abbey as she took out her concealer to repair the damage to her eyes. 'I'm lucky to have you guys.'

Mike worked at a small restaurant near Fisherman's Wharf, and Abbey spotted him almost immediately, carrying a tray of chowder to an outside table.

She called his name. When he saw her, Mike grimaced.

'Where's Cobey?' Abbey didn't waste time on pleasantries. She'd seen from his expression that he already knew why she was here.

'He's off working,' replied Mike.

'I know that!' cried Abbey. 'At least – I know that's what he said. I know he said he had a job on a cruise liner. But given that almost everything else he's ever told me has been a complete lie, I wondered if that was too.'

'Come on, Abbey.' Mike moved away from the diners, who were looking at them with undisguised interest. 'This isn't the time or the place.'

'It sure is, buddy,' said Solí. 'We're not going anywhere till you tell us what your friend is up to.'

Mike groaned. 'Look, I know he feels bad about this, Abbey. But the truth was that the company he was with was having problems and they were letting people go. Cobey knew it was only a matter of time. So when he was offered the job on the liner, it was a no-brainer.'

'But why didn't he tell me?' cried Abbey. 'We were living together, for God's sake.'

'Yeah, well, he saw it as an opportunity,' said Mike. 'To get out and do something new.'

'He was supposed to be setting up a business himself.' Abbey looked at him in bewilderment.

'But he decided on a new start,' said Mike. 'A new life.'

'What was wrong with his life with me?'

'Hey, he *loved* living with you,' Mike said. 'But . . . well, this was a great chance and so he took it.'

'What liner?' asked Abbey.

'I don't know,' Mike replied.

'Yes you do.' Solí's tone was scathing.

'Cobey's my friend,' said Mike defensively. 'But he's . . . well, he's not someone who stays in one place. He likes to move around, likes variety.'

'Likes not answering his phone, too,' said Vanessa. 'Least he could do would be to talk to her.'

'It doesn't matter.' Abbey spoke abruptly. 'He's gone. He's not coming back. It doesn't matter.'

She turned and walked quickly along the pier. Vanessa and Solí glanced at each other and then hurried after her.

None of them spoke as she continued to stride determinedly through the crowds and then along Jefferson Street, her back straight, her body tense. Eventually, though, Solí caught her by the arm.

'It's OK, Abbey,' she said.

'It's not.' Abbey turned to her, her eyes glistening. 'He's played me for a fool.'

'Men do that,' said Vanessa.

'No they don't. They might break up with you, sure, but how many of them leave you a note saying that they've got a new job and are never going to see you again?'

'Probably more than you think,' said Solí. 'You know they like to take the easy way out.'

'A cruise liner.' Abbey pressed her fingers to her temples. 'Why do people always want to get as far away from me as possible?'

'That's not true,' said Solí. 'We're here.'

Abbey gave her a watery smile.

'C'mon,' said Solí. 'Time for us to get wasted.'

Abbey didn't believe that the solution to life's problems, in particular problems with men, was getting wasted, but she didn't say no when her friends led her into a bar and ordered a pitcher of margaritas. She was happy to let the alcohol blunt her misery while Vanessa and Solí chanted empowering mantras at her and said that she'd done enough crying over Cobey, who should now be firmly put into the category of stupid-mistakes-I've-made-with-men.

Maybe they're right, thought Abbey. Maybe everyone has to have at least one shitty break-up. After all, every other time I've split with a guy it's been sort of amicable. I was due a bad deal. Mom would call it character-forming. But dammit, she said to herself as she allowed Vanessa to top up her glass, I thought my character was formed enough as it was. I thought I'd already paid my dues. Only goes to show how wrong you can be.

She wasn't sure whether her aching head the next morning was due to the margaritas, or if it was the start of another migraine. When she got out of bed, she poured herself a large glass of juice, took some pills, and decided that she had to deal with her future. The first thing to do was sort out her living arrangements, especially given the issue over the rent. She certainly couldn't stay in the apartment for much longer – she wasn't even sure if she should be there now, although nobody had yet come to turf her out. She didn't know what to do about it, though. Solí had offered to let her stay at her place for a while, but as Solí lived in a studio, that wasn't a very practical arrangement. Vanessa lived with her younger sister and didn't have a spare room either. Abbey clamped down on the sudden feeling of panic that washed over her as she tried to form a plan. Until she'd moved in with Cobey, she'd shared a place with two girls who also worked in the beauty industry. She hadn't been close friends with either of them, but they'd got on well together and she'd been very happy there. It was because she'd enjoyed sharing with

Maria and Caitlin so much that she'd never wanted to move in with a boyfriend before. She couldn't believe that she'd thrown it all away on Cobey Missen. And thrown it away she had, because the girls had rented out her room almost as soon as she'd left. So there was no going back.

She sighed and checked her Facebook page. No reply from Cobey to her messages (not that she truly expected one), but he'd changed his profile picture to one of him standing on board a ship, the blue sea in the background.

You should have told me, she said hotly as she stabbed the home button to get rid of the photo. But if you'd told me, then you couldn't have walked out owing me money. You shit! She was glad that she was angry with him. Angry was better than being miserable.

She was about to take a shower when her cell phone rang. She didn't recognise the number and her heart leapt traitorously. Maybe this time it was Cobey. Maybe he had a reason, an explanation for everything. Maybe he hadn't really cheated her after all.

Ten minutes later she was shaking. The call hadn't been from Cobey. It had been from the landlord, reminding her that she had to be out of the apartment by the end of the month and advising her that she would be pursued for the outstanding rent. When she tried to explain that she'd given the money to Cobey, he said that he didn't care what her arrangements with that douche bag were, he wanted his money and it didn't matter who he was getting it from.

Abbey wished she knew how he'd found out about her and got her number. But it didn't matter. The result was that her worst fears had been realised. Cobey had sold her out and left her to face the music. She was in deep trouble and none of it was of her own making.

In the end it was Pete, as always, who came to her rescue. Abbey hadn't wanted to contact him and ask for his help. The way she looked at it, her mom's ex-boyfriend had eventually moved on with his life and certainly had no obligation towards her, despite the fact that he still kept in touch.

Abbey was happy that Pete had finally met someone who loved him and wanted to share her life with him, even if she'd been surprised when he'd introduced her to the very glamorous Claudia, who, she thought, was the complete opposite of her own mother. But Claudia suited Pete and he now had a proper family of his own. The couple had two children – Grady, who was twelve, from Claudia's previous marriage, and Joely, now four, who was their own daughter. Even though Pete regularly asked her to dinner at his stylish house in Sausalito, Abbey strictly limited her visits. She was very conscious that her connection to Pete was tenuous at best, and didn't want to intrude on the Carusos' lives. While Claudia was always welcoming, Abbey was never a hundred per cent sure that her reception was as warm as the other woman made it seem. And she couldn't blame Claudia one bit. She was Pete's wife, they had a child together; Abbey was nothing more than a reminder of his past and the other woman in it.

So, ever since Claudia had appeared on the scene, Abbey had cut back on her time with Pete – the last time she'd seen him had been shortly after she'd moved in with Cobey. And the truth was, they hadn't parted on the best of terms. Pete hadn't liked Cobey very much; he'd said that Abbey's new boyfriend was too cocky for his own good. Abbey's view was that Pete was being overprotective and that he resented the fact that she'd finally found someone she wanted to be with. Jealous was the word she'd used (and immediately wished she hadn't). You're jealous of me having my own life, she'd said to him. Jealous that I don't need you any more.

But she needed him now.

'He what!' Pete had practically bellowed down the phone when she told him what had happened. 'And you're being harassed over the rent? That's a crock of shit, honey. Don't you worry. I'll sort it for you.'

And he had, meeting the landlord, agreeing on a reduced payment for the outstanding rent and getting the deal signed and sealed all within a few hours of her initial phone call.

'Sometimes it's good to have a lawyer in the family,' Pete told her afterwards as they had coffee in Union Square, a short walk from his office.

'I know. I can't thank you enough.'

'Honey, you don't need to thank me. You know I'm always here for you,' said Pete.

Abbey couldn't speak. She was always trying to prove to him that she could get by without him, but Pete was the one person who never let her down.

'Look, everyone has to cut their teeth on someone who isn't worth their while.' Pete took her hand and squeezed it. 'You came to the party a bit late, Abbey. It's no big deal.'

'So the girls keep telling me, but it's big to me.' She swallowed hard. 'I'm such an idiot. I thought he was more right for me than any of my other boyfriends, but the truth is, I was totally wrong. How could I be so stupid?'

'Live and learn,' said Pete cheerfully.

'I gave up so much for him,' Abbey told him. 'You didn't want me to. I should've listened.'

'Nobody listens to other people's advice.' Pete grinned at her. 'If they did, we wouldn't need so many lawyers in the world.'

She smiled shakily.

'I . . . there's something else.'

'What?'

She hadn't intended to tell Pete, but now she wanted to admit the full extent of her silliness. 'I lent him money,' she confessed.

Pete said nothing, but she could see his eyes darkening.

'It doesn't matter,' she said quickly. 'I mean, it does because I was so stupid, but . . . well, it's only money.'

'I guess if you're going to make a mistake over a man, you might as well make it big and get it over with,' said Pete. 'You need a bit of time out to take stock. So how about this, honey. You move in with us . . .'

'I can't do that,' Abbey said quickly. 'Thanks for offering, Pete, but I'm not going to mess up your family life.'

'. . . at the end of the week,' continued Pete, as though she hadn't spoken. 'We're heading off on vacation then. Three weeks in the Caribbean.' He made a face. 'Not that I really want to be out of town for three weeks, but I promised Claudia a long break this year and a promise is a promise. Anyhow, you can house-sit and dog-sit for us, because otherwise we'd have to put Battle into kennels. And I was feeling bad about that.'

Battle was the family's enormous but gentle golden Labrador.

'You'd be doing us a favour,' said Pete. 'Honestly you would.'

Abbey looked at him wordlessly. No matter what the problem, Pete would come up with a solution. He was a fixer. He always had been.

'So why don't you get your stuff together and I'll drop by the apartment this evening and we can get this show on the road,' said Pete.

She nodded slowly. 'Thank you. I . . . I don't deserve you in my life.'

'How many times have I told you to stop selling yourself short?' he demanded. 'You deserve the best and you should remind yourself of that over and over.'

'Right.' Her voice wobbled. 'I don't know what I'd do without you, though.'

'You'd manage fine. You're like your mom. A trouper.'

'I've never heard her called that before.'

'She's a strong woman.'

'Maybe. But I can't help thinking she let you down, Pete.'

Pete took her by the hands. 'You and your mom came into my life when I needed you most,' he said. 'Just because things didn't work out the way I'd hoped doesn't mean I won't always love both of you.'

'Please don't let Claudia hear you say that,' begged Abbey. 'She's your wife and you love her more.'

'I adore Claudia,' said Pete. 'You know I do. There's no need to worry. Love isn't like a pie, Abbey. It doesn't have a set number of slices. There's always enough to go round.'

'You're beginning to sound like Mom now.' But Abbey was smiling as they walked out of the café together, and for the first time since Cobey had left, her head wasn't aching, even if her heart was still sore.

Chapter 9

Abbey liked to sing in the shower. Given that she had the sort of voice that wouldn't have got her past *American Idol* auditions, the shower was the safest place for her to belt out the Venezuelan joropo music she'd grown up with, as well as the songs from the badly dubbed musicals she'd watched with her mom as a kid. Today, two weeks after her break-up with Cobey, was the first day she'd felt able to sing. And she was passionately informing herself that she was going to wash that man right out of her hair. *South Pacific* had been one of her mother's favourites, and she'd regularly sung this particular number when she was giving Abbey her bath as a child, belting out the tune as she lathered the shampoo into her daughter's long blond hair.

'I'm not sure I've entirely succeeded in sending him on his way,' Abbey murmured as she eventually turned off the water and wrapped herself in a bright yellow towel. 'But at least I don't feel like I'm going to burst into tears every few minutes.' She'd found that talking out loud to herself seemed to help, although she didn't know why. 'Anyhow,' she added, 'it's about time I got things into perspective. I'm twenty-eight years old and the worst thing that's happened to me has been him. At my age, my mom had worked overseas, had a baby, lost her husband and was getting ready to start a new job in Venezuela. By comparison I have it easy. I need to remember that.'

She gazed unseeingly into the misted mirror in front of her. If

83

things had worked out the way her parents had wanted, it would have been to them that she'd have run when she realised what Cobey had done. Maybe her dad, the tall, rugged, outdoors man she only knew from the single photo her mom had of him, would've gone after her missing boyfriend, smacked him in the jaw for hurting his daughter and demanded that he pay her back. And her mom would've put her arms around her and told her that there were plenty more fish in the sea. Instead of which, her father had died in Venezuela without ever having seen her, and she didn't know when, if ever, she'd tell her mother that she'd made a fool of herself over a man.

She took another towel from the rail and rubbed it briskly over her head. She wore her hair shorter these days and usually allowed it to dry naturally. So instead of using the professional turbo dryer in the drawer, she squeezed some serum from a tube and rubbed it through her damp locks. Then she padded into the bedroom and pulled on a vest top and a pair of baggy trousers before heading to the kitchen and using Pete and Claudia's gleaming top-of-the-range Nespresso machine to make herself a cup of coffee. She brought the coffee and a pastry she took from the cupboard out on to the first-floor deck.

The morning view of the bay from the deck never failed to take her breath away. She watched the tip of the Golden Gate Bridge appear and then disappear again as the receding fog swirled around it, while the sky grew brighter and brighter as the sun burned away the clouds and mist. And in the distance, she could see the grid of San Francisco itself as it got ready for another day.

She drained her coffee, then carried her cup and plate back into the kitchen and stacked them in the stainless-steel dishwasher. It was time for her to be part of the day too. Time to start living her life again.

She took Battle for his morning walk to the bottom of the hill and back, allowing her thoughts to wander skittishly as he tugged at the leash. Then she made sure he was secure in the garden with a bowl of water and another of dried food before letting herself in to Pete's enormous double garage. His Lexus RX was parked beside Claudia's convertible, but Abbey wasn't interested in the cars. She was borrowing Pete's Honda motorbike, which would get her to the salon in about twenty minutes.

The bike was Pete's pride and joy. When he'd first acquired it, Abbey had asked him if he was trying to regain his lost youth. Pete had looked slightly abashed and then said that you were only as old as you felt and he still felt about twenty. He'd offered to give her a ride, telling her that there was nothing like the exhilaration that being on a bike gave you. Abbey had been sceptical, but once she'd had a spin around the streets, she was hooked. She bought herself a full set of biking leathers (she'd once thought that it was the sight of her in full leather gear that had made Cobey think she was the girl for him – he said that she looked unbelievably hot wearing them), and whenever she visited Pete, he would allow her to take the bike for a ride.

She threw her leg over the saddle, pointed the remote at the garage doors, fired up the bike and set off towards the bridge. Crossing the bridge was her favourite part of the journey. She loved the buffeting of the wind and the buzz of the road stretching in front of her, water below. It was, she thought, the best way to start the day.

Pete had private parking in his office building and so she left the bike there before walking to the salon, thinking that maybe today was the day her heart would begin mending, because for the first time since Cobey's desertion she was conscious of the warmth of the sun on her shoulders and she was noticing the people around her and the window displays in the stores again.

When she walked into the salon she said a chirpy hello to Selina, who beamed back at her, delighted that her favourite employee seemed to have finally come out of her misery. Relieved, too, because part of Abbey's success as a member of staff was her unfailing cheerfulness towards her clients. Selina knew that Abbey's

85

smile had been forced recently and that she'd been struggling to keep it all together. But you have, she noted as she watched Abbey arrange the bottles of varnish on her desk. You have and I'm glad for you. And if I could get my hands on the man who took away your smile and your confidence, I'd wring his neck myself.

At two o'clock Abbey broke for lunch. She picked up a coffee and a wrap at Starbucks and ate sitting on the steps at Union Square. She watched the tourists jumping on and off the city tour buses and she counted herself lucky to be a native, not someone trying to cram in the San Francisco experience in a couple of days. Truly, she said to herself as she got up again, I'm incredibly lucky. This thing with Cobey – well, broken hearts mend. I know they do.

'Oh!'

She gasped as someone bumped into her, and then shouted as she realised that her cherry-red Kipling bag (which was her absolute favourite) had been snatched. The thief bounded down the steps while all around her people watched. And then, almost out of nowhere, a man grabbed the youth and prised the bag from his hand, allowing the thief to go free before returning it to Abbey.

'I don't believe that happened,' she said as he handed it to her while the knot of people who'd been watching applauded. 'Thank you.'

'You're welcome.'

'I guess I was careless.'

'He was opportunistic,' said the man.

'I shouldn't have given him the opportunity. I'm usually far more alert. I was daydreaming.'

'Because it's a lovely day for it.'

His accent was unfamiliar, soft and gentle. He was anything but soft himself, though, Abbey thought as she looked at him. He was tall and muscular and was dressed in a 49ers T-shirt, faded jeans and Converse boots. His eyes were hidden behind a pair of Ray-Bans and the whole effect was Hollywood star on a dress-down day.

'Isn't it?' she agreed. 'I was thinking that San Francisco was the best place in the whole world to be right now. But . . .'

'I'm sure it is,' he said. 'This sort of thing happens everywhere.'

'I know. Nevertheless . . .' She fished in her bag for one of her cards. 'If there's anyone you know who'd like their nails done – or if you'd like a manicure yourself – please have one on me.'

His eyes widened as he took the card. 'Do I look like a metrosexual man?'

'You look like a fit man,' she said, which made him laugh.

'Abbey Andersen,' he said out loud as he turned the card over in his hand (a hand on which, she noticed, the nails were short and well-kept). 'Nail technician and artist.' He put her card in his pocket. 'I love how every job in America is a major career.'

'Hey, nail care *is* a career,' she told him. '*My* career.'

'Sorry.' He took off his sunglasses and looked at her apologetically from eyes that were moss-green. 'I'm used to people being self-effacing and deprecating about what they do.'

'You're British, aren't you?' she said.

'Irish,' he amended.

'Oh, wow. My grandparents were from Ireland.' She beamed at him.

'They were?' His eyes lit up. 'Where?'

'Um . . . I'm not quite sure,' she confessed. 'Somewhere in the middle, I think.'

'Offaly, Meath, Tipperary?' He looked at her enquiringly.

She shrugged helplessly. 'I don't know. I never talked to them much about it.'

'Never mind,' he said. 'You should visit us one day.'

'Perhaps.'

'Lots of people come to Ireland to look for their roots,' he said.

'I've never thought that much about mine,' she told him.

'Oh, but roots are interesting,' he said. 'You should think about it. Meantime, if I suddenly find the need to get my nails done while I'm here, I'll definitely come in to your salon.'

87

'Great,' she said. 'I promise I'll send you out like a new man.'

Although, she thought, after he'd shaken her hand, said goodbye and melted into the crowd, you're not half a bad one the way you are.

After finishing work for the day, Abbey met Solí and Vanessa for pizza at Chiopino's and told them about the have-a-go hero in Union Square.

'Shoulda got his number,' said Solí. 'Being as he was all rugged and manly and you're a single girl again.'

'He has mine.' Abbey grinned at her. 'I gave him my card so he could have a comp treatment. Though regardless of the looks, I don't think he's a treatment sort of guy. A bit too European, you know?'

'I love that sexy British accent,' said Vanessa.

'He was Irish,' Abbey reminded her. 'But the accent was still cute.'

'Well, the encounter certainly seems to have cheered you up,' observed Solí. 'In fact you're looking a lot better.'

'I feel better,' said Abbey as she poured herself a glass of water from the jug on the table. 'Not exactly great yet. But definitely better.'

'How's life in Sausalito?' asked Vanessa. 'You all right all on your own in the house?'

'You know Pete. He has the most up-to-date security imaginable,' replied Abbey. 'It would be lovely to be able to afford a place like that.'

'It's pretty awesome,' agreed Vanessa. She was an accounts executive at the bank where Pete's firm had its business, and had been at a small party Pete had thrown a few months previously. 'I love the way the windows go opaque so you can't see through them.'

'Pete loves his high-tech stuff,' said Abbey. She added more water to her glass, then nodded her agreement at Solí's suggestion of sharing a couple of pizzas between the three of them. 'I'll miss it when I leave.'

'Any luck in finding a new apartment?' asked Solí.

'Not so far.' Abbey made a face. 'Rental in this city is beyond a joke.'

'You know you can stay with me while you're looking,' said Solí.

'Yes, and thank you,' answered Abbey. 'But I've got to get somewhere permanent soon. And preferably not some run-down dingy dump.'

'You certainly don't want a dingy dump,' said Vanessa. 'You've outgrown dingy dumps.'

'I'm struggling to find anything better,' said Abbey.

'Nobody you know looking to share?'

'Not right now. And the thing is, I'd love somewhere of my own this time. OK, living with Cobey turned out to be a complete disaster, but it was cool to have a place with no restrictions, and where I didn't only have one shelf in the fridge, or have to worry about sharing the bathroom.'

Vanessa understood perfectly. 'I'd hate to be in that situation. Of course I'm lucky. Shawna and I have lived together all our lives, so sharing with her is normal for me.'

'I'd love to say that I'd move out of the studio and share with you, but I'm pretty set in my ways,' admitted Solí.

'Which is totally OK,' Abbey assured her. 'I wouldn't expect you to mess up your life for me. Hopefully I'll find somewhere half decent before Pete and his family get back from their vacation. Claudia certainly won't want me moping around the place, and I don't blame her.' Abbey took a couple of slices from the pizzas that the waitress had placed in front of them and ground black pepper over them before continuing. 'I'm sure she looks at me and wonders why he bothers. I bet he wonders too! Here I am, nearly thirty, and I haven't achieved anything worthwhile.'

'What the hell are you talking about?' demanded Solí. 'You're the best nail technician in the Bay Area, that's for sure. And don't tell me that's not worthwhile, because I have a string of girls who say different.'

'No doubt about it,' Vanessa agreed. 'Just about every woman in my bank goes to you for nail work. Marian Marinari waxes lyrical every time she comes back from her manicure.'

Abbey couldn't help feeling pleased. 'Thanks,' she said. 'I know that I'm good at nails. It's . . . right now, I don't feel so good about everything else. It's like, having split with Cobey, I'm back at the bottom of the heap again.'

'Hey, we don't let men put us at the bottom of the heap!' Solí wagged her finger with mock-severity in front of Abbey's nose. Then her voice softened. 'You'll be all right, you know you will.'

'I *do* know,' Abbey agreed. 'It'd be nice to feel as though I'd properly achieved something, is all.'

Vanessa looked at her thoughtfully. 'You been talking to your mom lately?'

'No.'

'Because it's usually when you do that that you go all doubtful about your life and stuff.'

'I'm not doubtful,' said Abbey.

Vanessa's expression was only marginally less sceptical.

'Are you still moping because of Cobey?' asked Solí. 'You're not to be moping. No moping allowed here.'

Abbey held up her hands. '*So* not moping,' she said. '*So* not putting myself down. Honestly, ladies, I'm good. I promise you.'

'I hope you are,' said Solí. 'Chalk that man up to experience and get out there again.'

'I've no intention of getting out there for a bit,' said Abbey. 'I need to let my bruised heart heal first.' She drank some water, then put the glass down firmly on the table. 'So c'mon. We've done nothing but talk about me. What about you guys? Anything to tell?'

The conversation moved away from Abbey to Vanessa's run-in

with the senior president of her department, a complete jackass, according to her, who wouldn't know a good credit deal if ever he saw it. Then Solí, who'd studied art with Abbey and now worked for an auction house, talked about their forthcoming sale, which featured works from an up-and-coming New York artist.

'When are they going to sell your work?' asked Abbey.

'Hey, you feature it enough already,' said Solí.

'It's not quite the same,' Abbey said. 'Even though your cat picture is the most popular nail art in the salon.'

Abbey had used a painting her friend had done to create a template for a very distinctive nail art option. The Siamese cat, with its brilliant blue eyes and haughty expression, had turned into an absolute hit, being requested a couple of times a week by her clients.

'You're right.' Vanessa stretched her elegant hands out in front of her. 'When I had it done, everyone commented on it.'

'Because it was on your nails and not a canvas,' said Solí. '*King of Siam* is a nice painting but not a great one.'

'Now who's not being positive about her achievements?' demanded Abbey. 'What's happening to us tonight, people? Am I a gloom merchant or something?'

'Not at all.' Vanessa looked sternly at Abbey and then at Solí. 'Move the topic on. Did either of you see *Celebrity Meltdown* last night?'

'Oh my God, yes!' gasped Solí. 'What were they like!'

And the conversation moved away from being self-critical to criticising other people, a far safer bet for the rest of the evening.

By the time the three friends said goodbye to each other, Abbey was feeling the positive glow they'd insisted she needed. She promised herself that she'd find a suitable apartment where she could live on her own and feel grown-up and independent. And perhaps she'd also take a new direction in her career by giving in and doing as Selina often suggested, entering one of the many

91

competitions for nail technicians that took place around the country. Abbey had been reluctant before, both because she wasn't naturally competitive and because she didn't like leaving San Francisco for more than a day or two. She didn't know if the latter was because she was tired of travelling, or if it was because she didn't want to be away in case her mother came home unexpectedly. But the truth was that she couldn't live her life on the off chance that her mom might turn up. And she'd liked travelling when she was younger. It was time to give serious thought to it again.

As she hit the remote to open the gates to Pete's property, she noticed a black Escalade parked at the roadside. She closed the gates quickly behind her, vaguely uneasy at the sight of the car. The road was a private one, with only three other houses on it besides Pete's, and it ended in a cul-de-sac. There was no need for anyone to be parked on the street, because all the properties were as desirable as Pete's and all had plenty of parking space to accommodate both homeowners and visitors.

She thought about calling the private security firm which monitored the houses in the area, and then chided herself for being over-the-top. The Escalade owner could have parked there because he wasn't sure where he was going, or maybe he wanted to take a walk instead of driving . . . There could be a ton of reasons for the car being there, none of them sinister.

Nevertheless, after she'd parked the bike, she checked the garage before going into the house. The alarm was still on and showed no interruptions. Maybe I shouldn't live on my own after all, she said to herself as she disarmed it. I'm clearly paranoid. I can't believe I'm feeling edgy just because there's a car parked on the road. If Pete was here I probably wouldn't even have noticed it. Jeez, there were cars parked all over the street at the apartment!

Telling herself once again that she was being silly, and reminding herself that the best security of all was having a large Labrador in the house, she opened the back door and allowed Battle inside, rubbing him behind the ears and telling him that she was sorry she was late home. She didn't utter the word 'walk', as it always drove the dog into a frenzy of excitement, but Battle already knew that Abbey's return meant exercise for him.

'Without you I'd be locking myself away tonight and being a scaredy-cat girlie girl,' she told the dog as she allowed him to follow her upstairs and into her room (a practice normally forbidden by Claudia but which Abbey felt could be allowed for this evening). 'And you know I'm not girlie, don't you, Battle? You know I'm a tough cookie.'

The sound of the gate buzzer made her jump in fright and set her heart racing. Battle barked loudly and she shushed him by rubbing the top of his head. 'It's OK,' she told him as she went to the entry console on the upper landing. The figure of a man was illuminated by the security light outside the gates. She could see that he was wearing a suit and tie. He looked vaguely familiar yet she didn't recognise him as one of Pete's friends or acquaintances.

The buzzer sounded again.

'Yes?' Abbey knew that she sounded aggressive, but she reckoned it was better than sounding scared.

'Hi.' The male voice was distorted through the speaker. 'I'm looking for Mr Pete Caruso.'

OK, thought Abbey, at least this person knows who Pete is. But he doesn't know that Pete's away. Good or bad?

'Do you have an appointment?' she asked, thinking as she spoke that it was a stupid question. Who had appointments to see people at this time of the evening?

'I'm afraid not.'

'Well, why don't you make an appointment to see Mr Caruso and come back then,' said Abbey.

'I'm a bit pressed for time,' said the man. 'I tried to contact him at his offices but they said he wasn't available. So I came here.'

Damn you, Pete, thought Abbey. He never allowed his staff to say he was on vacation. Two reasons, he told her. One, I'm never properly on vacation because I'm in touch all the time and if something urgent comes up I don't want a client to think I'm not a hundred per cent committed. And secondly, I prefer not to let anyone know I'm out of town.

Abbey wasn't going to say that Pete was away now. She didn't want to appear like a vulnerable female. She reminded herself once again that she wasn't a vulnerable female. She was a tough cookie in biking leathers. With a dog.

'Why don't you tell me what you want to see him about, and I'll check when Mr Caruso can fit you in,' she said.

'My name is Ryan Gilligan,' the man told her. 'I wanted to talk to Mr Caruso about Ellen Connolly.'

Abbey felt her knees buckle beneath her and she leaned against the wall to steady herself. Ellen. Why did this man want to know about Ellen?

'What about Ellen Connolly?' She tried to keep her voice even.

'That's something I need to discuss with Mr Caruso,' said the man. 'D'you think I could talk to him now?'

'No,' said Abbey. 'No, you couldn't.' Her mind was in a frenzy and she didn't know what to say or do. She could hardly call Pete and ask for advice. She certainly couldn't call Ellen. But she couldn't let this man, this stranger, walk away without finding out why he was here.

'Perhaps I can help you,' she said eventually. 'Wait a moment.'

She walked downstairs again, Battle following her. She opened the cupboard beside the front door, took a can of Mace from the shelf and put it into the pocket of her leather jacket. Then she zipped the jacket up again and glanced at herself in the long mirror. She didn't look vulnerable. She looked like someone who could take care of herself. She pressed the button on the intercom and told the man that she was opening the gate. She watched the downstairs monitor as he walked inside and up the path towards the house. He looked even more familiar now, but she still couldn't place him.

Her right hand closed around the tin of Mace as, leaving the security chain in place, she opened the door with her left.

He was standing in front of her.

And then she recognised him.

It was the Irishman who'd recovered her bag in Union Square.

Chapter 10

'What the hell are you doing here?' She was clutching the canister of Mace now, getting ready to spray it into his face, while also hanging on to Battle's collar. (The man wasn't to know that Battle was the world's most placid dog and would undoubtedly lick him all over given half the chance.)

'This is a weird coincidence,' he said as he looked at her in surprise. 'I wasn't expecting to bump into you again.'

'You weren't?' She wasn't prepared to admit to a coincidence. No matter how astonished he appeared to be.

'Of course not,' he said. 'If I'd realised you and Mr Caruso were . . . are . . .' He looked enquiringly at her, but she said nothing. 'If I'd realised you knew each other,' he continued, 'I'd have talked to you in Union Square. I'd just been to his office when I . . . bumped into you.'

'How do I know that you didn't already know?' She winced as she spoke, realising that she was garbling her words.

'Um . . . I guess you'll have to trust me on that,' he said.

She hesitated. This man had chased after a thief and recovered her bag. Surely that made him trustworthy? Though perhaps it had all been a set-up, designed to catch her off guard now. Battle gave a gentle, welcoming woof and she glared at him, wishing that he could at least try to sound menacing.

'It's very late to be calling to people's homes,' she said.

'I realise that.' His tone was apologetic. 'I arrived earlier but there was nobody in. So I decided to wait.'

How long had he been sitting outside in the Escalade? Perhaps one of the neighbours had already phoned the police. She felt herself relax a little.

'You mentioned Ellen Connolly,' she said. 'Why do you want to talk about her?'

'May I come in?'

'No!' She almost closed the door on him, but Battle was in the way.

'Hey, sorry,' he said. 'I realise you might not want a complete stranger in your home. Here's my card.'

He reached into the pocket of his jacket. Abbey was on high alert, hoping that the gun laws in the state prevented random Irishmen from picking up pistols at the local gun store, on the off chance that they were murdering maniacs. He took a card from his pocket and handed it to her.

Celtic Legal, she read. *Legal and Investigative Services. Ryan Gilligan, Investigator & Legal Adviser.*

She glanced up from the card. An investigator? Like a PI? Surely not. For a brief moment she wondered if one of her friends was playing an elaborate joke on her. Although what kind of joke would involve sending a softly spoken Irish PI – albeit a very attractive one – to the house was beyond her.

She looked at the card again. Celtic Legal was based in Ireland. Why had he come from Ireland to talk about Ellen? Ellen wasn't in Ireland. She'd never even been to Ireland. Abbey was a hundred per cent certain of that.

'I'm working on behalf of Ellen Connolly's family,' he added. 'Can we talk?'

Ellen's family? Abbey looked at him in confusion. Ellen had no family. No other family. She would have known. She took a deep breath.

'We can't talk here,' she said. 'There's a bar near the ferry landing. About a five-minute drive. I'll meet you there.'

'Sure,' he said. 'Do you want a lift . . .' He stopped, then grinned. Quite suddenly he wasn't Hollywood-star-being-an-Irish-PI at all. He looked friendly and approachable. 'Sorry, I should get the terminology right. Can I give you a ride? We don't say that in Ireland,' he added. 'It has a completely different connotation.'

She almost said yes, because his sudden charm was disarming. But Abbey Andersen hadn't lived for twenty-eight years without being aware of her personal safety. So she told him firmly that she'd follow him.

As soon as the tail lights of the Escalade had disappeared from view, Abbey shut a disappointed Battle in the kitchen, returned to the garage and got on the bike again. By the time she arrived at the bar, the Escalade was already parked neatly in one of the spaces and Ryan Gilligan was standing at the entrance to the old wooden building, which was built over the pier.

'This the place you meant?' he asked.

She nodded and preceded him up the steps. She pushed open the door and went inside.

Abbey rarely visited Sausalito's bars, but sometimes she and Pete would come here. Both of them liked being able to see the water and the lights of the city across the bay.

'What can I get you?' asked Ryan as they sat in a booth near a window.

'Water,' she replied. 'Sparkling.'

He returned from the bar with a bottle of water for her and an alcohol-free beer for himself.

'Thanks for meeting me,' he said as he placed the water in front of her.

'How could I refuse?' she asked. 'You were my knight in shining armour earlier.'

He chuckled. 'Lucky break for me, otherwise I got the impression you were going to set that dog on me.'

'Not this time.'

'Sometimes you've got to ride your luck,' he said.

'You couldn't have planned it better.'

He heard the note of scepticism in her voice.

'A total fluke, I promise you,' he said. 'If you want to ring any of the numbers on my card to verify that I am who I say I am, please do. Although,' he added, 'it's the middle of the night back home, so that's not exactly helpful. Sorry.'

'I'm sure any number I ring will simply confirm anything you tell me,' she said.

'You're a suspicious girl, aren't you?'

'I'm careful.'

'And I'm a genuine person,' he assured her.

She wanted to believe him. But she'd believed Cobey, hadn't she? And look where that had left her. Nevertheless, this man was different. There wasn't any reason to distrust him. Besides, she needed to know where Ellen came into all this.

'So . . . what's the thing with Ellen Connolly?' she asked.

'Straight down to business,' he said.

'Yes.'

'Ellen's father is trying to trace her,' said Ryan Gilligan.

Abbey stared wordlessly at him.

'He hired my firm to do the search.'

'Who are you really?' Abbey drank some water directly from the bottle. 'Why are you saying such a thing?'

'Because it's true,' said Ryan.

'Ellen's father is dead,' said Abbey firmly. 'Both her parents are dead. I know because I was there when they died. You've got the wrong person.'

'Her adoptive parents may have passed away,' Ryan said. 'But I'm working for her biological father.'

The bottle fell from Abbey's grasp on to the wooden floor beneath. A pool of water spread across the boards. The bartender hurried across with a cloth and began to mop it up.

99

'Are you OK? Can I get you another one?' asked Ryan.

'No. Yes. I . . .' Abbey was looking at him with total disbelief in her eyes as she tried to process what he'd just said. But she was finding it very difficult.

Ryan went to the bar and returned with another bottle of water and a glass with a measure of spirits.

'Whiskey,' he said. 'You might like it. For the shock. Because clearly I've given you a shock. I'm sorry about that.'

Abbey picked up the glass and took a generous sip.

Ryan Gilligan watched her, a concerned expression on his face, but she swallowed the whiskey without spluttering and then took another mouthful.

'I only drink hard liquor when I've found out something that's knocked me sideways,' she said as she put the glass on the table again.

'I'm sorry to have knocked you sideways,' said Ryan.

'Oh, I shouldn't be all that surprised,' Abbey said. 'Ellen has a habit of doing that to me.'

'How well do you know her?' Ryan asked. 'Can you introduce us?'

'I know her very well,' said Abbey. She took a deep breath, then released it slowly. 'Ellen Connolly is my mother.'

This time it was Ryan Gilligan who looked shocked.

'I'm really sorry,' he said after a moment's silence. 'Ellen Connolly? Abbey Andersen? I didn't think . . .'

'Andersen was my father's name,' said Abbey. 'Mom didn't change hers after she married.'

'I'm sorry,' he repeated. 'If I'd known . . .'

'Hey, don't beat yourself up.' Abbey could feel the whiskey taking effect, mellowing her so that she wasn't as completely stunned as she'd been earlier. 'It's cool,' she said. 'I'm cool.'

'I'm not sure that you are.'

He called the bartender and ordered another whiskey for her.

'You definitely want that?' called Chet, the owner, who was behind the bar.

'Today I do, Chet, yes,' said Abbey.

'As long as you know what you're doin',' Chet said.

'I don't know what I'm doing at all,' murmured Abbey as Ryan put the drink in front of her. 'I don't know what any of this is about.'

'Mind if I ask you something?' asked Ryan.

'What?'

His expression was slightly uncomfortable. 'D'you have any ID? Anything to prove you're Ellen Connolly's daughter? Because as far as I know, you're Abbey Andersen and I found you in the house of Pete Caruso, which doesn't make much of a connection, does it?'

'I trusted you with that pathetic piece of cardboard you call a business card,' said Abbey. 'The very least you can do is trust me to be who I say I am.'

He smiled. 'Fair enough.'

'But . . .' She fumbled in her purse and took out her driver's licence. 'This is me. Obviously it doesn't prove I'm Ellen's daughter, but if you're a PI, you have to know that she *has* a daughter.'

'To tell you the truth, I didn't,' admitted Ryan. 'Just as I didn't know she was married.' He frowned. 'I should've been able to find a record of that, but I've been struggling to find any information on her at all.'

'Mom and Dad got married in Latin America. Maybe you were looking in the wrong place.'

'Maybe.' He looked thoughtful. 'It's a pity I didn't know about it when you handed me your card. I'm sure it would have set a bell ringing in my head.'

'If you'd said anything in Union Square, I would've been equally freaked out,' said Abbey.

'I suppose you would,' he conceded. 'So . . . well, I thought that perhaps Ellen might have married and had a family. I said this to her father. I have to be honest and say that his main concern was with finding his daughter, but I'm sure he'll be delighted to know about you too.'

'You think?'

'Of course. Now that I have actually tracked down one of his relatives, can I meet your mother?'

Abbey was stuck for words. The bottom line was that she had no idea if she wanted him to meet Ellen or not. Or whether her mother would even agree to such a meeting anyway. Besides, if anyone was going to talk to Ellen about this astonishing news, it was going to be Abbey herself. And even *she* didn't know when that would be. Because this was something that would have to be done face to face. And it was nearly a year since she'd spoken face to face with Ellen.

Her mother had never said anything about being adopted. So would this be as big a shock to her as it was to Abbey? Or had she found out? And if so, thought Abbey, had it influenced the choices she'd made after Gramps and Gramma died? But if she'd known, or had found out, why hadn't she said anything?

Ryan Gilligan was still looking at her, waiting for an answer to his question. Somewhat belatedly, Abbey shook her head and told him that no, he couldn't meet Ellen, who wasn't in San Francisco.

Disappointment etched itself on Ryan's face. 'Where is she?'

'You're the investigator.' Abbey took another sip of the whiskey.

'Clearly not as good an investigator as I thought.' Ryan looked rueful. 'Though tracking missing persons isn't usually my thing.'

The whiskey was warming Abbey, relaxing her more. She watched him as he mentally processed the information she'd given him.

'Can we get her back here?' he asked. 'It's important I speak to her soon.'

'Why?'

'Because my client is an old man and he wants to meet her before he dies.'

'What if she doesn't want to meet him?'

'I'm sure that when I explain the circumstances to her she'll agree.'

'You can explain it all to me. I'll tell her.'

'In a heartbeat I would.' The warmth in Ryan's eyes matched the tone of his voice. 'But my client hired me to find Ellen Connolly and ask her to come to Ireland to see him. I'm certain he'll be eager to know about you too, Abbey, but it's her I need to speak with.'

'What about my mother's mother? Doesn't she want to meet her too?'

'At the moment, all I can tell you is that Ellen's birth mother died shortly after she was born. If I can talk to Ellen and get her to travel—'

'I'm sorry, but that's not possible,' Abbey told him.

'Of course it is,' Ryan told her. 'Her father is prepared to pay for her to come to him if money's the issue.'

'It's not money.'

'Then what?'

'This has been a huge shock to me. I'm sure it'll be an equal shock to my mother. However, she really isn't in a position to come to Ireland, and I don't think that she'd even want to.'

'I don't think it's up to you to make that decision for her.' Ryan's voice, though pleasant, was determined.

Abbey hesitated. In the years since her grandparents' deaths, she'd guarded Ellen's privacy fiercely. Being honest with herself, it was as much for her own sake as her mother's. People could be judgemental, and she wasn't prepared to have troublesome discussions about the kind of life Ellen had elected to live.

'She's not immediately contactable,' Abbey said finally.

'How soon would you be able to get in touch?'

'I'm not sure.'

'But this is very important. She'd want you to make every effort to let her know.'

'You don't know what my mother would or wouldn't want,' said Abbey.

Ryan looked suddenly contrite. 'You're right. I'm sorry. The thing is, my client might not have a lot of time left.'

'Ellen's father is dying?' Abbey was shocked.

'He's not on his deathbed,' Ryan assured her. 'But he's elderly and he's had a few health scares, and he feels that time is running out to make amends.'

'Amends?' asked Abbey. 'For what?'

'For not being there.'

'He's looking for her because he wants to hear her say that she's all right with being adopted? That she forgives him?' Abbey shrugged. 'I know already that she'll forgive him, if that's what he needs.'

'You do?'

'I know my mom.'

'I still need to talk to her,' said Ryan. 'My assignment is to find Ellen, not her daughter. Although,' he added, 'I'm very glad to have met you.'

Abbey gave him a brief smile.

'Seriously,' said Ryan. 'I like you, Abbey. I do. Is there some reason you're keeping your mother's whereabouts a secret?'

'No, but . . .' She frowned. 'Look, all I want to say right now is that Mom can't travel to Ireland. It's simply not possible. Perhaps I can arrange for you to meet with her, although it could take a few weeks. But she won't travel. That's that.'

Ryan looked at her thoughtfully.

'Tell you what,' he said. 'I'll talk to my client. Tell him what you've told me. See what he wants to do and get back to you. OK?'

'Good idea,' said Abbey. Her fingers tightened around the glass in front of her and she waited a moment before she asked the question. 'What's he like?'

'My client? Like I said, an elderly man. A widower. He's in his eighties.'

'And he's my grandfather.' Abbey spoke out loud even though she hadn't meant to.

'I truly am sorry about how I broke that to you,' said Ryan. 'I should've thought a bit more.'

'It doesn't matter,' said Abbey. 'It's not your fault.' She exhaled slowly. 'I can't help thinking . . . I'm not who I thought I was. Gramma and Gramps weren't really my grandparents. At least . . .'

'I should've handled this differently.' Ryan looked at her with concern. 'Maybe when you get this sort of information you need to have a counsellor or someone standing by.'

'I don't need a counsellor.' She rubbed her forehead. 'But I do need to absorb everything you've told me.'

'Perhaps I've been watching too much Jerry Springer, telling you the way I did.' Ryan looked shamefaced. 'I didn't mean to upset you.'

'I'm not upset,' Abbey assured him. 'Just shocked.'

'What do you know about your mother's early life?' asked Ryan. 'It's OK to tell me that, isn't it?'

Abbey ran her finger around the rim of her glass. Her vision was slightly fuzzy now and she wished she hadn't downed the first whiskey so quickly.

'My grandparents came to America from Ireland in the nineteen fifties, when my mom was a baby,' she told him. 'They lived in Boston, where Mom trained to be a nurse. When she qualified, she moved away. Eventually she ended up in California, where she met my dad. They got married and worked together in Latin America, but he was killed before I was born.'

'Killed? How awful. What happened?' Ryan's voice was full of sympathy.

'It was a car accident in terrible weather. The Jeep he was driving went off the road. He died instantly.'

'I'm so sorry,' said Ryan.

Abbey smiled faintly. 'As it was before my time it doesn't much matter to me, except that – well, he was my father and I never got to know him. And it was obviously a tough time for my mom. Anyway, after that she decided to take a job in a small clinic in

Venezuela. We were there for a year before she moved again, and after that she changed jobs every few months, quite often to somewhere in a different country. The medical organisation she worked for had clinics across Latin America so it was easy to move around. Eventually, though, we went back to Venezuela and stayed there till I was twelve and she decided that I needed to get more of an American education.'

'Your mother dragged you around Latin America while you were a kid?' He sounded horrified.

'It was fun,' said Abbey. 'I had a blast.'

'Perhaps, but . . . some of those countries – and as a baby!'

'Babies are born in Latin America all the time,' Abbey reminded him with a smile. 'Just because some places get a bad press doesn't mean they're not good places with good people. My mother liked the rhythm of life there but she could never stay anywhere for very long, no matter how much she liked it . . . She was a kind of free spirit, I guess. She believed – she still believes – in following the road, and in peace and love and getting on with your fellow man.'

'Right. So what did she do when she got back?'

'While we were in Latin America all her work was with . . . well, needy people, I guess. But back in the States she got a job in a private clinic. That was where she met Pete Caruso. He'd been through a bad time, lost his only brother to cancer. A younger brother. It made Pete feel guilty but also turned him into something of a hypochondriac for a time. Mom helped him get over it and the two of them . . . well, they were good with each other. We all lived together. But then my grandfather – her adoptive father . . .' She stopped in sudden confusion. 'That's so weird. I always thought they looked alike, but of course they couldn't have, could they? Anyway, he had a stroke and my grandmother couldn't cope because she was elderly herself. So Mom and I went to Boston.' Abbey made a face. 'I'm not a Boston person. Neither is Mom. But she stayed with them until

106

my grandfather died. After that, my grandmother wanted to go into a home. She was in her eighties then. Mom didn't want her in a home, she wanted her to come back to California with us, but my grandmother insisted. She was a very strong-willed woman. So my mom agreed, but shortly after Gramma went into the home, she died.'

'I see.'

'After that, Mom decided she wanted to . . . to follow her own path,' said Abbey. 'I'm wondering now if Gramma told her something. If that's why . . .'

Ryan watched her intently as myriad expressions crossed her face.

'Anyway,' said Abbey eventually. 'She left San Francisco again and started a new life for herself.'

'As a free spirit? She's not living with Indians on a reservation, is she?'

Abbey burst into laughter.

'Obviously not,' Ryan said.

'Anyway, that's the story you can tell your client. My mother's father. My grandfather. Can you tell me more about him?'

'Let's both hold something back,' said Ryan. 'Let me talk to him first.'

'Tell him Mom will definitely forgive him,' Abbey said. 'She doesn't hold grudges, my mom.'

'You're saying a lot on behalf of your mother,' said Ryan.

'Because I know her,' said Abbey.

'Maybe this is something she needs to think about for herself.'

'Maybe.' Abbey finished her drink. 'Does he have any other children?'

'Ellen's father? Yes,' replied Ryan. 'That's another part of things, Abbey. Your mam has half-brothers and sisters she doesn't even know exist.'

But given that I exist and she's perfectly happy to be cut off from me, I don't think the lure of more people will mean much, thought Abbey. In fact, knowing that they're there will probably have the opposite effect to the one Ryan Gilligan so desperately wants.

Because Abbey had drunk the whiskey, she couldn't ride the bike back to the house. Ryan offered to take her home and she agreed, although she checked the pocket of her jacket and curled her fingers around the canister of Mace again, to be on the safe side.

'Nice place Mr Caruso's got,' remarked Ryan as she opened the door.

In the kitchen, Battle barked enthusiastically.

'He works hard, he's entitled to it,' she said.

'Of course.'

'I suppose you checked on him too.'

'He was easy to check up on. Where is he now?'

Abbey wasn't going to tell a stranger, even one who appeared as genuine as Ryan Gilligan, that she was spending the night alone in Pete's hillside mansion, so she didn't reply.

'D'you want me to wait with you until he comes home?' asked Ryan.

'No,' she said.

'I don't suppose you need me. You have the dog to protect you.' He glanced towards the kitchen, where Battle had stopped barking. 'Will you give me your mobile – I mean, cell number, so that I can contact you after I talk to Ellen's father?'

Abbey supposed that would be OK. She called out her number and Ryan entered it into his iPhone.

'Sure you're going to be all right?' he asked.

'Yes.' She straightened up. 'It was only two whiskeys, after all. I can cope with that, really I can.'

'You had a bit of a shock, though. Apologies again about that.'

'Oh, I can cope with shocks, too.'

'In that case, I'll leave you to it. Good night, Abbey.'

'Good night.'

She watched until the lights of his car had disappeared. Then she put the security lock on the door, checked all the windows and set the alarm. After that, she went into the kitchen, rubbed Battle's ears and made herself a cup of hot chocolate. As she sipped the hot chocolate, the dog sitting on her feet, she took out her phone and dialled her mother's cell. The voice of the operator told her that the number was no longer in service. But Abbey had known that already. There was never any point in ringing Ellen's cell phone. She wasn't sure why she still did it. But every so often, she did.

What was the best thing to do? she wondered as she listened to Battle snoring contentedly. She couldn't send a bald email saying what Ryan Gilligan had told her. Even if Ellen already knew about her adoption, it wasn't something they could discuss by email. She'd have to make an arrangement to meet. But it normally took a few weeks between deciding she wanted to see her mother and actually coming face to face with her. Abbey reached for her iPad and opened a website. She clicked on one of the menus and frowned. Even if she sent an email tonight, it would be at least two weeks before Ellen would be able to reply. She finished her hot chocolate and put the cup on the side table. Best to wait until Ryan Gilligan spoke to his client. Ellen's father. Abbey's grandfather.

She slid her feet from beneath the dog and let him into the garden for his late-night run. When he'd finished, she shut him in the kitchen again and went upstairs to her bedroom. Although she was utterly exhausted, she wasn't expecting to fall asleep. There was too much for her to think about. Too much information to process.

However, she dropped off almost at once. In her dreams she was a child again, packing her rucksack, getting ready to move on, trusting that Ellen knew where they were going, but sad that they were leaving the friends that they'd made. Ellen never seemed to mind starting over, but Abbey found it hard.

'People are the same no matter where you are,' Ellen would say. 'You'll make new friends.'

And she always had. But she'd always had to leave them too. Perhaps that was the real reason she didn't travel any more.

Chapter 11

When she woke the following morning, Abbey's tongue was a little furry from the whiskey but her head was thankfully clear.

She went into the kitchen and poured herself a cranberry juice, which, like the previous morning, she took out on to the deck. She was very grateful that today was her day off, because she knew that she was still keyed up after her conversation with Ryan Gilligan and even the slightest tremor in her hand would mess up her nail art. She finished the juice and decided not to bother with coffee. Instead she walked down to the waterfront and retrieved Pete's bike.

She wondered how soon it would be before she heard from Ryan Gilligan again. He seemed very clear that it was her mother he wanted to talk to, not her, but it would be unreasonable for him not to tell her more about her unknown family. He couldn't simply waltz into her life, announce that the two people she'd always thought of as her grandparents weren't her grandparents at all and leave it at that. Besides, she was still his only route to Ellen.

He probably thinks we're nutters, she thought as she placed her helmet on the garage worktop. He probably lives a well-ordered life, knowing everything there is to know about everyone in his family. Although, she reminded herself, weren't PIs supposed to be maverick loners struggling with some kind of addiction? In all the TV programmes she watched, they generally lived and worked by themselves and tried to overcome their problems with alcohol or gambling or whatever demon the writers had given them. Perhaps Ryan Gilligan had his own worries after all.

She'd left the garage and was making the coffee she hadn't bothered with earlier when her phone rang.

'It's me,' said Ryan. 'Hope you're feeling all right.'

'Of course I'm all right,' she said.

'I've spoken to my client. I told him I'd met you and what you'd said. He's extremely disappointed.'

'That's understandable.'

'Indeed. Especially as he's spent a lot of money looking for Ellen.'

Abbey hadn't thought of that before. Sending a PI across the Atlantic to find someone must be incredibly expensive. Did that mean that Ellen's dad was rich? The thought startled her. Ellen wasn't a materialistic person. Pete had confided in Abbey that he thought it was one of the reasons she'd refused to talk about marrying him. She'd known that he wanted to do well in his career, and had known, too, that success brought material rewards.

'I can see why that might be a bit annoying for him,' said Abbey.

'So he's asked me to talk to you some more instead.'

'I'm happy to talk to you but I'm not sure what more I can tell you.'

'Let's meet anyway,' said Ryan. 'Um – at that bar again?'

'Where are you staying?' asked Abbey.

'The Holiday Inn.'

'Columbus or Beach?'

'Beach,' he said.

The hotel was only a few blocks from one of the Mariposa salons.

'I'll meet you at Pier 39,' she told him. 'There are plenty of places there for coffee and a snack. About an hour?'

'Perfect,' said Ryan Gilligan. 'I look forward to seeing you.'

He was standing at the entrance to the concourse when she

arrived. Today he was dressed in a Gap T-shirt and shorts, with Aviator sunglasses on his face and deck shoes on his feet. This time he looked like a Hollywood star playing an American tourist.

She went up to him and said hello and he gave her his bright smile and said it was good of her to come. She steered him through the crowds of tourists to a small coffee and doughnut place beside the restaurant where Cobey's friend Mike worked. The restaurant hadn't opened yet and there was no sign of Mike. She wondered if he was in touch with Cobey. If he'd told him that she'd come looking for him. And if Cobey had cared. She clenched and unclenched her fist and then realised that a waitress was standing by their table and that Ryan was looking at her expectantly.

'Breakfast,' she said as she ordered a ring doughnut and a black coffee.

Ryan asked for a black coffee too, but passed on the doughnut. 'I had breakfast earlier,' he said.

'I need the sugar more than I don't need the calories,' she told him as she bit into the doughnut. 'Sugar's good for shock, isn't it?'

'I think so. Although shouldn't it be in tea? Hot sweet tea with milk?'

Abbey made a face. 'I *so* don't drink tea like that.'

'Neither do I,' said Ryan. 'But that's how my mam makes it.'

She liked the way he pronounced it. Mam. Not mom. Kind of cute, she thought.

'So,' he said. 'Down to business?'

'I'm all ears.'

'Mr Fitzpatrick is a retired businessman with a grown-up family. Your mother was born before he married.'

'Fitzpatrick,' said Abbey slowly. 'My mom's real name is Fitzpatrick.'

'You mam's name is Connolly,' Ryan corrected her. 'After James and Ellen Connolly adopted her—'

'My grandmother was known as Mamie,' Abbey interrupted him.

'Oh. OK. Well, James and Mamie adopted Ellen when she was a few weeks old, and that made her a Connolly.'

'What about her mother?' asked Abbey. 'Her birth mother, who died?'

'Her name was Ita Dillon. My client knew her as Dilly. Ita was only sixteen when she got pregnant with your mother.'

'Oh, wow. That must have been a shock.'

'In Ireland, in the nineteen fifties, it was more than a shock. It was a disaster.' Ryan's voice was grim. 'Unmarried mothers were – well, it was not a good situation to be in. Ita was sent away.'

'Sent away?' Abbey looked at him in astonishment.

'It was a massive shame on the family to have a pregnant, unmarried daughter,' explained Ryan. 'I don't know how it was looked on here either; I'm guessing America was more liberal, but even so, I'm sure being an unmarried mother wasn't a great life-style choice.'

'No,' agreed Abbey.

'But, like I said, in Ireland it was a complete disaster. Have you ever heard of the Magdalene laundries?'

Abbey shook her head.

'Not a good chapter in our history,' said Ryan. 'Pregnant girls were sent to these institutions, which were run by religious orders. The nuns pretty much considered the girls to be fallen women, sinners who needed to be punished.'

Abbey looked startled. '*Nuns* thought that? They were judgemental?'

'Back then, the Catholic Church had a very firm grip on Irish society. And its views on sexual matters were pretty . . . well, like you said, judgemental. A girl who got pregnant outside marriage was a fallen woman who deserved punishment.'

'I understand how society might feel that way, but nuns? Nuns are supposed to be caring and charitable.'

'And I'm sure most of them are,' said Ryan. 'But there are always exceptions. Many of the nuns in these institutions believed

114

that the girls had to be punished for their sins. They treated them badly. Ita Dillon tried to run away.'

'Poor thing.'

'She was caught and beaten. She went into labour, and died soon after the baby was born.'

'Oh my God.' Abbey looked at Ryan in horror.

'Her baby was given up for adoption. The couple who adopted her, James and Ellen, sorry, Mamie Connolly, were in their forties. Which back then was very old as far as having a child was concerned. After the adoption, they emigrated to the States.'

'It was a big move at that time of their life too,' observed Abbey.

'James was an engineer. He had skills that were in demand.'

Abbey nodded. She knew that her grandfather had worked for an engineering company.

'James and Mamie thought it would be a good move. They didn't have family in Ireland. They thought that it would be better to bring their daughter up in America, where there was hope and opportunity.'

'I understand. Did my mom's actual father . . . Mr Fitzpatrick, you said, meet them before they went?'

'Not at all.' Ryan sounded apologetic. 'Back then, the father's rights were pretty negligible. Besides, Fred Fitzpatrick was equally horrified by Ita's pregnancy and was relieved when she was sent away.'

'No!'

'It was another time,' Ryan said patiently. 'You've got to understand that. I know it seems callous, and it was, but people's attitudes were very different back then. Fred put it all behind him.'

'Did he even know that Ita had died?' demanded Abbey.

'Yes, but – well, there was nothing he could do at that point, even if he'd wanted to. Obviously Ita's parents wanted nothing to do with him. Mind you, they hadn't wanted anything to do with her either, even though she was their only child. Anyway, Fred got on with his life. Married Ros. Had three children. Built up his business. Didn't think any more about it until he saw a documentary on TV about the Magdalene laundries. A lot of information has emerged over the last few years. People are appalled at how the girls were treated. Fred feels guilty about what happened to Ita. He blames himself for not doing more to help her. He wants to meet her daughter – his daughter – and apologise.'

'Like I said, my mom will forgive him.'

'He wants to apologise in person.'

'I appreciate that,' said Abbey. 'But it's not possible.'

'That's what I told him,' said Ryan. 'And he's decided that he'd like to meet you instead. He thinks that if you hear what he has to say, you'll understand that he's a genuine person and will put us in touch with your mother, his daughter, and persuade her to come to Ireland.'

'So is he going to come here to see me?' asked Abbey.

'No,' Ryan said. 'He wants you to visit him.'

'But . . .' Abbey was dumbfounded.

'He doesn't want to travel to the States,' said Ryan. 'He doesn't want his family to know about Ita yet.'

'They're going to find out, surely, if I turn up on the doorstep.'

'Of course. But that can be managed at a time and in a way of Fred's own choosing,' said Ryan.

'I can't leave everything here to go to Ireland,' Abbey protested. 'I don't travel much any more. I like staying put. Besides, I have a job. I have commitments . . .'

'Mr Fitzpatrick will pay all your travel and other expenses,' said Ryan.

'It's not about the money,' said Abbey.

'Look, Abbey. Mr Fitzpatrick is an old man. He wants to meet your mam, of course, but at least if he meets you he'll feel as though he's made some progress. It's the least you can do.'

Abbey didn't know what to say.

'You don't have to decide right now,' Ryan said. 'But in the next day or two.'

'Right.'

'He's not a bad person,' Ryan told her.

She said nothing.

'Think about it.'

'I will,' she said as she stared out across the bay. Alcatraz, silent, unmovable, brooding, looked back silently at her.

PART 4

THE MEETING

Chapter 12

Suzanne Fitzpatrick was sitting in the boardroom of the bank. Her friend and accountant, Petra Summers, was with her, along with the two other businesswomen, Beatriz and Concha, who made up the consortium interested in buying the Mirador Hotel. The four women were seated on the opposite side of the table from the bank's representatives, four middle-aged men in navy business suits. Although they were also wearing business clothes, Suzanne's skirt and jacket were bright red, Concha's floral dress was teamed with a canary-yellow jacket, Beatriz was striking in emerald green and, while Petra's trousers were mocha brown, her own jacket was orange. Walking into the boardroom, Suzanne had remarked that they looked like a packet of Starbursts, which gave Petra a fit of the giggles and caused Concha to look sternly at her.

Perhaps we should've consulted about our wardrobes, though, Suzanne said to herself as she listened to the lending manager picking holes in Petra's financial plan for the purchase, renovation and reopening of the Mirador. Perhaps boring blue is good when it comes to bankers. She continued to allow her mind to wander. She knew the bank wasn't going to lend them the money, even though the plan was a good one. Picking holes in it was simply an excuse. Ever since the financial crisis more than five years earlier, the banks had become ultra-cautious about lending. A joke, in Suzanne's view, given that most of the people looking to borrow had already propped up the institutions through taxpayer-funded rescue plans. She wanted to scream this at the boring bankers, but there wasn't any point. They wouldn't care. They were going through the motions. And they were wrong to be cautious about the Mirador. Suzanne knew she could make it work. Petra, Concha and Beatriz thought so too. That was why Concha and Beatriz were prepared to put money into the venture. They were expecting a profit. And Suzanne would give it to them. If only they could get the project off the ground.

Alberto Gonzales, the lending manager, was talking about the decline in the tourist industry and the fact that the Mirador wasn't in the centre of a town and the hard work it would take to turn it into the sort of hotel Suzanne was proposing. She turned her attention to him, tuned in to his latest objection and then stood up.

'I see we're wasting our time,' she told him briskly. 'We will talk to someone else. Someone who has a better understanding of what we're trying to do.'

He looked at her in surprise.

'Yes,' said Beatriz. 'There are clearly lots of other banks with more *cojones* than you.'

The four women swept out of the boardroom and walked to the elevator.

'Shit,' said Petra. 'I was sure they'd be interested. They've invested in this sort of thing before.'

'And probably lost money,' said Concha.

'True,' agreed Beatriz. 'But we could've made it work.'

'Ladies – wait.'

They turned to see Alberto, flanked by his colleagues.

'It cannot work for us with the amount of borrowings you need. But if you could come up with additional funding yourselves . . .'

'If we had additional funding we wouldn't be here today,' said Suzanne impatiently.

'You need to be more flexible,' said the bank manager. 'We would like to help.'

'You haven't been very helpful so far,' she said.

Petra put her hand on Suzanne's arm. 'Make a proposal,' she told the manager as she pressed the call button on the elevator.

'These times are difficult. But if you could reduce your requirement a little . . .'

'We'll discuss it,' she said. 'But you need to put something more concrete to us first.'

Once they were inside the lift, Petra turned to Concha and Beatriz and asked if they could raise additional capital.

'I could increase my investment a little,' said Concha. 'But not more than another ten per cent. Not for a hotel project.'

Beatriz nodded. 'I could do the same.'

Suzanne looked regretful. 'As you know, I'm bringing the expertise, not the money. At least, only the money from the bank. I don't have enough personal finance to make up the amount we need and I can't honestly see where I'd get it from.'

'If this is so, then I am sorry,' said Beatriz. 'I would like to be involved, but I have to be realistic also.'

'I have to say the same,' said Concha.

'Let's not give up just yet,' said Petra. 'Let's see if they come up with anything. Meantime, Suzanne and I will go through the figures again. We could still make it work.'

'If you can, let me know straight away,' said Beatriz as the lift reached the ground floor. 'I will keep my interest open for another four weeks. After that, well, I will begin to look at other investments.'

'That seems reasonable,' said Concha. 'I also will wait for four weeks.'

'OK.' Suzanne smiled brightly at them, although she couldn't help feeling that the opportunity to acquire the Mirador was slipping away. 'I'll be in touch with you.'

As the two investors left the building, Suzanne looked gloomily at Petra.

'It can't be done,' she said.

'We'll try harder,' said Petra. 'In the context of what we need, it's not such a large amount. A few hundred thousand.'

'It might as well be a few million,' said Suzanne.

'Maybe we can get someone else to join the consortium,' said Petra. 'I'll run through my client list again. We'll come up with something, I promise.'

'I wish I was as optimistic as you.' Suzanne pushed open the door of the bank and stepped outside.

They walked in silence through the narrow streets of the old town until they reached Petra's office. She said goodbye to Suzanne and went inside. Suzanne, who'd taken a day off work, got into her car and drove out to the Mirador again. It was as beautiful as before, its views over the water unparalleled.

I know this is a good business, she thought. I know I can make it work. It's not as risky as the bank thinks. Unbidden, a memory of her father came to her. Talking to her mother about his own business. 'Risk comes from not knowing what you're doing,' he had said. 'I read that somewhere. It's true. My alarm company is doing well because I know exactly what I'm doing all the time.'

Suzanne wondered if Fred would think she was a good risk. She felt sure he had the money, but would he be prepared to invest in her project? She inhaled sharply. 'I must be really desperate if I'm thinking about Dad,' she muttered under her breath. 'He's never supported me in anything before. Why should he start now.' Besides, she told herself, it would be a disaster. He'd want to control her every step of the way. He had no faith in her whatsoever, and her brief, failed marriage had only hardened his view. Not that he'd known Calvin. They'd married in the States and hadn't invited anyone from her family to the wedding. She hadn't seen the point. Afterwards, when it had all gone so horribly wrong, she'd been glad.

'Not relevant,' she said out loud in order to dislodge those memories. 'Nothing to do with my current situation. I need to be thinking about real people who can help.'

Although right now, she couldn't come up with anybody.

Zoey was trying on her party dress when she heard Donald's key in the front door. She immediately pulled it over her head (swearing softly under her breath because she should have unzipped it properly) and stepped out of it. Then she hung it in the wardrobe. She'd told Donald that he couldn't see it until the day of her birthday.

Donald wasn't overly enthusiastic about the party. When she told him what she'd planned – an evening in their home for fifty guests with canapés being provided by the local delicatessen – he'd looked appalled.

'It's going to cost a bloody fortune,' he protested.

'Not at all,' she assured him, while making a note to keep the deli's bill (as well as those for the helium balloons and party flowers) out of his sight. 'I've sourced everything locally, nothing is too extravagant.'

'Too late to do anything now that you've invited people, I suppose,' said Donald. 'Who exactly is coming?'

Zoey ran through the guest list, an eclectic mix of her family and friends, his colleagues and, of course, Gareth, Lisette and Fred.

'You think my dad will want to come to a birthday party for a thirty-year-old?' asked Donald.

'And why wouldn't he?' Zoey beamed at him. 'It'll make him feel young and virile again to see me.'

'I don't want him feeling virile,' said Donald in alarm.

Zoey chuckled. 'He likes looking at me, Don. Mind you, if he looks for too long, he might have a heart attack and keel over.'

'What a way to go.' Donald couldn't help laughing too.

'It's such a pity our house is so small,' said Zoey. 'We could've had a really big bash.'

'It's not that small,' objected Donald, although he was the one who usually compared it unfavourably with the Clontarf home that his ex-wife lived in. He always felt a band of anger squeeze his chest when he thought of leaving the house he'd loved. A house with way more character than the current one had.

'For a party it is,' amended Zoey. 'But never mind, sometime in the future I'm sure we'll move onwards and upwards.'

She was so enthusiastic, thought Donald. So full of energy and hope and expectation. That was what he loved about her, even though he sometimes felt that life had squeezed all the hope and expectation out of him already. He was fifty, for God's sake. There was more behind him than in front of him. Zoey would still be around long after he'd gone. The thought depressed him.

'What's wrong?' Her voice was full of concern.

'Nothing,' he said. 'Nothing at all. And the party is a great idea with or without my dad.' He put his arms around her and drew her close to him, inhaling the apple-scented shampoo from her hair.

Zoey held him tight. She knew that sometimes he could get depressed and down on himself. It was her job to make sure that he didn't stay that way. Her job to look after him. And to keep him happy and in love with her.

Lisette was posting a status update on Facebook when Gareth walked into the room, a glass of red wine in his hand.

'I thought you'd be up there for ever,' she said.

'Class 3A would try the patience of a saint.' Gareth sat down beside her and sipped his wine. 'God, I needed that.'

'I know how you feel,' said Lisette. She closed her laptop, went into the kitchen, found the wine bottle and poured herself a glass too, before returning to the living room and sitting in the armchair opposite Gareth.

'Honestly,' he said. 'I don't know how much longer I can go on like this. I know everyone says that teachers have a great life, and when you think about the holidays, you can't blame them, but – BUT – none of them have to sit in front of a group of Neanderthals like 3A. Tony Mitchell seemed to think that farting continuously throughout the lesson was hilariously funny. So did his mates. I found it excruciatingly disgusting and unamusing.'

'As would I,' agreed Lisette.

'They're monsters, you know. All of them. Full of delusions about their own brilliance. I blame bloody *X Factor* and *Celebrity Whatever*. Everyone has a dream. Everyone thinks they can be somebody. Well, not class 3A, that's for sure.' He closed his eyes.

Lisette reopened her laptop and updated her status again. **Other half ranting about school. Can't honestly blame him. But no point in ranting to me.**

She wasn't worried about posting it. Gareth wasn't on Facebook; he called it 'another step on the slippery slope to social disintegration'. Lisette didn't care what he thought. It allowed her to keep in touch with her friends and family in France in a way that had been impossible when she'd first come to Ireland twenty-five years earlier.

When she'd met Gareth back then, he'd been an enthusiastic, involved teacher. It was a combination of things, not all to do with the educational system, that had knocked the enthusiasm out of him. The boom and bust had a lot to do with it. In the time when the economy had been racing ahead, teachers had been regarded as almost incidental in the fabric of society. Because they didn't set up businesses or employ people or generate money, they'd become unimportant nobodies, their role devalued and their opinions discounted. Respect for teachers had been lost, while pupils and parents were adamant that their own rights should be upheld. Lisette firmly believed that respect had to be earned, and she herself made sure that she did her best to earn it in the classroom, but she knew that parents looked down on her for not being an entrepreneur. Stupid people, she often thought. Stupid people who can't see what they're doing to themselves and their families.

With the subsequent bust, the attitude towards teachers shifted again, but this time the focus was on the fact that they were paid too much for too few hours and that they had safe, secure jobs. Lisette wondered if anyone who had to spend time with Gareth's 3A class would ever think it was a safe, secure place to be. She would've bet any money that a businessman faced with Noel (the Mucker) Kelly and Tiernan (the Truck) Scallon would walk out of the room and drive away in his prestigious car.

No matter what people thought, the job wasn't easy. And no matter what they said, it didn't pay a fortune either. Which was a pity. Because both Gareth and Lisette could've done with a fortune to get them out of their property nightmare. A nightmare that had only happened because they'd taken the words of those who'd sneered at them to heart and tried to be entrepreneurs as well as teachers.

It had seemed like a great idea back in the mid noughties, when everyone was piling into bricks and mortar. The annoying thing was that initially they hadn't even gone hell-for-leather at it like so many other people.

With some unexpected help from Fred, they'd put a deposit on their current home, Thorngrove, before selling their three-bedroomed house on the Kilmore Road. It was then that what had seemed like a brilliant stroke of luck led them down the dark path of property investment. While they were waiting to move into Thorngrove, house prices continued to rise. By the time they actually sold their house, they'd made much more money than they'd dreamed possible. The bank manager had suggested that perhaps they might like to use some of that money to invest in more property. Which they'd done, flipping a city centre apartment profitably. And that had led them to buying a four-bedroomed house for rental in Artane, another Dublin apartment and, of course, their house in La Rochelle.

Lisette had been astonished at how easy it all was. In a few months they'd made more playing the property market than they ever did as teachers. It made her wonder what the point was of the years of studying and the hard graft of the classroom, when you could coin it in by buying and selling an apartment in a matter of weeks. Additionally (and to her secret shame), she'd felt superior to Donald for the first time ever, because he'd had to downsize after his divorce from Deirdre. She clamped down on her smugness but every so often allowed herself to think that for once in his life Gareth had beaten his older brother and his family unit had come out the best.

Notionally, she and Gareth had made fifty grand on the second apartment when they put it on the market. They'd turned down an offer that would've got them out at a profit of twenty-five because they hadn't believed that prices would go much lower. But of course they had. So dramatically that they'd been left reeling, and in more debt than they knew how to manage. The only way they had kept their heads above water was by giving grinds after school and at the weekends (it was fortunate that so many students wanted extra tuition), and they also occasionally had foreign students stay with them at Thorngrove. It was the foreign students that had kept them going the previous winter, but Lisette wasn't sure that she'd have the same number this year.

Now, even though they'd said no more about it, the knowledge that Gareth had been checking prices of La Rochelle properties was still a barrier between them. No matter how hard things got, she couldn't bear the idea of selling Papillon.

A message alert pinged on the laptop and she looked at it.

Just a reminder about my upcoming birthday party, she read. **Hope to see you bright and early.**

She groaned. Going to Zoey's thirtieth birthday was the last thing she felt like doing, being surrounded by her flighty friends and Donald's boring colleagues, made to feel ancient and irrelevant by one lot and useless by the others, and forced into being nice to Gareth in public when she was still angry with him.

Stop it, she said to herself. You're not useless, you're not ancient

129

and you're not irrelevant. And you're angry with Gareth because he's looking at every option. The real problem is that you're broke. And trying to hide it. Which is a difficult place to be in. But hopefully not for ever. Things will change. They always do.

She thought again about her father-in-law and his will. She wished she hadn't seen it, because she didn't like thinking of Fred's ultimate end. She was fond of him no matter how exasperating he could be, and it was awful to think that she was pinning her hopes on his death to get them out of the hole they were in. Yet the last time Gareth had talked to their bank manager, Bill Hogan had asked him about Fred's estate and Gareth had assured him that they stood to inherit a substantial amount. Bill had believed him, which was why he was cutting them more slack than they deserved. Lisette wondered if Fred knew exactly how important he was to their future. Knowing him, he probably did. She turned her attention back to the laptop.

Wouldn't miss it, she lied in response to Zoey's message. **Am sure will be the event of the year.**

She closed her laptop. Gareth had fallen asleep on the sofa beside her. She leaned her head on his shoulder and closed her eyes. But she couldn't sleep herself. There were too many worries still whirring around in her head for that.

Chapter 13

Abbey told Ryan Gilligan that she'd go to Ireland and meet Fred Fitzpatrick, but not before Pete and Claudia arrived home from the Caribbean at the weekend.

'I'm house-sitting,' she explained. 'And dog-sitting. I can't just walk out.'

'Fair enough,' said Ryan. 'Mr Fitzpatrick will be delighted. I'll try to organise flights for as soon as possible. My client . . .' He broke off and considered for a moment before continuing. 'I should stop saying "my client" and call him your grandfather, shouldn't I?'

'Whatever.'

'Anyway, he'll be delighted to see you, and the sooner the better.'

'I guess it's costing him a fortune keeping you here,' she said. 'I'm sorry.'

'It's OK. I'm not on billable hours this week.'

'You're on vacation?' Abbey grinned at him. 'I should show you a bit of the city in that case.'

'I've done the bus tour,' Ryan said.

'I guess that takes in most of it,' agreed Abbey. 'Have you been to the Rock yet?'

'No. I've seen the movie, though. As well as *Escape from Alcatraz* and the TV series,' he added.

'It's my favourite place,' she told him. 'You should come with me. I'll try to get tickets for tomorrow.'

'OK,' said Ryan. 'Should be fun.'

As the ferry docked at the island, Ryan remarked that the chill breezes and damp mists that the brochures had threatened hadn't materialised and that the heavy fleece he'd brought with him was totally unnecessary.

'People like to think of Alcatraz as cold and grim.' Abbey glanced down at her T-shirt and capris. 'But sometimes it can be warm and welcoming.'

They turned towards the prison block and Ryan murmured that welcoming wasn't exactly the word he'd use for it. It was smaller than he'd imagined, he told her. And cramped.

'It's like stepping back in time,' she said. 'That's why I like it. It doesn't matter that the world has changed so much outside; in here it's always 1963.'

'And you prefer the past?' asked Ryan as he looked at the breakfast menu (assorted cereals, steamed wheat, scrambled eggs, stewed fruit and toast) for 21 March 1963, the day on which Robert Kennedy had ordered the closure of the prison.

'No,' said Abbey. 'But I think it's important.'

'So do I,' said Ryan. 'So does Mr Fitzpatrick.'

She glanced at him, but he was still staring at the menu.

Ellen would've been five years old when the men in the prison were tucking into that breakfast, thought Abbey as she looked at it too. She'd have been in Boston, with Gramma and Gramps, not knowing that in Ireland there was another family waiting for her. Or not, obviously. She chided herself for being sentimental. The Fitzpatrick family hadn't been waiting for Ellen. Only Mr Fitzpatrick had even known of her existence, and he'd conveniently forgotten about her until now.

She shivered.

'Cold?' There was a mixture of concern and surprise in Ryan's voice.

132

'No,' she said. 'Just, you know, thinking.'

'Come on.' He led her out of the prison block and into the fresh air. The sun scorched down from the cloudless blue sky as they walked to one of the walls and stared back across the bay towards the city.

'It's emotional,' said Ryan.

'You're the first person who's come here with me to ever say that.'

'Of course it's emotional,' he said. 'To be so near and yet so far . . . but,' he added briskly, 'they were hardened criminals and deserved it.'

'That's what Pete says too.'

'I think I'm going to like Pete,' said Ryan.

And Abbey couldn't help thinking that Pete would probably like Ryan too. He was an easy person to like.

'Stay there,' she said suddenly.

'Why?'

She opened her bag and took out a notebook and pencil.

'Don't move,' she ordered. 'Keep looking in that direction.'

Her pencil raced over the paper while, in between shooting glances in her direction, Ryan stared out over the bay. After a few minutes she stopped, tore out the page and handed it to him. He looked at it and then at her, a surprised expression on his face.

'This is brilliant,' he said. 'Really good. Although I didn't think you saw me quite like that.'

She'd drawn him as a prisoner, staring across the water, a pensive expression on his face.

'When we were first talking about my mom, you had that expression on your face,' she said. 'And suddenly it came back to me and I wanted to capture it.'

'You're very talented.'

'Adequately talented,' she told him. 'Anyway, I did it as a present for you. For being good company.'

'I've enjoyed the company too.' He looked from her to the

drawing and then at the dilapidated prison block. But he didn't say anything else.

As she'd already suspected, Pete and Ryan got on well together from the moment she introduced them. Pete quizzed the Irishman on his background, and Ryan explained that although he had a legal qualification, the firm where he worked had an investigative division and that was what he specialised in.

'I'm not exactly a PI,' he said, which Abbey couldn't help feeling disappointed Pete. 'I mostly do corporate work.'

'Industrial espionage?' asked Pete hopefully, and Ryan said it was a bit more mundane than that usually, but from time to time, yes.

The two men spent a lot of time discussing differences in US and Irish law before turning to the issue of Fred Fitzpatrick and his sudden desire to meet the daughter he apparently hadn't thought about for over fifty years. When Pete heard about Ita Dillon and the Magdalene laundries, he was as shocked as Abbey had been and their eyes met in a complicit look that Ryan didn't see.

'Abbey is going to Ireland simply to meet with this guy and talk about her mom?' said Pete. 'There's no other reason?'

'Well, Mr Fitzpatrick is hoping she'll be able to persuade Ellen to visit him too,' said Ryan. 'I appreciate that there seem to be logistical difficulties about this, but I'm sure it can be arranged eventually.'

'What d'you think, Abbey?' asked Pete.

'It can do no harm to talk to the man,' she said. 'I'll tell him everything he needs to know about Mom.'

'Is it likely she knew about the adoption?' she asked Pete later that evening, after Ryan had gone.

'She never told me,' he replied. 'Not that she had to, of course, but we talked about a lot of things, back in the day.'

'I can't make up my mind whether she knows or not.' Abbey looked at him with a worried expression. 'Although if she does – d'you think it explains anything?'

'With your mom, anything's possible,' said Pete.

'I keep wondering if I should contact her straight away,' said Abbey. 'I feel as though this man, her father, deserves something from her, and that she should know what's going on too. But it seems wrong to email her out of the blue, and besides, I don't know what to say.'

'I understand,' he said. 'I think you should go to Ireland. Tell him everything and let him decide what he wants to do. Then you can worry about your mom. Keep in touch with me the whole time. You don't have to stay for a second longer than you want.'

'He's paying for the flight and putting me up in a hotel for as long as it takes,' said Abbey. 'It's a bit weird, someone doing that. It must matter a lot to him.'

'Hey, I paid for you to stay in a hotel once,' teased Pete. 'Remember when we all went to Santa Barbara?'

Abbey grinned. 'Sure do. Poolside room, great food. Can't imagine it'll be like that in Ireland.'

'I'm sure it'll be awesome.' Pete leaned forward and ruffled her hair. 'You'll have a great time.'

'Hmm.' Abbey looked at him doubtfully. But she felt an unexpected thrill at the idea of travelling again. Besides, she didn't want Ryan Gilligan to have to report that he'd failed in his mission to bring at least one member of Fred's family home. And, quite unexpectedly, she also wanted to see her unknown grandfather for herself.

The flight arrived in Dublin at 8 a.m. Abbey stared out of the window as the plane descended over the steel-blue sea followed by a chessboard of green fields before touching down gently on the runway and taxiing to the gate. As she gathered up her things, she was conscious of a sudden increase in her heart rate. Until now she hadn't felt as though coming here was really happening. Now, quite suddenly, it was real. She was in her mother's homeland, preparing to meet her mother's father, someone she hadn't even known existed a couple of weeks earlier. She hesitated for a moment.

'Everything all right?' asked Ryan as he took his computer bag from the overhead bin.

'It's all been a bit of a whirl, to be honest.'

'I know.'

'However, now that I'm here . . .'

'You'll love it,' he assured her. 'Ireland's a great place.'

'So I've heard.'

She stepped into the aisle and moved towards the exit. She was reminded of her childhood, getting off planes with her mom, wondering if this time they'd arrived somewhere they were going to stay for ever.

'We'll collect the cases and then get a taxi to your hotel,' said Ryan as he steered her towards the baggage hall.

'If Mr Fitzpatrick and I don't get along, it'll be a short stay,' observed Abbey.

'You can leave any time you like.' Ryan's voice was reassuring.

'He might not even want me to hang around,' Abbey remarked as they stopped at the carousel. 'He might be madly disappointed in me.'

'Hey, I thought all you American girls were full of confidence and no false modesty,' said Ryan. 'He'll love you.'

Abbey laughed. 'You have some skewed notions about the States,' she told him.

'Too many reality shows.'

She laughed again, and then clapped her hands in delight as her case appeared on the carousel.

'Good omen,' she said as she grabbed it. 'My bag has never appeared this quickly before.'

'They obviously threw the smallest out first.'

Ryan had been surprised at the size of her luggage when he'd met her at San Francisco airport, but Abbey told him that she always travelled light.

They walked through the arrivals hall and out of the terminal building. Abbey stood still for a moment, then smiled.

'It's warm,' she said.

'That surprises you?'

'Gramma hardly ever talked about Ireland. But when she did, she said that it was cold. And that it rained.'

'She wasn't wrong,' agreed Ryan. 'But occasionally we can surprise the visitors and ourselves by having a bit of an Indian summer. It's been nice for the past fortnight, apparently. And they're hoping for another week of it. Which would be a total heatwave.'

'Excellent,' said Abbey as they got into a taxi.

'Howth,' Ryan instructed the driver, and got in beside her.

Abbey didn't speak until the car pulled into the pretty Northside village, but then she exclaimed in pleasure.

'It's lovely,' she said, looking at the harbour with its multitude of sailing boats and the clusters of people already strolling along the pier. 'Pretty.'

'Like Sausalito,' suggested Ryan, which made her smile.

'A little, I guess.' She sounded doubtful.

'Wait till you see the views from your grandfather's house. He overlooks Dublin Bay. Not quite the same as San Francisco, I'll admit, but still amazing.'

She said nothing.

'This is your hotel.'

The cab pulled up outside a double-fronted building which faced directly on to the street and therefore had views across the harbour and towards the sea.

'It's a small, family-run place,' he said. 'Boutique is how they describe it. I hope it's OK.'

'It looks perfect,' she told him, thinking that although it certainly looked boutique, she'd been right in thinking it would be a far cry from the uber-luxurious hotel that Pete had arranged in Santa Barbara.

Ryan paid the taxi driver and ushered Abbey inside. The entrance hall was small but pristine, with a black and white tiled floor and a large floral arrangement in an empty fire grate surrounded by brass trims.

'Hello,' said the receptionist, who Abbey thought must have come direct from central casting, because she had glorious red-gold Irish hair, green eyes and a smattering of freckles across her nose. 'You're very welcome, Miss Andersen.'

'Thank you,' said Abbey.

'I know you've had a long journey and you're probably tired. Your room is already prepared, so you can go straight up. But if you'd like breakfast, it's being served now.'

'That would be nice,' said Abbey, who, although she'd eaten everything that had been put in front of her on the plane, was feeling hungry again. She turned to Ryan. 'Would you like to join me?'

'That's very kind of you,' he said. 'But I've got to check in at the office and catch up on some paperwork. So . . .'

'Sure, no problem.' It occurred to Abbey that over the last few days she'd thought of Ryan Gilligan as a friend. As someone who had her best interests at heart. Someone who cared about her. But he was nothing of the sort, just someone doing a job. She'd forgotten that. 'Thanks for looking after me so well,' she said.

'No problem. It was good to meet you.'

'You too.' She held out her hand and he took it, before dropping a swift kiss on her cheek.

'Take care of yourself,' he said. 'A cab will be here at one o'clock to bring you to Mr Fitzpatrick's. OK?'

'Sure.'

'Good luck.' He released her hand and walked out of the hotel. She wanted to call after him, to tell him that she was nervous

and ask him to stay with her. But she knew she was being ridiculous. She took her room key from the receptionist and picked up
her bag.

She suddenly felt very alone again.

The room was beautiful, and the views across the water were
breathtaking. Abbey stood in the bay window, watching the sailing
boats as they skimmed across the entrance of the harbour, and a
tug boat as it chugged its way to its moorings. She was glad that
she was staying here, near the sea, in a place that, although nothing
like San Francisco's Fisherman's Wharf, was still a working harbour.
She could smell the salt of the water and the hint of tar through
the open sash window, and she could hear the screech of the gulls
as they wheeled overhead. It was comforting.

Her phone rang, startling her. She took it out of her bag and
answered as soon as she saw Pete's name.

'How're you doing?' he asked.

It was good to hear his voice.

'I'm standing in the cutest little hotel, overlooking a miniature
harbour,' she told him. 'The sun is sparkling off the water, there
are fishing boats and artists and people walking along the pier.'

'Sounds like home from home,' said Pete.

'Not entirely,' she said. 'But it's very pretty. You're up late.'
She glanced at her watch and realised that it was the middle of
the night in San Francisco.

'Wanted to make sure that my girl was all right,' he said. 'Besides,
I needed to do some catch-up, and night-time is good for that.
No interruptions. What are your plans?'

'I'm going to have breakfast in a few minutes,' she told him.
'Then I'll take a walk around the town. And after that, I'll be
meeting Mr Fitzpatrick. My grandfather.'

'You're OK about talking to him?' asked Pete.

'I'll tell him everything he wants to know,' said Abbey. 'I guess
he deserves that. Though I'm not sure how he'll feel about it.

But hey, what odds? He's here, Mom's in Los Montesinos, they're both doing their own thing, and I'll assure him that one way or another she definitely forgives him.'

'Are you nervous?' asked Pete.

'I don't know exactly,' admitted Abbey. 'I feel a bit weird about it, but it's not like I'm going to get involved with the whole family or anything.'

'Are you sure you're all right?' said Pete.

'I'm fine,' Abbey assured him. 'Now go to sleep.'

'Good night, honey.'

'Good night,' she said and ended the call.

The hotel breakfast was lovely – lots of fresh fruit and yogurt, meats and cheeses, all of which Abbey loved. Usually her breakfast was a coffee and Danish from Starbucks, and although she was a big fan of their coffee, a skinny latte and Danish on the go couldn't match having a sit-down breakfast overlooking the ocean. (Sea, Abbey reminded herself when she thought this. She wasn't near an ocean. Dublin overlooked the sea.)

After breakfast she went outside and walked along the pier, the lower level first, where it was warm and sheltered, and which seemed to be popular with mothers and babies out for a morning stroll. When she reached the lighthouse at the end, she stared across the water at the small island known as Ireland's Eye, which was accessible to visitors by boat. She thought about taking a trip, but decided to wait for another day. After all, she had a whole week for tourist things. Unless she bailed out early.

She turned around and followed the walkers returning to the town along the higher pier wall. The sun was still warm but the wind buffeted her as she picked her way along the uneven surface. It was exhilarating, though, and she felt awake and refreshed when she'd completed the walk. She continued her stroll around the marina and then back through the town towards the hotel.

All of a sudden she experienced another flashback. To a time when she and her mother had walked along a pier together, towards the hotel they were staying in. She'd been young at the time and she couldn't remember what country they'd been in. All she remembered was Ellen pointing at the building and saying 'home at last' because it had been a long walk and Abbey had complained about feeling tired. She remembered thinking that the hotel wasn't home, but that it was somewhere she could lie down and rest. She remembered wishing that her mother wasn't so energetic, always wanting to be different places, do different things. She remembered promising herself that when she was old enough, she'd find a place she loved and live there for the rest of her life. Ellen had done that now, in Los Montesinos. Abbey had tried to achieve it in San Francisco. She thought she had. She felt more at home there than anywhere else in the world. She had everything she wanted on her doorstep. She hadn't had the slightest desire ever to cross the Atlantic. But now that she was here, she was glad she'd come. Even if things didn't work out the way her new grandfather wanted them to.

Chapter 14

When she got back to the hotel, she changed into a pair of skinny jeans and a loose floral top. Then she went down to the reception area and sat in a deep armchair near the window, where she was able to watch the activity on the street outside while waiting for her taxi. Clara, the receptionist, asked her if she needed anything.

'No, everything's good so far,' said Abbey.

'Have you ever been to Ireland before?'

'No.'

'Lots for you to explore, so,' she said cheerfully.

'I guess so. If I have the time.'

'Sure, of course you'll have the time,' said Clara. 'Dublin's easy enough to get around. You can catch the Dart into town from here and you'll be there in twenty minutes.'

Abbey looked at her in confusion.

'It's the suburban train,' Clara explained.

'I thought this was the town,' said Abbey.

Clara shook her head. 'Howth is a village,' she said. 'Town is Dublin, the city.'

'Right,' said Abbey.

'It does sound slightly bonkers,' Clara said cheerfully. 'But that's the way it is. If you get the bus, it will say City Centre on the front. As well as An Lár. That means city centre but in Irish.'

'OK.' Abbey was feeling confused again.

'Ah, you won't get lost,' said Clara. 'Dublin's too small for that.

We've plenty of brochures here for all the main tourist sights. Let me know if there's anything special you want to do and I'll help you organise it. And if you're here to trace your roots, I can help you with whatever you need.'

'Thank you,' said Abbey. 'But I'm pretty much being organised for now, roots and all. And I think this might be my cab.'

A red taxi had pulled up outside the hotel and the driver came inside.

'Ms Andersen,' he said.

'That's me.' Abbey got up, said goodbye to Clara and followed the driver outside.

'Right you are, love,' he said. 'Furze Hill. Great location.'

The driver kept up a running commentary as he drove up the steep road towards the summit of Howth Hill.

'Gorgeous here in this sort of weather,' he said. 'A bit bleak in winter. Though that's just my opinion.'

He was right about its beauty today, thought Abbey as they reached the summit. A carpet of yellow gorse stretched out in front of her, leading to the now aquamarine blue of the sea. In the distance, on the other side of the crescent bay, she could see a peak in a ridge of purple mountains.

'The Sugar Loaf,' said the driver. 'Wicklow. The other side of the city obviously. Another place worth visiting.' He pulled up outside a high double-sized wooden gate. 'Furze Hill.'

She looked out of the car window. The gate was at street level but the land behind it rose steeply and she could make out the edges of the house, shielded by shrubs, at the top. It was spookily reminiscent of Pete's home, both in the way it was hidden from casual view and the way it overlooked the water.

She opened her purse. 'How much?'

'On the account, love,' said the driver.

'Oh.' She fumbled for some coins and handed him a couple, unsure of the correct tip.

'Ah, no need,' he said. 'But thank you.'

143

She got out of the cab and waited until the driver had disappeared around a bend in the road before turning towards the gates of the house again. She guessed that these gates led to a garage. There was a wooden pedestrian gate a little further on, with an intercom beside it. She looked at it hesitantly.

She realised that, despite what she'd told Pete, she was nervous. She wasn't sure why. All she had to do was give Fred Fitzpatrick information about Ellen and listen to him saying sorry. And yet her heart was pounding in her chest and her hands were trembling. She wished that Ryan Gilligan was beside her now, telling her there was nothing to be nervous about. Ryan had been a sort of steadying influence. Although, she reminded herself once again, all he'd been doing was his job.

What would this man want to know about her mother? What would she tell him? How would he react?

She took a deep breath. It didn't matter how he reacted. None of it mattered. They were connected by blood, but that was all. They didn't mean anything to each other. His opinion was irrelevant. She pressed the button.

After a few seconds, a rasping, slightly breathless voice said, 'Yes?'

'This is Abbey Andersen,' she said. 'Here to see Fred Fitzpatrick.'

'I was beginning to wonder if you were ever going to ring the damn thing,' he said. 'Come in. Come in.'

The pedestrian gate clicked open. She pushed against it and stepped inside.

Uneven steps were carved into the hillside and led through a tumble of tall grasses, trees and flowering shrubs to the house. She walked up them slowly, stopping once to look behind her and over the beautiful bay again. The sun was warm on her shoulders and she could feel beads of perspiration forming on her forehead. Her heart was racing. She remembered Ryan Gilligan suggesting that maybe she needed some counselling after he broke the news about Ellen's father. She'd scoffed at the idea then. But she was wishing now that she'd talked to somebody about it, someone who could put things into perspective for her. Because right now she was wondering if she was out of her mind.

The house, when she reached it, was a single-storey building with a very retro look. It had a wide paved area at the front, huge picture windows and a stone-clad chimney. The walls were painted a buttercup yellow. The front door, in honey pine, was ajar.

She tapped at it nervously and then pushed it further, poking her head around it, her eyes struggling to adjust to the dim interior after the bright sunshine.

'In here,' said a voice.

She stepped inside. The hallway was a big square, tiled in terra-cotta with a large Aztec-patterned rug in its centre and rooms leading off from each side. The walls were covered in an eclectic mix of small paintings, prints and photographs.

'This way,' the voice said.

It had come from the right-hand side of the hallway. She walked across and entered what she realised at once was the main living room. It was long and wide and the floor-to-ceiling windows on both sides overlooked the sea.

'So you're Abbey.'

She'd glanced at the view before looking at the man who was sitting in an armchair in a corner of the room. She knew that he was in his eighties, but he held himself well. His pale blue eyes were clear and alert in a round face with an almost bald head. He was wearing a suit and tie, the jacket tightly buttoned over a stomach that was also rounded.

'Mr Fitzpatrick?' she said.

'Who else?' His laugh was rasping and he coughed afterwards.

'Stupid question,' she agreed and walked over to him. 'Abbey Andersen. Pleased to meet you.'

'My God,' he said slowly as he took the hand she'd extended politely towards him. 'You're the image of her.'

'My mother?' Abbey was startled. This man had never known her mother. Anyway, she wasn't at all the image of Ellen.

'No. Dilly. Her mother. She was just like you. Same eyes. Longer hair, but . . .'

He sniffed loudly while Abbey stood uncertainly in front of him.

He took a hanky from his pocket and blew his nose. 'I don't know what's got into me,' he said. 'I hadn't thought of that woman for years and now I'm snivelling over her. Sorry.'

Abbey said nothing.

'Maybe all I wanted was for you to be her.' He returned the hanky to his pocket. 'Now that I look at you . . . well, you're like my daughter too. But she's darker; there aren't that many natural blondes in Ireland. Dilly was one of them. She was beautiful. So are you.'

Abbey was finding it difficult to take in that she was apparently the image of a woman she'd never even known had existed until recently. And that the old man considered her beautiful, which she knew she clearly wasn't.

'I'm sorry about how things turned out,' she said.

'Sit down, sit down.' He waved at her and she pulled an upright chair from its position near the wall until it was facing him before sitting on it. 'I'm sorry too. Now, I mean. I didn't think of her much back then. It was a silly love affair. It didn't mean that much. I was probably tired of her before she even got pregnant.'

Abbey was silent.

'She was fun. A bit of devilment in her, that's what attracted me. That and the looks, of course. But they broke her spirit in the end.'

'She was very young,' said Abbey.

'Yes, but these days . . . well, girls her age wouldn't put up with that sort of stuff now.' There was a mixture of support and irritation in Fred's voice. 'You see them in their short skirts and their long hair and their low-cut tops, yapping away like demented

146

parrots, phones clamped to their heads, doing their make-up on the bus or the train . . .' He coughed again. 'Got a bit of a cold,' he explained. 'Excuse me. Anyway, if what happened then happened now, it'd have an entirely different outcome.'

'It was a difficult time,' said Abbey, paraphrasing what Ryan had told her.

'It was a disgraceful time,' said Fred. 'Men behaved disgracefully.'

Abbey looked startled.

'I did too,' said Fred. 'I abandoned her. I didn't care. What d'you think of that, Abbey Andersen? That I didn't care?'

'I don't know the circumstances so I can't pass judgement, can I?'

'Very diplomatic,' he said. 'You don't have to be. The truth is, I left her to it and they sent her to that terrible place and she died and that was my fault.'

Did he want her to forgive him? wondered Abbey.

'I don't think . . .' she began.

'I didn't think either,' said Fred. 'For a long time. Until I learned about it. And now I do think. A lot. About how I acted and how I behaved. I have a book for you.' He picked it up from the table beside him. 'It's about the laundries. About what went on. It disgusts me to know what happened to those girls. I don't know what happened to Dilly, but as she died there . . . I can only imagine it wasn't good. That her last days were miserable and hard. But I never once thought about it. And I was relieved that I didn't have to worry about your mother. Who is my daughter.' His fingers tightened around the book. 'I completely put her out of my mind, you know. As though she didn't exist.'

'To her you didn't,' said Abbey. 'At least, maybe not. Because she never said anything about being adopted. So she might not even know about you.'

'Which is terrible, don't you think? I let those people take her and change her name and bring her to America. I was pleased about that, back then, because it meant that I wouldn't have to

147

worry about her popping up and demanding to know me and wanting to be part of my life.'

'She didn't. She doesn't,' said Abbey.

'Have you spoken to her?' His voice was eager. 'Does she know I'm looking for her?'

'No,' said Abbey. 'I haven't been able to talk to her about it.'

Fred's brow furrowed. 'Are you estranged?' he asked. 'Because I'm telling you, that's not a good thing. I know all about it. Families should stick together. Support each other. Look out for each other.'

'We're not estranged,' said Abbey. 'I know she loves me. But she's built a certain life for herself and I . . . I'm not a big part of it.'

'She abandoned you?' asked Fred. 'Like I did with Dilly?'

'No. No,' said Abbey, while at the same time remembering the day her mother had left, remembering that she had indeed felt abandoned. 'She – she does her own thing. It's . . . she . . .'

'That's what the investigator told me.' Fred didn't wait for her to finish. 'I said to him that I didn't care. I wanted her found. But then he suggested I talk to you instead.'

Abbey was surprised. She'd thought that her visiting the old man was his own idea, not that Ryan Gilligan had put it into his mind.

'He said I'd like you,' Fred told her.

'He did?'

'He said you were feisty.'

Abbey thought about the tin of Mace she'd carried with her when she'd met Ryan in Sausalito, and smiled.

'You get it from her,' added Fred. 'From Dilly. She was feisty too.'

'Was she?'

'I suppose you think I'm crazy.'

'No.' She spoke slowly. 'No, it's not crazy to want to . . . to make your peace with people.'

He chortled. 'Before I die, you mean.'

'Wow, no, I didn't mean that you were going to die,' she said quickly.

'Of course I am,' he returned. 'I'm an old man. Old people die, that's the way life is. We don't talk about it, though, do we? And these days it's like we pretend it doesn't happen. Hush it up in words like "passed on" when we mean dead. It was different when I was a kid. More people died then, I suppose, at younger ages. So you knew about it. Got used to it. Mind you, I've got along pretty well so far and I might have another few years in me yet. All the same, you're right. I think of dying and I think . . . well, let's say there is a place where you have to account for yourself, or a place where you bump into the people you knew. I want to be able to say I tried to make a difference, even though it was too late for Dilly.'

'I understand,' said Abbey.

'You're quieter than I expected,' Fred said. 'When Ryan said feisty, I thought you'd come in here all guns blazing and blame me for the death of your grandmother and for anything that ever went wrong in your mother's life.'

'I didn't even know about Dilly until he told me,' Abbey said. 'As far as I'm concerned, my grandmother isn't that woman. And as for my mom, well, I guess she's happy with her own life. Which is obviously different to the life she'd have if you and her mother had got married and lived here together.'

'I keep wondering about it,' confessed Fred.

'But if you'd married Dilly, you wouldn't have the family you do now,' said Abbey. 'So I guess it's swings and roundabouts, isn't it?'

'That's true. Although who knows . . .' Fred made a dismissive gesture.

'My grandparents were good to my mom,' said Abbey. 'They gave her lots of freedom.'

'Hmm.' He looked sceptical. 'Not always a good idea.'

'We live in the land of the free,' Abbey reminded him.

'And the home of the brave.'

'Absolutely.'

'You were,' he said. 'Brave. Coming here on your own. Not knowing me or anything. I was surprised when you agreed.'

'So was I.'

'That investigative guy is very persuasive, though.' He chortled and winked at her.

'Mr Gilligan was a total professional,' she said, wondering if she'd misinterpreted the wink.

'How is the hotel?' Fred changed the subject.

'Lovely.'

'So are you going to stay?'

'In Ireland?'

'Of course.'

'Until I've told you everything you want to know about my mom.'

'Excellent,' he said. 'I want to introduce you to the family, too.'

'How much have you told them?' asked Abbey.

'Nothing yet.'

'Nothing?' She looked worried. 'They don't know anything about Dilly? Or Mom? Or me?'

'No,' said Fred. 'But they'll be OK about it.'

'Are you sure?'

'Oh yes,' said Fred. 'I reckon they always guessed there was something. I wasn't an angel, you know.'

Abbey wasn't so certain that the old man's family knew anything about his younger days. And she couldn't help thinking that there were plenty of reasons why they wouldn't be too impressed by the news that he had a secret daughter and granddaughter. She looked around her. 'Do any of them live here, with you?'

'No,' he said. 'I'm an independent person. A bit of a crock at the moment, what with my bad wrist, bloody cold and all, but independent all the same. My daughters-in-law drop in from time to time and I have a woman who does light housework twice a week. I do everything else myself.'

'I was wondering how you get up and down those steps,' said Abbey. 'If you're crocked.'

He laughed. 'There's a lift from the scullery to the garage. No problem.'

'Cool,' she said.

'Want to see?' he asked.

'Love to.'

He got up from the chair. He walked slowly, but he wasn't as infirm as she'd initially thought, although she could see that beneath the long-sleeved shirt there was some light strapping on his right wrist. He brought her through the kitchen of the house and then into a utility room which contained a boiler, a washing machine and a dryer as well as the lift. He pressed the button and the doors slid open.

It only took a couple of seconds to reach the garage. Abbey was astonished to see a restored Volkswagen Beetle and a Mercedes there, along with a Ford Focus.

'I used to love driving,' he said. 'Cars were a hobby that became a business and eventually turned back into a hobby again. I worked on the Beetle and the Merc but I'm stuck with the Ford for day-to-day driving. Not that I drive much any more.'

'What were you?' she asked. 'A salesman? A mechanic?'

'No, no. All I did was install car alarms,' he replied. 'Afterwards I moved into home alarms and security systems. But the car business meant I got to work on some great motors.' He pressed a button and the garage doors slid open. 'Come on,' he said. 'I'll walk you around the rest of the property.'

At this level, with the high surrounding walls, it was impossible to see the sea any more. But the garden, as they walked along a narrow twisting path, was lush and green, although a little overgrown, and crammed with multicoloured flowers.

'I fired the gardener a while back,' said Fred. 'Haven't got a new one yet. But I will.'

'I like it,' Abbey told him. 'The whole untamed look you've got going outside works.'

'Too much land,' Fred said. 'Relative to the size of the house. But I always wanted space. Where I first lived in Dublin all we had was a small yard, so this is heaven for me. When we moved here, I spent a lot of time in the garden and the garage. Then the old ticker started to give me some trouble so I don't walk around it as much as I used to.' He pulled a dead blossom from a rose bush. 'This place was worth a fortune at the height of the property boom. Not so much now, I'm afraid.'

'Oh, that doesn't matter in the slightest when you're living in it, does it?' she said. 'I think it's beautiful.'

He looked pleased. 'You really do, don't you?'

She nodded enthusiastically. 'I love being near the sea and being able to see it from the house. In California . . .' She stopped. She'd been about to tell him about Pete's place, but she wasn't sure if he'd want to know.

'I'd like to know all about you,' he said when she faltered. 'And I want to know about your mother and your lives. Unvarnished truth,' he added. 'No sugar-coating.'

'OK,' said Abbey.

'Let's sit in the garden,' suggested Fred.

They walked slowly to the back of the house, where there was a large patio area with outdoor seating.

'Why don't you sit down and I'll make us some tea,' said Fred.

'That would be lovely,' Abbey said. 'But I should do it. You've a sore wrist . . .'

'I'm perfectly capable of doing it myself.' Fred's voice was testy. 'But of course – you're American. Would you prefer coffee?'

She smiled at him. 'Yes please.'

'Coming up,' said Fred, and went into the house.

It was peaceful in the garden. Enormous bumblebees lumbered

from flower to flower, while graceful butterflies alighted then departed from the small green bush to the side of the seat where Abbey was sitting. Amid the sweet smell of honeysuckle and later summer blooms, she could detect the tang of the sea, which sparkled in the distance. Furze Hill was both similar to and different from Bella Vista Heights. But it struck Abbey as a happy coincidence that both Pete and Fred's homes had magnificent views over water.

She tapped her fingers anxiously against the arm of the seat. Fred had asked for the unvarnished truth. She wasn't sure how that would present either her or her mother from his perspective. She wondered if he was still holding a grudge against these Magdalene laundry people (she'd googled it after her meeting with Ryan Gilligan and been appalled) and if he'd expect her and Ellen to hold a grudge too. But how on earth would Ellen feel about that? She wished now that she'd emailed her mother before coming here, no matter how difficult that would have been for her. It would have been good to have found out how much Ellen herself already knew.

She strained her ears to hear if Fred needed any help with the coffee. Despite his protestations that he was able to manage, she was very conscious of his age. He could be weaker than he thought and she didn't want him putting himself to any trouble for her. She thought she'd heard the sound of beans grinding earlier (and had been impressed that he had a grinder and hadn't succumbed to Nespresso like everyone else she knew), but she hadn't heard any sounds from the house for the last few minutes. Still, she thought, making decent coffee took time. She didn't want to hassle him.

She leaned back in the seat and closed her eyes. She truly could be on Pete's deck, she thought, as the sun warmed her face. There was the same sense of serenity. Calming. Soothing. She felt herself drifting into sleep. It had been a busy few days, and despite sleeping on the flight (she'd always been good at sleeping on planes), her body clock was completely out of synch. Her head lolled to one side. She was only half conscious now, thinking that her mother was sitting beside her, talking of how her father had abandoned her and her mother and of how lonely that made her feel.

'But you can't be lonely,' she told Ellen seriously. 'You have me.'

And then she heard the crash and she woke up.

Chapter 15

More than fifty people had been invited to Zoey's thirtieth birthday party. Too many, really, for the house in Baldoyle, even with the double doors between the living and dining room open. Now that the rooms had been festooned with balloons and banners, as well as vases of fresh flowers, the space looked even more limited. But, thought Zoey, as she looked at it critically, people could drift into the garden because the warm spell of weather still hadn't broken. So all things considered, it would probably work out OK.

She walked upstairs to the bedroom and looked at her dress. It was firecracker-red and plunged pleasingly both front and back, showing off her sleek body and its generous curves to their best advantage. She'd bought a set of matching costume jewellery with ruby-red stones (so totally cutting back by not asking for real gems) which complemented the dress (Harvey Nicks, expensive but definitely worth it) and the almost identically coloured shoes (Topshop, absolute bargain). She reckoned that she was putting together a fabulous look for a fabulous party as cheaply as was humanly possible. There was the slight issue of her hair, to which she'd added more extensions for the evening, which weren't cheap, but by and large she felt that Donald couldn't complain. And he wouldn't, she knew, when he saw her in her gorgeous dress, looking beyond stunning. He wouldn't be able to help comparing her to her sister-in-law, Lisette, who'd undoubtedly be wearing something supposedly understated and chic, but which in reality would be safe and boring. Zoey knew that Lisette thought she was sophisticated, but she wasn't, she was dull. And as for her hair – Zoey reckoned the older woman could knock at least ten years off herself if she'd get a decent colouring job done. Or even if she bought a bottle of Clairol and did it herself!

Not that it mattered how Lisette looked tonight. The attention would all be on Zoey herself and how great she looked for thirty. Thirty. She repeated it to herself. It was only a number, after all, but there was a small part of her that thought it also sounded a lot more grown-up than twenty-nine. Maybe that was what had happened with Lisette, she thought in a sudden spurt of amusement. She hit thirty and decided to be a grown-up. Only she went straight to being a middle-aged grown-up.

Anyway, thought Zoey, the party would be grown-up and sophisticated but with a fun dimension. All her friends would be there, after all, so it couldn't get boring; and thankfully this would also be a family occasion at which there'd be no unwanted appearance from Disgruntled Deirdre and her equally disgruntled daughters. Zoey hoped that Donald was finally coming to realise that she was far more important to him than his former wife and just as much a part of his family as his pampered girls. And that she was worth every single cent he spent on her.

Lisette wasn't looking forward to Zoey's party in the slightest. If it had been at all possible to get out of it, she would have, but she hadn't been able to come up with a single excuse not to go. It wasn't that Lisette didn't enjoy parties and going out, but her idea of a good time was very different to Zoey's. Besides, her sister-in-law's family would be there too, and they were far too raucous for Lisette. They all talked at the same time, didn't listen to each other, drank too much, laughed loudly at unfunny jokes and generally took over any gathering they were at. Not that she could blame them for taking over Zoey's birthday – it was her night after all – but Lisette truly would have preferred a quiet evening in a restaurant, with good wine and equally good conversation.

She couldn't remember what she'd done for her own thirtieth birthday. Fifteen years ago, she realised with a sense of dismay. Where had those years gone? Years when she didn't have to worry about anyone other than herself and when she could go where she liked and do what she liked. She hadn't appreciated them at the time. Hadn't appreciated how good living and working in Dublin as a young, free and single girl could be. Only the thing was, she hadn't really lived a hectic young, free and single life. She'd actually been quite lonely, spending most of her free time studying her English and traipsing around the city's cultural highlights, until she'd met Gareth at Dublin's Alliance Française. They'd both come to a talk about French painters (not a topic she was madly interested in, but she was feeling homesick and wanted to hear French accents), and she'd noticed the bearded Irishman with his grey eyes, narrow chiselled face and unfashionably long hair almost at once. He looked like an artist, she thought, as she observed him sitting in his seat making notes in a spiral-bound book. After the talk, when people were drinking coffee, she'd manoeuvred her way to his side and asked him, in her still less-than-fluent English, what he'd thought of it.

She'd been surprised when he spoke to her in more than passable French, which had led to a much longer conversation than she'd expected. And then he'd opened the notebook and shown her that the notes she'd thought he was making were in fact profile sketches of her, which delighted her even more.

'You have an interesting face,' he told her. 'It's worth drawing.'

She'd been told before that she had an interesting face, although it wasn't something she'd ever taken as a compliment. Good bone structure, which she undoubtedly had, didn't necessarily lead to beauty. In her case it gave her a slightly aloof, angular appearance that, together with her hair, generally made people think she was older than she was.

But Gareth liked her hair. He told her that it was soignée, which made her smile. But he meant it.

He asked her out and she accepted. She liked the coincidence of them both being teachers, art and history being his subjects, while she specialised, not surprisingly, in French. At a boys' comprehensive school, which, she told Gareth, could be tricky.

'But I love it,' she added. 'I love the boys and I love being here.'

She eventually fell in love with him too, thinking that he was one of the gentlest men she'd ever met, thoughtful and kind. He was a good teacher and a good painter and a good person. Unfortunately, as it turned out, he wasn't a good businessman.

God, she thought, as she looked at the pile of bills stuffed on to the kitchen shelf, we're in such damn trouble here. Over the past few months they'd cut everything back to the bone. They'd got rid of their multi-room satellite TV and downgraded their phone and internet packages. Lisette took advantage of any money-saving coupons she could find and she was now a pathological switcher-off of electrical appliances. But none of these savings could possibly make a dent in the mortgage payments on the investment properties they owned, which were now less of an investment and more of a millstone.

Except for Papillon. She felt an almost physical pain in her heart when she thought of selling it. When she was in her twenties, all she'd wanted to do was to leave France, which she'd always believed was too bureaucratic and too stuffy and too much – as she used to say – up its own derrière. But when Jerome was born and she'd brought him home, she suddenly felt French as well as Irish, and she wanted her son to feel as though he was a citizen of both countries. She wanted that for Fleur too.

Buying the house in La Rochelle had been a culmination of that desire. It was more than a holiday house. It was their home in another country. Unfortunately it had become a major bone of contention between them, the elephant in the room in every single conversation they had these days. And because they were in such a deep financial hole, every conversation they had was about money. It had never been like that before. Money hadn't been important to them. They'd joked about Donald, who seemed to believe that as Fred's elder son, and because he worked in the business with him, he had a certain image to maintain. They secretly mocked his apparent obsession with sales targets, profitability and income, even though, back then, they were both quietly envious of his beautiful home in Clontarf.

Not that he had that any more, thought Lisette. Somehow, Donald too had slid backwards, because his house in Baldoyle wasn't anything like the one he had left behind. Even his new wife was a cheaper model. Or, Lisette amended, a model who looked cheaper but who might actually be more expensive to maintain. Deirdre used to buy sparingly but well. Zoey, from what Lisette could make out, took a more scattergun approach. Both Lisette and Gareth had been sad when Donald and Deirdre split up, and at first Lisette had tried to maintain her relationship with Donald's wife, with whom she'd got on well. But that friendship had faded since her brother-in-law's remarriage. He didn't like anyone being in touch with Deirdre, who, Lisette had to admit, had taken him to the cleaners in the divorce.

Funny how things had all started to change after Ros had died, she thought. Fred's wife had been a quiet sort of woman but somehow her influence seemed to hold the entire family together on every level. And now it had splintered apart and nothing was the same as it had been before. Although perhaps nothing had been as wonderful as she was remembering. That was the trouble with looking back. You couldn't help doing it from the perspective of where you were now.

She got up from the kitchen table, ignoring the pile of bills, and not wanting to depress herself still further by deciding which ones they could pay this week. The thing to do, she told herself, was to get off her high horse about tonight, take full advantage

159

of Zoey and Donald's hospitality and have a great time. Maybe even drink too much. Lisette rarely drank too much. But sometimes letting the alcohol take you over wasn't entirely a bad thing.

I'll trawl through my wardrobe, she decided, and find the most suitable outfit I have for a bling-bling night, even though my bling-bling days are far behind me. And I'd better remind Gareth that we're picking up his dad too. She knew that Fred was looking forward to the party, despite the fact that he was more than twice the average age of Zoey's friends. He was probably convinced that one or two of them would fancy him!

What is it about men, she asked herself as she climbed the stairs and went into the bedroom, that no matter what age they are, they think they're eternally attractive to women? Whereas we perpetually worry about lines and wrinkles and looking older and undesirable? She glanced at her reflection in the dressing-table mirror and frowned. If she didn't make a big effort tonight, people would think that she was Fred's wife, not his son's. And that would be one blow too many to take. She opened her make-up bag. She had a lot of work to do.

Chapter 16

It took Abbey a few seconds to realise where she was. The half-dream had seemed so real that she was sure Ellen was physically there beside her and reached out to touch her. Meeting nothing but thin air, she blinked a couple of times, and then the noise of the crash filtered back into her consciousness. That was what had jerked her into wakefulness again. She rubbed her eyes, got up from the chair and made her way to the kitchen, where she expected to find Fred fussing over whatever he had dropped.

But there was no sign of him. She called his name tentatively, not wanting to appear as though she was checking up on him. She'd already gained the very strong impression that Fred didn't like being thought of as old or helpless, despite their conversation about age and mortality.

'Mr Fitzpatrick?' she called, slightly louder. And then, with a touch of embarrassment, 'Fred?'

There was still no response, and she stood uncertainly in the kitchen, thinking that although being on the patio outside had reminded her of Bella Vista Heights, the inside of Fred's home was very different. The airy kitchen was cluttered and untidy, with a selection of unwashed mugs on the worktop beside the sink, a pile of newspapers on another worktop and a variety of empty bottles on a third. There were also two cups beside the kettle. One contained a tea bag and the other a spoonful of instant coffee. Which meant, she thought, that the sound she'd heard of grinding beans hadn't been Fred making her coffee at all.

She tried calling again, but there was still no reply.

He could be a bit deaf, she supposed, and unable to hear her. Yet she couldn't help feeling a little bit concerned. She walked slowly out of the kitchen and paused in the hallway. Once again she called his name, without reply. She looked into the living room where he'd been sitting when she first arrived, but there was no sign of him.

She crossed the hallway to a smaller, more comfortably furnished, television room. In the centre, a Lay-Z-Boy recliner faced an enormous wall-mounted flat-screen TV. It was connected to a state-of-the-art speaker system. He'd be with Pete on that one, thought Abbey. Pete loved his gadgets. Cobey had been a gadget fan too. She remembered, with a dart of anger, that she'd bought him the latest iPad as soon as it had hit the Apple store on Stockton Street, even though he already had the previous one. He'd taken both of them when he'd left.

She moved through the house, still calling Fred's name, but it wasn't until she pushed open the door to a home office with a desk that she let out a cry of shock.

Fred was lying, half on his side, half on his stomach, stretched across the floor. A small printer was upended beside him.

'Mr Fitzpatrick!' cried Abbey. 'Fred? Are you all right?' The question was instinctive. She already knew that he was in big trouble.

She dropped to her knees and rolled him on to his back. His eyes were closed. Her first priority was to see if he was breathing. He wasn't. Nor could she find a pulse.

'Oh shit,' she said. 'Shit, shit, shit.'

She grabbed the phone from the desk and, kneeling beside Fred's prone body, dialled 911. There was the sound of an unconnected number. She looked at the phone in anger. 'Nine one one,' she said out loud. 'Emergency. Come on!' And then she remembered that some countries used 999 as an emergency code.

This time her call was answered straight away. She told the dispatcher that Fred was unconscious and not breathing. The dispatcher asked if she could do CPR, and Abbey, giving thanks to Ellen, who had taught her, said she could.

'The ambulance is on its way,' said the dispatcher. 'It should be with you very shortly.'

Abbey placed her hands on Fred's body and began chest compressions, counting in her head, keeping the rhythm even. But she was horribly afraid that they weren't having any effect.

'Come on, Mr Fitzpatrick,' she muttered. 'Come on, Fred.'

She glanced up. Directly opposite her, on the wall, was a painting of a large rock in a stormy sea, lit by a shaft of sunlight spearing through the dark clouds.

'Be strong,' she urged Fred. 'Like the rock. Please.'

She continued with the CPR until she heard the siren of the ambulance on the street outside. She pressed the button for the gate and the paramedics hurried into the office, where Fred was still prostrate and unresponsive. They immediately took over from her, and, after she'd quickly told them how she'd found Fred, asked her to wait outside.

Abbey's knees were like jelly. She sat on the floor of the hallway, her back against the wall and her legs bent. She listened to the sounds from Fred's office, where the paramedics were continuing their attempts to revive him, and felt sick. She leaned her head on her knees and closed her eyes, trying to compose herself. It wouldn't do any good for her to faint now and be another emergency for the ambulance crew to deal with. She took a few deep breaths and then got slowly to her feet.

She wasn't the right person to be here, not when his life was at stake. It should be someone close to him. Someone from his family. But she didn't know any of his family and they didn't know her. Her hands were shaking as she opened her purse and took out Ryan Gilligan's business card. She dialled the number, which seemed to ring for ages before he answered, sounding tired and vague.

'It's me,' she said. 'Abbey Andersen.'

'Abbey!' This time he was more alert. 'Is everything all right?'

'Um . . . no, not exactly.' She told him what had happened and was met with a shocked silence. 'Are you still there?' she asked.

'Yes, yes, of course. What's happening now?'

'They're continuing to work on him,' she said. 'But . . . I don't know . . . he was in a bad way, Ryan. I kept on and on with the CPR and it wasn't having any effect, and I don't know how long they can keep trying.' She began to cry.

'Oh, don't cry, don't get upset.' Ryan's voice was concerned. 'I'll get to you as quick as I can.'

'Thank you,' she said. 'Please hurry. I don't know what to tell them if . . .'

'I'll phone my colleague Alex and get him to alert the family,' said Ryan. 'He's Fred's solicitor and they all know him.'

'OK,' she said, and sank back to the floor again.

Through the closed door of the office she heard the sound of a defibrillator being used. She felt herself tense even more, praying that it would work.

Oh Fred, she thought. Don't give up now. Not when you haven't properly talked to me about anything. Not when I could have told you everything you wanted to know about Mom. Stick with it, please.

The door to the office opened and one of the paramedics came out.

'Are you all right?' he asked.

She nodded. 'How is he?'

The paramedic's face was calm. 'Unresponsive,' he said.

'Unresponsive?' Abbey stared at him. 'That means nothing's working, doesn't it?'

She could tell that the paramedic was choosing his words with care. 'He isn't responding to our efforts,' he said.

'He's dead?'

'We're continuing our efforts to revive him.'

But they'd been working on Fred for over half an hour, thought Abbey, and unresponsive wasn't a good result.

The buzzer sounded, and this time Abbey went down the steps to open the gate. Ryan Gilligan looked at her paper-white face, concern in his eyes.

'Are you all right?' he asked.

'Yes, I'm fine,' she replied. 'But poor Mr Fitzpatrick . . .' She bit her lip. 'I should have gone to find out what was wrong sooner. Maybe if I had . . .' Suddenly the tears that hadn't fallen before slid down her cheeks and she sniffed loudly. 'God, I'm sorry. I . . .'

'This isn't your fault.' Ryan put his arm around her shoulders and hugged her. 'I'm sure you did your best, and you never know, miracles can happen, he could be all right.'

She shook her head. 'I don't think so. Not this time. He . . . he . . .'

Just then a blue Ford pulled up outside the door and a middle-aged man with a doctor's bag got out.

'I'm Mr Fitzpatrick's family doctor,' he said. 'Alan Casey.'

'The paramedics are with him now,' said Abbey.

Dr Casey hurried past her, up the steps and into the house. Abbey and Ryan stayed outside. He continued to hold her and she leaned against his shoulder, suddenly dizzy again.

'Come back to the house,' said Ryan. 'You need to sit down.'

Even though the sun was warm on her shoulders, Abbey was shivering. Ryan led her into the kitchen and put the kettle on.

'I'll make tea,' he said. 'For shock.'

'Mr Fitzpatrick was going to make tea for me,' said Abbey. 'I asked for coffee instead. I shouldn't have let him make anything. I should've been the one to make it. He was an old man.'

'You were a guest in his home,' said Ryan gently. 'He wouldn't have wanted you making coffee for him.'

'We're talking as though he's died.' Abbey's teeth chattered. 'And I think he has, Ryan. I think he was already dead when I started doing CPR on him.'

'Look, they can do amazing things these days,' said Ryan. 'You hear about it all the time. Please don't worry.'

Why was it, she wondered, that people always told you not to worry at exactly the time you needed to worry most? She picked up the mug that Ryan had put in front of her and looked at him apologetically.

'I'm sorry. I can't drink this,' she said. 'It's got milk in it.'

'It's good for you,' he said.

'It's really not.' She put the cup back on the table and sighed. 'I'm nothing but trouble. I've been nothing but trouble ever since you met me.'

'Of course you're not trouble,' said Ryan, as Dr Casey walked into the kitchen.

'How is he?' Ryan asked.

'I'm afraid there was nothing anyone could do,' said Dr Casey.

Abbey stifled a sob, and Ryan put his arm around her.

'I've spoken to the paramedics and to Donald Fitzpatrick, Fred's elder son,' continued the doctor. 'He's on the way here now. There's no need for Fred to be taken to hospital and Donald says that his father would have wanted to be here.'

'But I can't be here.' Abbey looked horrified. 'He can't see me. He doesn't even know me.'

Dr Casey looked at her with interest. 'And you are?'

'It's a complicated situation,' said Ryan.

'I need to wait until Donald arrives,' said the doctor. 'I have time for you to explain it to me. You were the last person to see Mr Fitzpatrick alive, and—'

'You're surely not suggesting that she had anything to do with his death!' Ryan looked at the doctor in astonishment.

'Of course not,' said Dr Casey. 'According to the paramedics, she did a good job on him before they arrived. But I'd like a little more detail about what happened before I certify the death.'

Feeling that she should make a recording of it, because she was sure this wasn't going to be the last time she told the story, Abbey gave Dr Casey an account of Fred's last minutes.

'You acted with great presence of mind,' he said. 'Fred had been suffering from heart problems – he'd been to see me a few days ago. Sometimes the heart has just had enough.' He gave her a sympathetic look. 'I'll tell the paramedics that they can leave.'

'OK,' said Abbey. She watched the doctor as he walked out of the room. She and Ryan sat silently while the medical people talked to each other. Abbey was acutely aware that Fred was still in his office.

'Something should be done for him before his son gets here,' she said. 'He won't want to see him . . . Well, we should move him.'

'I'll speak to the doctor.'

Ryan got up and left Abbey sitting alone. She closed her eyes and pictured Fred as she'd last seen him alive. An old man, a touch infirm, but alert all the same. She couldn't help wondering if it was because of her that his heart had suddenly had enough. If the tension and excitement of looking for Ellen and then Abbey's own visit had been too much for him.

Her eyes were still closed when Ryan returned.

'The doctor and I moved him to a bedroom,' he said. 'You were right. I wouldn't have liked Donald to see him on the floor like that.'

'I should go,' Abbey said.

'They're going to have to meet you,' Ryan told her. 'You might as well stay.'

'But they'll be in shock!' cried Abbey. 'Meeting me will only make things worse.'

'You were there when he died.'

'It wasn't my fault!'

'They'll know that. The doctor knows. I told him all about you.'

'I guess he thinks it's not surprising that Mr Fitzpatrick had a heart attack.'

167

'I don't think it was because of you, Abbey.' Ryan's words were consoling. 'From what I gather, he'd had bypass surgery before. His time had come, that's all.'

Her mother had said that to her when her Gramma and Gramps had died. That their time had come. Of course, thought Abbey suddenly, they weren't her real grandparents. Fred Fitzpatrick was. And now he was gone too.

'You were great.' Ryan squeezed her arm. 'Calling the emergency services, doing CPR . . . So don't worry, everything will be fine. And you'll be grand,' he added.

You'll be grand. She smiled slightly at the expression, which sounded as though it had come from one of the old black-and-white movies about Ireland that her grandmother had occasionally watched. Where everyone said things like 'grand' and 'begorrah' and 'top of the morning'. Until now, she hadn't heard a real person use any of those phrases, but Abbey liked hearing 'grand' the way Ryan said it. With a totally different meaning to the way she'd use it. But she knew what he meant. That she'd be all right. It was just that 'grand' sounded a much, much better way to be.

Chapter 17

In her party-ready house, Zoey scrolled to the playlist of hits from the eighties that she'd made, and set her phone into the dock. (Not that she remembered any of the actual songs, but she thought it would be nice to have music from the decade she was born.) Donald would certainly remember them. In fact they'd pretty much be his era. She grinned as she thought of Donald moving and shaking to the sounds of George Michael in his Wham! years. Although she rather thought her husband had been a Madonna fan. She knew he had a greatest hits CD gathering dust somewhere. Despite having an early generation iPod, Donald preferred to listen to music on CDs. He thought they were more authentic than downloads, something that made her grin and call him 'old man' with amused affection.

She was moving a set of balloons from one side of the room to the other when she heard his key in the door. She felt a rush of love for him. It was good of him to come home early on the day of her party. No matter how irritating he could be sometimes about her ability to spend money on fun things, he always embraced whatever she'd organised.

'Oh my God.' He strode into the room and looked around.

'Like it?' she asked, linking her arm to his. 'It's going to be a brilliant evening.'

'No,' he said. 'I'm sorry, Zoey.'

'What?' She removed her arm and looked at him. 'What's the matter?'

When he told her about Fred, she immediately put her arms around him and held him tight.

'Oh Donald, how awful. Poor Fred. What happened?'

'I'm not sure,' said Donald. 'Alex didn't go into details, but Dr Casey is still at the house and he'll fill me in.'

'Why was Alex Shannon at Fred's?' Zoey raised her head from his shoulder.

'I don't know. I was a bit shocked. I didn't think to ask.'

'It seems odd,' said Zoey as she released her hold on him. 'That your dad would be visited by his solicitor at home.'

'It does, doesn't it?' Donald looked pensive. 'We'll know soon enough. You'd better get changed.'

'Why do I need to come?' Her voice was a squeak. 'I don't want to see Fred . . . dead.'

'Of course you're coming,' said Donald. 'We all have to be there. Gareth and Lisette are on their way already.'

'What about my party?' asked Zoey.

'Zoey! You can't possibly have a party. Not now.'

Zoey had known from the moment Donald had told her about Fred that she wouldn't be having a party. But she couldn't help feeling peeved that Fred had chosen today, of all days, to kick the bucket.

'I'm sorry, I know. What I meant was that I'll have to contact people to tell them it's off. It'd be better if I did it from here, wouldn't it?'

Donald considered for a moment, then shook his head.

'I need you with me,' he said. 'You can contact people from the car.'

Zoey knew that arguing with Donald was futile. Besides, he had a point. They couldn't let Gareth and Lisette be the ones to take over. Donald was the eldest, and as his wife she had a certain position in the family. He was right. The party wasn't as important as taking charge.

'No question.' She kissed him on the cheek. 'I'll find something more appropriate to wear and then we'll go.'

They arrived at exactly the same time as Gareth and Lisette, who'd had to arrange for a neighbour to look after Jerome and Fleur. The four of them embraced and then Donald opened the gate and they walked up the steps to the house.

Dr Casey was at the door to greet them, telling them that he was sorry for their loss but that for Fred it had been mercifully quick. He led them into the bedroom where he and Ryan had brought Fred. Lisette muffled a sob, while Zoey tried not to look at the immobile body of her late father-in-law. Then Lisette stepped forward and kissed him on the forehead, an act that was copied by both Donald and Gareth. Zoey hung back until the last minute before leaning towards Fred, allowing her lips to hover for a moment above his head without actually touching it.

They stood in silence, the two brothers either side of the bed and their wives at its foot. Zoey positioned herself behind her sister-in-law so that her view of Fred was partially blocked. She could feel her phone vibrating in the pocket of her jacket and she knew it was from responses to the message she'd sent out to everyone telling them about Fred's death. She'd seen a few of the replies before she and Donald had arrived at the house – one of the messages had been accompanied by a glum emoticon. It wasn't clear if the sender was sorry that Fred had died or because the party had been cancelled.

Oh well, she thought, he had to die sooner or later. At least he had the decency not to peg out at the party itself. That would've been spectacularly awful.

Lisette was thinking of the last time she'd seen Fred. It had been two days previously and the old man had been in great form, excited about something but not telling her what. She'd thought he looked younger and more animated than he'd appeared for ages.

171

'You'll see,' he'd told her. 'I'll surprise you yet.'

She'd said that she hoped it would be a happy surprise and he said that it was for him. Now she wondered what it might have been. And if it mattered any more.

'Did you call Suzanne?' she murmured. Both Donald and Gareth looked shocked at the sound of her words. Then they glanced at each other.

'I didn't,' said Gareth.

'Bugger,' said Donald. 'Neither did I.'

'One of you'd better,' said Zoey.

'Stay with him a little longer.' Donald moved away from the bedside. 'I'll phone her now.'

As he walked out of the room, Donald could feel himself growing into the role as head of the family already.

There was a hum of conversation coming from the kitchen. Dr Casey, he presumed, and maybe Alex. He needed to talk to them and find out exactly how his father had died. Zoey's question about the solicitor's presence in the house was bothering him. As far as he knew, Fred had always visited Alex in his offices. Why had he called him to the house this time? Because he was feeling suddenly unwell? Because he needed immediate legal advice?

Donald stood outside the bedroom, vacillating between phoning his sister and talking to the people who had been the last to see his father. What the hell, he thought. Another few minutes wouldn't matter to Suzanne. And if he talked to the doctor and solicitor now, he might have more information to give her.

He strode across the hallway and into the kitchen, stopping abruptly at the doorway.

Alex and Dr Casey were standing together, drinking coffee. And sitting at the table were two people Donald had never seen before in his life. A young couple, the man tall and slightly tanned, dressed in jeans and a sweatshirt, the woman pale and fair-haired, an anxious expression on her face. Donald stared at her. Because he recognised the blonde stranger, even though he'd never seen her before in his life.

Zoey had had enough of being at Fred's bedside. Standing guard over a corpse wasn't her idea of the way to spend her thirtieth birthday. She murmured to Lisette that she needed to use the bathroom, and then opened the door and went outside before her sister-in-law could do anything to stop her.

She heard Donald's raised voice straight away.

'Who the hell are you?' he was saying. 'What in God's name are you doing here?'

Zoey hurried into the kitchen and then stopped. She hadn't expected to see so many people there already. She recognised the doctor again, of course. And she supposed the silver-haired man in the sharp suit was the solicitor. But she'd no idea who the younger couple were. Neither, she gathered, had Donald, who was looking at them intently. At least, Zoey realised, he was looking at the girl intently. For a fleeting second Zoey wondered if she was Fred's bit on the side. It wouldn't have surprised her in the least if he'd had someone. She'd always considered him to be a desperate old lech, the way he ogled her! But this girl . . . Zoey looked at her again. She seemed vaguely familiar, even though she was sure she'd never seen her before.

'This isn't the ideal way for you to meet,' Alex was telling Donald. 'I know you must be very upset.'

'Of course I am!' cried Donald. 'My father has just died and there are people I don't know in his house and she . . .' He stared at Abbey. 'She's . . . she's . . .'

'Maybe we should all sit down,' suggested Dr Casey.

'I'm perfectly all right the way I am.' Donald crossed his arms over his chest.

'What's going on, Don?' asked Zoey. 'What's all the fuss?'

'These people,' said Donald. 'Why? And her – why her?'

'D'you know her?' asked Zoey.

'No.' Donald's eyes still hadn't left Abbey. 'No. I don't. But . . .'

'Do sit down,' said Alex. 'Then we can discuss this properly.'

'Discuss what?' Gareth, followed by Lisette, walked into the kitchen. After Zoey had left them alone with Fred, they'd decided that they would be better off joining her and Donald. Just in case, Lisette had said softly as she dabbed at her eyes with a tissue, there was anything they needed to know about.

And now Gareth was thinking that there definitely was. Because he too was looking at Abbey in utter astonishment. And thinking that, although this girl was blonde and his sister was dark, there was could be no denying that she was a younger version of Suzanne.

Chapter 18

'Who the hell are you and what are you doing here?' Donald found his voice first and directed his words at Abbey, who was looking from one brother to the other.

'That's what we need to discuss,' said Alex. 'It's a complicated situation.'

'My father is dead and there's a complicated situation?' Gareth was unable to take his eyes off Abbey.

'Yes,' said Alex. 'It's why I'm here.'

'What's complicated?' asked Zoey. 'What's the problem?'

'She is.' Lisette looked from Abbey to her sister-in-law. 'We don't know her. But I think we should.'

'Why?'

'Sit down,' said Alex again. 'Sit down and let me introduce you.'

The Fitzpatricks pulled out chairs and did as he asked. Then he spoke.

'Abbey Andersen, this is Donald, Gareth, Zoey and Lisette Fitzpatrick. Donald – this is Abbey, your father's granddaughter.'

There was a stunned silence around the table.

'I'm so very sorry about your dad,' said Abbey. 'I—'

'What d'you mean, Dad's granddaughter?' Donald stared at her.

'Yes,' said Abbey. 'And I'm sorry—'

'Where did you spring from?' asked Donald.

'I . . . I'm from San Francisco,' said Abbey. 'I didn't really know your dad, but I—'

'This is unbelievable.' Gareth interrupted her. 'Dad is dead and somehow you've appeared from San Fran-bloody-cisco? And who are you?' he demanded, turning to Ryan.

'Ryan Gilligan,' said Ryan. 'I'm a colleague of Alex. I was the one who found Abbey.'

'Found her?' said Donald. 'Who asked you to find her? Who said she needed to be found? Who says she's any relation to my father?'

He knew, even as he spoke, that those words were ridiculous. Because he knew that Gareth and Lisette had seen it too. In the shape of the girl's face and the sweep of her hair. She was a Fitzpatrick. She looked like his sister and his father. He and Donald had always been more like their mother. Everyone had said so. But Suzanne had been pure Fitzpatrick. And this girl was too.

'It's a long story,' said Alex. 'How much do you know about your father's early life?'

The Fitzpatricks looked at each other. Donald cleared his voice and spoke.

'Like everyone of his age, it was tough. He was brought up on a farm and worked there for a few years before he came to Dublin. He shared a run-down place off Blessington Street when he started off in a bakery. After that he was a driver in a butcher's and later a garage worker. He eventually set up his own business, married my mother, moved to East Wall. And the rest – well, he worked hard and loved his family. It wasn't a complex life.'

Gareth said nothing. It had been more complex than Donald had wanted it to be. He remembered the times when Ros had waited stoically for her husband to come home from his nights out. Her face had been set as she'd told them that men needed to let off steam a bit. As he grew older, Gareth had heard the occasional rumours. That Fred was a bit of a ladies' man. That he had a fancy woman on the other side of town. Gareth had tackled his father about it once and Fred had cackled with laughter.

'It would do you good to have a woman of your own,' he'd said. 'Make me proud of you as a son. But you're too involved in your so-called art for that sort of thing. You're an embarrassment, that's what you are.'

But I never embarrassed my wife by having affairs, Gareth had thought. And I'll never treat my own daughter with the disrespect you showed Suzanne.

'It's true that Mr Fitzpatrick worked hard like most of his generation.' Ryan was the one to speak. 'But in recent years he was concerned about his early life, while he was still living on the farm.'

'I don't even know where that farm was,' said Donald.

'Tipperary,' said Ryan. 'It wasn't a big place, and, as you rightly say, your father eventually left it to come to Dublin. But before he did, he had a relationship with a girl in the town.'

Abbey watched the faces of Fred's children as they listened to Ryan retelling the story of Fred and Dilly.

'Oh my God,' said Lisette when he'd finished. 'This is why he was so obsessed with the Magdalene laundries. This is why he was upset about what happened to the girls.'

'Yes,' said Ryan. 'And that's why he asked me to find his daughter.'

'But you're not his daughter,' said Donald to Abbey. 'Alex says you're his granddaughter.'

'Yes,' said Abbey. 'My mom . . . couldn't be here.'

'So when did you turn up?' demanded Donald. 'My father isn't even cold in his grave and somehow there's a long-lost grand-daughter in his kitchen?'

'Abbey arrived in Ireland yesterday. She met with Mr Fitzpatrick earlier today,' said Ryan. 'She was with him when he died.'

'What!' Donald stared at him. 'This woman – someone we didn't even know existed – was the last person to see my dad? How could that be? Who left them alone together?'

Abbey cleared her throat. She was dizzy with shock and with

exhaustion, but she knew that Fred's sons must be shocked too, and they deserved to know about their father's final moments.

'Mr Fitzpatrick wanted to meet me,' she said. 'When I arrived, we talked a little and he showed me around the house. Then he went to make some coffee. I sat outside and I think I was half asleep when I heard a crash. I went inside and found your dad.'

'Abbey began CPR immediately,' said Dr Casey. 'She was very capable.'

'Capable?' Donald exclaimed. 'Dad is dead!'

'Abbey continued with CPR until the paramedics arrived,' said Dr Casey. 'She did as much as she could.'

'Are you a nurse?' asked Donald.

'No,' said Abbey. 'But I knew what I was doing.'

'Because often unqualified people can make things worse.'

'Indeed,' said Lisette.

Abbey blinked a couple of times. Surely they weren't accusing her of killing the old man?

'Everyone is very tired,' said Dr Casey. 'And you've all had a shock. You must be distressed, too. Perhaps this conversation should wait.'

'We're all very upset,' agreed Lisette. 'Nobody was expecting Fred to . . . to pass away so suddenly. We need some time to grieve. And then we have arrangements to make for the funeral.'

'Of course you all want to be alone,' said Abbey. 'I didn't mean to intrude.'

Donald snorted.

'I'll bring you back to your hotel,' said Ryan. 'And when the rest of the family is ready to talk to you, we can meet up again.'

'That sounds like a good idea,' agreed Alex.

Abbey stood up and Ryan escorted her out of the house. Alex and Dr Casey followed them.

'That was difficult,' said Dr Casey.

'Unfortunate timing,' said Ryan.

'It's very upsetting for them,' Abbey said.

'For you too.' Ryan looked sympathetically at her.

'I hardly knew him,' Abbey said. 'He's their father.'

'It'll all get sorted,' Alex told her. 'I'll go back and talk to them. Arrange a proper meeting with you.'

'Should I . . . should I go to his funeral?' asked Abbey. 'I want to do the right thing, but I don't want to cause trouble.'

'I'll let you know what the arrangements are,' promised Alex. 'We'll sort everything out. Don't worry.'

But it was hard not to, Abbey thought, when you'd met and lost a grandfather in a single day. And when you were the one who hadn't been able to save him.

Back in the kitchen, the Fitzpatricks were sitting in stunned silence.

Not only were they struggling to come to terms with Fred's unexpected death, they were also dealing with their utter shock at Abbey Andersen's existence. But even as Fred's sons thought about Abbey's situation, they were both coming to the conclusion that she wasn't as much of a surprise as they'd initially believed. Donald had been aware of his father's affairs, but had always assumed that Fred's liaisons were trouble-free. As, indeed, they seemed to have been. Given that Fred had had an unwanted child before, Donald was certain that he'd have taken precautions that it wouldn't happen again. Gareth, meanwhile, was wondering about Fred's daughter, Abbey's mother. Why hadn't she travelled to Ireland to see her father herself? Why had she sent her daughter instead?

Lisette was wishing she'd quizzed Fred further about the Magdalene laundries. If she'd taken more interest that day, she might have found out about this unknown daughter and then it wouldn't have been landed on them in such a shocking way. She was very conscious that Fred had clearly been looking over his will then too. A niggling worry that he might have been considering altering it was taking root in her brain. But he wouldn't have done anything before meeting his daughter. And now, thankfully, it was too late. Lisette released a relieved, yet guarded, breath. She shouldn't be glad that her father-in-law had died, but she was certainly glad that he hadn't been able to mess things up.

Zoey wanted to go home. Nobody else seemed to be concerned about the fact that there was a dead body in the house. But she couldn't help thinking about Fred lying there in the bedroom and it was freaking her out.

When Dr Casey returned, he spoke to them for a couple of minutes about Fred's heart attack, assuring them that his death had been pretty much instantaneous and hadn't been because of any inadequacies on the part of the emergency services or, indeed, Abbey Andersen. He then talked about the funeral arrangements and Donald said that he'd organise things now. That he hadn't been able to think of it before, what with the shock of learning about the Andersen woman.

'And Suzanne?' asked Gareth, after the doctor had gone. 'You'll have to tell her about Abbey Andersen too.'

'Oh God, Suzanne. I forgot all about her,' said Donald.

'You mean you haven't told her about Dad yet?' Gareth sounded appalled.

'I was going to ring,' said Donald defensively. 'And then I heard them in the kitchen. It drove everything else out of my mind.'

'You'd better call her straight away,' said Lisette. She hesitated for a moment, then added, 'Didn't you think that Abbey looked very like her?'

'Not a bit,' lied Donald, and Gareth shot him a surprised look. 'I'll tell Suzanne about Dad, but I'm not going to go into the whole thing about this Andersen woman over the phone.'

'You have to tell her,' said Lisette. 'You can't have her arrive home and suddenly discover her.'

'We did.' Donald sounded truculent.

'But she doesn't have to,' his sister-in-law said.

'Lisette is right,' said Zoey. 'Tell her now, get it over and done with.'

'I can't do everything.' Donald was irritated. 'I have to look after the funeral arrangements first. Then Suzanne.'

'Suzanne first, then the arrangements,' said Lisette.

'She's waited this long. Another half-hour won't make any difference.' Donald got up from the table and went into the living room. He was the eldest. He was the one calling the shots. Lisette wasn't going to tell him what to do.

Suzanne was going through her folder on the Mirador Hotel when her phone rang. She saw Donald's caller ID and she nearly didn't bother answering because she was absorbed in what she was doing and the idea of talking to her brother for the first time in months wasn't very appealing. But the very fact that she hadn't spoken to him in so long was what made her decide to take the call. It must be important.

When he told her about their father, she couldn't speak. She'd always had a dream in which Fred would one day admit to her that she was the cleverest and most successful of all his children. In it he'd apologise for not having realised that before and admit that it was his fault she'd left home. And she'd forgive him and hug him and he'd be grateful for her understanding.

But now the old git had gone and she'd never have the chance to hear him say that she was the smart one and that he was sorry for doubting her. She wouldn't be able to invite him to the Mirador Hotel and see the expression on his face when she told him it was hers. He was the person who'd won, in the end. He'd left her with her feelings of bitterness and regret and with no way of getting rid of them. And he'd left her to face her two brothers on her own.

'Suzanne?'

Donald's words brought her back to the present.

'I'm sorry,' she said. 'I – I'm stunned. I thought that you'd ring one day and say he'd been taken ill and could I come home. I didn't expect this.'

'Yes, well, neither did we,' said Donald.

'What happened?'

Donald gave a brief summary of Fred's heart attack, sticking only to the medical details and saying that Alex had been the one to let the family know.

'I suppose it was a good thing Alex was with him when it happened,' said Suzanne.

He couldn't not tell her. She'd be spitting mad if she came home and didn't know.

'Alex arrived later,' he said. 'The person who was with Dad when it happened was a girl called Abbey Andersen.'

As Donald told her about their meeting with Abbey, Suzanne found herself speechless again. She too had known about Fred's affairs, and the idea that he'd fathered another child wasn't entirely surprising – more surprising, maybe, was that nobody had appeared before now – but the story of the young girl dying in the convent was deeply upsetting.

'So where is she now?' asked Suzanne. 'Our . . . our half-sister?'

'She's not our half-sister!' Donald's tone was explosive. 'She's nothing to do with us. She was adopted and brought to the States and she's nobody we know.'

'First of all, she *is* our half-sister,' Suzanne said. 'And the fact that her own daughter has turned up means she is something to do with us.'

'I don't want to have anything to do with her,' said Donald. 'She's nothing to this family. Nothing.'

'Dad obviously thought differently.'

'He was an old fool.'

'No argument from me there,' said Suzanne. 'But we have to talk to Abbey. Find out about her and her mother. See what Dad already told them.'

'After the funeral,' said Donald. 'We can talk then.'

'All right,' Suzanne said. 'I'll try to book the morning flight.'

'Let me know.'

'I will,' she said.

After she ended the call with her brother, she opened her laptop and searched for flights home. She scrolled through the options, wondering how many people came home for a funeral and then had to face people they'd rather not bother having to talk to at all. And how many others felt cheated when someone died before they had the chance to say the things they'd always meant to say.

Chapter 19

'How are you feeling?' asked Ryan as he and Abbey, having finally left Furze Hill, walked into the reception area of the Harbour Hotel.

'It's been a hell of a day,' Abbey replied. 'I feel like I'm going to collapse, but I don't know if that's because I'm jet-lagged or because of everything else.'

'I'm surprised you haven't collapsed already,' said Ryan. 'You had to deal with a lot of stuff.'

'And there'll be a lot more when I meet the Fitzpatricks again,' she said. 'They're not happy about me and I don't blame them.'

'Well obviously today's weren't the ideal circumstances for them to find out about you, but they'll come round,' said Ryan.

'I admire your optimism.' Abbey said. 'But I'm not expecting a warm welcome when we meet again.'

'These things take time,' Ryan told her. 'Have you eaten anything since this morning? Would you like something now?'

'I think I'll have some coffee in my room,' she said. 'Thank you so much for everything. You must be shattered too – I woke you up this afternoon, didn't I?'

'All part of the job.' He smiled. 'If there's anything else you need, let me know, OK?'

'OK.'

He gave her a brief hug and she went up the stairs to her room. Despite not having eaten, she wasn't very hungry and she was perfectly happy to make herself some coffee and eat the small pre-packed slice of fruit cake that she'd seen on the tray earlier.

After she'd kicked off her shoes and poured herself the coffee, she picked up her phone and called Pete.

'Well whaddya know!' Pete was gobsmacked when she related everything. 'So what happens now?'

She explained that there would be a further meeting with the Fitzpatrick family, depending on how the schedule for Fred's funeral turned out.

'You need representation when you meet them,' said Pete. 'They can't imply that your actions hastened the old man's death. I can come over, honey. Stall them till I get there.'

'It's OK, Pete,' she said. 'The doctor certified the cause of death as a heart attack. He said there was nothing more I could have done. So did the paramedics. There's no problem.'

'People can say and do stupid things,' said Pete. 'My job is to stop that. Or to make sure that if they do cross a line, they pay the penalty.'

'I'm sure everything will be all right,' she said. 'If there's a problem, I'll let you know. In the meantime, though, the Irish lawyers are taking good care of me.'

'That Ryan Gilligan guy seemed to have his head screwed on the right way,' conceded Pete. 'But he was working for Mr Fitzpatrick, not you. So don't let him push you around either.'

'He didn't push me around,' said Abbey. 'He was nice.'

'Yeah, well, don't let his niceness fool you,' warned Pete.

'Pete, Pete, I've got to trust someone!' cried Abbey. 'And the doctor and the lawyers have been on my side. Not that there should be sides. The family was upset, is all. I understand that. I'd be upset too.'

'You were a hero,' said Pete. 'You tried to save him and you called for help and they should've been thanking you.'

'Maybe they will when we meet again,' said Abbey. 'They had too much to process this time.'

'Given that they freaked out when they met you, do I gather that you haven't had time to talk to them about your mom?' Pete asked the question warily.

'No,' said Abbey.

'That might be another shock,' he observed. 'You sure you don't want me over? Because it's no trouble.'

'Moral support would be nice,' Abbey admitted. 'But I think it would worry them even more if you turned up all sharp suits and lawyerly on my behalf.'

'Maybe,' conceded Pete.

'I'll talk to them,' Abbey said. 'Tell them everything. What difference does it make anyway? I doubt very much that after that conversation I'll be hearing from any of them ever again.'

'Which in some ways would be a pity,' said Pete. 'They're your family, after all.'

'No,' said Abbey. 'You and Claudia are. Even if I'm a bit of a cuckoo in the nest.'

'You're a very welcome part of our family and you know it,' said Pete. 'If you think you can manage without me, that's fine. But any sign of trouble, you call. No matter what time it is.'

'You're my Alcatraz,' said Abbey. 'My rock.'

And he was, she thought, as she ended the call. Always there for her. Even though he didn't need to be.

Suzanne Fitzpatrick arrived in Dublin at midday the following day. Although Gareth and Lisette had asked her to stay with them, she'd elected to book in to the Harbour Hotel instead. Gareth might be her brother, but she hadn't seen him in years and she didn't want to stay in his home.

Abbey, who'd slept late and had decided to go for a long walk to clear her head, noticed the tall, slim woman checking in as she herself crossed the reception area. A vague sense of recognition nagged at her mind, but as she'd only glanced in Suzanne's direction it didn't really take hold, and she walked out of the hotel without a further thought. Suzanne didn't see Abbey at all; she was too busy filling in the registration card and thinking that the Harbour Hotel wasn't a million miles away from what she wanted the Mirador to be. Chic and exclusive, but friendly.

Like Abbey, Suzanne told the receptionist that she was perfectly able to carry her own bag to her room. She took the lift rather than the stairs to the top floor, thinking that the art deco one in the Mirador was a million times nicer. The style of the reception area would be dictated by that lift, she thought, as she reached her room and opened it with the card key. It would be the Mirador's signature feature. Always provided that she somehow managed to raise the money she needed.

She walked into the room and put her bag on the bed, still thinking about the Mirador. Having got over the shock of her father's sudden death, she couldn't help feeling frustrated at being in Ireland when she needed to be in Spain, raising finance. Typical of Fred that even in death he interfered with her plans. She felt a surge of guilt at the thought, but she couldn't help herself. Just because the old man was dead didn't mean he hadn't caused anything but trouble for her when he'd been alive. And what additional trouble had he intended to cause, she wondered, by asking this hitherto unknown granddaughter to meet him?

She exhaled slowly. Donald had been overwrought when he'd called the previous night, but she knew that he was both upset and angry about the discovery of another Fitzpatrick. Although she was an Andersen, Suzanne remembered. And what about the mother? Her father's first child. Well, the first they knew of. God knows what other surprises Fred might have had up his sleeve.

She unpacked her things from her cabin bag and freshened up before ringing Gareth.

'Come to the house when you're ready,' he said. 'We're having the removal to the church this evening; the funeral will go ahead tomorrow.'

Suzanne thought about having something to eat at the hotel

before going to her brother's, but she knew that was only to put off the inevitable, so she changed from the jeans and T-shirt she'd travelled in into a navy dress which would be suitable for wearing in the church later. Then she slipped into a pair of mid-height shoes and left the hotel.

Gareth and Lisette's house was only a twenty-minute walk. Suzanne had never been in it before and was impressed by its location. Not bad, she thought, for a couple of teachers. Of course they'd got into property a number of years back, hadn't they? She vaguely remembered her father cackling about it one Christmas when she'd made her obligatory phone call home. 'Think they're property modules,' he'd said, and she'd corrected him, telling him he surely meant 'moguls', and he'd retorted that whatever his second son and his wife were, moguls certainly didn't describe them. He'd never given Gareth much support, Suzanne thought. He'd fought with her and wanted to mould her into a certain type of person, but he'd simply dismissed her older brother, scornful of his more sensitive nature. Donald was the favourite, she reckoned. But even Donald had never been good enough for him.

She rang the bell and the double gates swung open. Gareth was standing on the front step, shielding his eyes from the glare of the sun. (Suzanne had been surprised by its warmth when she'd walked out of the terminal building in Dublin and had immediately taken off the heavy jacket she'd dug out of the back of her wardrobe specifically for the Irish weather.)

'Hi,' he said as she walked up the path. 'Welcome home.' He gave her a perfunctory hug.

'Thanks. Although obviously the circumstances . . .'

'Yes, well, we all knew it would happen sooner or later. But it's been a shock all the same.'

Suzanne followed her brother into the house, and along the hallway to the large kitchen at the back.

'Suzanne, *chérie*, it's nice to see you again? Did you have a good flight?' Lisette got up from the table where she'd been sitting with the children.

'There was a time when it was worth asking that question,' said Suzanne. 'But these days there's no such thing as a good flight. All you can hope for is that it won't be too awful. And it wasn't.'

'True,' agreed Lisette. 'Jerome, Fleur, say hello to your Tante Suzanne.'

'Hello, Tante Suzanne.' Fleur briefly looked up from her colouring book while Jerome, engrossed in his iPad, muttered a greeting.

'I'm sorry,' said Lisette. 'I am trying to teach them manners but I think I'm failing.'

'They're fine,' said Suzanne.

'Would you like coffee?' asked Lisette.

'That'd be great.'

Lisette got up and poured hot water into a cafetière, releasing an aromatic hit of ground beans.

'So – all the drama,' said Suzanne as her sister-in-law poured the coffee. 'The way Donald talked last night, I thought he was convinced that this American girl had a part in Dad's heart attack.'

'Was Gran'père killed?' Jerome looked up from the iPad, his eyes wide. 'That would be so cool.'

'Of course he wasn't,' said Lisette. 'I told you, he hadn't been well.'

'He died because he was ancient,' said Fleur. 'I heard you say it to Papa. You said, "It's time that ancient old man did us all a favour and died."'

'Fleur!' Lisette's face flamed red. 'You shouldn't have been listening to our conversation. Anyway, I'm sure you didn't hear me properly.'

'I did.' Fleur put her crayon on the table. 'And I heard you say that you thought a man with a dicky ticker shouldn't be so healthy.'

'What I meant . . .' Lisette's voice was filled with forced patience, 'was that your *gran'père* was a very active man for his age.'

'A cranky man, you usually say,' remarked Jerome.

Suzanne tried to keep a straight face. She understood perfectly the conversations her brother and Lisette might have had with each other, but it was amusing to hear it rehashed by their children.

'Why are you both inside anyway?' demanded their father. 'It's too nice to be indoors.'

'Maman said we should stay in and say hello to Tante Suzanne.'

'Well, you've said hello,' said Gareth. 'Now go outside and play.'

He watched as the two of them scrambled down from the table and went into the garden.

'Why did we keep them off school today?' he asked Lisette.

'Out of respect for your father. And because it would have been awkward to pick them up from school and then go to the removal,' she said.

'Less awkward than having them spout nonsense in front of our guest.'

'Your sister,' Suzanne reminded him. 'Not just a guest.'

'Sorry,' said Gareth.

'So tell me about this woman,' said Suzanne. 'This long-lost relative who conveniently happened to show up as Dad dropped dead.'

'I'm glad you think that's suspicious,' said Gareth, who filled her in with more detail than Donald had on the previous day's events.

'So why didn't the mother come too?' asked Suzanne.

Gareth shrugged. 'I've no idea. We only barely got to talk to her and the next thing that sidekick of Alex's ushered her out of the house. I don't like it, though.'

'Why?'

'There's something not right about it all,' said Gareth. 'Why now? And, like you said, where's the mother? What do they want? What did Dad want with them?'

190

'He was very upset about the Magdalene laundries,' said Lisette. 'I suppose he wanted to find out that they were OK.'

'A bit strange,' remarked Suzanne, 'given that he never gave a toss about whether the rest of us were OK or not.'

Gareth shot her an understanding look.

'Maybe he'd mellowed in his old age,' said Lisette.

Gareth grunted. 'As if.'

'So we're meeting her after the funeral,' said Suzanne. 'That makes today a right barrel of laughs, doesn't it?'

Gareth said nothing. Lisette got up from the table and fetched some biscuits. Suzanne sipped her coffee.

Home, sweet home, she thought.

It was nine o'clock by the time Suzanne arrived back at the hotel. The removal service, where Fred's coffin had been taken to the church in readiness for the funeral the following day, had been lengthy, with a steady stream of friends turning up to console the Fitzpatricks on the death of their father. People she hadn't seen for years had queued to shake her hand and murmur words of sympathy, but the truth was that she'd felt a fraud for thanking them. And she'd felt a fraud too for the sudden feeling of loss that had engulfed her after they'd left the church. It was ridiculous to feel anything, she thought, for a man who'd been nothing but a thorn in her side and who'd carried the secret of his . . . well, she supposed love child would be the term that was used now . . . anyway, the man who'd kept his other child a secret from them all.

Don and Gareth were still furious about it, although Suzanne got the impression that they were more angry about him having invited the American granddaughter to see him than the fact that she existed in the first place. Lisette had been notably quiet, but Zoey had remarked that these things happened and they should all get over it because wasn't the girl going to go back to the States immediately the funeral was over? So what was the point in stressing about it all? Forget it, was Zoey's mantra. Forget it, forget her.

Suzanne was quite impressed by the attitude of Donald's second wife. It was perfectly clear to her that Zoey had married Donald for position and security – a kind of Jane Austen combination that shouldn't have been relevant in the modern world but obviously still was. Whatever her reasons, though, Suzanne thought that Zoey was good for her brother. There was no doubt that she looked sensational, and she managed him well too, saying the right thing at the right time and deferring to him when it seemed important to him.

But then, Suzanne mused as she accepted yet more condolences from someone she didn't even know, Zoey had her eye on another prize. She knew this because she'd heard her sister-in-law murmuring to her husband about Fred's will and the fact that Alex was going to talk about it after the funeral, which was all very Agatha Christie-ish, and did Donald think there was the slightest possibility that Fred's exit had been hastened in some way by seeing Abbey Andersen? Had he been so shocked by her appearance that he'd just keeled over? Suzanne had eavesdropped shamelessly as her brother reminded his wife that there was no evidence of that and that Dr Casey had said that Abbey had done a good job on the CPR, but Zoey had sniffed and muttered that old men were total fools and it was easy to give them a heart attack. At which Suzanne herself had had to turn away because she'd wondered if Zoey was talking about Donald himself.

Anyway, they'd gone back to Gareth and Lisette's after the removal. There'd been an awkward moment when Deirdre, Donald's ex-wife, had asked if she was invited and then said that she didn't want to go anyway, before flouncing off with her two daughters in tow, leaving the rest of the family to continue thrashing out the whole situation about the American girl. But Suzanne had no interest in going over and over things with them. So she'd told them that she was very tired and wanted to go back to the hotel, and even though Gareth had offered to drive her, she'd said that she was perfectly happy walking.

She was deep in thought as she strode across the reception area to the lift. As she waited for it to descend, she glanced towards the bar. It had been a long day and the idea of a drink was suddenly appealing. She left the reception area and walked up to the bar counter instead, where she ordered a Jameson and ice.

She took the glass and looked for somewhere comfortable to sit. Somewhere she wouldn't be disturbed. And then she saw the woman sitting at the table near the window. She was wearing jeans and a light knitted top. Her blond hair was carelessly scrunched around her face and one leg was crossed lazily over the other. She had a glass of rosé in front of her and was engrossed in a red-covered Kindle.

Oh my God, thought Suzanne. That's her. It has to be. I recognise the way she's sitting. I recognise her. She's Dad. She's me. She's the American.

She hesitated for a moment, and then crossed the room.

'Excuse me,' she said. 'I think I know you.'

Abbey Andersen looked up from the book she'd downloaded that day. And her eyes widened in shock.

'I see you know me too,' said Suzanne.

'You're Mr Fitzpatrick's daughter, aren't you?'

Suzanne nodded. 'Suzanne.'

'You remind me of my mother,' said Abbey. 'Although you're a lot younger,' she added hastily. 'More my age, I guess.'

Suzanne smiled slightly. 'I suppose I'm your aunt. I should be older and wiser than you.'

'Half-aunt,' said Abbey. 'Though that sounds kind of weird.'

'The whole situation is weird. Mind if I sit down?'

'Of course not.' Abbey was pleased to have the chance to talk to one of her newly discovered relatives in a less emotionally charged atmosphere than before.

'It was a shock, finding out about you,' said Suzanne.

'For me too,' Abbey told her.

'And your mum?'

'She's been out of touch,' said Abbey. 'She doesn't know about any of this yet.'

Suzanne looked startled.

'I'll tell her soon,' Abbey said.

'How will she react, d'you think?'

'As shocked as the rest of us,' said Abbey. 'But she's good with stuff, my mom.'

'As you are, it seems,' said Suzanne. 'I believe you tried to resuscitate Dad.'

'And failed.'

'At least you tried.'

Abbey said nothing. She still felt raw about the whole thing, but it was a welcome change for someone to appreciate the effort she'd made.

'Did you like him?' asked Suzanne.

'I didn't have the chance to get to know him,' Abbey replied. 'We only spoke for a few minutes. Walked around the garden. But he was nice to me.'

'Dad. Nice. That's a first.'

'Oh?'

'He was never nice to me,' Suzanne said. 'Ugh. This is why I hate the whole thing around death and funerals. The past gets dredged up and you rediscover old hurts you thought you'd plastered over.'

'What hurts do you have?' asked Abbey.

Suzanne shrugged. 'They're in the past. They should stay there.'

If only the past could stay in the past, thought Abbey. But it had a nasty habit of coming back to haunt you.

'So tell me a little about yourself,' said Suzanne. 'What d'you do?'

Abbey told her about her nail art and Suzanne involuntarily checked her own nails, which were square and buffed. Then

Abbey took out her phone and opened the Mariposa website. She scrolled to the pictures of her work and Suzanne gave a low whistle of appreciation.

'Gosh, that's good,' she said. 'So vibrant and electric. And, well, artistic.'

Abbey grinned. 'I studied art before I got into this,' she said. 'I still like painting but I get a great buzz out of nails.'

Suzanne continued to look at the pictures. The Mirador Hotel didn't have a spa or a beauty salon and there wasn't a lot of room for anything too grand, but the idea of offering nail treatments to guests was a good one. Women liked to look good on holiday, and blinging nails was a great way of jazzing up your appearance, especially if you were make-up-free around the pool. Perhaps if she managed to buy the hotel, she could get some advice from Abbey on the treatments a manicurist could offer. Though she was getting ahead of herself, wasn't she? She still hadn't managed to put together enough of a consortium to make an offer on it.

Abbey, realising that Suzanne had lapsed into a daydream, and supposing that she was thinking about her father, sat in silence. It was a few minutes later before Suzanne, whose mind had wandered off into worries about the finance, blinked a couple of times and apologised for her lack of attention.

'I've had a long day,' she added. 'And it'll be equally long tomorrow. I should go to bed.' She drained her glass and stood up. 'It was nice meeting you.'

'You too,' said Abbey.

'Are you coming to the funeral tomorrow?'

'Yes.' Abbey looked at her anxiously. 'That's OK, isn't it? It won't upset you?'

'Not in the slightest,' said Suzanne. 'As for the rest of them – I'm sure they'll have got over the shock. Actually, it's good of you to come.'

'I'm glad you think so.'

'Family situations are never easy. Believe me.' Suzanne's tone was heartfelt. 'Anyway, we'll all be on our best behaviour, I'm sure. So don't worry. You'll be grand.'

I'll be grand, thought Abbey, as she watched Suzanne walk out of the bar. Ryan says so. Suzanne says so. I hope they're right.

PART 5

THE WILL

Chapter 20

The day of Fred's funeral was the hottest of the year so far. Temperatures were in the high twenties and the sun shone from a perfect blue sky. Clara, the receptionist at the Harbour Hotel, told Abbey that there hadn't been a month like it since she could remember. Clara had been amazingly kind when she'd learned about Mr Fitzpatrick's death and had been as helpful and supportive to Abbey as she could possibly be. She was the one who'd given advice about going into Dublin so that she could buy something suitable to wear, because Abbey felt her own clothes were far too casual for a funeral.

After her conversation with Suzanne, she felt a bit more relaxed about her decision to attend the service. Ryan Gilligan had already told her that good turnouts were mandatory at Irish funerals, and it was a question of the more the merrier. Abbey still wasn't entirely sure this applied in her case, and she planned to hang back and not get in the family's way at all.

However, Ryan had called her before breakfast to say that they were now prepared to meet with her after the funeral and find out more about her and her mother. Abbey wasn't entirely sure what she'd say to them. She'd only come to Ireland so that Fred could be reassured that Ellen forgave him for abandoning her as a baby. She hadn't intended to have any contact with his family at all. Left to herself, she'd have been quite happy to return home straight away. But she knew the Fitzpatricks had questions and she hoped that she'd be able to put their minds at rest, whatever those questions might be.

The phone in her room shrilled and Clara told her that Ryan Gilligan had arrived to collect her. She picked up her bag and went downstairs. It was the first time she'd seen Ryan in a shirt and tie and she was struck by how formal and how much less approachable he appeared. Then he smiled at her.

'Great day for a funeral,' he said as he led her outside. 'I'm sure Fred would've liked it.'

'You think?' She got into the passenger seat.

'Definitely,' said Ryan. 'I bet he was an outdoors man.'

'I don't know what sort of man he was,' said Abbey. 'Which, despite everything, makes me feel a little uncomfortable about showing up today.'

'You're doing the right thing,' said Ryan. 'And the family will be grateful for your support.'

Abbey glanced at him. There had been a hesitation in his voice. A sudden lack of conviction. Which made her wonder if he knew something about them that she didn't.

Although Abbey had been brought up as a Catholic, she hadn't spent much time inside churches. The last time she'd set foot inside one had been for the wedding of one of her clients in the red-brick St Patrick's Church on Mission Street. It had been a joyous day, photos had been taken in the Yerba Buena Gardens afterwards, and Abbey had felt connected to everyone around her thanks to the warmth of the ceremony.

Her most recent experiences of funerals had been those of her grandparents, but that had been ten years earlier and at a Boston crematorium. This was different. The pews nearest the altar were already occupied by Fred's family, while other friends were scattered throughout the rest of the church. Organ music, vaguely recognisable, was being played softly in the background. Abbey shivered, even though the building was warm inside.

She chose an empty pew halfway up the aisle and sat down. She had a spray of flowers for Fred's coffin but she wasn't sure if she should place it there yet or not. It seemed that many people had left their tributes at the service the night before.

'I'll put them up for you,' said Ryan softly. She handed the spray to him. He walked up the aisle with it and left it near the altar. Abbey was grateful to him for being with her and for supporting her. It was, she thought, beyond the call of duty for a legal firm to take such care of someone who wasn't even a client. But perhaps Fred had been a good one. Perhaps Ryan was still being paid by him.

There was a rustle at the side of the altar as the priest walked out, the organ music grew louder and the funeral Mass started. Abbey allowed her thoughts to drift as the priest spoke. She knew the words even though she seldom used them. She wondered if they were a comfort to the Fitzpatricks. She hoped they were.

When the priest talked about Fred, he described him as a much-loved member of the community and a man of strong faith. He added that he was sure that Fred and his beloved Ros were now happy together for all eternity.

Abbey couldn't help wondering how things worked out in the afterlife in circumstances such as Fred's. When there were other women involved. What kind of welcome would be waiting for him? Had Ros and Dilly met? Had they spoken about him? How did they feel about him, always providing you felt anything at all after you died? She would've liked the answers to those questions, but they weren't the ones the priest was addressing.

Nor did he say anything about Fred having had another daughter. Of the fact that latterly he'd been consumed by guilt about what had happened to her. Or that he'd eventually found a grand-daughter he hadn't known about. Those topics were clearly ones for another day. Or, thought Abbey as she glanced at her watch, ones for a few hours' time.

Suzanne listened to the priest's words and bit her lip. Not because they made her sad but because she had to restrain herself from jumping up and shouting that it was all a lie and that her father hadn't given a shit about anyone other than himself. And in making contact with Abbey Andersen, nice and all though she appeared to be, he still wasn't thinking about anyone other than himself, because he clearly hadn't cared about the impact knowing about her would have on the family. But what was the point in creating a scene? she asked herself. There was nothing to be gained by saying that he'd made her life and her mother's life a misery with his attitude and his philandering and that it was fortunate there wasn't a whole pew full of his extramarital offspring instead of a lone girl.

Put it out of your head, she told herself. It'll all be over soon and you can forget about Dad and forget about Don and Gar too. You'll soon be back in Girona getting to grips with business which is far more important.

That morning, while she was getting dressed, she'd received a phone call from Petra saying that she was working on another potential investor and that she was keeping her fingers crossed. Unfortunately, though, Beatriz was getting twitchy about the enterprise as she'd been approached by someone else looking for money. Swings and roundabouts, said Petra. If we can land one more member for our consortium, we'll get the deal done. The call had frustrated Suzanne. Why was money always such a damn problem? Why did it always get in the way?

She glanced at her father's coffin and tried not to think that he might have left her something. He'd been so hard on her before, so unwilling to understand her or to listen to her, that she could think of no reason why he might have changed now. But she was the successful one, wasn't she? She mightn't have had the chance to prove it to him, but she was. She deserved some damn recognition from him. It didn't matter that he was dead.

Donald was thinking about his speech after the funeral Mass. As the eldest son, it was his task to say a few words about his father, to bring him to life (at least metaphorically) for the people who'd come to say goodbye to him. Donald was quite good at this sort of thing – being able to talk about every conceivable topic was an important part of being a sales director – but it was hard to know what to say about Fred. He'd been a tough father and an even tougher boss. He'd been cantankerous and difficult. He had a daughter that nobody knew about. Donald wasn't planning on mentioning her. There was no need to pick at wounds, new or old. He'd stick to the positives and recall how Fred had worked hard at building the company from humble beginnings to the success it had become. A success which meant that he had died in his beautiful home on the hill instead of the two-up, two-down terraced house he'd started his married life from.

Zoey slipped her hand into her husband's. She was thinking of Fred's house too and planning what she would do to it if Fred had left it to her and Donald as he should have done. She remembered telling Fred how much she liked it, and, one day, him asking her if it was the sort of place she'd like to live, at which she'd nodded eagerly and said that it was perfect. She didn't say that on moving in she'd immediately hire decorators because it needed a lot of upgrading to turn it into anywhere she'd actually live. It was a trophy home in a trophy location and that was what mattered. It would be great to invite her friends there and show off the magnificent views. They'd envy her more than ever then. And she deserved to be envied. She really did.

Gareth knew that Donald and Zoey had designs on the house. His brother had said as much a short time ago when they'd met for a drink. It had been after Fred had hurt his wrist and Donald had rung Gareth to discuss their father's long-term care. Gareth had been quite insulted by the call, because, as he'd told Donald, Lisette spent a lot of time looking out for Fred. She did his shopping every week, he'd said. Called in to see him every Saturday.

Which wasn't always convenient, but she did it anyway. And she'd continue to do it. Donald had been taken aback at that, Gareth knew. Donald and Zoey dropped in to Furze Hill from time to time, but not regular as clockwork like Lisette.

Gareth had seen the flicker in Donald's eyes when he realised that Gareth had a greater toehold in Furze Hill than him. Nevertheless, he'd made his comments about being the eldest and Fred's business partner (a low blow that) and had said that their father had talked about a family member taking the house over after his death. Gareth had said that Lisette loved Furze Hill, a comment that he knew had startled his brother. Seeing the look on Donald's face had given Gareth great satisfaction. Sometimes, he thought, Donald could be too damn cocky for his own good. But maybe he had a reason to be. Maybe he knew things that nobody else did.

Lisette had a headache. It had been with her ever since the news of Fred's death, and nothing seemed to shift it. The previous evening Suzanne had seen her reaching for the Panadol and had offered her some tablets from her own bag. Like horse tablets, Suzanne had said, and with a dosage to match. Got rid of the worst of everything. But Lisette didn't like taking tablets at all; she'd only started swallowing Panadol out of desperation. She'd tried meditating later on, in the bedroom, but of course that had been useless because the only meditation she'd done had been on Fred's will. She wished she'd looked at the copy she'd seen peeking out from under the papers that day. Maybe he'd even wanted her to look. Maybe it would have been worth a row with him.

She rubbed the back of her neck.

Or maybe not.

Because her grandparents had been cremated, Abbey had never been to a burial before. She followed the crowd of people as they gathered around the open grave. She heard one of the mourners comment that Fred was joining Ros at last, and she supposed that the Fitzpatricks had some kind of family plot. Which was a bit spooky, she thought, if practical.

In fact the whole thing was vaguely spooky from Abbey's perspective. There was a finality about putting a coffin in the ground that passed you by at a cremation. It was more primeval, somehow. The heat of the sun was scorching the backs of her bare legs and she moved a little so that she was in the shadow of another mourner. Ryan glanced enquiringly at her but she mouthed back that everything was fine, even though the heat was making her feel slightly dizzy.

The words of the priest were being carried away on the warm breeze, so it was difficult to hear the latest set of prayers. A man and a woman, like her at the edges of the crowd, were holding a whispered conversation about whether it would be OK to slip away immediately afterwards or if they needed to go to the nearby hotel where the family had organised refreshments for the mourners. Abbey wished she could slip away too. But the plan, according to Ryan, was that she'd accompany him back to the hotel, and then afterwards the family would get together and talk with her.

The day after tomorrow, she thought. All this will be over and then I'll be back home. And my worries will be my own again. Worries like sorting out my finances and finding a place to live. The previous night, after she'd gone to her room, she'd googled apartments in San Francisco and had despaired of finding anything suitable. Nearly everything seemed to be out of her reach, but she hadn't been able to keep her attention on her search anyway. Looking for an apartment had seemed like part of another life.

She realised that the priest had finished speaking and that the crowd around the grave was beginning to disperse. Ryan took her by the arm.

'It's only a few minutes to the hotel from here,' he said.

'Is it formal?' she asked.

'Huh?'

'The refreshments. Do they make speeches, that sort of thing?'

'No, no, nothing like that,' Ryan told her. 'It's just a way of people being able to say a few words to the family in more relaxed surroundings. They have some food, something to drink . . .'

'Like a wake?'

'Well, no. The body's usually there for a wake,' Ryan explained. 'This is very relaxed, I promise you.'

'That suits me. All I want is for the family to know that I'm sorry about Fred and that it was good meeting them.'

'Sounds perfect,' said Ryan. 'Ah, Alex, there you are.'

His colleague from the law firm had come over to them.

'What a day,' said Alex as he ran a finger around the inside of his collar. 'You'd swear it was high summer.'

'A cracker, isn't it?' agreed Ryan. 'You feel like you should be going to the beach rather than a cemetery.'

'You're coming back to the hotel?' There was a question in Alex's tone and yet Abbey could also hear that it was a command.

'Of course,' said Ryan.

'Good,' said Alex.

Abbey looked from one to the other. There was something going on here, she thought, although she had no idea what it was.

'Are you?' she asked.

'What?' Alex turned to her.

'Coming back to the hotel?'

'Yes,' said Alex. 'Fred was a friend as well as a client. He used our firm from the start. Worked with my father before me.'

'Did you like him?'

'He could be difficult,' conceded Alex. 'But I got on well with him.'

They walked along the gravelled pathway towards the car park. Alex's Lexus was at the opposite end to Ryan's Golf.

'I'll see you there,' said Alex, and walked away from them.

The sun had been shining directly into the car, and Abbey gasped as a blast of warm air hit her when she opened the door.

'I should've bought a convertible,' said Ryan.

'I like convertibles,' said Abbey.

'D'you have one?'

She shook her head. 'Are you crazy? I can't afford a car. Jeez, right now I can hardly afford an apartment! Although when me and my mom were in Latin America, we drove everywhere in . . .'

'Convertibles?' He sounded surprised.

'No.' She laughed. 'Open-topped jeeps.'

Ryan laughed too. Then he put the car in gear and joined the queue to leave the car park.

Chapter 21

Suzanne recognised many of the people who came to the hotel after the funeral, among them Mrs Farrell, who'd lived across the road from the Fitzpatricks in East Wall, along with her daughter Adrienne. Mrs Farrell looked exactly the same as she always had – squeezed into a suit that was at least one size too small for her and cheerfully allowing her white blouse to strain across her size-able chest. Suzanne had always envied Adrienne her easy-going parents; she'd been one of the clique of cool girls who wore short skirts and copious amounts of make-up and had a different boyfriend for every day of the week. Though she wondered whether she should envy her now. Adrienne, while still trowelling on the make-up, wore a permanently dissatisfied expression and looked older than her thirty-nine years. Would that have been me if I'd stayed? wondered Suzanne. Did Dad actually do me a favour by making me leave? The thought shocked her.

Adrienne Farrell was looking in her direction and Suzanne, not feeling able to talk to her even though she knew that the aftermath of a funeral was exactly the place for meeting up with old acquaint-ances, turned to the long trestle table from where a waiter was dispensing tea and coffee. She asked for a black coffee and then moved to a corner of the room where she could observe other people without being seen herself.

She watched Lisette walking around the room shaking hands with people as though she was the hostess for the day – which,

Suzanne supposed, she might well be. She was the senior Mrs Fitzpatrick these days after all, wasn't she? Not that Deirdre would feel too happy about that. Suzanne had already seen her ex-sister-in-law shoot a few daggered looks in Lisette's direction. As well as in the direction of the woman who'd usurped her, the beautiful Zoey. Seeing Deirdre prowl around the room, Suzanne felt a bit sorry for her. It was as though she hadn't been able to let go, hadn't been able to leave the Fitzpatricks behind.

Am I the only person in the world to happily extricate themselves from a marriage? she wondered. The only one who sailed through a divorce without acrimony? She hadn't heard from any of her ex-husband's family since her split from Calvin. They'd never been very close, of course. But the Fitzpatricks weren't all that close either. Maybe it was different in Ireland, though. Maybe in a country with fewer than five million people, it wasn't possible to completely cut the ties that had once bound you. That was why she'd been right to go.

She saw Abbey Andersen, looking cool and smart in a black and white dress and high-heeled sandals. She was alone, and Suzanne walked over to her.

'How are you today?' she asked.

'Grand,' said Abbey, pleased to be able to use her favourite new word. 'I'm grand. And you?' Her voice softened. 'The priest said some nice things about your dad. Donald, too.'

'Never speak ill of the dead.' Suzanne gave her a wry smile. 'Nobody would've got up there and said that Fred was a womanising sod who lobbed a grenade into the bosom of his family before he departed this life.'

'Am I the grenade?' asked Abbey.

'Sorry, that was a bit insensitive,' said Suzanne.

'Oh, not really. I understand.'

'Will your mother be very upset when you finally get around to telling her about all this?' Suzanne looked curiously at Abbey.

She'd meant to tease out a little more about the American girl's mother when they'd spoken, but she'd been too tired.

'I'm sure she'll deal with it,' said Abbey. 'At least I was here to say goodbye for her.'

'It's good to say goodbye.' Suzanne looked surprised at her own words. She wasn't sure why she felt the way she did, but she suddenly realised that despite everything, she was glad she'd come.

'When do you go back to Spain?' asked Abbey. 'It is Spain, right?'

'Yes. I'm staying till the day after tomorrow.' She made a face. 'It seemed right when I was booking it, but to be honest, I'd be quite happy to go back tonight.'

'But you're having the family meeting with me,' said Abbey.

'Indeed.' Suzanne gave a quick smile. 'I'm sure that'll be fun.'

'I'm sure it won't.' But Abbey couldn't help smiling too.

Lisette wondered what Suzanne and Abbey had found to talk to each other about. They seemed to be getting on well together, even laughing occasionally, though Lisette couldn't imagine what there was to laugh about. She'd be glad when all of this was over and everything had got back to normal.

She groaned inwardly as Edie Farrell walked over to her. Fred's former neighbour wanted to talk, and Lisette didn't feel like talking right now. She tacked a smile on to her face. Only a little longer to go, she said to herself. Only a little longer.

In fact it was nearly three hours later before only the family (including Deirdre, her daughters and Abbey) remained. As well as Alex and Ryan, the legal people. Abbey was standing beside Ryan, who'd stuck to her for the majority of the afternoon, keeping her amused with anecdotes about his work with Celtic Legal and shielding her from Fred's neighbours and acquaintances who, once or twice, tried to strike up conversations with her. Abbey was very grateful to him for looking after her so well; despite the solemnity of the occasion, she'd enjoyed his company. Not that the occasion had stayed overly solemn. After about an hour it had become more of a celebration than anything else, with people chattering and laughing and every so often recounting stories about Fred.

But now the friends and neighbours had left and the family was alone.

Donald spoke briefly to Alex and the solicitor cleared his throat and asked everyone to gather round.

'You all wanted an opportunity to talk to Abbey Andersen,' he said. 'And this is that opportunity. However, I thought that perhaps it would be a good idea for me to talk to you too, especially with regard to the late Mr Fitzpatrick's will.'

The Fitzpatricks shared glances.

'We would certainly welcome the opportunity to hear what Dad wanted for us,' said Donald. 'But it doesn't concern Abbey. Does it?'

'Why don't we sit down and talk,' suggested Alex.

'Aren't you the executor of Fred's will?' Zoey asked her husband quietly. 'Why should Alex be talking about it?'

'I may be the executor, but Dad didn't keep me informed of all the changes,' replied Donald. 'And I'm guessing the old man left something to his damn illegitimate daughter.'

'You can't say illegitimate any more!' Zoey squeezed his arm. 'It's not PC. Maybe Fred left her something nice and Alex wants Abbey to bring it home to her.'

Donald grunted. 'Even so, I don't like the idea of her being part of a family gathering.'

'Oh, who cares.' Zoey plonked herself down on one of the well-upholstered sofas. 'Let's get this over and done with and then we can move on.' And hopefully, she thought, me and Don will be moving to Fred's house.

'I know the whole thing about reading someone's will aloud is usually confined to period detective novels and movies,' said Alex when everyone had found a seat. 'But I think under the circumstances it might be worth making Mr Fitzpatrick's wishes quite clear to you all.'

'What circumstances?' asked Donald as the rest of them gathered round.

'Everyone who has any interest in it is here,' said Alex.

At his words, Deirdre Fitzpatrick straightened in her seat and her two daughters exchanged happy smiles. Abbey felt tense. Had Fred left something to her mother? No matter what it was, Ellen wouldn't be able to accept it. She exhaled slowly. She been steeling herself all day to talk to the family about her mother. She hadn't anticipated that Fred might have left her anything. As if things weren't complicated enough already.

The extended Fitzpatrick family sat in a semicircle and looked at Alex expectantly. The solicitor was calm and controlled, his expression neutral as he glanced at the papers in his hands. He cleared his throat before starting to speak.

'Mr Fitzpatrick Senior's estate is made up mainly of cash and property,' he told them. 'The cash, which amounts to somewhat over four hundred thousand euros, comes from the recent liquidation of his equity portfolio; he decided to sell all of his shareholdings at the beginning of the year. The property is his home.'

The family nodded. Not a bad amount from the share portfolio, thought Gareth. Dad had done OK, despite the rocky markets of the past few years. He was a canny old devil, you had to hand it to him. Yet to look at him you'd think he hadn't a red cent!

'As you probably all know,' Alex continued, 'Mr Fitzpatrick, like many older people, liked to tweak his last will and testament from time to time.'

Lisette reached for Gareth's hand and gave it a squeeze.

'The last time I met Mr Fitzpatrick about his will was a little over a week ago,' said Alex.

'A week ago?' Donald looked at him in shock. 'I thought the last time he changed it was at the beginning of the year! Why did he need to talk to you a week ago?'

'He was advising me that he had made some alterations.' Alex's voice was steady. 'And he wanted me to be the executor of his new will.'

'Alterations?' Donald was horrified. 'What sort? And why am I not the executor? I always was.'

'Oh for God's sake, Don, who cares?' Deirdre spoke impatiently. 'Let Alex get on with it and tell us what the hell Fred has left us.'

'Before I do,' said Alex, 'I want to point out to you that Mr Fitzpatrick was perfectly entitled to draw up his own will without any input from me.'

'Is that what he did?' asked Gareth.

'In this instance,' said Alex. He cleared his throat. 'Mr Fitzpatrick's previous wills had always been drawn up by our firm, but he wanted to do this one himself. He said that he was very clear about his wishes and that he didn't need to waste time leaving it with me and having someone here draw it up again. When he called in to the practice, all he wanted was for two people to witness his signature.'

'Oh my God,' said Deirdre. 'The old bugger has left it all to the cats and dogs.'

'He hasn't done that,' Alex assured her, and Deirdre's face cleared.

Donald and Gareth exchanged tight smiles. Zoey tried to look unconcerned. Lisette tightened her hold on Gareth's hand. Suzanne stared straight ahead of her.

Alex took a document from his inside pocket and unfolded it. 'With that in mind, he bequeathed equal sums of money to his four grandchildren.' He glanced down at the paper in front of him and read from it. '". . . as a means of starting out in the world. Which my two oldest granddaughters have already done. But hopefully this will stop them leaning on their father so heavily in the process."'

Sorcha and Karen exchanged glances, while Deirdre hid a smile.

'Twenty-five thousand each,' said Alex.

The two girls hugged each other. Deirdre looked pleased. Donald's face was expressionless while Zoey's eyes were hard. Lisette leaned her head on Gareth's shoulder. She hadn't expected that sort of generosity from Fred towards his grandchildren. No matter how difficult a man he'd been, he'd still been mindful of the next generation and she was grateful to him for that. Whatever happened, at least her son and daughter would have money to go to college. She allowed herself a sigh of relief.

'The money for Jerome and Fleur is to be placed into a trust until they are eighteen,' said Alex.

'That's fine by us,' said Gareth.

'He's left five thousand to the former Mrs Fitzpatrick,' said Alex.

'What?' Deirdre looked affronted, while Zoey smiled surreptitiously. 'Five bloody K! For crying out loud! I kept in touch with him. I called to see him. I cut his grass. And that's the thanks I get.'

'If you were doing it for the money, you should have charged him,' said Suzanne. 'I'm sure he would've paid the going rate.'

Donald looked at his sister in surprise. He hadn't expected her to be the one to spring to his father's defence.

Alex looked at her too. 'As far as you're concerned, Suzanne, I'll read to you from the will. "I realise that as a father I failed with my daughter, Suzanne. I didn't appreciate her spirit and her drive. That was my loss."'

Suzanne felt her eyes well up with tears. She remembered how she'd wanted to come back as a success and see Fred's face. She'd never thought that he already considered her to be successful. She never dreamed he'd felt that it was a loss to him not to know her better.

'"To my daughter Suzanne,"' Alex continued, reading from the will, '"I leave the sum of two hundred and fifty thousand euros."'

Suzanne's mouth fell open. She realised that she had been steeling herself to receive nothing at all from her father. He'd cut her out of his life so comprehensively in the past (and to be fair, she'd allowed it to happen) that she'd been quite prepared to accept that he'd left everything to her brothers. In fact, as soon as Alex had started talking, she'd been thinking of ways in which she might be able to persuade either one of them (or both) to become part of her hotel consortium. But now she could bring some money to the table herself. Not enough, she thought, as she took out a tissue and wiped her eyes. Not enough to put the whole thing to bed, but enough, surely, to influence the bank a little. *If that happens, I can have my hotel. And it would be because of Dad.* She crumpled the damp tissue and covered her face with her hands.

'Congratulations, Suzanne,' said Donald, his voice clipped. 'You deserve it. You should consider yourself very lucky.'

Suzanne couldn't say anything. She was still overcome. Still shocked.

'"I have previously settled a considerable amount on my two sons, Donald and Gareth, and their wives",' read Alex. '"At the time, I told them that I wanted them to have the benefit of my good fortune before I died. I wanted them to enjoy the money."'

Suzanne raised her head and looked at both of her brothers in surprise. This was the first she'd heard of any previous settlement.

'He gave you money before?' she said. 'When? Why?'

'After Mam died,' Donald replied. 'He said that he'd expected to be spending the money on her, but he decided to give it to us instead. I was working with him, after all. I deserved something for that.'

'And you?' She looked at Gareth.

'I suppose he thought I could do with a bit of a leg-up,' said her brother. 'Teaching doesn't pay all that well, you know.'

'I always knew he favoured you both.' Even though she was still reeling at her own bequest, Suzanne couldn't help feeling hurt that Fred had given money to the boys already.

'You were living abroad at the time,' Gareth said. 'You hadn't been home in years. And when you did come home, for Mam's funeral, you made no secret of the fact that you couldn't stand him.'

'He's given you money now,' said Lisette. 'You should be happy.'

Suzanne knew that Lisette was right. The past wasn't important. The future was the only thing that mattered. And her father had – so unexpectedly – looked after her future.

'It's always unfortunate when a parent favours one child or children over others,' said Alex. 'I don't think that Mr Fitzpatrick intended to hurt anyone's feelings. He wanted to do the right thing by everyone.'

He returned to reading the will.

'"I know that the economic situation has affected both my sons, and Donald's domestic situation hasn't been as easy as he would have liked, and so, taking into account the money I gave them a number of years ago, I am making an additional settlement of twenty-five thousand to each of them, as well as leaving them my two classic cars to help them smooth out their affairs."'

The brothers exchanged glances again. Getting such a small cash sum was somewhat insulting – especially compared to Suzanne – but not if they also shared the house between them. But, each of them was also thinking, what if Fred had left the house to the other brother? How would he have made that decision? And what then?

'"To Lisette Fitzpatrick, Gareth's wife",' read Alex, '"I leave five thousand euros and my silver collection, and I thank her for looking after it and polishing it for so many years."'

Not that damn silver, thought Lisette. None of it special and nothing but trouble to keep clean. Is he having a laugh? As for five thousand – even added to Gareth's money, that's still not enough to clear all our debts.

'"To Zoey Fitzpatrick I also leave five thousand and my late wife's jewellery, which I hope she will enjoy as much as Ros did."'

216

Bloody hell, thought Zoey. He's left me some God-awful neck-laces and a few unwearable rings. And five grand is hardly pushing the boat out, is it? But once he's done right by Donald, it doesn't matter. What's mine is mine and what's his is mine too. And one way or another, Furze Hill will be mine.

Alex took a sip of water and cleared his throat before continuing to read. '"By now you are all aware of events in my past life. I hope you have found it in your hearts to forgive me."' He looked up from the will. 'Mr Fitzpatrick had intended to talk to the family after meeting Miss Andersen. Obviously things didn't turn out like that.'

Abbey shifted uncomfortably in her seat as the family's eyes fixed on her.

'"It's only in recent times that I realise the consequences of those actions",' read Alex. '"A woman I cared about died in appalling circumstances. I deprived her daughter of her true family."'

'You know, I think my mom was happy,' said Abbey tentatively. 'Your dad was beating himself up for no reason, at least as far as she was concerned.'

'"I was never punished for what I'd done",' continued Alex.

'What the hell does he mean, "punished"?' demanded Donald. 'He fathered a child. So what? Loads of men have fathered children they've had nothing more to do with. Why should Dad be any different?'

'When Mr Fitzpatrick came to me to talk about it, he was quite distressed,' said Alex. 'He'd seen programmes about the treatment of unmarried mothers on the TV. There was a particular programme on the Magdalene laundries that upset him considerably. He was very angry at the treatment meted out to the girls by the religious orders and upset about his former girlfriend who herself had been placed in an institution during her pregnancy.'

Lisette wished Fred had never seen that damn TV programme and had stuck to the war movies and blockbusters he usually watched.

'"Recently I discovered that I had not only a daughter I had never met but also a granddaughter."' Alex returned to reading the will. '"I want to compensate them for what happened to Ita Dillon and for not having bothered to find out anything about them before now."'

There was an audible intake of breath among the Fitzpatricks, triggered by the word 'compensate'. Now their eyes turned to Alex, who looked up at them. 'Mr Fitzpatrick wrote this will after Abbey Andersen had agreed to meet him but before she left the States,' he said. 'And so he has made a provision for her of five thousand euros, specifically for coming to Ireland without any knowledge of what lay ahead of her.'

A relieved expression appeared on the faces of the Fitzpatrick brothers and their wives. Five grand to the long-lost relative wasn't too bad after all.

'That's the last of Mr Fitzpatrick's cash,' Alex said. 'Except for a small balance in his current account which doesn't exceed a thousand euros.'

So now to the meat of it, thought Donald. The house. What has Dad done? Shared it equally between me and Gar? Or has he cut Suzanne in too? But he's already left her a quarter of a million. Why should she get anything more?

'"It's only in recent years that I realise the emotional and physical distress that the mother of my daughter went through. And I regret that I didn't make an effort to help her, or to keep my daughter in the country."'

'It was more than fifty years ago!' cried Donald. 'He couldn't have been expected to look after a baby on his own back then.'

'"I want to make amends for what happened",' read Alex. '"Unfortunately, the only way I can do that is materially."'

Donald and Gareth shared a tense look.

'"To Abbey Andersen and Ellen Connolly jointly, I leave my home, Furze Hill, and its contents except those already bequeathed",' finished Alex.

218

For almost half a minute there was complete and utter silence in the room.

Then the Fitzpatricks started to talk all at once. And none of them had anything good to say.

Chapter 22

Abbey was in complete shock. Her grandfather, a man she barely knew, had left his home to her and Ellen. And he'd done that before he'd even seen her or spoken to her. Why? She hadn't told him anything about Ellen's life. And she hadn't had time to talk about herself either. What if they'd had a chance to discuss things? Would he have changed his mind again? She had no problem understanding why the family was stunned. She was stunned herself.

'Surely you can see that this is insane?' Donald's voice rose above the others' as he confronted Alex. 'My father was clearly out of his mind.'

'Mr Fitzpatrick seemed very lucid and clear when he came to see me,' replied Alex.

'He couldn't have been!' exclaimed Donald. 'He's given away our inheritance to complete strangers.'

'Mr Fitzpatrick didn't see it that way.'

'It was up to you to make him see it that way!' Donald's face was red and veins stood out at his temple. 'You've been his solicitor for years. You must have known this is nonsense.'

'I advised your father that it could cause some concern,' agreed Alex. 'I urged him to think about it again. But he was insistent.'

'Why didn't you send him off to a shrink?' demanded Deirdre. 'How can he leave everything to this money-grabbing woman and her mother!' She turned towards Abbey, her face almost as red as her ex-husband's.

'I advised Mr Fitzpatrick that he should wait until he met both Miss Andersen and Ellen Connolly before changing his will,' said Alex. 'I told him that at that stage he should come to me and I would draw up a document that would meet his desire to compensate his daughter and granddaughter. I pointed out that he'd written this will without even knowing them. He said that wasn't their fault and that Ellen Connolly was his daughter and deserved something from him.'

'Something maybe!' cried Gareth. 'But the house and everything in it? I don't bloody think so. He should've left it to me and Don.'

Suzanne opened her mouth, but closed it again without speaking.

'I told Mr Fitzpatrick that he should reconsider,' said Alex. 'However, he was adamant that his wish was for cash bequests to his immediate family and the house and contents to Ellen Connolly and her daughter.'

'It's not only about the amount involved.' Donald gritted his teeth. 'It's about – about implying that they have some right to be considered part of our family. They aren't. They never have been and they never will be.'

'Mr Fitzpatrick's view was that he wanted to acknowledge his daughter,' said Alex.

'Acknowledge, fine,' growled Gareth. 'But turn over the family home – no way is that right.'

'Did you plan this?' Donald turned to Abbey, his voice laden with fury. 'Did you? Did you contact him? Stalk him? Make him feel sorry for you?'

'Of course not!' cried Abbey. 'I didn't even know he existed until a couple of weeks ago.'

'You say that.' Gareth was equally angry. 'But how do we know?'

'Because I was the one who found Miss Andersen,' said Ryan. 'She had no idea about Mr Fitzpatrick's place in her life before then.'

'He didn't have a place in her life!' cried Donald. 'And she doesn't have a place in his. Or ours. My father couldn't have been more wrong about that. The truth is that she's nothing but a money-grabbing gold-digger who hastened Dad's death—'

'Donald, I strongly advise you not to talk about Miss Andersen in those terms.' Alex spoke slowly and steadily. 'I understand you're upset, but—'

'Too right I'm upset,' raged Donald. 'Too bloody right I am.' He glared at Alex. 'You said that my father drew up this ridiculous will himself. Are you sure it's properly done? After all, my father wasn't a solicitor.'

'You don't need a solicitor to write a will,' said Alex. 'When he brought it to me, he confirmed that he wished me to be the executor and that he wanted to have his signature witnessed. I urged him to wait until he'd met Miss Andersen before signing it. He told me that if he disliked her on sight, he'd shred it. If not, then this was a valid will and he'd shred the previous one so that there wouldn't be any doubt.'

'And did he?' asked Donald.

'I don't know,' replied Alex. 'However, as you can see, this one is dated a week ago, and certainly after the last one I prepared for him.'

'Maybe he changed his mind. Maybe there's another one.' Gareth looked hopeful. 'If he was going round drawing up wills himself, there could be more. Ones that leave things properly to the people who deserve them. To his real family.'

'There must be something you can do,' said Donald to Alex. 'You advised him against it, after all.'

'But he chose not to take my advice,' Alex reminded him.

'I'm very sorry.' Abbey looked at them all in distress.

'I doubt that,' snapped Deirdre. 'I'd say you can't believe your luck. You walk in and take the lot from under our noses. Well done. You didn't have to put up with the moody old tosser all these years and you've still hit the jackpot.'

'Don't talk about my father like that,' said Donald.

'Now you're defending him?' cried Deirdre. 'You're a fool,

Donald Fitzpatrick. But then you always were. You were a fool over me and a fool over Miss Social Climber there too, because I'm sure your bottle-blond bombshell will have changed her tune about you now.'

'Who the hell do you think you are?' Zoey's eyes flashed angrily. 'Say one more word and I'll see you outside.'

'Zoey!' Donald caught her by the arm. 'Please.'

'She has no right to talk to me like that,' said Zoey. 'Disgruntled Deirdre, all high and mighty and pushing her weight about. Still thinking that she's entitled to be part of this family when she was the one who had the affair, the slut!'

There was a sudden silence and everyone looked at Deirdre.

'This isn't the time or the place.' Donald looked pleadingly at both his wife and his ex-wife.

'That was a complete misunderstanding,' said Deirdre. 'Which Donald already knows.'

'My arse,' retorted Zoey.

'None of this matters,' cried Lisette. 'What's important is what Fred has done. Everything else . . . is secondary.'

'If we don't discover another, later will we're going to contest this travesty.' Donald turned to his siblings for support. 'I don't care what ideas he had about acknowledging his . . . his . . . love child. There's no way Dad would want to leave so much to Abbey Andersen and her mother when he knew that we were depending on him for financial help. I'm sorry, Abbey,' he added, although there was no regret in his voice. 'You may be an innocent party in all this, but you're not a Fitzpatrick and you've no right to my father's house. Of course we'll pay you the five thousand for coming here – I can give that to you today if you like – but anything else just wouldn't be fair.'

'Seems to me that fairness and Dad have never gone hand in hand,' remarked Suzanne. 'But it only bothers you when you're at the wrong end of it. You clearly didn't kick up a fuss when I was left out before. You didn't even bother to tell me about it.'

'Those were entirely different circumstances,' said Donald. 'You were always going to get something sooner or later, and now you have. So there's nothing for you to complain about. This involves almost everything Dad owned going to a complete stranger. We haven't even had the opportunity to talk to her yet! There's no way that can happen, and I won't let it.'

'Well, not everything,' said Suzanne. 'Like you said, I'm getting quite a bit of money. You, Gar, your children and your wives – current and previous – are getting a generous enough wedge between you all. It's only the house that's the problem.'

Gareth stared at her. 'Are you saying that this is OK by you?' he asked. 'That you're all right about our family home being given to two people you've never heard of before? Because that's what's happening here. We're being sold short.'

'Going on past form, I'm lucky to have got anything,' remarked Suzanne. 'So I guess it's no skin off my nose. Besides, it's not the family home. None of us ever lived here. It was Dad's home, not ours.'

'Don't be stupid,' said Donald. 'Nobody is getting any of Dad's assets except his family. And we are his family, not some American blow-in. Alex, we're contesting this will and I want you to set the wheels in motion straight away.'

'I have to advise you that there are very limited circumstances under which you can contest a will.' Alex had expected this kind of response from the family. He'd warned Fred about it, but Fred had said it was his money to leave as he chose. He'd done a lot for his children over the course of their lives. He'd fed them, clothed them, brought them on holidays and given them significant sums of money to ease them on their way. But he'd done nothing at all for Ellen Connolly or Abbey Andersen and that was why he wanted to fix things now. Despite all his powers of persuasion, Alex couldn't change Fred's mind. There was a part of him that wondered if Fred had wanted his children to flare up as they had, if the old man was enjoying the opportunity to cause trouble after

224

his death. 'Additionally, as I'm the executor, I can't help you do it. It's my job to ensure that Fred's wishes are carried out,' he added.

'I think disgraceful advice from his solicitor is damn good grounds to contest this nonsense,' said Donald. 'Allied with the fact that Dad had clearly lost his marbles completely.'

'What makes you think he lost his marbles?' asked Suzanne. 'OK, it was a weird decision, but it was his to make and he appears to have weighed up a lot of things.'

'He was an old man and his mind was going,' said Lisette. 'He didn't weigh up anything. There were days when he couldn't remember his own name, for heaven's sake.'

'There are days when *I* can't remember my own name,' returned Suzanne, 'and there's nothing wrong with my mind.'

'Naturally you don't want to lose your money, Suzanne. I understand that,' said Zoey. 'Donald and I will guarantee that when this will is overturned, you'll get what's due to you, won't we, Don?'

'It's not about my share of the money,' said Suzanne.

'Don't make me laugh.' Zoey was scornful. 'It's always about the money.'

'All Abbey has to do is say that she and her mum will give up their rights to Dad's property.' It was Gareth who stood up and faced the rest of them. 'Then we can avoid all this hassle.'

'I have to advise you not to do that, Abbey,' said Ryan.

'Why?' Abbey looked hunted.

'This is a pressurised environment,' said Ryan. 'You can't make decisions under duress. Nor can you make decisions on behalf of your mother.'

'Hey, lawyer man, you're working for us, not her,' said Donald.

'I was working for your father,' said Ryan.

'Well you can consider that particular job at an end,' Gareth told him.

'It ended when I brought Miss Andersen back here,' said Ryan.

'But Ryan is right,' said Abbey. 'It's not just up to me, is it? It's up to my mother too. I'll have to talk to her.'

'I thought you *couldn't* talk to her,' said Gareth. 'I thought she was uncontactable. Which in itself is bloody suspicious. Nobody is uncontactable these days.'

'I always intended to contact her when I returned to the States,' said Abbey. 'Even if it took some time.'

'Oh, so now you're changing your tune?' Donald looked at Abbey accusingly. 'Previously she was holed up somewhere incommunicado. Was that so my father couldn't see that she was a totally unsuitable person? A crackhead pole-dancer maybe? There's no way our inheritance is going to some madwoman in the States. No way at all.'

Ryan was looking at Abbey intently. 'How long before you can talk to her?' he asked.'

'I have to make specific arrangements,' said Abbey. 'A week, maybe two.'

'Is she in prison or something?' asked Zoey. 'I doubt Fred would want his house to go to a convicted criminal.'

'Of course she's not a criminal,' said Abbey. She looked apologetically at Ryan. 'My mother lives in a monastery. She's a Benedictine nun.'

Chapter 23

There was another stunned silence, this time eventually broken by Lisette.

'A nun? A Catholic nun? That can't be possible. She's your mother! She's had a child!'

'My mom is a widow,' Abbey said. 'And there's no problem with a widowed woman who's had a child becoming a nun, as long as the child isn't dependent. In any event, the monastery she's a part of isn't exclusively Catholic. It's Christian.'

'Monastery? You mean convent,' said Suzanne.

'No. Benedictines live a monastic life.'

'Holy Mother of God,' cried Deirdre. 'He's left his house to the Moonies.'

'No,' said Abbey steadily. 'This is a proper Christian community of sisters.'

'You have *got* to be kidding me.' Donald's face was like thunder. 'You're saying that Dad's house, the house he's always loved and worked so hard to get, is now half owned by a gang of lunatic lesbian nuns?'

'They're not lesbians!' cried Abbey. 'Although even if they were, there's no need for you to be so insulting.'

'There's something very weird about a gang of women holing themselves up together behind high walls,' said Donald. 'I think I'm perfectly entitled to call them whatever I like.'

'Why didn't you tell me about this when I first met you and

227

asked about your mother?' asked Ryan, who'd been listening in total astonishment.

'People can be very judgemental about religion. They can be equally judgemental about choices,' said Abbey. 'Especially when they concern someone who had a late vocation, like Mom. I wanted to protect her.'

'I wouldn't have been judgemental,' said Ryan. 'I'm a solicitor. I don't get to be judgemental.'

'But my father bloody well would have been!' Gareth cried. 'After all, he decided to leave you all this because he wanted to compensate your mother for what allegedly happened to her own mother in those damn Magdalene laundries. Which were run by nuns. So you can't tell me that he would've left her anything if he'd known she was a nun herself.'

'I think this strengthens our hand,' said Donald. He looked at Alex. 'Dad would never have left his property to a nun.'

'Just because he was upset by what happened to children in the care of religious orders years ago doesn't mean he wouldn't have left the money to his daughter all the same,' said Alex.

'Never!' cried Gareth. 'And you know what – Abbey Andersen probably knew that. Which is why she pretended she couldn't contact her mother and why she came here herself. And now she's found that she's getting what's rightfully ours and all you want to do is help her.'

'That's not true,' protested Abbey. 'I didn't even want to come.'

'You were playing hard to get,' said Gareth. 'Making him feel even more guilty. Pushing sob stories at him until he had a heart attack.'

'No!' Abbey was close to tears. 'Of course I wasn't.'

'And you were keeping your mother out of it because you knew that her being a nun would muddy the waters.'

'You don't understand,' said Abbey. 'I didn't have the opportunity to tell him about Mom.'

'You had plenty of opportunity, but you decided to come here and see what was on offer before reporting back to your mother in her zealots' commune,' retorted Donald.

'I did not. And it's not a commune. Nor is it a laundry. It's a place of quiet and solitude and reflection and ministry.' As Abbey spoke the words, she realised that it was the first time she'd truly believed them. Because when Ellen had taken off to the monastery, she'd had the same view as the Fitzpatricks about it. She'd thought that her mother was a crackpot. That she'd allowed herself to be brainwashed. But Ellen was quite insistent that her decisions – first to spend six months with the community on what they described as an 'estancia', where she learned about their everyday lives, and then to serve a further number of years as a postulant before moving on to her novitiate – were the only possible ones she could take. Because of her background, she was now spending an extended time of temporary commitment with the order before making her final profession, something that Abbey knew she hoped to do the following year.

'Bollocks.' Donald's voice was emphatic. 'I think you should leave. You've no business being here.'

'Well, actually,' said Ryan, 'she does. As a beneficiary of the will—'

'There is no way on earth that a court will uphold that will!' cried Gareth. 'No way.'

'What happens to me and my daughters if it's set aside?' Deirdre interrupted him.

'If there's no other will, Mr Fitzpatrick will be deemed to have died intestate,' said Alex. 'The estate will be divided up between his family in accordance with the 1965 Succession Act.'

'We're his granddaughters, that makes us family.' Karen sounded pleased.

'Yes, although any share to those other than his direct children might depend on how the court interprets Mr Fitzpatrick's wishes. Family usually means the immediate family, which in this case would be his children, Donald, Gareth and Suzanne. I should also warn you that this would be a very expensive process.'

'Bloody hell,' said Sorcha to Karen. 'We've got our money. Maybe we should tell Dad to leave well enough alone.'

'Will enough alone,' muttered Karen, which made her sister giggle.

'It's not funny!' Donald was so angry, his face was almost purple. 'Dad has made fools out of all of us.'

'I'm sure we can work something out,' said Abbey.

'You think?' There was a hint of wickedness in Suzanne's voice. 'I'm quite sure that if the nuns know that your mother has a huge inheritance, they'll definitely want their part of it. I don't care whether it's Catholic or ecumenical or just plain crazed, with all these religious orders you end up giving them all your worldly goods.'

Abbey was silent.

'Over my dead body is this house going to a gang of nuns!' cried Donald. 'We're contesting and that's that.'

'I think you all need a bit of time to reflect before you start talking about legal action,' said Alex. 'I realise this isn't what any of you expected. I raised all these issues with Mr Fitzpatrick, although clearly neither of us had any idea of his daughter's . . . calling at the time. All I can say is that he was adamant that he wanted to provide for her and for his granddaughter and he thought this was a fair way of doing it.'

Lisette looked at Abbey. 'Surely you can see that you have no right to my father-in-law's house,' she said. 'You must give it up.'

'I . . .' Abbey didn't know what to say. She couldn't help feeling that Lisette was right, and yet she didn't want to rush into doing or saying anything stupid.

'Y'see!' Donald's expression was triumphant. 'She's got her hand in the honey pot and she won't let go.'

'I need time to think,' said Abbey.

'Any normal, decent person wouldn't think twice about doing the right thing,' said Donald.

'Any normal, decent person would've mentioned to his sister

230

that he'd got a great wedge of cash from their father a few years ago,' Suzanne observed.

'Get over it,' snapped Gareth. 'That's not the issue here now.'

'We'll see them in court,' said Donald. 'And we'll win. Because we're Dad's family, we're Dad's heirs, and we're the people who really mattered to him.'

'Do we all have to contest the will?' asked Deirdre. 'After all, my girls are being looked after. Maybe not as much as they should've been, but . . .'

'They'll be better looked after when we get it overturned,' said Donald.

Gareth looked at him. 'Are you saying that you'll sell the house and give extra money to your children?' he asked.

'Uh, no, not exactly.' Donald sounded flustered. 'Of course I'll look after Jerome and Fleur too. I'll make sure that everyone is better off,' he said, recovering his composure. 'Except the last woman to see my father alive and her allegedly monastic mother.'

'That sort of talk isn't helping anyone.' Ryan glanced at Abbey, who was white-faced.

'There might still be another will,' said Gareth.

'I can assure you there isn't,' Alex told him. 'As far as this one is concerned, I would seek counsel's advice. Abbey and her mother could possibly renounce their rights to the bequest, but—'

'That's all that needs to happen,' interrupted Donald. 'They admit that they're not entitled to a cent. Get the paperwork ready, Alex, and have them sign it. Let's face it, we need to get a move on so that we can plan our futures.'

'I can't make any decisions until I talk to my mom,' said Abbey. 'I don't know what the situation is regarding an inheritance when she's in the monastery. But the last thing she'd want is for you to be upset.'

'I think the best thing now is for all of you to go home and think things over,' said Alex.

'I don't need to think a single thing over,' Donald told him.

231

'Dad has acted like a fool, but I'm not going to let him make a fool out of me.'

'C'mon, Don. Let's go.' Zoey took him by the arm.

Donald hesitated and then allowed her to lead him from the room. One by one the rest of the Fitzpatricks followed him.

Finally, only Ryan, Alex and Abbey were left behind.

'That went pretty much as I expected,' said Alex. 'Though the nun part of things has pretty well put the cat among the pigeons, hasn't it?'

'I'm truly sorry I didn't say anything before,' Abbey told him. 'I didn't think it would matter. After all, as far as I was concerned I was coming to meet with Mr Fitzpatrick and tell him a little about me and my mom. Obviously I would've told him about her vocation. I didn't expect him to die and leave us everything!'

'You should have told me.' Ryan sounded hurt. 'I thought you trusted me. I'd have gone to the monastery and dealt with things in a sensitive manner and we could've headed all this nonsense off at the pass.'

'I did trust you,' Abbey said. 'But . . . well, first of all, Mom was leading a retreat when you came to the States and so I couldn't get in touch with her. I didn't say why because I didn't think it would matter in the end, especially after Mr Fitzpatrick asked to see me instead. I was going to tell him about her life. I had to, because she was never going to be able to visit him and I needed to explain why. But I didn't want you going to the monastery, Ryan. It's not the sort of place where you fetch up with a sheaf of legal papers and tell one of the nuns that you need to have a chat about her long-lost dad.'

'So how does it work? How often do you talk to her?'

'Not very often,' replied Abbey. 'The Benedictines live a monastic life. They don't go out into the community like other nuns. They spend a lot of their time doing contemplative stuff. Praying mostly. Growing vegetables, tending the garden, that sort of thing. They have a certain amount of interaction with people outside of the monastery too. They do art work – stained-glass ornaments that they sell. And, of course, they run the retreats and other prayer ceremonies. But it all fits in around their day, which is still sort of old-fashioned. They get up very early, they go to bed early. They don't talk at certain times . . .'

'Bloody hell!' exclaimed Ryan. 'That's medieval.'

'It's not something we're accustomed to in the modern world,' Abbey acknowledged.

'How did you know your mother was running a retreat, in that case?' asked Ryan. 'And how do you contact her?'

'The monastery has a website,' said Abbey. 'I know that sounds a bit odd given what I've told you, but it makes a lot of sense when you think about it. It's a way of them reaching out to people while living a more cloistered life. They post information on their retreats and services. I check it every week and I contact my mother by email. The nuns are allowed a certain number of personal emails every year. It wasn't like that when Mom first joined, but the monastery has developed quite a big social media presence since then. You can send prayer requests and the nuns tweet Bible quotes and inspirational messages and stuff like that.'

'Now you're really having me on,' said Ryan.

'No,' said Abbey. 'They put out their message to the world, you see. But . . . but they don't talk to the world in the same way as you or I do.'

Ryan rubbed his forehead. Abbey understood how difficult it was for him to understand. It had been difficult for her too, at the start, and the truth was that it was still difficult. Because no matter how happy Ellen insisted she was, Abbey couldn't help feeling that a woman who had loved to travel and meet people must surely feel like a trapped bird inside the four walls of the monastery, even if she could look outwards in a virtual way.

'We'd better get a move on,' said Alex, who had been making notes as Abbey spoke. 'Obviously Ellen's situation is unusual, but she's still a beneficiary of the will. That hasn't changed, and I want to make sure that whatever you or the Fitzpatricks decide to do, I have the files and paperwork ready. You said you can speak to your mother in a week or two?'

'I need to contact the prioress of the monastery,' said Abbey. 'She'll let me know when I can talk to Mom.'

'Why can't you talk to her whenever you want?' asked Alex.

'Because it's the rules.'

'Presumably you can make an appointment to see her, though?'

'Only occasionally. Obviously if there's an emergency the prioress will be extra accommodating.'

'And this is an emergency,' said Ryan.

'Well . . .' Abbey looked doubtful. 'We might think so, but the prioress might view it differently.'

'Bloody hell.' Ryan scratched his head as he looked at her. 'I never thought it would end up like this.'

'Neither did I,' said Abbey.

Ryan drove her back to the Harbour Hotel, but the journey was conducted in near silence. It was an awkward silence too, Abbey thought, quite unlike the easy comfort she'd felt in his company until now. She knew that he was disappointed in her for having kept her mother's way of life a secret from him, and she could understand that. Things might have been a bit easier today if she'd shared the information sooner. But she still wouldn't have allowed him to hotfoot it to the monastery and demand to see her mother.

When Ellen had told her of her decision more than eight years earlier, Abbey hadn't at first realised how life-changing it would be. After she learned more about the way of life at the monastery, she'd been appalled. She'd felt as though her mother was abandoning her and shutting her out, and that she herself must have done something to push her away, even though Ellen had insisted that joining the nuns at Los Montesinos was a true vocation. A calling from God, she had said, which had made Abbey snort in derision, because they'd encountered more than one God in their travels and numerous different types of beliefs in him. She couldn't accept that her mother had decided that the Christian God was real, and someone (something? Abbey wasn't quite sure) she was going to devote the rest of her life to. Religion, in any form, had never been high on Ellen's agenda before, and back then, Abbey couldn't help thinking that her decision to shut herself away was a reaction to the death of her parents. And perhaps to having lost Jon, Abbey's father, too. Abbey had sometimes wondered if their nomadic lifestyle had been a result of Jon's death – if her mother had been looking for something to help her cope. Perhaps she'd kept on looking, even when they were living in San Francisco and even when Pete came along. Abbey had been very sure for a long time that Ellen's so-called vocation was more to do with her personal life than any calling from God.

Yet the nuns didn't take in people who were going through personal crises, which was why Ellen was spending such a long time with them before making her final profession. They wanted to be sure, and Ellen, in her last conversation with Abbey, had said that she was happy to walk a slow road. This was another thing that had shocked Abbey, because Ellen had never taken a slow road anywhere before. She'd always been in a hurry to move on, find somewhere new, do something different. Realising that she had changed was probably the hardest thing for Abbey to accept. If her mother had been the same woman as always when she saw her, she might have believed in it more. As it was, she thought that Ellen had been seduced by the serenity and the support of the community and the fact that her life was ordered and measured when, in the past, she'd had to work everything out herself.

The hardest thing, initially, had been the fact that she couldn't speak to her mom whenever she wanted. Even when she'd had a major life crisis on her hands, she hadn't been able to call, although in fairness, her major crises were usually to do with work or boyfriends and never seemed so bad in the light of day. In any event, they nearly always resolved themselves. The monastery's rules often made people outside take a slower road too.

'I'm sorry,' she said again as Ryan drew the car to a halt outside the hotel. 'I should've told you.'

'I would have done some things differently,' he said.

'Yes. I realise that.'

'But you weren't to know that Fred Fitzpatrick had already changed his will. And you certainly weren't to know that he'd have a heart attack within a couple of minutes of meeting you.'

'I've never been great at timing,' said Abbey.

'It wasn't your fault.'

'I've made things tough for you.'

'That's why I'm paid the big bucks.' His tone was lighter but still carried a hint of disillusionment.

'Um . . .' She spoke hesitantly. 'Can I go back to the States right now, or do I have to wait here for things to be sorted out?'

This time Ryan chuckled. 'You're talking about the law, and that never moves quickly,' he reminded her. 'I'll speak to Alex, but I don't think there's a compelling reason for you to stay. You're correct in that you can't do anything independently of your mother, and no matter what happens, it'll take time before you can access the estate. But Abbey, you need to think long and hard about what you want to do. It was Fred's wish that you and your mom share that house. He wouldn't want you to give it up.'

'I was delighted when he left me the five K,' said Abbey. 'But the house is a different matter. I know what you mean, though, and – well, I have to admit that it's the only chance I'll ever have of getting my hands on that kind of money. All the same . . .' She looked worried. 'What have I done to deserve it?'

'What you've done or haven't done isn't the point,' said Ryan. 'What Mr Fitzpatrick has done, because he wanted to, absolutely is. And perhaps when the others calm down, they'll see that some kind of negotiated settlement is best.'

'The two brothers were pretty mad, weren't they?' observed

Abbey. 'The others not so much, though they all got cash . . . but Donald is furious at the very idea of Mom's existence. I understand it, I honestly do, but I'm not sure that spending a fortune on legal action is the right way to go about things. Sorry,' she added. 'I'm sure you have a different view, it's your livelihood after all.'

Ryan looked amused. 'Most legal professionals spend a huge amount of time telling people not to go to court at all,' he said. 'It's messy and expensive and you don't always get what you want. As far as I know, if Mr Fitzpatrick's will is contested, everyone's money will go back into the estate. Some of the lesser family members might be worse off.'

Abbey sighed. 'Life without money can be hard, but life with the possibility of having it might be even worse. All the same, the house isn't in the best of conditions, so I guess it isn't a fortune we're fighting about, especially after taxes.'

'How much would a similar property in Sausalito be worth?' asked Ryan.

'Pete's is worth about four million dollars,' Abbey replied. 'But everyone knows that real estate prices in Sausalito are crazy and Bella Vista Heights is an exceptional property.'

'Furze Hill is in a very desirable location,' Ryan told her. 'Abbey, I think you should expect to get close to a couple of million for it.'

'Oh my God.' Abbey was completely shocked. 'I never imagined it was anything like that amount! No wonder the family have gone postal over it. He really did leave us most of his wealth.'

'Exactly,' said Ryan.

Abbey got out of the car. She couldn't think of anything else to say.

Chapter 24

There was a lot of discussion in the Fitzpatrick cars as the various members of Fred's family drove home. Deirdre and her daughters veered from being happy that they'd been left something to being insulted that it wasn't enough, then anxious about how things would turn out if it all ended up in some kind of legal battle.

Donald was saying very little as he drove, but that was made up for by Zoey, who wanted to know as much as possible about the law regarding wills and inheritances and who broke off halfway through the conversation to phone her mother and share the news with her. Predictably, Lesley was hopping with rage and told her daughter that she hadn't married Donald, had she, to be left to rot on the sidelines while someone else swooped in and took what was rightfully hers. Donald kept his eyes firmly on the road ahead of him, although he was able to guess at most of Lesley's comments by his wife's replies.

In Gareth's car, Lisette was regretting once again that she hadn't looked at the will the day she'd seen it on Fred's table, because she knew she would've torn it up there and then and saved them all a lot of heartache. She would have done it in front of Fred and told him that he was being foolish, and she knew he would have listened to her because he always said that the French were very practical people. She was worried about the cost of taking legal action and how that might turn out. If they lost, they'd have spent even more money and not got anything in return. She couldn't help thinking that the only way forward was to persuade Abbey Andersen that the acceptable thing to do was to return her share to the family, even if the nuns insisted on getting their hands on her mother's half. After all, how could anyone seriously expect to be left such an enormous amount by a person they hadn't even known existed up until a few weeks earlier? It wasn't right. It couldn't be.

Suzanne had declined the offer of a lift from Lisette and Gareth and was instead walking back towards her hotel. She too was mulling over the events of the day. She was trying to decide if she was delighted by what her father had left her, hurt by the knowledge that he'd given the boys money years ago while ignoring her, or even more hurt that this time he'd left the house to two complete strangers. On the one hand, being singled out for a large amount of cash while seeing the boys get a couple of old cars was vindicating. On the other, learning that she was in third place behind Abbey and her mother was another kick in the teeth.

You were such a fool, Dad, she thought, as she neared the harbour. You were a fool to get that woman pregnant fifty-odd years ago and a fool to suddenly feel guilty about it now. It was almost certain that Abbey Andersen and her mother had had a perfectly good life without any input from him. The fact that Ellen Connolly had ended up in a monastery was a bit freaky, but it was her choice to make. The daughter, Abbey, seemed nice enough, but realistically, how likely was it that she'd say no to an unexpected inheritance? Not bloody likely, in Suzanne's view. Why should she? She had no earthly chance of making that kind of money from doing people's nails, after all.

However, regardless of how things worked out, Suzanne had to admit that financially she herself was a lot better off than she'd been a couple of weeks ago. And that meant, for the first time in her life, that she should be grateful to her father, even if she couldn't quite find it in herself to forgive him.

*　　*　　*

After saying goodbye to Ryan, Abbey went into the hotel and up to her room. She eased her feet out of her shoes, curled her legs beneath her on the bed and stared out of the window at the boats bobbing in the harbour. She was trying to get her head around the idea that after meeting her for less than five minutes, Fred Fitzpatrick had made his decision to leave her and her mother a house worth around two million dollars. Two million dollars, half of which was hers! Even after taxes, it was still a huge amount of money.

She closed her eyes and tried to think of herself as a millionaire. She didn't succeed. Because, of course, she wasn't that person. And if the Fitzpatrick family got their way, she never would be. But she was part of the Fitzpatrick family too, wasn't she? Just because she hadn't known about them before didn't mean that they couldn't get to know each other now. Maybe even get to like each other. And come to some kind of agreement about the will. Because she couldn't simply walk away from owning a house worth two million dollars. With that sort of money she could . . . well, the first thing she could do was to stop worrying about where she was going to live. She could afford to rent an apartment way better than the one she'd shared with Cobey. Hell, she could buy an apartment of her own! She thought of Pete and how he'd light up when she told him. He'd be thrilled for her, she knew he would. So would Solí and Vanessa. Selina too. Thinking about other people's reactions made her realise that it would be cool to be the one to be envied for a change, cool to be the one with great news. She was exhilarated by the feeling.

She opened her eyes again and wondered about her mom's reaction. She was pretty sure the Fitzpatricks were right in thinking that it wouldn't be up to Ellen alone to decide what to do about her inheritance, that the monastery's prioress, Sister Inez, would be the one calling the shots. Perhaps Ellen would want to decline it but not have any choice in the matter. So it might come down to a court case after all, although she wondered how successful the family's argument that Fred hadn't been in his full senses might be. Perhaps they'd be able to roll out a doctor to say that he was suffering from some kind of mental illness. Anything was possible. How reasonable was it for someone who was in his full senses to leave a house to two people he didn't know, even if one of them was the daughter he'd given away?

She massaged the back of her neck. Things were far more difficult than she'd ever expected when she'd agreed to come to Ireland and meet her unknown grandfather. She should've followed her initial instincts and said no. He would have been disappointed but it would surely have stopped him from making such a radical change to his will and prevented all this bitterness.

She would have to call Pete soon and tell him what had happened. He'd be able to give her a legal perspective on things. But although she took her phone out of her bag and scrolled to his name, she didn't select it. She wasn't ready to talk to him and to hear his advice, which she was certain would be to sit tight and fight for what she'd been left. Pete wouldn't understand the uncomfortable feeling that told her that she wasn't really entitled to anything at all. He would be all for getting the house, selling it and securing her future. And, she muttered aloud to herself, he would be utterly right.

She opened the email app and took a deep breath. Even though she didn't want to talk to Pete, she had to set the wheels in motion to meet with her mother. She thought long and hard for a few minutes and then began composing a message to Sister Inez. In it she said that an urgent family matter meant she needed to meet with her mother as soon as possible. She didn't give any more details, didn't talk about Magdalene laundries or unknown relatives and inheritances.

She sent the message and put the phone back in her bag. Then she unfurled her legs and stretched her arms over her head. She couldn't sit here thinking about things any longer. She needed to get out and clear her head.

*   *   *

241

She'd timed it badly, she thought, as she walked out of the hotel door and almost collided with Suzanne Fitzpatrick coming in. The two women looked awkwardly at each other for a moment.

'Ah, the heiress,' said Suzanne finally. 'Where are you off to?'

'A walk,' replied Abbey. 'I need to clear my head.'

'I'm not surprised,' said Suzanne. 'I'm sure you have a lot of things to think about. All the same – would you like to join me for coffee in the village?'

Abbey wasn't sure if she could deal with being told again that she didn't deserve what Fred had left her. But Suzanne didn't seem aggressive, and there was a hint of sympathy in her eyes. So she said that she'd be delighted to have coffee with her.

The two of them walked towards the harbour and Suzanne stopped outside a small café with pavement tables.

'Here?' she asked.

'Suits me,' replied Abbey.

'I'm sure you're exhausted after the day you've had,' Suzanne remarked after the flat whites they'd ordered arrived.

'No more than you,' said Abbey.

'It was hard for you.'

'Funerals are hard at the best of times.'

'I don't think there is a best of times for a funeral,' said Suzanne.

'No, you're right. I'm sorry. You must be devastated at your loss.'

'I wouldn't exactly go that far,' said Suzanne. 'But there is a part of you that thinks your parents will last for ever. My dad was stubborn. I thought he'd hang on till he was a hundred.'

'Didn't you get on with him?'

'Not especially,' said Suzanne. 'Not that it matters now anyway.'

Abbey sipped her coffee and said nothing.

'Anyway, he's really stirred things up,' Suzanne said. 'He was always good at that, but this has outdone anything that went before.'

'I can imagine.'

'My brothers are not impressed.'

'I wouldn't expect them to be.'

'Their wives are even less impressed.'

'And you?' asked Abbey.

'I don't know what to think,' said Suzanne. 'Obviously I was delighted when he left me money. I need it. But it was hard to hear that he'd given something to the boys before. Not that I should've been surprised.'

Abbey wondered if she was going to be approached by each individual member of the family, each with their own version of what should happen with Fred's will.

'And what he did for you . . .' Suzanne stirred her coffee idly, 'well, it leaves me wondering about the justice of it all, from everyone's perspective.'

'Me too,' admitted Abbey.

'We didn't know anything about his relationship with the woman before my mother,' Suzanne said. 'Getting her pregnant obviously made it significant, but the truth is that Dad had plenty of other relationships afterwards that could have been significant too.'

Abbey's eyes widened. 'Afterwards? After he got married, you mean?'

'He was an unfaithful sod,' said Suzanne. 'God knows how many other half-siblings we might have.'

'You can't be serious.'

'*You* exist,' Suzanne pointed out.

'I'm not actually your half-sibling,' Abbey reminded her. 'My mom is. So if there are others, they're probably a lot older than me. At least . . .' She wondered for how long Fred had carried on his extramarital affairs. If he was the sort of old stud that Suzanne seemed to think, he could have been having relationships after his wife had died, right up to his own death. Which left all sorts of possibilities open. 'Regardless,' she added, 'he didn't mention them in his will. I don't think they can come chasing you for more of a cut, if that's what you're worried about.'

Suzanne was startled by the sudden waspish note in Abbey's voice as she finished the sentence.

'I wasn't thinking that,' she said. 'I was wondering if . . . if there could be more Fitzpatricks out there, that's all.' She could see that Abbey wasn't convinced. 'You believe that all I care about is what my father left and who might claim it. That's not true.'

'Seems to me it's what all of you believe,' said Abbey. 'At least as far as me and my mom are concerned.'

'Is she really a nun?' There was an edge of scepticism in Suzanne's voice. 'That's so bizarre.'

'Sure is.'

'D'you know, if you'd said she'd become a Buddhist monk or something I'd have believed it quicker,' Suzanne said. 'The whole Catholic thing seems so out of date.'

Abbey couldn't help smiling. 'I once said that to her too. She was always a bit hippy-freaky. And a bit of a rebel. So I find it hard to believe that she's contentedly living by the rulebook in the monastery. Which, as I said already, is a Christian community, not specifically Catholic, not that it makes much difference, I guess.'

'So have you been in touch with her?'

'No. I've sent a request to the prioress to meet her. But to be perfectly honest, I haven't a clue what I'm going to say. Or what she'll say either.'

'Maybe she'll take a very Christian view and say that no matter what happens, she'll gift it back to the family.'

'That's what all of you want, isn't it?'

Suzanne hesitated. 'Part of me thinks that's what's fair,' she said eventually. 'But then I think of your mom being handed over to strangers and hauled off to America and airbrushed out of my dad's past, and I can't help feeling that she's entitled to something.'

'But not that I am,' observed Abbey.

'It's a lot,' said Suzanne.

'I know.'

The two of them sat silently for a while, then Suzanne spoke again. 'I'm using my share of the money for a hotel,' she said.

Abbey looked at her curiously and Suzanne explained about the Mirador.

'That's very entrepreneurial of you,' said Abbey.

'I like to do my own thing,' Suzanne said. 'I love managing the El Boganto, but this would be a step up.'

'It sounds lovely.'

'Why don't you come?' Suzanne made the suggestion without giving it much thought. 'Stay with me for a few days.'

'So that I can see that you need more of your father's money?' asked Abbey.

'I wasn't thinking like that,' said Suzanne. 'But I guess you have a point.'

Abbey stayed silent.

'You're not as sweet and helpless as you seem, are you?' Suzanne's tone was thoughtful.

'Do I seem sweet and helpless to you?'

'A little,' said Suzanne. 'But you've clearly got some Fitzpatrick blood in you somewhere. You've got some inner toughness too.'

Abbey was taken aback. Nobody had ever called her tough before.

'Do you want to visit?' asked Suzanne. 'No strings, Abbey, I promise. I'd like . . . well, y'see, I was the only girl. It's interesting to have another female Fitzpatrick around. It would be nice to get to know you a bit better.'

'I'm not a Fitzpatrick, I'm an Andersen,' said Abbey. 'Besides, I have to get back to the States.'

'Why?'

'I have a job.'

'Doing nails.'

'And what's wrong with that?' Abbey hated sounding defensive.

'Nothing at all. But you can surely take some time out from it without the world crashing down around your ears?'

'I'm not sure most of my clients would agree,' Abbey told her. 'If the world was crashing down around their ears, they'd want to be sure that at least their nails looked good while it was happening.'

Suzanne laughed. 'Fair enough. But I'd like you to come. I'd like to get to know you better.'

So that you can ask me to hand over more money to you? wondered Abbey. So that you can buy your hotel?

'I'll think about it,' she said.

'OK, I'll admit it.' Suzanne looked sheepish. 'I want to freak the boys out.'

'Why?'

'One of us getting friendly with the heiress,' she said. 'They wouldn't take that at all well.'

'Divide and conquer?'

'Something like that.'

Abbey finished her coffee. 'I don't know what my plans are yet, but I'll tell you when I do.'

'Sure.' Suzanne drained her cup too and then stood up. 'No matter what we think, and no matter what I might say to you, you're entitled to whatever Dad gave you. Don't feel bad about it.'

'If your brothers get their way, I won't be seeing any of it,' said Abbey. 'So don't you feel bad about that either.'

'You're definitely tougher than you look,' murmured Suzanne.

'Perhaps everybody is,' said Abbey.

'Coming back?' Suzanne slung her bag over her shoulder.

'I think I'll stay here a bit longer,' Abbey told her. 'My head still hurts.'

She finally rang Pete and told him everything. He gave a long, low whistle before saying that it was a good thing she'd gone to Ireland because otherwise the old man wouldn't have given her anything. Obviously Fred had drawn up the will in anticipation of meeting her, and if he hadn't liked her, he would've torn it up. If she'd refused to meet him, he wouldn't have left her anything at all. It was possible, remarked Pete, that the grinding sound she'd heard had been him shredding the previous will. Abbey said that it would've been far more sensible for him to have drawn up the will that favoured her and her mother but not to have signed it until after they'd met. Pete said that older people did strange things sometimes but it was as well he hadn't waited to sign it, because otherwise he would've popped his clogs without leaving her anything. He also said that he was certain the courts would find in her and Ellen's favour. After all, Fred had brought the will to his solicitor to be witnessed, the solicitor himself was the executor, and there was no obligation on the old man to leave anything to his children. Families often wanted to contest wills because they didn't like what was in them, but the courts weren't concerned with what they liked or didn't like. The courts only wanted to ensure that the dead man's last wishes were carried out. Given that Fred had no dependent children it was entirely up to him what he did with it.

'So I doubt they'll succeed in changing it,' he finished. 'If it was my case, I'd be very confident fighting against them.'

Abbey explained about Fred's dislike of nuns and the Fitzpatricks' belief that they could use that as a basis to challenge the will if necessary.

'Not relevant,' said Pete. 'You've hit the jackpot, honey.'

'That seems to be the general view, but I didn't come here to hit the jackpot.'

'All the same, you have. And I'd take up the sister on her offer to visit her in Spain, too. Find out what makes her tick. Of course she has her own selfish reasons for asking you. Do likewise. Keep your friends close and your enemies closer.'

'She's not an enemy.'

'Don't be so naive,' said Pete.

'Hmm. Well, right now I'm not sure about staying with her. I only have a few hundred left in my checking account and I don't want to load up my credit card . . .'

247

'Abbey Andersen! Didn't you just say you've been left a house worth a couple of million?'

'Me and Mom.'

'And five thousand in cash?'

She'd completely forgotten about that. The drama about the house had pushed it out of her mind.

'So you can afford to spend some of it.'

'I'm sure I won't see that for ages yet. Besides, I don't feel it's mine to spend.'

'Yes it is,' said Pete. 'You're a good person, Abbey. Your mom is a good person. Why shouldn't you both be rewarded?'

'What sort of karma is it to take what we're given when the rest of them will hate us for ever?'

'Your mom doesn't believe in karma,' Pete reminded her. 'She's a reward and punishment person. And it's time for you to collect your reward.'

'It sounds almost reasonable the way you say it.'

'Because it is,' said Pete. 'You're entitled to that money and you're taking it for yourselves and for that girl, Dilly, too. Don't forget her. She's why he wanted you to have it.'

'I can't forget her,' confessed Abbey. 'I keep thinking about her and how terrible things were for her.'

'She was your grandmother, Abbey. She was connected to you. That's why Mr Fitzpatrick is leaving you and your mom the house,' said Pete. 'So suck it up, honey. Take what you've been given and move on.'

'It all seems so black and white when I'm talking to you,' she said.

'Good. That's how you've got to see it. In the meantime, though, don't let any of them pressurise you. Go to Spain, get to know this Suzanne woman. Think of this as a business opportunity.'

Abbey could understand why Pete might have that view. He was a lawyer, after all; they saw opportunity all the time. But she didn't have that perspective and she couldn't help thinking that perhaps this apparent inheritance was nothing more than a millstone around her neck, making people hate her and her mom. She'd never felt hated before. But then she'd never been rich before either.

Chapter 25

She was at breakfast the following morning when Donald and Gareth Fitzpatrick strode into the hotel and sat down at the table opposite her. She felt at a total disadvantage because when they arrived she was tucking into what was known as a full Irish, with bacon, sausage, tomato, egg and mushrooms, along with granary toast and home-made marmalade. It felt to Abbey as though she were feasting on their father's account as she wiped away the crumbs from her mouth and offered them coffee.

Even though Donald said that they hadn't come for coffee and pleasantries, neither he nor his brother objected when the waitress placed two cups in front of them and brought another cafetière, along with more toast, to the table.

'My father is paying for it,' said Donald as he filled his cup. 'So I suppose we might as well have something.'

Abbey didn't know what to say to the two men. She wondered if Suzanne (who she never saw at breakfast) knew that they were here.

'OK,' said Donald after he'd added milk and sugar to his coffee and buttered himself a slice of toast. 'We're here to tell you that you'd better do the right thing and give up any thoughts of getting your hands on our house.'

'You're not entitled to anything from my father,' Gareth told her. 'And for you to think otherwise is nonsense.'

'We want to do this as cheaply and as easily as possible,' Donald continued. 'We'll offer you and your mother twenty-five grand each to forget this ever happened.'

'Quite frankly, we think that's more than enough to assuage our father's misplaced sense of guilt,' said Gareth. 'It's the same sum as he left us and his grandchildren, so it seems perfectly fair to us.'

'We assume you'll do the right thing,' said Donald.

'Especially given that your mother is apparently a religious person and will immediately realise the injustice of what's happened here.'

'If you don't give it up, we'll go to court and we'll win,' said Donald. 'Don't underestimate our ability to get this done.'

'Or our ability to portray you as a money-sucking leech.' Gareth spoke bitterly as he refilled his cup.

'We're Dad's true heirs,' Donald said. 'His sons. We're entitled to that house and we're going to have it.'

'What about Suzanne?' asked Abbey as the brothers finally stopped talking.

'Suzanne has been well looked after,' replied Donald. 'A quarter of a million! She can probably hardly believe her luck.'

'But didn't you two get money before?' asked Abbey.

'That was different,' said Donald. 'Dad was entitled to give it to us.'

'But not to Suzanne?'

'Suzanne is none of your damn business,' Donald said. 'Nothing that goes on in this family is any of your damn business and you'd better get that into your head. You and your mother are nobody to us. Nobody.'

'We're the people who've been left your father's house,' said Abbey. 'That means we're somebody.'

'You don't have any rights to that house,' said Gareth. 'You have to see that.'

'So what happens if we give it up?' asked Abbey.

'You get your fifty grand and you're out of our lives for ever,' replied Donald.

Abbey stared at the brothers. 'You don't want to keep in touch or anything like that? You don't want to get to know me, or Mom?'

'Why would we?' asked Gareth. 'You're nothing to do with us.'

'But we are,' said Abbey. 'I saw it myself. Suzanne is so like my mom it's untrue.'

'Wishful thinking.' Donald's words were dismissive.

'No,' said Abbey. 'Inherited genes.'

'You're not part of the family,' said Gareth again. 'You live a different life. On a different continent, for heaven's sake. You've nothing to do with us and you never will have. This . . . situation should never have arisen in the first place. It only happened because Dad was old and easily confused.'

'I see,' said Abbey.

'So you've got to do the right thing,' Donald told her. 'Look, maybe you're thinking that we're here playing the big bad wolf, trying to grab money for ourselves when we're already loaded. But that's not the case. I'm a divorced man with a demanding first family and an extravagant second wife. I have debts and obligations and I need the money that the house will bring.'

'All right.' Abbey turned to Gareth. 'And your reason for wanting everything is . . .?'

'The financial crisis of the last few years has caused me a lot of trouble,' said Gareth. 'My property investments are under water and it'll take a long time for them to come back to the surface again. I need hard cash, and soon.'

'So you see, Abbey, we're under a lot of pressure and you can't spend time swanning around thinking about things. You've got to do the only right thing now and end this once and for all,' Donald said. 'Most importantly, neither you nor your mother were relevant to my father and we shouldn't have to be worried about what you want now. Dad lived his life without you and without caring about you and you got on fine without him. There's no need to try to make us all one family. We're not and we never will be.'

'Regardless of what I think or what I might do, I still have to talk to my mom,' Abbey reminded them.

'You mean you haven't spoken to her yet?' Donald looked incredulous.

'I've emailed the monastery. Sister Inez will set something up as soon as my mom is available.'

'When will that be?' demanded Gareth.

'I don't know.'

'Call her again,' ordered Donald. 'Tell her how urgent it is.'

'It's the middle of the night on the West Coast right now,' Abbey reminded him. 'But Sister Inez knows it's urgent. She'll organise the meeting as soon as she can.'

'See that she does,' Donald said. 'My brother and I don't have time to faff around. We want our inheritance and we don't need you delaying matters.'

Abbey looked at them enquiringly.

'Suzanne doesn't fit into it at all as far as you're concerned?'

'What's your obsession with Suzanne?' demanded Donald. 'Is this some girl-power thing? Do you think she will be on your side? She won't. Suzanne only looks out for herself.'

'She was never here,' said Gareth. 'She left us. She doesn't deserve anything.'

'You clearly link deserving something with being in Ireland,' said Abbey.

'Too right,' said Donald. 'We put up with him. Me and Gar and Zoey and Lisette. We looked after him. We're the people who matter.'

'And we damn well need the money!' Gareth's voice rose as he spoke and a few of the other guests looked around at their table.

'You don't realise what we've been through over the last few years,' he said more quietly. 'Everyone in Ireland has lost money. So have we. We need to be compensated.'

'You messed up your lives and your investments and now you want your dead father to bail you out?'

'Don't get stroppy with us.' Donald's eyes narrowed. 'You don't want us as enemies, Abbey Andersen.'

'I think you already are,' she said.

'We've made you a fair offer,' Gareth told her. 'Take it and get out of our hair.'

'I'm not sure that anyone else would think fifty K was fair,' she said.

Donald turned to his brother. 'Y'see,' he said. 'Like I told you. A couple of weeks ago she didn't know we existed. A couple of weeks ago she probably would've jumped at the chance of fifty K, but now she wants everything.'

'I don't!' cried Abbey. 'But . . .'

'But nothing.' Donald stood up. 'You have twenty-four hours to accept our offer, and after that we're going to court.'

'Don't be so damn silly,' said Abbey. 'What are the chances of you winning a court case against me? Your father left me and Mom that house and you don't have a good case.'

'Who told you that?' asked Gareth.

'I spoke to my . . . a friend back home,' Abbey replied. 'He's a lawyer. He—'

'So you haven't been able to talk to your mother but you've already been in touch with a lawyer!' Donald's face was like thunder. 'That takes the biscuit, it really does. My father was off his trolley when he wrote that will. And I'm still not convinced that you didn't say or do something to cause him to have that heart attack.'

Abbey's eyes widened, but Gareth put his hand on his brother's arm.

'Cool it, Don,' he said.

'Whatever.' Donald shook himself free. 'What's happened is plain wrong and I want to fix it. For me and my family. Which doesn't include you, little Miss American Pie. Twenty-four hours. And that's that.'

He stood up from the table. Gareth did too. Then they both walked out of the breakfast room, leaving Abbey staring after them.

* * *

254

While Donald and Gareth were meeting Abbey, Zoey decided to call to her mother's. As soon as she walked into the house, Lesley told her to sit down and fill her in on what was going on.

'Let's face it, Donald is right. That woman and her daughter aren't family. You are,' she said.

'Too right,' agreed Zoey. 'But what we believe and what the court says . . .' She tapped her fingers on the arm of the chair. 'Oh Mum, I want that house. I've always wanted it.'

'It's a nice property,' agreed Lesley. 'Take a lot of cash to bring it up to scratch, though.'

'We could borrow.' Zoey made a face. 'Aargh, this is *so* not how I expected things to turn out when I married Don!'

'Do you love him?' Lesley had never asked Zoey that question before.

'Of course I love him,' Zoey replied. 'He's a good man. But I didn't think I'd have to be listening to him whingeing on about his bloody ex all the time, or paying off those daughters of his. I put up with it because I thought we'd win out in the end, but now . . .'

'You're still young,' said Lesley. 'If you don't think you're going to get what you want from the marriage, maybe you need to reconsider.'

'That makes it sound like I only married him for the money,' said Zoey. 'It was more than that and you know it. He's good and caring, and he can be generous when he puts his mind to it. It's just that he doesn't have as much to be generous with as I thought.'

'I'm trying to be practical,' said Lesley.

'I know.' Zoey leaned back in the armchair and closed her eyes. 'Stupid old fool, why didn't he keep it in his pants?'

'He was in his twenties back then,' said Lesley. 'None of them do then. None of them do any time, if you ask me.'

Zoey opened her eyes again and laughed. 'They're so easily led, aren't they?'

'Too right. What about the jewellery he left you? What's that like?'

'His dead wife's jewellery.' Zoey made a face. 'How could he even think I'd want any of that! Some of it isn't too bad – there's a couple of gold chains and a silver bracelet that aren't too horrific – but mostly it's crummy costume jewellery and old-lady brooches. I don't think it's even worth trying to flog, and if I did I'm sure Don would have a fit anyhow. But until we sort out the whole will thing, I can't even get my hands on that.'

'Maybe you should get to know the American girl a bit better. Try to appeal to her good side.'

'She'd see right through that,' said Zoey. 'She pretends to be syrupy sweet but I don't think she is at all.'

'I know men always go headlong into things,' said Lesley. 'But there's more than one way to skin a cat.'

Her mother was right, thought Zoey. Although she wasn't entirely sure that Abbey Andersen was a cat who'd let herself get skinned.

Lisette was searching the internet for information on inheritance law. None of the cases that she was reading about sounded like Fred's. Mostly it was old men who'd left their fortune to a young second wife and completely neglected the first family. Understandably in these cases the family insisted that the dead man had been coerced into it by his new wife. The other cases usually concerned old dears who'd left millions to their pet cat or dog. There were no cases of men leaving money to women who were the antithesis of everything he believed in. Lisette was a hundred per cent certain that if Fred had known that his long-lost daughter was a nun, he wouldn't have left the house to her. As for Abbey – Lisette's views echoed Donald's as far as she was concerned. She was convinced that the American girl had somehow persuaded Fred to include her in the bequest. Maybe because she was afraid there'd be a problem about a legacy to her mother. Perhaps the courts would see that too. But even so, Abbey would get half the value of the house.

Lisette grimaced. Half of Furze Hill divided between Gareth and Donald would be better than nothing. But it wasn't anything like what they'd originally hoped for. In the meantime, she couldn't even take the bloody silverware that Fred had left her. She hadn't said anything to Gareth, but she was hoping that maybe one or two of the pieces could be valuable. Not *Antiques Roadshow* material. Not the kind of valuable that made you gasp in surprise. But worth a few thousand anyway.

Still, none of that was enough. None of that could set them back on the road to security. None of that could stop Gareth looking at Papillon and thinking that selling their beautiful French home would solve everything. Damn you, Fred, she thought. Damn you for snatching away everything we hoped for. She leaned her head on the table and started to cry.

Chapter 26

The double doors leading on to the tiny terrace outside Abbey's room at the El Boganto hotel were open, and the sound of laughter and conversation wafted up from the street below. Through the windows she could see a hodgepodge of buildings of various heights, backed by the magnificent cathedral – the pealing bells of which had woken her at seven that morning. She'd got up straight away and followed the aroma of coffee to the breakfast room – a converted cellar with narrow windows which allowed diners to see the feet of the people in the street outside.

She'd been finishing her second cup of coffee (and thinking that the El Boganto was far better at it than the Harbour Hotel had been) when Suzanne came in, expressing surprise that she was up so early.

'The bells,' explained Abbey, and Suzanne nodded.

'I'm used to them by now,' she said. 'But they can be a bit of a shock.'

Suzanne told Abbey that, having been in Dublin for the best part of a week, she had lots to do, but she armed her with maps and informational leaflets and told her to explore the city.

'We can meet up for dinner if you like?' she offered, and Abbey said she looked forward to it.

Abbey had spent most of the day wandering around the old city, losing herself in the narrow maze of streets, hearing the excited clamour of voices, recognising the Spanish and remembering the times she and her mom had walked through the streets of cities or towns in Colombia or Venezuela or Ecuador. She recalled those days with a mixture of happiness and regret. She'd loved being part of her mom's life. 'You and me against the world,' Ellen had sometimes said, and her words had strengthened Abbey, made her feel important. Yet she'd also felt angry with Ellen too – when her mother told her that they were moving on, leaving whatever town it was she'd come to love, to start over somewhere else, thinking that it wasn't really her mom and her together but her mom alone who took on the world.

When they'd returned to San Francisco, Abbey was utterly determined that there would be no more uprooting, although even then they'd ended up in Boston when her grandparents had fallen ill. She hadn't wanted to go to Boston either, she remembered, crying bitter tears the night before they left, saying that Pete wouldn't be waiting for them when they got back.

But Ellen had insisted. They were her parents, she said. She loved them and it was her duty to care for them. She was prepared to put their needs ahead of her own, and ahead of Abbey's too. That didn't surprise Abbey, who knew that Ellen was the sort of woman who made it her mission in life to look after people, whether they were close to her or complete strangers. It was her nature and she couldn't have gone against it. But what she'd done afterwards, shutting herself away in the monastery, was something Abbey still didn't understand. Before she'd gone, Ellen had said that she'd be looking after people spiritually instead of physically, and Abbey had suggested that in that case she should become a counsellor instead, but Ellen had shaken her head and told her that this was the path she wanted to take.

Yet even though it was a long time since Ellen had chosen to go to Los Montesinos, and even though she knew that her mother would soon make her final profession, there was still a part of Abbey that expected her to throw it all in and turn up on her doorstep again. It was hard for her to believe that a woman who hadn't been able to stay in one place for more than a couple of years would have so contentedly set down her roots on the border between California and Mexico. Abbey had never stopped imagining the day when Ellen would return to San Francisco, telling her that it had all been a terrible mistake.

Which made it all the more extraordinary that she'd gone to Ireland to see Fred and had then made the sudden decision to come to Girona after all. Her reasons were complex and not entirely clear even to herself. But of all the Fitzpatricks it was Suzanne who seemed to be the least hostile and the most sensible. And the one most likely to give her some good advice. I could be wrong about her, of course, thought Abbey. Just because she reminds me of Mom doesn't mean she's in any way like her.

They hadn't travelled together. Suzanne's flight was fully booked and so Abbey had to wait until a day later, which had allowed her time to meet with Alex before she left. Alex was surprised when she told him that she was going to Spain, and asked if Don and Gareth knew about her proposed trip.

'I don't know,' replied Abbey, who went on to tell him about their visit to the hotel.

'Fools,' said Alex. 'They shouldn't harass you like that.'

'Do you think I'd be better off not visiting Suzanne either?' asked Abbey. 'I guess they'll freak out at that.'

'I don't imagine they'll be very pleased. But it's entirely up to you, Abbey. What's not up to you, though, is that you absolutely have to inform your mother about this situation as soon as possible.'

'I spoke to the prioress last night,' said Abbey. 'I'll be able to see Mom as soon as I get home.'

'Good.' Alex was pleased. 'Once I know how you're both thinking, I can be fully prepared for every eventuality.'

'Everyone's so emotional about it,' said Abbey. 'It scares me sometimes.'

'People can get extremely emotional about wills,' said Alex. 'You'd be surprised how often they fight about them. I've had to defend myself as an executor before, and the whole process can split families for good.'

Abbey looked at him curiously. 'Do you think it's right to get into a fight over it?' she asked.

'Fred Fitzpatrick was perfectly clear in what he wanted, and even though he drew up that will himself, he knew what he was doing,' Alex told her. 'You and your mother can, of course, renounce your inheritance, which would go back into the estate and be divided up among the children. But if either of you renounced your half solely, it would go to the other one of you. For instance, if you yourself decided you wanted to give up your share of the house, it would automatically go to your mother. Which would bring us back to square one as far as everyone else is concerned.'

Abbey groaned. 'How much more tangled can this get?'

'The big thing that I want you to think about,' said Alex, 'is what Mr Fitzpatrick wanted. The will represents his wishes. Not his family's. He wanted you and your mum to have something. So even if both of you wanted to hand it back to the family – for whatever reason – I have to tell you that Mr Fitzpatrick would be very hurt by that.'

'Mr Fitzpatrick is dead,' said Abbey. 'He can't be hurt. But other people can.'

'Nevertheless,' said Alex. 'It was what he wanted, so that he could rest in peace.'

Abbey was startled. She didn't believe that Fred Fitzpatrick was watching over them, or that he would be unable to live some kind of eternal life unless his wishes were carried out.

'Maybe it'll be clearer after I talk to my mom.' Perhaps Ellen agreed with Alex, although Abbey was sure that the monastery frowned on the idea of restless spirits wandering around in the afterlife.

'Let me know as soon as you speak to her,' said Alex as she got up to leave. 'Meantime, I'm going to delay probate on the basis that there might be a challenge to the will from the rest of the family. Or from Donald and Gareth, at any rate.'

'OK,' said Abbey.

'Enjoy your trip to Spain.'

'Hopefully I will,' she said, although a part of her was expecting some kind of onslaught from Suzanne too.

It was almost nine before she and Suzanne met for dinner, but it was still warm outside and the streets were thronged with people. Suzanne steered her towards a café-bar near the church of St Felix. Students were sitting on the church steps chattering into mobile phones while watching tourists kiss the replica of the nearby stone lion – a tradition to ensure they'd return, Suzanne said as she found them a table and then waved at a waiter.

'Did you have a good day?' she asked when they'd ordered food and drink (tuna for Abbey, prawns for Suzanne and a glass of Viña Esmeralda each).

Abbey gave her a detailed account of her tour of the city and Suzanne looked impressed, although she remarked that Abbey must be exhausted.

'To be honest, it's such a long time since I was anywhere new, I couldn't help myself,' Abbey told her.

'What about Dublin?'

'I was too busy in Dublin for sightseeing.'

'Of course you were. Busy trying to save Dad's life and then busy talking to the hunky solicitor,' said Suzanne.

Abbey hadn't got used to the fact that lawyers and attorneys seemed to be called solicitors in Ireland. To her, it sounded like a form of prostitution. Although Pete had once remarked that being a lawyer kinda was.

'I think he's ticked off at me for not telling him about Mom.'

'It was a big omission,' said Suzanne.

'I know. But there was a part of me that didn't quite believe his story and I didn't want anyone trying to hassle her.'

'You're very protective of her,' said Suzanne. 'But she's a grown woman, she can look after herself, and I bet they all flock around each other in that convent anyway.'

'It's a monastery,' Abbey corrected her. 'And yes, it's a big support for her. Sometimes I think that's why she joined in the first place.'

'Oh?' Suzanne was interested. 'What makes you think she needed that kind of support?'

Abbey hesitated before speaking. 'It seemed to me that as she didn't have to look after me any more, and after the death of her parents, she needed something else.'

'Could be.' Suzanne sounded doubtful. 'Or it could be that she's just a religious woman.'

'She's certainly a very caring woman,' said Abbey. 'And she's had a lot to deal with.' She told Suzanne about her own father's death. 'So I guess I can't complain that she found God. It's not how I deal with stuff, but each to her own.'

'And how do you deal with stuff, Abbey Andersen?' asked Suzanne.

'Oh, I don't have anything much to deal with right now.' Even as she spoke, Abbey realised that she hadn't thought about Cobey Missen and his treatment of her for ages. What a way to mend a broken heart, she thought. She couldn't help thinking too that her wallet would also be mended if everything went her way.

'Are you a career girl? How's the nail business?'

'It's not exactly a major career, but it's good,' said Abbey.

'Those pictures you showed me were amazing,' Suzanne said. 'I can hardly slap on a coat of varnish without making a mess of it. It must be very difficult.'

'I guess it's a skill like any other,' said Abbey. 'I've always been good at it.'

'Can you teach it?' asked Suzanne. 'I mean you personally, can you teach people how to do it?'

Abbey looked at her curiously. 'I've never tried.'

Suzanne told her about her idea to have a pretty nail bar at the Mirador, offering manicures and holiday designs to the guests.

'You haven't got the hotel yet,' Abbey reminded her.

'True.' A worried expression flitted across Suzanne's face. 'But I'm a determined person. I'm doing my damnedest.'

'You're like my mom, how she used to be,' said Abbey. 'When we travelled around together. She was very determined then. Religious life has softened her.'

'How did you really feel when she said she was joining the nuns?' asked Suzanne.

'Shocked,' confessed Abbey. 'Especially because of the life they live. If she'd said she was becoming a nun and going to work with the disadvantaged in the city, I could have understood it more. But locking herself away . . .'

'I can't believe anyone would cut themselves off from the world any more,' said Suzanne.

Abbey explained about the website and the social media, which made Suzanne laugh.

'Religion in the digital age. I must check out the site.' She sat back and looked at Abbey. 'So on the basis that she's not locked away in a dungeon somewhere praying her socks off, why didn't you email or call your mother the minute you heard about Dad?'

'Because I don't know if she knows about being adopted or not. I realise she should be able to fall back on God and her faith and all that sort of stuff, but it wouldn't have been right to spring it on her like that. In any event, she was leading a retreat at the time, which meant it wasn't possible to get in touch with her.'

'How often do you two talk?'

'I email her occasionally and we meet up once or twice a year, but . . . I'm not a major part of her life any more, to be honest, and I'm never sure what to say to her.'

'You've had more contact with her than I had with my mum after I left Ireland,' remarked Suzanne.

'It's all a question of perspective, I guess,' said Abbey. 'I think she probably gets on better with people she doesn't know personally.'

'Do they do a lot of praying?' asked Suzanne.

One of the reasons Abbey rarely talked about her mother was because she got tired of replying to a barrage of questions similar to the ones Suzanne was posing now. But talking to Suzanne was different. Talking to Suzanne was like talking to an old friend. She explained that the nuns' days were crafted around prayer and meditation, although every nun had her own particular work to do within the monastery too.

'It wouldn't be my thing,' said Suzanne.

'Mine neither,' agreed Abbey. 'But it seems to suit Mom, and the nuns are lovely people, even if they're bit too good sometimes. It can be exhausting.'

Suzanne looked pensive. 'There's probably all sorts of petty rivalries and intrigue under the surface. It's a gang of women living together, after all. A potent mix.'

'Possibly,' said Abbey. 'But they present a very calm exterior.'

'What do you think your mum's reaction to her inheritance will be?'

'A normal person would be shocked, but nothing seems to shock her.'

'You know my brothers are convinced you and your mum already have a strategy worked out, don't you?'

'They think you have one too.' Abbey recounted their visit to Suzanne, who pursed her lips.

'They're so fecking self-centred,' she said. 'And they don't give a toss about anyone other than themselves. Maybe that's why Dad decided to leave the house to someone else entirely.'

Abbey looked surprised. 'He didn't know us.'

'But he knows Gar and Don,' said Suzanne. 'Only too well. I'm surprised at Gar, though. He's normally the more sensitive of the two.'

Abbey told her about Gareth's plummeting property portfolio and Suzanne's eyes widened.

'What an eejit,' she said. 'He hasn't a commercial bone in his body. No wonder it all went pear-shaped.'

Abbey said nothing, but busied herself with her food. She was thinking that perhaps Suzanne really was the one with the strategy, or that her brothers had secretly charged her with the task of sussing Abbey out, softening her up even. But if that wasn't the case, and the family was split about it, Suzanne clearly had her own agenda too. Perhaps suggesting that Abbey train her as yet non-existent staff in nail art was part of a plan to butter her up, get her to trust her.

Money was such a game-changer, whether you had it or you didn't, she thought. Ellen had always said that the pursuit of money was a soul-destroying exercise. Pete believed that with money came choices. Abbey supposed that they were both right to some degree but that neither had the right answer.

'You OK?' asked Suzanne after Abbey hadn't spoken for a few minutes.

'Oh, sure. Thinking about stuff.'

'Lots to think about,' agreed Suzanne. 'Listen, tomorrow I'm going out to the hotel I'm trying to buy. Want to come with me? See what sort of place it is – advise me on a good spot for the nail bar?' Her eyes twinkled and Abbey couldn't help smiling, even though Pete's advice about keeping your enemies close was still fresh in her mind.

She told Suzanne she'd be delighted to come along, and then spent the rest of the evening listening to her mother's half-sister talk about growing up in Dublin and leaving home. She couldn't help thinking that Suzanne was very much like Ellen had been when she was younger – full of brightness and enthusiasm and a belief that you could do anything you wanted. Which, as it turned out, Ellen had.

*   *   *

266

The next morning, Suzanne drove down the coast to the Mirador Hotel, stopping at the offices of the estate agency to pick up the keys from Jaime.

'There are other people interested,' he told her as he handed them to her. 'If you want to buy this property, you will need to make a move.'

'Has anyone else put in an offer yet?' she asked.

He hesitated, then shrugged. 'Not a serious one.'

'Tell me if they do.'

He winked at her, and she hurried out of the office and back into the car. She hoped he was just trying to scare her. She didn't want to think that this thing could get competitive.

When they drew up in front of the hotel, Abbey exclaimed with pleasure, both at the building and at the views across the Mediterranean.

'Nearly as nice as Big Sur,' she said. 'Maybe even a little better because there's no mist. It's superb.'

'It's better still from the top floor,' said Suzanne. 'C'mon. Follow me.'

She unlocked the building, and once again Abbey exclaimed in delight, this time over the old-fashioned lift that had so charmed Suzanne herself.

'You're right about the views,' she said when they were standing on a tiny balcony leading off one of the rooms. 'It's stunning. Are you really hoping to buy this place?'

'Yes,' said Suzanne. 'And obviously Dad's money would come in handy.'

'I hope it all works out,' said Abbey.

'So do I.' Suzanne stepped back inside the room. 'I'm meeting my bank manager and my other investors tomorrow. I'll be showing the bank a copy of the will. Hopefully on the back of that they'll lend me the money Dad left me.'

'You're going to put *all* of it into the hotel?' Abbey was surprised.

'It's my life,' said Suzanne. 'My passion. It's what I always wanted to do.'

'But you surely need more than what your father left to buy this.'

'Of course I do. That's why there's a consortium. And I know you're thinking that's the reason I asked you here too. Maybe it'd be a great investment, but you'd never be able to sell Furze Hill in time, and it could all be horribly delayed anyway by whatever madness the boys cook up. Besides, even though I meant it about you giving advice regarding a nail bar, it's not always a good idea to go into business with your family.'

'You can't truly think of me as being part of it,' said Abbey. 'I'm only your half-sister's daughter after all.'

'Good enough for me.' Suzanne's blue eyes sparkled and Abbey couldn't help smiling.

So like Ellen, she thought, as she followed Suzanne downstairs again. Although thankfully without the desire to do good in the world. There was only so much of that you could take in a family.

Chapter 27

Abbey had to stop over in Ireland again before catching her flight to the States. She called Ryan Gilligan to let him know she was back on Irish soil, even though she'd barely spoken to him since the moment she'd revealed that Ellen was a nun.

His voice was warm but, she thought, more reserved than previously as he told her that he'd received a letter from Donald and Gareth's new solicitors claiming that Fred had been of unsound mind and unduly influenced when he wrote the will.

'By me?' she asked. 'That's not possible.'

'Doesn't matter. They'll have a go anyway. There's always something they can pursue.'

'Pete Caruso wanted me to study law,' she remarked. 'I'm so glad I didn't. It's a battlefield. And relatively speaking this is a small thing, isn't it?'

'Small in one sense but big for the people involved,' said Ryan. 'Which is something we always try to remember.'

'Is it?'

'Yes.' His voice softened some more. 'Yes, it is.'

'That's good to know.'

'What time's your flight?' he asked.

'Three o'clock,' she replied.

'Well, look, have a good one. I'll be in touch as soon as there's any news.'

'Sure.'

She ended the call. It would probably be ages before she heard from him again.

She didn't stay in the Harbour Hotel this time, but booked into the Clarion, which was located in the grounds of the airport itself. From there she took a bus into the city centre and acted like a tourist, visiting Christ Church Cathedral (so that she could tell her mom she'd given a few moments of her time to God), then Dublin Castle and Trinity College before buying herself an authentic Aran jumper in Dawson Street. The jumper would be useful, she thought, in the chillier days that were beginning to roll in. And it would be a reminder of her tenuous roots here. She didn't know when or if she'd be back. She supposed she'd have to return sometime in the future for the legal action, if it got that far. But that would certainly be a long way off.

She wore the jumper the following day because the weather had turned cold and grey. She liked the feel of the rough wool against her bare arms and the way the jumper seemed to insulate her from the chill breeze. It felt good to be protected.

She got off the courtesy bus from the hotel and pulled her case into the terminal building. She'd already checked in online and so she only had to make her way to the departure gates. She was standing on the escalator when she heard her name being called. She looked around in surprise to see Ryan Gilligan a few steps behind her.

'What are you doing here?' she asked when he joined her on the upper level.

'I came to say goodbye, of course.'

'I didn't think you wanted to see me again,' she said. 'I thought you were sore at me for not telling you about my mom.'

'Ah, now, don't be like that.' His voice was gently teasing. 'My pride was hurt because you hadn't trusted me, but I'm over that now. I had to come and say goodbye. But I nearly didn't recognise you, and you all done up like an Irish cailín.'

'An Irish what?'

'Don't you know anything about your roots?' he demanded, though his eyes were twinkling. 'A cailín. A young girl.' He tapped the Aran jumper. 'Anyone would think you'd been born and raised here.'

She laughed. 'I haven't seen any Irish person wearing one of these jumpers yet. But they're cute. And warm.'

'There's a bit of a myth that the patterns are individual family designs,' Ryan told her. 'So that if the wearer – originally fishermen – was drowned and his body washed up, he could be identified by the pattern.'

'Ugh!' She looked horrified.

'It's only a story,' he assured her. 'The designs are probably done by computer or something. But yours is a genuine home knit, isn't it?'

'I hope so,' she said. 'That's what they said in the shop.'

'You can wear it the next time you go to Alcatraz,' said Ryan. 'When it's properly misty and cold like they warn you.'

'Good idea.'

They stood in silence for a moment, then Ryan asked if she'd like a coffee before she went through the departure gates.

'I'd love one,' she replied.

When they were seated in the café, he asked her about her trip to Spain and what Suzanne's view of the will was. Abbey said that Suzanne could do with lots of money but that she seemed to be fatalistic about whatever would happen.

'She's like my mom in a lot of ways,' she finished.

Ryan raised an eyebrow quizzically.

'She is!' said Abbey.

'But she's quite glam, isn't she, and I can't see a nun being glam,' Ryan protested.

'I'm talking about her personality not her looks!' Abbey laughed, and Ryan grinned at her.

'D'you think she's friendlier than her brothers?'

'Less hostile, but who knows what that means.' She shrugged.

271

'I'm sure she'd be glad if she ended up with more of the estate, however that might happen. The extra money would come in useful for her.'

'Fred Fitzpatrick's legacy would be useful to you too, wouldn't it?'

'Yes. It would.'

'You're entitled to it,' he said. 'Despite everything they might tell you.'

'Alex made that perfectly clear.'

'Legal battles can be demanding,' Ryan said. 'Don't let them stress you out.'

'Is that you remembering that every one of your clients is a person?' She smiled at him.

'No,' he said. 'It's me being concerned for you. Like I said, battles can be stressful. Battles with money are the most stressful of all.'

'Maybe I should just join Mom in the monastery,' remarked Abbey. 'Then money would be irrelevant to me.'

'Ah no, don't do that.' Ryan looked at her in mock horror. 'You'd be totally wasted in a monastery, Abbey Andersen.'

She couldn't help smiling. 'You think?'

'Without a doubt.'

She stood up. 'I'd better go. Last thing I want is to miss my flight.'

Ryan waited while she gathered her things together.

'So, did you enjoy your time here?' he asked.

'Enjoy might be pushing it.' She grimaced. 'It was certainly interesting.'

'Well, look, we'll keep in touch about the will, and hopefully I'll see you again soon.'

He was a nice guy and she didn't mind the idea of seeing him again too. But right now all she wanted was to go home and leave Ireland behind.

'It was good meeting you,' he said.

'You too.'

They looked awkwardly at each other. Then he leaned forward and kissed her gently on the lips. She was startled by the sudden closeness of him, the scent of his body spray and the feeling of his mouth on hers.

'It's an Irish goodbye,' he told her.

'It is?' Her heart was racing.

'My Irish goodbye at any rate,' he said.

'Thank you,' she said. 'For everything.'

'See you again, Abbey Andersen.'

'Sure,' she said.

Although, she thought as she breathed slowly to calm her heart, maybe it would be better if she didn't.

The moment she stepped off the plane at San Francisco, she felt a wave of relief wash over her. She hadn't realised how tense the whole situation with the Fitzpatrick family had made her feel, and even the slightly less strained time she'd spent with Suzanne in Girona hadn't been entirely relaxing. When she walked into the arrivals hall and saw Pete waiting for her, she nearly cried with relief.

'Hiya, honey.' He wrapped her in a bear hug and then led her towards the car park. 'Welcome back to the good ol' US of A. How're you doing?'

'Exhausted,' she admitted. 'Though I think that's more from waiting for something horrible to happen rather than the jet lag.'

'Don't you worry, you're home now and we'll look after you.'

With every mile they drove, Abbey felt herself unwind more and more. Eventually Pete swung his 4x4 into the garage at Bella Vista Heights.

'You're staying here tonight,' he told her when she mentioned this. 'No question.'

She didn't argue. There was nowhere else for her to go.

Claudia was in the kitchen waiting for them when they entered the house. She greeted Abbey warmly and told her that it was

273

good to see her. Then she lifted a pot off the stove and said that she'd made pasta and salad for dinner.

'You're the best,' said Abbey.

'Thank you.' Claudia turned to Pete. 'Would you bring Abbey's case upstairs, honey? She has fifteen minutes to freshen up before we eat.'

Claudia was always precise in her timekeeping. Abbey was sure that Pete's wife had been watching the flight arrival time on the internet so that she could have the food ready almost as soon as they walked in the door. In reality, she would have loved to go straight to bed, but she couldn't ignore Claudia's hospitality. Besides, she was trespassing in her home again. She was definitely going to have to get her life into some kind of order, she thought. And soon.

When she came downstairs, Claudia and Pete as well as the children, Grady and Joely, were already sitting at the table waiting for her. Pete kept the conversation light and focused on the touristy things that Abbey had done until the two children had excused themselves and gone into the playroom to watch TV. Then he quizzed her in detail about the events of the past couple of weeks.

'Did they seem like family to you?' asked Claudia.

Was that a note of hope in her voice? wondered Abbey. A hope that perhaps she'd found some relatives of her own so that she didn't keep gatecrashing Claudia's home and family? She couldn't blame Claudia for thinking like that. It probably drove her nuts that Pete still cared for Abbey as though she were his daughter. Her own father, Jon, hadn't had any close family. She'd sometimes talked to Ellen about the Andersens when they were travelling together, but Jon's parents had divorced when they were younger and his father had moved to Tampa with his new wife. Jon hadn't kept in touch with his mother, who'd died shortly after he'd started med school. Abbey hadn't wanted to hear much more about her father's family after that, thinking that they'd all died young, and scared that they'd passed the gene on to her. (She knew that she was being irrational, especially as her father's death had been an accident, but she'd only been a kid at the time.) She suddenly thought of Fred Fitzpatrick, and wondered if she'd inherited his long-life gene as well as the supposed Fitzpatrick toughness.

'Abbey?'

She realised that she hadn't answered Claudia.

'Abbey's tired,' said Pete.

'No, no, I'm fine now,' she said. 'I've got my second wind after the food, thanks to Claudia.' She sat back in her chair. 'They were a weird bunch,' she said in answer to the other woman's question. 'They didn't seem to like each other very much.'

'I suppose if the old man had made different bequests at different times it would cause some friction,' observed Claudia, who'd been filled in on the situation by Pete.

'Yes, but there was something else,' said Abbey. 'A feeling that they were all in competition with each other.'

'That happens in families,' said Pete.

'And with me now as well, obviously,' said Abbey. 'And Mom too. Even though the brothers made it perfectly clear that they want nothing to do with us outside of the current situation. But until it's resolved, I guess we're fighting. Mom won't like that.'

'Your mom isn't a fool,' said Pete. 'She'll want to look after you. The way I see it, you're going to win this case. Ellen's father was very clear in his wishes.'

'I'm not at all sure what Mom's own wishes will be,' said Abbey. 'The nuns aren't allowed to have money or possessions of their own.'

'She can't walk away from millions.' Claudia looked horrified at the idea.

'Nobody's walking away from anything,' Pete told his wife. 'Abbey just has to clarify things with Ellen. When are you seeing her?' he asked, turning towards her.

'I'm waiting for a time and date from the prioress,' said Abbey.

'When I spoke to her, I impressed upon her how urgent it was, so I'm sure it'll be pretty soon. But that's the thing, Pete. Mom gave up her actual family and the nuns became her family instead. Given that she hardly ever sees me, she won't care much about a dead father she never met or his last wishes.'

Pete and Claudia exchanged glances.

'It's not because she doesn't love you that she doesn't see you,' said Pete.

Abbey yawned. 'Whatever.'

'She'll certainly want to see you about this,' said Claudia. 'The nuns might not have possessions of their own, but I've never known a religious community turn away hard cash.'

'I'm sure Ellen will want to see Abbey regardless.' Pete shot a warning look at his wife. 'For the moment, what she needs is to get a good night's sleep.'

'Oh God, sorry. I swear I'm not tired now.' Abbey tried hard not to yawn again. 'And if I go to bed, I'll wake up at some ridiculous hour of the morning. How about I go and play with Joely for a while? In fact, why don't I sit with the kids if you two would like to go out?'

'I don't think you'd stay awake,' Claudia said. 'But thank you for offering.'

'It's the least I can do. You keep looking after me and I know it must be a pain for you.'

'Of course it isn't,' said Pete.

'Poor Claudia didn't sign up to looking after me,' said Abbey.

'Hey, I don't know what impressions you got about people when you were in Ireland, but we have family values here,' said Pete. 'Claudia cares about you as much as I do.'

'When Pete married me, he knew Grady was part of my package,' said Claudia. 'And I knew that you were part of Pete's package.'

'But here's the thing.' Abbey looked seriously at both of them. 'I'm not part of your package at all. Not yours, Claudia, or yours, Pete. You've both been nothing but wonderful to me, but you're not my family and you shouldn't have to care about me. The trouble is that the people who are . . . well, I don't matter to them.'

'Oh, sweetie, don't upset yourself.' Claudia put her arm around Abbey's shoulders. 'As far as we're concerned, you're part of the Caruso family. And you always will be.'

Which was all very well, thought Abbey later that night. But she wasn't a Caruso. She wasn't a Connolly. She wasn't a Fitzpatrick. And she wasn't really an Andersen either. Despite the fact that she'd tried to put down roots for herself, she was someone who could be anyone. Because she didn't matter very much to any of the people who were actually related to her by blood. And that was something she'd have to learn to live with. No matter how abandoned it sometimes made her feel.

When Abbey finally went to bed, she fell asleep almost instantly. On opening her eyes the following morning, she was wide awake and refreshed, so despite the fact that it was only six thirty, she pulled on the guest robe that hung on the back of the bedroom door and made her way downstairs. The sun was barely rising and the ocean was still wreathed in mist as she stood by the kitchen window and drank a glass of orange juice. Because it was Saturday, the family still hadn't woken, although during the week Pete was usually in his office before seven thirty.

She made herself a coffee and was sitting at the breakfast bar with it when Claudia walked into the room. She too was dressed in a robe, and her brunette hair was pulled into a lazy ponytail. She looked younger than her forty years, although without the make-up she normally wore, the fine lines that were beginning to appear on her face were more evident.

'I hope I didn't wake you,' said Abbey.

'Of course not,' said Claudia. 'I'm an early riser. You get to be when you're a mom.'

'I bet.'

'You wake up and then you start thinking about your family and you can't go back to sleep,' added Claudia.

'You have a great family,' said Abbey.

'I know. And I meant what I said last night. That I accept that Pete looks on you as a daughter.'

Claudia's words were warm, but Abbey could hear a certain guardedness in her voice.

'He's always been great to me,' she said. 'But I know I can't depend on him for ever.'

'Exactly.' Claudia looked suddenly relieved. 'And that's why, Abbey, you have to fight for this inheritance and not let those horrible people persuade you out of it.'

'I can understand why the Fitzpatricks are angry, though. It's their house, not mine. Not Mom's.'

'Yes, but their father already helped them in life,' said Claudia. 'It's their tough luck if they didn't make the most of it.'

'I guess so.'

'How many chances do they want?' demanded Claudia. 'You get one, you take full advantage. You know that.'

'I do know,' agreed Abbey. 'It's just that sometimes you don't always grab the opportunity when you should.'

'Exactly.' Claudia spoke firmly. 'And you've got to grab this opportunity. Besides . . .' She looked at Abbey from her big hazel eyes. 'Pete has done something for you and I admire him for it, but it has to be the end of it.'

'Excuse me?'

'He acted rashly. A trait he usually manages to keep under control, but when he heard about your situation . . .'

'What the hell did he do?' asked Abbey. 'What's it got to do with me?'

'Pete bought an apartment for you,' replied Claudia.

'He what!' Abbey stared at her in shock.

'Well, he said he was buying it as an investment. But then he told me it was for you to live in until you got your money from

278

the house. He said you needed somewhere decent to live. He thinks that after you collect your inheritance you can buy it from him, if that's what you'd like to do.'

'Is he nuts? If my mom refuses to accept it, if it all goes pear-shaped for me – I'll never be able to buy it.'

'I know,' said Claudia grimly.

'But . . . but . . . what was he thinking?' demanded Abbey. 'Why on earth would he go out and buy somewhere and think that I'd even want to buy it from him afterwards?'

'It was a foreclosure and he had the inside track on it so he acted real quick. But he's using his heart, not his head. He said he knew that you'd want this apartment.'

'I can't believe this,' said Abbey. 'He's lost his mind, surely.'

'Who has?'

Pete walked into the kitchen. He was wearing a grey leisure suit which didn't entirely hide the few extra pounds he'd put on over the years, weight that Claudia was determined he should lose.

'Claudia was telling me about the apartment,' said Abbey. 'Are you out of your mind?'

'I agree it was a bit of a left-field move,' said Pete. 'But when I saw it, I couldn't pass it up. And don't look at me like that, Abbey Andersen. I know you'll want it.'

'Where is it?' asked Abbey.

'Dolores,' said Pete.

'Oh.'

'The Torreblanca building.'

'Oh,' said Abbey again.

'Apartment number 12.'

'Pete!'

It was the apartment she'd lived in with her mom when they'd first come to San Francisco. At the time, the district had been a bit tired and rough around the edges, so they'd been able to afford the rental of the two-bedroom unit. Both the area and the building had undergone considerable gentrification over the past years, and it was now a very desirable place to live. She would never have been able to buy an apartment there because the prices were unaffordable on her pay – even the rentals were outside her budget. But now Pete had done this and he was telling her that she could live in the place where she'd felt the most secure in her whole life. And that she could buy it from him when she could afford it.

But she couldn't. Not without accepting everything that Fred had left her. Possibly not even then. Pete was crazy. It was unworkable.

Except she desperately wanted to live in number 12 again. It was the one place she'd always considered home.

'Oh, Pete . . . I'm not sure about this.' She looked at him with worry in her eyes.

'Abbey, sweetheart, it's time you took the bull by the horns,' said Pete. 'You've got to do something with your life, make something of it. And you're getting the opportunity now.'

'Seems to me that you're forcing me into it,' said Abbey. 'And forcing me to be part of the fight over Mr Fitzpatrick's legacy, because you know I'd need every last cent for that apartment.'

'You need forcing,' said Pete. 'You're too nice and kind and . . . well, I hate to say it, but you're passive, Abbey. You don't go after something, you wait for it to come to you. You could set up your own nail bar, but you're happy to stay at the Mariposa, letting Selina take a cut from your earnings. I've heard the girls in my office talking about you – they think you're a genius.'

'I don't—'

'Genius,' repeated Pete firmly. 'That you can do things with nails nobody else can. That you make them feel beyond fabulous. But you don't sell yourself like that.'

'I don't want to sell myself at all,' said Abbey. 'It's not who I am.'

'I know,' Pete told her. 'That's your mother in you. But you've got to change, Abbey. We live in a world where you have to make the most of yourself, otherwise people will trample all over you. And I've seen lesser talents do better than you.'

280

'You keep an eye on the nail business?' Abbey asked.

'I keep an eye on every business,' said Pete. 'C'mon, honey. You need to ramp up your act a bit. And Fred Fitzpatrick is giving you the opportunity to do it.'

'So you think I should take my share, buy an apartment I can't really afford and set up in business for myself?'

'Now you've got it,' said Pete.

'I can't, Pete. I . . .' She looked at him helplessly.

'Yes you can. Abbey, you can shoot for the stars, make lots of money, live a great life. It's the American way.'

'My mom doesn't live her life that way.'

'Your mom is a whack-job,' said Claudia.

Abbey stared at her.

'I'm sorry, but it has to be said.' Claudia tightened the belt of her robe around her waist. 'How many women would abandon their own daughter to join a monastery, for heaven's sake. It's not natural.'

'Claudia.' Pete looked anxiously at his wife.

'You've said it yourself,' said Claudia. 'She broke your heart and Abbey's heart too. Only a fruitcake would do that.'

Abbey said nothing. She was wondering how many times Pete and Claudia had talked about her and her mother. And if Pete truly believed that Ellen was crazy.

'Look, Abbey.' Pete took her hands in his. 'Maybe Claudia is being a bit . . . forthright . . . but she's nailed one thing. Living the way your mom does, doing what your mom did by walking out on you – and me – isn't . . . isn't the usual way of getting on with life.'

'Unless you've got a vocation,' said Abbey. 'Unless you believe that God has called you.'

'But very few people have that belief or that calling.' Pete was choosing his words carefully. 'And just because you don't have it doesn't mean that you have to live the kind of life you seem to think your mom would want you to live.'

'I'm not!' she cried. 'Far from it. You know what she thought about the beauty business.'

'Yes, and I think that's why you haven't given it your best shot.'

'That's nonsense!'

'Is it?'

Abbey's shoulders slumped. She didn't know. Pete and Claudia had completely confused her with their comments. In some ways, she wasn't surprised at what Claudia thought. But Pete – she'd always believed that he was on her side. Only he wasn't, was he? He thought that Ellen was mad and that she herself was a hopeless idiot.

'Abbey.' Pete's voice was gentle as he released his hold on her. 'Your mom would want you to grasp the opportunity. What was that Bible story – you know, the one about the man who buried his talents, which wasn't what God wanted at all.'

'I didn't know you were into Bible study,' said Abbey.

'I remember some of it,' Pete told her.

'The talent you're talking about now, though, is the talent for accepting money from someone I didn't even know existed,' protested Abbey.

'To kick-start your own talents,' said Pete. 'And maybe to allow you some time to develop others.'

'What others?'

'Like your painting.'

'Stop with the painting stuff,' she said. 'We already agree that I'm good but not brilliant. And you need to be brilliant.'

'Who says? You set yourself impossible standards like that, you're always going to fail.'

'Oh Pete . . .' She buried her head in her hands. 'I'm so mixed up. I don't know what's right any more.'

'Move into the apartment,' said Pete. 'We'll work out a rental until you've got your inheritance. And don't feel guilty about him having left it to you. Allow yourself to have some good things in your life.'

'I do have good things,' she protested.

'Have fun,' Pete told her. 'Have fun and don't worry.'

But that, thought Abbey, was a lot easier for him to say than for her to do.

Chapter 28

Lisette was in the living room of Furze Hill. Given that the house was going to be unoccupied for a considerable amount of time, she'd asked Alex if she could look after the maintenance. After all, she'd said, no point in it falling into disrepair. Alex had consulted the rest of the family, including Abbey Andersen, before agreeing that Lisette could call in once a week to make sure that everything was OK. It annoyed her considerably that she'd had to have everyone else's permission to do something she'd done on a regular basis when Fred was alive. It annoyed her even more that she might be doing this on behalf of the hitherto unknown Americans. But Lisette still loved Furze Hill, and she couldn't bear to think of it damp and dusty and uncared for.

Her first task had been to check Fred's den for any other wills. Gareth had come with her, but they hadn't found anything, even though they'd opened literally every drawer in his desk. They had, however, found sheaves of the heavy parchment he'd used to draw up the one leaving the house to Abbey and Ellen. The following day, Don and Zoey had rummaged around the den too, but had also come up empty-handed. They had all had to reluctantly agree that Fred's ridiculous will really was his last one, and that they had no option, therefore, but to contest it.

Now, having spent the last couple of weeks cleaning and tidying, Lisette walked through the rooms of the house, unable to clamp down on her usual dream of what she'd do to it if it were hers.

Open it out, she thought. Replace the heavy drapes with something more modern. Change the kitchen. Let in the light. Only she'd never get the chance to do any of it, would she, because she'd never be the chatelaine of Furze Hill.

She stood at the patio windows and looked out over the garden. What Fred had done was wrong, she thought furiously. He must have known how much it would upset them. So why the hell had he done it? Of course he hadn't expected to die so suddenly. Maybe he'd intended to show the stupid will to Donald or Gareth, use it to influence them in some way and then change it back. That would've been typical, in a way, of Fred. He liked to have his children exactly where he wanted them. Regardless of his ultimate intentions, however, he'd left behind a nuclear bomb.

She went over to the large display cabinet in the corner of the room where the majority of the silver pieces were kept. The silver pieces that were supposedly hers, although she couldn't have them while everything was still up in the air. She took out a small snuff box and a set of six bishop's spoons. Of all of the items, these were the only ones that she truly liked. The snuff box, oblong and carved with what seemed like unfurling leaves around a navy blue glass container, was distinctive and eye-catching and reminded her of a bygone age. She'd always liked the spoons, each with a carving of a bishop's head on the handle, even though they probably weren't worth anything. Fred's personal legacy to her was a pittance as far as the overall estate was concerned. But it was her pittance and she wanted to bring it home. It annoyed her that she couldn't, especially as nobody would actually miss the snuff box or the spoons. Lisette doubted that there was a single person in the family that knew they even existed. It wouldn't matter if she took them.

The sudden shrill of the doorbell startled her so much that she dropped the snuff box on to the granite hearth. The lid immediately detached from the base and the glass container cracked.

'*Merde*,' she muttered as she picked it up and put it on the

285

mantelpiece, before walking into the hall and pressing the intercom button.

'Hello?' she said.

'It's me,' said Zoey. 'Let me in.'

The idea to drive by her late father-in-law's house had come to Zoey after having lunch with a friend in Howth village. Friend wasn't the right word for it, she thought; Esther Canaletti was more of an acquaintance, someone who wanted her to become involved in a protest march about traffic-calming measures on their housing estate. Zoey had no intention of becoming involved, but she'd been bored and thought lunch was a good idea. It occurred to her, as she said goodbye to Esther, that it would do no harm to drive past Fred's house while she was in the area, even though, unlike Lisette, she didn't have keys and so couldn't go inside. When she saw her sister-in-law's car parked outside, however, she pulled to a halt immediately.

'Cleaning?' she asked when Lisette opened the door.

'I said I'd keep an eye on the place.' Lisette pushed her hair behind her ears. 'You know that.'

Zoey walked into the hallway. Lisette followed her.

'So what have you been doing?' Zoey ran a finger along the console table and looked at the streak that it had left in the dust. She raised an eyebrow at Lisette.

'Tidying up,' said Lisette defensively. 'Fred had loads of junk in the house.'

'What have you done with it?'

'Put it in the garage mostly. D'you want to see?'

Zoey recognised a challenge in Lisette's voice. 'Sure,' she said.

The two of them went to the garage, where Lisette pointed out the multiple boxes of papers, gadgets and alarms that she'd taken from the living areas and stored away.

'Honestly,' said Zoey as she gazed at them. 'What are men like?'

'I'm sure Donald doesn't hoard junk like this,' said Lisette.

'Are you having a laugh?' Zoey led the way out of the garage and back into the house. 'Not stuff like Fred's, of course. But technological bits and pieces. CCTV cameras. Alarms. And all sorts of computer-related gizmos. I've no idea what most of them are and couldn't care less. But I'm always having to move them out of my living room and outside into his den.'

'I didn't know Don had an outside den.'

'Damn right he does,' said Zoey. 'It's one of those wooden rooms like sheds that you can set up at the end of the garden. Men need somewhere they can sit in private and think manly thoughts.'

'Manly thoughts?' asked Lisette as they entered the kitchen.

'Not porno thoughts, if that's what you mean,' said Zoey. 'Though I suppose he has them too, even when he's not with me. But you know what guys are like. They don't talk to each other about things; they mull life's injustices over in their heads instead.'

'Is Donald doing much mulling lately?' asked Lisette.

'What d'you think?' Zoey's tone was dark. 'Since we didn't find another will, he's done nothing but. Here, put the kettle on. Let's have a cup of coffee. No chance that Fred has a proper coffee machine, I suppose?'

'Are you joking?'

'Green tea? Camomile?'

'Lyons Green Label tea. And Nescafé.'

'I'll have the coffee.' Zoey perched on a high stool beside the old-fashioned breakfast bar. 'So how's Gareth holding up?'

Lisette put the two cups sharply on the counter. 'Stressed,' she said shortly, her back to Zoey.

'They're both stressed. And we are too. Aren't we?'

'I'm tired of being stressed,' said Lisette.

'Me too,' said Zoey. 'It's not the payday I was looking for.'

'None of us was expecting this,' agreed Lisette.

'Was there an inventory done of the silver?' asked Zoey suddenly. 'Or of anything else in the house for that matter?'

Lisette turned to look at her. 'What are you implying?'

'Nothing,' said Zoey. Her eyes were wide and innocent. 'I was wondering, that's all.'

'Well I'm not sure I like the tone you're wondering in,' said Lisette.

'All I'm saying is that it would be easy for the person who's looking after things to . . . to accidentally take something home, that's all.'

Lisette thought of the damaged snuff box and swallowed hard.

'I 'aven't taken anything from this 'ouse,' she said, her accent deteriorating under pressure. 'I wouldn't.'

'I would.' Zoey was unfazed.

'Well I didn't.'

'More fool you then,' said Zoey. 'If you ask me, we should try and secure as much as we can in case it all goes horribly wrong and that oh-so-innocent American and her barmy mother get their hands on everything.'

'You mean take things? We can't do that.' Lisette's voice was a mixture of horror and wistfulness.

'Who's to know?' asked Zoey. 'You've already gone through a heap of junk that nobody had a clue about. What else is here that we've never seen before?'

'Nothing valuable,' said Lisette.

'You've looked?'

'I've done a lot of clearing up,' she replied. 'I would have noticed.'

'Pity,' said Zoey.

'If it comes to it, do you think we'll win in court?' asked Lisette. 'Do you?'

'If Alex says that Fred ignored the advice he gave him, I can't see how we can prove otherwise,' said Lisette. 'I've said this to Gareth but he insists they can show that Fred was off his rocker. Only thing is, I don't think he was. He might have been a bit doddery, but he knew exactly what he was doing.'

Zoey tapped her finger against the side of the breakfast bar. 'Did you know that if this ends up in the High Court, the fees alone could cost fifty grand a day.'

'What!' Lisette was horrified.

'For each side,' Zoey added. 'If we challenge and lose, we might have to pay their costs too.'

'That can't be right,' said Lisette. 'We don't have that sort of money.'

'Neither do we,' said Zoey.

'But . . . but . . . I'll have to talk to Gareth,' said Lisette. 'He hasn't said anything to me about this.'

'Donald hasn't opened his mouth either. He's probably afraid to.'

'How do you know, in that case?' asked Lisette.

'I thought somebody needed to take an analytical look at it,' Zoey told her. 'I did a bit of checking.'

Lisette looked surprised. She'd never thought of her glamorous sister-in-law as being the analytical type before.

'We can't let them do this,' she said. 'They could ruin us.'

'Only if they have to take it to court,' said Zoey. 'Only if Abbey Andersen and her mother keep what they've been left and we fight it.'

'But they will do that!' cried Lisette. 'You saw her. She pretended not to care, but she's not a rich person and she wants the money. Who wouldn't?'

'Of course,' agreed Zoey. 'So you and I have to come up with a plan, don't we?'

'What sort of plan?'

'We have to make it attractive for her to settle with us. And not with threats and bluster like the boys. By making her an offer she can't refuse.'

'But we have no leverage over her. She can refuse anything.'

Zoey made a face. 'Our leverage is the fact that her mother is a nun. I know that we talked about the convent wanting the money, but the truth is that nuns are supposed to be charitable. And I got the impression that Abbey was . . . well, disposed towards being charitable too.'

'I need more than her charity!' cried Lisette. 'I need . . . I need . . .' She started to cry, and Zoey put her arm around her shoulders.

'Hey, don't get upset,' she said.

'It's hard not to.' Lisette sniffed. 'I thought when Fred died it was the answer to all our prayers. But it's been nothing but a nightmare ever since.'

'Are you really up shit creek on those properties?' asked Zoey.

'We're so far up it they don't make paddles big enough for us,' replied Lisette. 'The only property we'd possibly break even on if we sold it is Papillon, which means Gareth is eyeing it up as a lifeline. But I love Papillon. It would break my heart to lose it.'

'I didn't realise things were that bad,' said Zoey. 'I thought it might be a bit rocky for you but that you were riding it out.'

'I wish.' Lisette sniffed again. 'We've made a complete mess of everything.'

'We could do with the money too,' said Zoey. 'Don keeps giving cash to Disgruntled Deirdre because he's afraid she'll turn the girls against him, even though she's a lying, scheming bitch who cheated on him.'

'I liked Deirdre,' admitted Lisette. 'We got on well.'

'Yeah, well.' Zoey made a face. 'She can be charming when she wants to be. Apparently. I wouldn't know, of course, she's never been charming to me. Anyhow, Don was a bit too generous when they divorced. He wanted to appear magnanimous even though the whole thing was her fault.'

'Is it true she had an affair?' asked Lisette. 'She never told me she was unhappy.'

'A fling with her gym instructor,' Zoey replied. 'She claimed that they never slept with each other, but come on, nobody would believe that.'

'She always seemed devoted to Donald and the girls,' said Lisette.

'That woman is devoted to herself,' Zoey said scornfully. 'Anyhow, given that Alex was his solicitor then too, he's not exactly Donald's favourite person. Plus we're in negative equity on our own home. I thought if we got Furze Hill, we could sell it and be set up for life.'

'But why should you get Furze Hill and not us?' demanded Lisette.

'I didn't say we would. Only that I hoped we would. That your dad would treat the elder son with more respect.'

'He hasn't exactly treated any of us with respect,' said Lisette. 'What about you and me? We did a lot for him and ended up with a measly five grand each and some silverware and jewellery that we can't even take.'

'The idea of owning a dead woman's jewellery creeps me out,' said Zoey. 'Unless it belonged to Liz Taylor I'm not interested.'

Lisette gave her a watery smile.

'Anyway,' said Zoey. 'Bottom line is that our father-in-law was incredibly daft and we need to do all we can to fix the mess he's left us in. I still think we should make some kind of offer to Abbey Andersen and sort of throw ourselves on her mercy. But maybe there's a temporary solution to our problems.' She looked pensively at Lisette. 'Are you absolutely sure there aren't any heirlooms in the attic?'

'There isn't an attic,' replied Lisette. 'Everything was in the spare bedrooms.'

'Did he have a safe? When we were looking for the will, Don said he hadn't, but perhaps Fred kept it secret.'

Lisette looked at her doubtfully. 'I didn't think so either.'

'Why don't we look?' Zoey finished her coffee and slid off the chair. 'Old man like him, maybe he kept other bits and pieces hidden away. Or money. Or shares to a diamond mine or something.'

'You're getting carried away,' Lisette told her.

'I can dream.'

'The best place to look is the study,' said Lisette.

'I helped Don look for the will in the study,' said Zoey. 'That creeped me out too, to be honest. After all, he actually died there!' She shuddered.

'Best place,' repeated Lisette as they left the kitchen. She had to admit that she also felt slightly uneasy in the room where the old man had died. It was as though he were still here, watching them. Zoey, though, had apparently got over her squeamishness very quickly. She surveyed the room and then lifted the seascape painting that Abbey had admired off the wall.

'Damn,' she said. 'In spy movies the safe is always behind a painting.' She worked her way through the dozen or so other paintings in Fred's office, without any luck. 'Maybe it's under the floorboards,' she said.

'A bit difficult to access beneath a fitted carpet,' Lisette pointed out. She opened the doors of a cupboard in an alcove. A blue file, filled with cuttings, fell out.

'*Zut!*'

She picked it up. The cuttings were about the Magdalene laundries and the fight that the survivors were having to get justice and compensation. She held it out to Zoey.

'This is what it's all about,' she said angrily. 'His damn obsession!'

'I saw those cuttings when I was here with Don.' Zoey said. 'I can't imagine what it was like for those girls. But Fred was stupid to get so fixated on it.'

'How will they prove this obsession in court if it comes to it?' Lisette asked.

'We don't want it to get that far, which is why you and I are going to think of a way to sort things out by taking action ourselves, instead of putting our faith in our emotional and probably equally irrational husbands. But in the meantime . . .' Zoey's eyes narrowed and she stalked across the room to another cupboard. 'I don't remember looking in here.' She yanked the door open and a mountain of books, videos and DVDs toppled out. 'Oh for God's sake!' she cried as she dodged them. She looked down at the pile on the floor. 'John Wayne, Clint Eastwood, Tommy Lee Jones. He was into the whole macho man thing in a big way, wasn't he?'

'He liked to think of himself as a tough man,' agreed Lisette.

'Where else could he have hidden stuff?' asked Zoey.

'Perhaps upstairs,' suggested Lisette. 'Perhaps in his room.'

She'd only been in Fred's bedroom a couple of times before, both times when he'd had bad chest infections and wasn't able to get up. The decor hadn't changed since Ros had been alive – the room was still floral and pink, colours that were at odds with Fred's personality. The dressing table was reproduction Louis XV and the framed print over the bed showed a French pastoral scene from the same era.

'Bloody hell,' said Zoey as she stepped inside.

'Don't you like it?' Lisette looked at her with a sudden hint of mischief in her eyes.

'I like pink,' said Zoey defensively. 'But this is something even my granny would've rejected as being over the top.'

'It's pretty awful, isn't it?' Lisette agreed. 'I suppose it reminded Fred of his wife.'

'A woman with no taste whatsoever,' said Zoey.

'Perhaps it was tasteful when they did it.'

'I doubt that. Right. A safe.'

Zoey opened the first of the fitted wardrobe's three doors. Seven shirts were neatly hung on the rail, along with seven pairs of trousers. Seven pairs of shoes were arranged on a rack on the floor.

'Ugh,' she said. 'His clothes. That's definitely creepy, and a bit sad too.'

'He didn't spend his cash on clothes,' observed Lisette as she opened the second door. 'This is all his casual stuff. Sweat shirts and jogging pants. Not that he jogged much.'

'Hey, if I get to eighty-odd, I'll be happy to sit around and let people bring things to me,' said Zoey. 'I hate the gym.'

'Are you a member of one?'

'How d'you think I keep this body?' demanded Zoey. 'It's not from sitting on my arse all day. I have to work at it, you know. I'm not naturally thin like you.'

'I'm not naturally thin either,' said Lisette. 'But I eat well.'

'I try,' Zoey told her. 'It's hard.'

'Not if you cook the food yourself,' said Lisette. 'That's the problem with people today. They own lots of cookbooks but they still buy ready-made meals.'

'Because there are better things to do than slave over an oven,' Zoey said.

'No, there are not,' Lisette disagreed. 'Cooking is the most important thing you can do. Proper food keeps your body in balance. It is ridiculous that people spend more money on clothes and computers and other things than food. What is the point in paying for an expensive dress if the body it covers is like shit?'

Zoey stared at her. 'I've never heard you sounding so French before. But you guys eat frogs' legs, you know.'

'They are delicious,' said Lisette. 'Like chicken wings.'

'Gross,' said Zoey.

'All I'm saying is that more care with your food means less hard work in the gym.' Lisette opened the final door. 'Oh my God!'

'What? What?'

'He kept her clothes,' said Lisette.

'Yeuch!'

'They're OK.' Lisette ran her fingers over a selection of dresses and trousers. 'Not so bad, actually. Good quality.'

'They're over ten years old!' cried Zoey.

'I keep clothes for more than ten years,' said Lisette. 'It's not a crime.'

'But she's dead!' cried Zoey.

'Perhaps he got comfort from them.'

Zoey shuddered. Then she dropped to her knees to inspect the interior of the wardrobe more closely.

'Look,' she said. 'Half hidden by those trousers.'

Lisette knelt down too. They both looked at the safe. It was similar to the type found in hotel bedrooms, small and oblong, with a keypad to enter a code.

'Well, well,' said Zoey.

'We found it.'

They exchanged glances.

'So what's the code?' asked Zoey.

'I have no idea,' said Lisette.

'Think,' said Zoey. 'What interested him? What could he remember? He was an old man, after all, so it couldn't be too difficult.'

Lisette keyed in 1234, but the safe remained closed.

'Bugger,' said Zoey. She sat back on her heels and considered it. 'Birthdays?' she suggested. 'His, Don's, Gareth's?'

Lisette keyed in 0205, which was Gareth's birthday, but nothing happened. Then Zoey keyed in Don's with the same effect.

'This is hopeless,' said Lisette. 'We'll never guess. And we're wasting our time anyway, because there probably isn't anything in it.'

She keyed in Fred's own birthday, but still had no luck.

'Maybe it's her birthday,' said Zoey suddenly. 'His wife's.'

'Ros?' Lisette rolled her eyes. 'I have no idea what her birthday is.'

'Or maybe their anniversary,' said Zoey.

'I do know that.' Lisette punched in 2111, and much to their surprise, the door of the safe swung open.

They stared inside. The contents comprised a red leather box and a large brown envelope.

'Family secrets?' whispered Lisette as she looked at the envelope.

'Something better?' said Zoey, lifting out the red leather box.

She opened it slowly. Inside were two dozen gold coins. She picked one of them out. 'What the hell is this?'

'Bullion,' said Lisette. 'He must have kept some of his money in bullion.'

'Real gold?' Zoey looked at her hopefully.

'It looks like it.'

'What's it worth?' asked Zoey.

'I don't know,' said Lisette. 'But gold has soared in value over the last few years, so . . . a few thousand?'

'That's all?' Zoey looked disappointed.

'We could check online,' said Lisette.

'What's in the envelope?' asked Zoey.

Lisette removed it from the safe and opened it.

'Oh!' she exclaimed. 'Money.'

'Cash? How much?'

'I don't know. I . . .' Lisette withdrew six bundles of notes and started counting. Zoey watched her intently.

'My God, it's thirty thousand,' breathed Lisette. 'He must have been mad, keeping this in the house.'

'And there's the proof you need.' Zoey flicked through the notes. 'Oh Lisette, you know what some old people are like. They need to have hard cash tucked away somewhere. He didn't make any mention of this in the will, did he?'

Lisette shook her head. 'Though I suppose it's included in the contents of the house, isn't it?' she asked. 'Which means it's Abbey bloody Andersen's money.'

'Only if she knows about it,' said Zoey.

'She'll have to know about it.'

'Why?' asked Zoey.

Lisette stared at her.

'Who's going to tell her?' demanded Zoey. 'You? Me?'

'But . . .'

'What was the point in looking for a safe if we weren't going to take whatever was inside?' asked Zoey.

'I don't know,' said Lisette.

'Look – this money isn't going to make a whole lot of difference, is it?' asked Zoey. 'To you or to me. Even with it, you and Gareth will still owe whatever you owe on the mortgages. Don and I will still be living in our poky house. But what the hell, Lisette, *we* deserve something for ourselves, and we deserve it now. Even if the Americans see sense sooner rather than later, it'll still take ages to get the whole thing sorted out.'

Lisette looked longingly at the envelope and the leather box. She thought of her kitchen shelf, crammed with envelopes full of gas bills, electricity bills, insurance bills and a whole heap of other things that she couldn't afford to pay.

'We can't take it all,' she said.

'Five grand each,' decided Zoey. 'That doubles what he left us, which seems perfectly fair to me. We're entitled to more than Disgruntled Deirdre. And not a word to the boys, because they'd let something slip.'

'What about Suzanne?' asked Lisette.

'What about her?' Zoey was dismissive. 'If we get a deal done, we'll make sure she doesn't lose out.'

Lisette nodded slowly.

'So come on,' said Zoey. 'We're entitled. Don't you think so?'

Lisette nodded again, more vigorously this time.

'All the time you spent looking after him,' said Zoey. 'Suzanne didn't. And I visited him too. Never even said a word when he spent most of the time looking down my blouse.'

'He used to pinch my bum,' said Lisette.

'There you go,' Zoey told her. 'Payment for services to old men.'

Lisette made a face.

'You in or not?' asked Zoey.

'Yes. Yes, I am.'

Lisette took the money from the envelope again. Meanwhile, Zoey divided some of the coins between them.

'We won't take them all,' said Zoey. 'That way, it makes sense that he'd have the safe for both the money and the gold.'

'Good idea,' said Lisette.

Then the two of them closed the doors of the wardrobe and walked out of the room.

Chapter 29

Moving into the apartment changed everything. The moment she stepped over the threshold, Abbey felt it was her place, her home, and she wanted to stay there for ever. It had been altered significantly in the ten years since she and Ellen had lived there; both the building and the apartments inside had been remodelled and upgraded so that the living area with its open-plan kitchen seemed bigger and brighter than before. The space in the bedrooms was better utilised too, and the bathroom . . . well, that sealed the deal as far as Abbey was concerned, because the old acrylic bath with its constantly dripping shower had been replaced by a sleek tiled wet-room which she fell in love with at first sight. Additionally, the overgrown garden behind the building had been made over and now consisted of paved and grassy areas containing fruit trees and flowering shrubs.

In a million years she wouldn't have been able to afford a place like this on what she made at the Mariposa salon, either renting or with a mortgage. But Pete had insisted that he wasn't going to charge her rental until after everything to do with the will was settled. At which point, he said, you'll hopefully be in a position to buy it off me. Abbey had never seriously considered buying San Francisco real estate before. But standing in the apartment, she knew that it was an option she definitely wanted to consider now. And, like Pete said, she deserved it, didn't she?

Pete was right about so many things. Why should she feel bad for the Fitzpatricks, who'd had a proper family life and had already been looked after by their father? As for Suzanne – well, she might have been hard done by in the past, but she was a smart business-woman who'd been left a lot of money now, so she didn't have anything to complain about either.

So it's not my fault, thought Abbey. Nothing to do with them is my fault. It was Fred's right to leave his house to whomever he wanted, and if he hadn't liked me he would have shredded that will.

She wondered if her mother would take the same point of view. She would be meeting her at the weekend, having received an email back from Sister Inez to say that Sister Benita – as Ellen was now known – would be available on Saturday. Abbey was both pleased and nervous. She was glad to finally have the opportunity of talking with her mother about everything, but anxious as to how Ellen would react, especially if she was unaware of her adoption. She was also unsure how she herself would react if Ellen told her that she had known but had kept the information from her.

Abbey felt the weight of responsibility on her shoulders grow as the weekend approached. She tried not to think about it too much by immersing herself in her work, which included studying a website for a nail art competition which would shortly be taking place in LA. Although she'd always refused to participate in competitions in the past, Pete's recent words about her being passive, about setting impossible targets and not using her talents, had hit home. Part of the reason she'd said that she didn't want to take part was that she didn't like leaving San Francisco. But how could she use that as an excuse when she'd recently travelled to Ireland and Spain? And if she wanted to prove to herself (and maybe to Ellen too) that she'd made the right decision in choosing to do nail art, perhaps entering a competition was the way to go. If she won . . . well, she wasn't thinking that far ahead, but maybe the experience would be worth-while. And so she studied the entry requirements, filled in the online form and hit send before she could change her mind.

She also contacted Ryan Gilligan to let him know that she was finally going to see her mother and discuss the inheritance. He sounded quite pleased at the prospect of things finally moving on. Billable hours, she reminded herself. All lawyers love 'em.

She wasn't thinking about the will, or the competition, or billable hours, or indeed anything other than the fact that she hated flying in bad weather as her plane made a bumpy landing at San Diego airport. Even as they taxied towards the terminal, however, the heavy rain began to ease, and by the time she parked her rental car outside the downtown hotel where she'd reserved a room, the skies had almost cleared.

She walked up to the reception desk and checked in. The receptionist, whom she'd never seen before, welcomed her back to the Old Inn. Abbey knew that because she always stayed in the same place near the Pacific Highway when she visited her mom, her details were already in the hotel's system, which meant that even the newest person on the desk could welcome back previous guests.

'Have a nice day,' said the receptionist as Abbey took her key card and made her way to the fourth floor.

She was pleased to have been given a room that overlooked the bay and not the car park, and she stood gazing out at the ocean for a couple of minutes before telling herself that it was the same damn water that she saw every single day and that she should unpack and get on with it. She knew that she was wasting time so as to delay the moment when she set off for the monastery of Santa Ana in Los Montesinos, which was a little under an hour's drive from the hotel.

She'd told the prioress that she'd be arriving at the monastery mid afternoon, which meant that she didn't have too much time to spare. Sister Inez, a kindly and efficient woman, had said that she'd allocate one of the visitors' rooms to her and Sister Benita, and that she hoped they'd have much to share.

Sister Inez would get her wish, thought Abbey, as she left the

301

room and went downstairs again. She had far too many things she needed to share with her mother. Her heart was tripping in her chest as she went over them all again. She wished (as she'd known she would) that she'd accepted Pete's offer to come with her. But when he'd suggested it, she'd told him that she'd prefer to meet Ellen by herself. Pete had looked a little wounded at that, but Abbey pointed out that Ellen would immediately assume something terrible had happened if she saw him, and she didn't want her mother being defensive straight away. Besides, she wasn't sure that Claudia would approve of Pete seeing his ex again, even if she was now a celibate nun!

'Call me as soon as you've spoken to her and let me know how it went,' he ordered, and she'd promised that she would.

As she drove along the dusty road that led to the monastery, she toyed with the idea of calling him now but quickly dismissed it. Ellen (Abbey never thought of her as Sister Benita) was her mother and her family. And this was between the two of them, even if Pete now had a vested interest in their inheritance. She pressed the on button for the car radio and listened to the pre-set station, a Mexican one playing a selection from Linda Ronstadt's *Jardín Azul* album. The songs were traditional, and Abbey remembered singing them with her mother during their Latin American days. She wondered if Ellen had felt the tuggings of a vocation even then. Had she wished that she could leave Abbey somewhere and join the nuns? Many of the health facilities that Ellen had worked in had had religious volunteers as well as lay staff. Abbey hadn't recognised all of them as nuns then, because not all of them wore habits. Sister Teresa – young, pretty and vivacious – came to the clinic every day dressed in jeans and a checked cotton blouse, and it wasn't until they were leaving that Abbey discovered she was a nun at all.

Had Ellen wished that she lived Sister Teresa's life, going back to a peaceful convent instead of the shabby apartment she and Abbey had shared? She must have thought about it, Abbey mused, but how could she have done anything about it when she had a child to look after? Had Ellen resented her? She'd never made her feel anything but loved and wanted back then, but perhaps it had all been a facade. Yet she'd come back to California for Abbey's sake. And she'd had a loving relationship with Pete.

Gramps and Gramma dying had been the catalyst, Abbey decided. After that, Ellen had gone on the retreat that had obviously been enough to make her give up everything, Abbey and Pete included.

She clearly remembered the day that Ellen had told her. It had been shortly after Abbey had given her the news that she was doing the nail technician's course and that she was going to move in with some friends. Ellen had frowned at the idea of the course, asked about her art studies, told her that she was cheapening her life and focusing on the wrong things. There'd been a row, Abbey had stormed off in a rage and then, when she came home ready to apologise to her mother, Ellen had sprung the bombshell about wanting to spend some time at the monastery to see if the life was the right one for her. Abbey had been dumbstruck by her decision, but at the time had thought it was an easy way of allowing both of them to do their own thing for a while. Living together had become claustrophobic, which was part of the reason why Abbey had been so keen to move out of their apartment, even though she'd loved it. She had, however, been devastated for Pete, because she'd been sure that he and Ellen had a future together. Shortly after Ellen's decision, Pete had called Abbey and met her for coffee, asking her what it was that he'd done to drive Ellen away. It was a question that Abbey hadn't been able to answer.

Although she'd grown even closer to Pete, she couldn't, in all honesty, say that she'd missed her mother in those early months. And even when Ellen said that she'd decided she wanted to stay with the community as a postulant, Abbey had dismissed it as a fad. She'd told Pete to hang in there, that she was sure her mother would be back and that she'd be looking to both of them for support after her mad venture. But that wasn't how things had turned out. And as Ellen grew more distant, Abbey realised that this wasn't like the times when her mother had decided she needed a change and had upped sticks and moved to a different town to use her nursing skills there. She'd formed a bond with the monastic community which seemed stronger than the bond she'd had with Pete. Stronger, even, than the bond that she and Abbey had once shared. The realisation had hurt Abbey deeply. Mothers were supposed to care for their children above everything and everyone else. But she wasn't enough for Ellen. She never had been. That was why her mother had spent so much time looking after other people. Abbey herself had never measured up. But then, she asked herself, as the music switched from traditional Spanish songs to something more upbeat and recent, who on earth could measure up to a relationship with God?

After about fifty minutes, she saw the monastery building. Dating back to the early 1800s, it had originally been a convent consisting of a hacienda-style adobe construction around a central courtyard. At that time, many of the nuns were women who had been sent there by family, either for protection or because they wanted to get rid of them. When the convent closed nearly seventy years later, the building fell into disrepair, and it wasn't until the 1950s that a group of nuns who wanted to live a monastic lifestyle took it over and restored and remodelled it. They retained the courtyard layout, rebuilt the walls and the campanile and founded the Hermanas de Santa Ana, a community that now had almost fifty sisters. That number was down from over a hundred in the initial years of its existence but was nevertheless a sizeable community for modern times. Abbey knew that the average age of the nuns was creeping inexorably higher. Despite the fact that a surprising number of young people came to the monastery on retreats, very few girls wanted to live their particular lifestyle. Abbey didn't blame them. She wouldn't have been able to put up with it herself.

There was a small parking area covered by a corrugated-iron

roof outside the monastery walls. Three other cars were parked there, and she pulled into a space beside a dusty red pick-up. She got out of her rental and locked the door, although, she thought to herself in amusement, the likelihood of it being stolen was pretty remote. For as far as she could see in either direction, the ribbon of road was deserted.

Abbey took a few deep breaths, then pressed the buzzer on the gate. A bead of sweat traced its way along her spine. She didn't know if it was from nerves, or because without the protection of the iron roof, the heat of the sun was intense.

It was Sister Esperanza who opened it. Abbey remembered her from the last time she'd been to Los Montesinos, a tall, ebony-skinned woman wearing the coffee-coloured skirt and jacket with white blouse that was the habit of the monastery. When Ellen had first talked about joining the enclosed community, Abbey had visualised her in a long black tunic and veil, but Ellen had smiled and said that fortunately the nuns were a bit more up-to-date than that and that spending the day wearing heavy black in the heat of southern California would be madness. Abbey had eventually put away many of her preconceptions about monastic life, but what she couldn't avoid was knowing that Ellen's choice meant that she would be permanently living in Los Montesinos and would rarely step outside its exquisitely maintained garden.

Sister Esperanza led her along the terracotta-tiled inner corridors to a small room, redolent of beeswax and hibiscus, with a narrow stained-glass window which reflected reds and blues on to the opposite wall. In the centre of the room were two chairs either side of a round wooden table. A jug of iced water, containing mint leaves and a slice of lemon, and two tall glasses were neatly placed on the table.

'Sister Benita will be with you shortly,' said the nun, before leaving Abbey alone in the room.

Abbey realised that her hands were shaking as she poured herself a glass of water from the jug. She sipped it slowly, willing herself to be calm and relaxed as she strained her ears for the sounds of someone approaching. But the door opened without her having heard any footsteps. And then she was looking at her mother for the first time in nearly a year.

Abbey stood up as Ellen crossed the room. Like Sister Esperanza, she was dressed in the coffee-coloured skirt and jacket. Before she'd joined the monastery, she'd liked to wear vibrant primary colours. But it wasn't the vibrancy of her clothes that people noticed when Ellen – Sister Benita – came into a room now. It was the brightness of her smile and the intelligence that shone from her blue eyes that drew immediate attention. Her face, smooth and barely lined, would have done justice to an anti-ageing-cream advertisement. She's hardly changed, Abbey thought, from the days when she lived in San Francisco, although perhaps she's a bit more serene now.

'Hello, Mom,' she said.

'Hello, Abbey.' Ellen opened her arms and embraced her daughter. And suddenly Abbey felt the years roll back so that Ellen was the mother she'd always known.

'How have you been?' asked Ellen.

'Oh, not bad.' Abbey gave her a quick resumé of her working and social life. 'What about you?'

'I'm very well, thank God,' said Ellen. 'I've led lots of people in prayer and contemplation since I last saw you. I've treated a variety of ailments, stitched a few cuts and popped a dislocated shoulder back into place.'

Ellen was in charge of the monastery's infirmary. Her undoubted nursing skills were one of the reasons, Abbey had always thought, that she had been so readily accepted into the community, despite being a late vocation and having a daughter.

'But you're not here to talk about these things, are you?' asked Ellen. 'You want to discuss something else with me.' She looked steadily at Abbey.

'Yes.' Abbey took another sip of the cold water. 'I . . . I'm not sure exactly how to start.'

'At the very beginning.' Ellen's face broke into a smile. 'Didn't Julie Andrews say it was a very good place to start?'

Abbey laughed. 'Is *The Sound of Music* compulsory viewing here?' she asked.

'Well, it shows nuns as very resourceful people,' Ellen told her. 'And the music is lovely.'

'OK then.' She felt slightly more at ease. 'I guess the place to start is to ask you if you knew you were adopted.'

She kept her eyes fixed on Ellen as she spoke. She was sure the answer would be yes, but when she didn't see any flicker of expression cross her mother's face, she wondered if she'd been wrong. And if she'd shocked Ellen so much that she didn't know what to say.

'How did you find out about that?' asked Ellen after a long pause.

'So you did know?'

'Yes.'

Abbey clenched her fists and her nails dug into the palms of her hands. 'Always?'

Ellen shook her head. 'My mom told me when Dad was sick,' she said.

'Why didn't you say anything?' asked Abbey. 'Why didn't you tell me?'

Ellen said nothing for a moment, and Abbey could see that she was gathering her thoughts.

'I was very shocked at first,' Ellen admitted. 'And with Dad being so ill, it wasn't something I had time to process properly. Then Mom got sick too and . . . I guess I kind of put it to one side.'

'You still should have told me,' said Abbey.

'I know.' Ellen looked contrite. 'I'm not sure I was thinking very clearly myself back then. I was angry at my mom for not having said anything sooner, even though in those days people weren't always as open about adoption as they are now. I was frustrated that I hadn't been able to talk to my parents about it. I'm sorry I didn't tell you. I'm sorry you found out about it from someone else.' She looked at Abbey curiously. 'And surprised. Who told you? And when?'

Ellen was completely still after Abbey finished her account of meeting with Ryan Gilligan and her stay in Ireland. Abbey continued to sip her glass of water while she watched her mother's face. Once again it was almost expressionless, but she could see that Ellen's mind was working hard, because her eyes gleamed with the intensity that she remembered well.

'You've had a traumatic time,' said Ellen eventually.

'Challenging,' agreed Abbey.

'And you've learned a lot about me. More than I knew myself.'

'I have?'

'I didn't know my mother's name,' Ellen said.

'Didn't Gramma and Gramps tell you? Didn't they know?' Abbey was astounded.

'Maybe they knew her full name,' said Ellen. 'But if so, they didn't share it with me. All they said was that she was a mother who'd died in childbirth.'

'Ryan Gilligan, the investigative lawyer, told me she died shortly after you were born,' said Abbey. 'Not, I suppose, that it makes a huge difference, but . . .'

'But perhaps she knew I existed,' said Ellen. 'Dilly.' She said the name slowly. 'Poor, poor girl. It must have been an awful time. Imagine how she was feeling.'

'Fred Fitzpatrick said I looked like her.'

'In that case, she was beautiful,' Ellen said.

'Fred told me that too,' said Abbey. 'But that's just an old man and a biased mother talking. Besides, I don't look like her. If anything, I think I might look a bit like him. Because I look like his daughter Suzanne. So do you.'

Ellen blinked a couple of times. 'I never thought I'd know anything about my birth family,' she said. 'After Gramma told me,

I wondered about them. Anyone would. But they had their own lives and there was no reason for me to try to find out about them.'

'Your father felt differently.'

'Eventually.'

'Do you resent it?' asked Abbey.

'It took me a while to come to terms with the knowledge when I first found out,' admitted Ellen. 'Not because of being adopted, but because I hadn't known. I felt like a different person. But then – then I discovered my vocation and nothing else mattered.'

That was true, thought Abbey. But the fact that Ellen had joined the monastery so soon after learning about the birth mother she hadn't known existed was surely more than a coincidence.

'Mom . . .'

'Yes?'

'Is she why you became a nun?' asked Abbey. 'I mean – she died in a convent. The nuns treated her badly. Are you sure you're not simply trying to make amends?'

Ellen looked at her, startled. 'Of course not. I didn't know she'd died in a convent. All I knew was that she'd died and that her family couldn't cope. My vocation might have been triggered by events, but it's very real. I'm not trying to make amends for what happened to her, even though it was so very dreadful.'

'Now you know the full story, does it make a difference?'

Ellen contemplated silently for a moment before speaking.

'The past is the past,' she said. 'There's nothing I can do about it. I have to live my life the best way I can in the present.'

'So joining the monastery wasn't some sort of . . . of penance?'

'Everyone wants to find reasons when somebody does something unexpected,' Ellen replied. 'But the only reason is – and this is the truth – I truly found God. Which I know sounds very cultish and strange in the modern world. People are far more accepting of New Age stuff than they are of Christianity, and I understand that, honestly I do. But all the time I was working in the hospitals and all the time we were travelling, I was searching for something. I've found it here. Nevertheless . . .' She looked intently at Abbey. 'I'm sorry that in doing that, I left you behind.'

'Oh.' Abbey caught her breath. Ellen had never apologised to her for her vocation before.

'I should have talked to you about it.'

Abbey said nothing.

'But the way I saw things, you had your own life to lead. Your friends had asked you to share an apartment with them. You were doing your art course and your nail course too. You were making your own decisions and I was confident that you could manage without me.'

'So was I,' said Abbey. She didn't want her mother to know how much she'd been hurt by her decision. It didn't matter now, after all.

'And I was right, because you're doing wonderfully well.'

Abbey's emails to her mother, though short, only ever talked about the good things going on in her life. What was the point, she often thought, in worrying someone who couldn't do anything to help, other than pray?

'Generally speaking I'm . . . I'm grand.' She smiled to herself as she used Ryan Gilligan's expression. 'But there are other things to consider now. You and me and the Fitzpatricks.'

'You did a good job on Mr Fitzpatrick,' said Ellen. 'I'm proud of you.'

'He died, Mom,' Abbey reminded her. 'Not such a good job after all.'

'You did the right thing, though. You were there with him. And you were right to stay on and tell the family what had happened.'

'That's what I was thinking at the time. Of course when the whole thing about the will came out – then I kinda wished I'd legged it sooner.'

'I'm sure it was a big shock to them.'

'Not as big a one as it was to me.'

'Indeed. So – let me get this straight. He's left us his house but the family are furious, and unless we give up everything, they'll take a court action to overturn the will.'

Abbey nodded. 'I guess I can't blame them. They had no idea we existed, and then – bam! We get what they consider to be the jewel in the crown.'

'And how do you feel about that?'

Abbey gazed into the distance. 'At first I felt terrible for them. And guilty. But . . .'

Ellen waited for her to continue.

'But now I'm thinking – why not, Mom? What happened to Dilly was terrible, and it's easy to understand why he'd want to . . . to make reparations for that. Our lives and his would've been so different if he'd faced up to his responsibilities and hadn't abandoned her and her baby. You. He might even have married her!' As she had on various occasions since learning about Dilly, Abbey tried to visualise what life would have been like if her mom had been raised in Ireland by Dilly and Fred. And then, as always, she wondered what her Gramps and Gramma would have done without Ellen.

'How did he feel about me being in a monastery?' asked Ellen.

'He didn't know,' said Abbey.

'Nobody told him? Why?' Ellen was surprised.

'When Ryan Gilligan came looking for you, I didn't know if you'd already been told about being adopted or not. I wasn't having him barge in here with that sort of information. I didn't want him making judgements about you and the sisters either. Besides, you were on a retreat, so I told him I couldn't get in touch with you. I thought I'd go to Ireland, check things out, see what was going on and then let you decide if you wanted to contact him or not. I didn't for a second expect Mr Fitzpatrick to drop dead in front of me.' Her voice suddenly wavered and Ellen looked at her sympathetically.

'Of course you didn't.'

Abbey took a deep breath before continuing. 'But unsurprisingly, the family went ballistic when I said you were a nun. They think I kept it quiet for some nefarious reason and that you'll give all your money to the monastery.'

'The bell tower does need replacing,' murmured Ellen.

'Mom!'

'What?' Ellen's expression was innocent.

'I thought . . .' Abbey hesitated. 'I thought you'd think it was wrong to accept the inheritance.'

'Really?' Ellen looked at her with interest. 'And do *you* think it's wrong?'

'I don't know what to think,' admitted Abbey. 'At first I sympathised with the family and I thought Mr Fitzpatrick had made a terrible mistake. But then the two sons were horrible to me and implied that you were a nutter and that I'd killed their father.'

'You're joking!' exclaimed Ellen.

'I don't think they were entirely serious about the killing him part,' said Abbey. 'But they were throwing out some pretty nasty accusations. All the same, their sister, Suzanne, is lovely and she made up for them.'

'You seem to have got on well with her.'

Abbey told Ellen about her visit to Girona and her mother looked at her in surprise.

'You've been quite the globetrotter,' she said. 'She must be an interesting person if you stayed with her for a time.'

'There's no love lost between her and her brothers,' Abbey told her mother. 'She thinks we should take what we've been left. So do the legal people. So does Pete.'

'Of course Pete would think that,' said Ellen.

'And the thing is, Mom, my situation has changed since I first learned about it.'

'How?'

Abbey explained about Pete having bought the apartment.

'He did what!' exclaimed Ellen. 'Is he out of his mind?'

'He did it to inspire me,' said Abbey. 'A kick in the butt to make me fight for my rights.'

'Hmm.' Ellen's eyes were suddenly flinty.

'He thinks I'm too passive.'

Ellen looked thoughtful. 'Obviously fighting the Fitzpatrick brothers would be a fairly active thing to do.'

'It's not that I want a fight,' said Abbey. 'But I'm beginning to think that the old man had his reasons for doing what he did. And besides, I can't help loving the apartment.'

'You have to let go of the past,' said Ellen.

'Thing is, Mom, it's not the past. It's been renovated and it's very different. It's exactly right for me. And – well, I deserve something to go right in my life.'

'Why?' asked Ellen. 'I thought you said that you were . . . grand. Have things been going wrong?'

Abbey grimaced. 'There was this guy . . .' She told her mother about Cobey, and Ellen's eyes darkened.

'I'm sorry that happened to you,' she said. 'He treated you very badly.'

'I know.'

'And getting the house, or at least the money for it, is a bit like getting him back, isn't it?'

'Partly,' agreed Abbey.

'Obviously the Church preaches turning the other cheek,' Ellen reminded her.

'I'm *so* not convinced about that policy,' said Abbey. 'I can't entirely turn the other cheek anyway. Pete dug me out of a hole with the rental too by negotiating a deal. I owe him. Big time. And this way I can pay him back.'

'You do realise, I'm sure, that I can't keep anything myself,' said Ellen. 'We don't have personal items here and we certainly don't have bank accounts with large inheritances. I wouldn't accept it and hand it all to the monastery; that wouldn't be right either. So the reality is that I'd be giving my half to you.'

'You would?' Abbey was astounded.

'Of course I would,' said Ellen. 'And from that you could make a donation towards the upkeep of the bell tower, if that was what you wanted.'

'I can't quite believe you're saying I should have everything.'

'If the man wanted to leave something to us, and if you want to take it, then the logical conclusion is you take my share too,' said Ellen.

'But . . .'

'But what?'

'It's worth a lot of money,' said Abbey.

'And?'

'And I don't know if it's right.'

'Why?'

'I . . .' Abbey thought about it for a moment. 'The family don't think I deserve it. I wasn't there to look after their father.'

'And he wasn't there to look after me,' said Ellen.

'Mom!' Abbey was shocked. Ellen had passed judgement on Fred and she never passed judgement on anyone. At least, not since joining the monastery.

'That's the argument you're using, isn't it?' said Ellen.

Abbey took a sip of water before speaking. 'Actually, the argument that the legal people are using is that Mr Fitzpatrick was perfectly entitled to do whatever he liked with his money.'

'I know it well,' said Ellen. 'Sometimes benefactors leave us a legacy. The families aren't always happy about that either. D'you think if I wasn't a nun it would make a difference to them?'

'I'm not sure,' said Abbey. 'It would certainly have meant that challenging the will would've been more difficult for them. Basically they're saying he never would have left you anything at all if he thought you were a nun, because they were the ones who treated Dilly so badly.'

'Makes sense,' said Ellen.

'You know, I liked Mr Fitzpatrick in the few minutes that I knew him,' said Abbey. 'Although I'm not so sure his own children did. But I wish he hadn't left us quite so much. It would've made things a lot easier.'

'It was somewhat overgenerous,' agreed Ellen.

'I tried to say that we could talk about it,' Abbey told her. 'But Gareth and Donald are really angry with their father. They don't like me and they like you even less. They don't think we should have anything at all. Well,' she added, 'they offered us fifty thousand and I was supposed to accept that straight away. I couldn't, not without talking to you, but they said that if I didn't take it, they were going to court, and I guess that's what they're doing.'

'There are times when I can't help thinking God was having an off day when he created men,' said Ellen. 'They accuse us of being emotional, but when they get an idea into their heads, they start to think with the stubborn part of their brain. It becomes a win or lose situation, and they hate to lose.'

'I thought you loved all God's children equally,' said Abbey.

'I can love them all equally while acknowledging design flaws,' Ellen said.

Abbey couldn't help laughing. 'You know, sometimes you're like a regular person.'

'I *am* a regular person.' Ellen looked offended, but there was laughter in her voice. 'I haven't lost my sense of perspective just because I spend my days here.'

'Don't you get bored?' asked Abbey.

'I'm far too busy to get bored,' replied Ellen.

'Busy praying?'

'And working in the infirmary and with the sisters and on the retreats. There's lots to do. But our dilemma is something I have to pray about. I want to honour Mr Fitzpatrick . . . my father.' For the first time since she'd come into the room, she sounded

315

uncertain. 'Well, I want to honour his wishes, but I do understand the family's issues.'

'I thought perhaps if we offered them half they might come round,' said Abbey tentatively. 'We're being true to what Mr Fitzpatrick wanted but also giving them a lot.'

'That sounds very reasonable to me,' said Ellen.

'Do you really think so?'

'Yes, I do.'

'I thought you'd be against accepting anything at all. Either for you or for me.'

'I might have renounced all my worldly goods, but that doesn't mean you have to,' said Ellen.

'But I didn't know him,' said Abbey. 'And it's a lot of money.'

'Would you be uncomfortable having so much?' asked Ellen.

'Not if I was spending it all on the apartment,' replied Abbey.

'Ah yes, the apartment.' Ellen looked thoughtful.

'Do you think it's wrong to want it?'

'I think it was wrong of Pete to buy it and put you in a difficult situation,' said Ellen. 'But that's an entirely different issue. So I think you have to try to negotiate with the Fitzpatricks and then decide what you want to do about Pete and the apartment.'

'Mom, for a spiritual woman you have a great grasp of the material world.'

'I'll take that as a compliment,' said Ellen.

'Um, right.'

'And I'll do the praying.' Ellen added. 'For Dilly too.'

'Would you like to have known her?'

'Of course,' said Ellen. 'It wouldn't have affected how I felt about your Gramma and Gramps, but – yes, I think everyone needs to know where they came from. And even if the Fitzpatricks are being difficult right now, I'm glad to know they're there.'

'You might not be if it all gets messy,' said Abbey. 'I'm still not sure that Donald and Gareth are interested in negotiating.'

'I'll pray,' repeated Ellen.

'I think we need more practical stuff than prayer,' remarked Abbey. 'Much as I'm sure you're good at it.'

'I'll get the sisters on the job too,' Ellen said. 'When all of us get going, God knows we mean business.'

'I hope He's listening.'

'He's always listening.'

'Fingers crossed,' said Abbey. 'It'll be interesting to see if a bolt of lightning from heaven arrives with a message.'

'We won't need lightning,' said Ellen.

'But until then, I make the offer and we run with the punches.'

'Yes.' Ellen stood up. 'I have to get back now.'

'Already?' Abbey glanced at her watch and was surprised to see that over an hour had passed. 'Can't we have longer together?'

'It's almost time for the Lectio Divina, the sacred reading,' said Ellen. 'That will put me in a good frame of mind for the prayer bombardment.'

'Can you be a bit more worldly about things for another moment,' said Abbey. 'If they get in touch and there's something I need to talk to you about – what will I do? Will the prioress allow us to have another discussion so soon?'

'You can send an email. I'm sure the prioress will pass it on under the circumstances. In any event, I'll talk to her about it so that she knows what's going on. She'll understand. She'll pray too.'

Abbey looked at her in frustration. 'You'll probably have to sign things. Even if you're handing your half over to me and even if I'm doing a deal with the Fitzpatricks, the house was left to us jointly, so I'm sure there'll be paperwork. You can't ignore it.'

'The modern world is all about paperwork,' said Ellen gloomily. 'Maybe it was all the form-filling I used to have to do that drove me into the arms of the Lord.'

This time Abbey laughed.

'It's good to see you smile,' said Ellen. 'When I first saw you it seemed that you were very burdened.'

317

'Still burdened,' said Abbey. 'But . . .' She looked around. 'It's hard to stay tense in here.'

'I know.'

'It's a good life,' Abbey told her.

'But you're telling me the truth when you say you're all right, aren't you? The occasional cheating boyfriend notwithstanding?'

'I guess so,' said Abbey. 'I have good friends and I like my job.'

'Who would've thought there was a living to be made in painting nails?' Ellen couldn't hide the scepticism in her voice.

'I thought you'd come round to the whole nail-care thing,' said Abbey.

Ellen glanced at her own perfectly plain nails. 'Perhaps we should get portraits of the saints on ours,' she mused.

Abbey stifled an exclamation and Ellen looked at her quizzically.

'I suddenly thought of *Two Mules for Sister Sara*,' Abbey explained. 'Remember, that movie with Shirley MacLaine and Clint Eastwood. Where she was a nun?'

'Posing as a nun,' recalled Ellen. 'As I recall, though, she was a prostitute. I do hope you're not drawing comparisons.'

'Of course not!' exclaimed Abbey. 'If you must know, I'm a bit shocked at hearing you use the word.'

'Don't be silly,' said Ellen. 'I had to deal with a lot of problems to do with prostitution when I worked in the clinics. And we deal with the effects here sometimes too.'

'I can't help thinking you're too earthy to be a nun,' said Abbey.

Ellen laughed. 'You'd be surprised at how earthy nuns can be.'

'In all of your modes – earthy, worldly and spiritual – do you have any idea how things might work out?' asked Abbey.

'Things have a way of working out for the best in the end,' said Ellen.

'In a fairy story maybe,' muttered Abbey.

'Believe in God's plan,' said Ellen. 'Trust in Him.'

Which was all very well if you were the sort of person who

placed your trust in some kind of higher force, thought Abbey, as she hugged her mother before leaving. But if, like her, you thought life was a series of random events, then all the faith in the world wouldn't make the slightest bit of difference.

Chapter 30

Abbey arrived home at lunchtime the following day. Even though it was grey and dank in San Francisco, walking into her very own apartment lifted her spirits. She loved it here, no question. She wasn't harking back to the past; she was setting herself on the road to her future. A future in which she would inherit a house worth two million dollars from the grandfather she hadn't known about. Things like this happened all the time. Well, she thought, maybe not all the time, but people did receive money from unknown relatives. So why shouldn't she?

She sat down and composed an email to Ryan Gilligan, telling him that she and her mother were prepared to give up half the inheritance, thinking even as she hit the send button that this was an offer the Fitzpatrick brothers had to take seriously, and also that Pete would freak when she told him how much they were prepared to hand over. But, she reasoned, basically she was keeping everything she was entitled to; it was Ellen who was sacrificing her potential wealth. And since potential wealth meant nothing to her mother any more, it was hardly a big sacrifice for her to make.

Later that afternoon she met up with Solí in a café close to the gallery where she worked. She'd messaged both her and Vanessa when she was in Ireland, telling them about the Fitzpatricks and that Fred had left her something in his will, but not saying how much. Solí had posted on Abbey's Facebook wall, saying that she looked forward to hearing news of her grand inheritance, which had in turn resulted in a lot of jokey comments about her potential wealth. Abbey's response had been to joke back – she didn't want casual acquaintances knowing the true extent of what had been left to her – but now, drinking coffee with Solí, she filled her friend in.

'You're not serious!' Solí's huge brown eyes were wide with disbelief. 'He's cut his family out for you and your mom? It's like a movie.'

'That's what I thought,' said Abbey. 'But Hollywood has a habit of resolving things quickly. This is taking a bit longer and it's not an entirely pleasant experience.'

'No, I gathered that,' said Solí. 'All the same, it's pretty amazing to think that you're an heiress.'

'I didn't quite see it that way myself,' said Abbey. 'Sounds kinda cool to be an heiress, doesn't it?'

'And how.' Solí looked excited. 'But you deserve it, Abbey. You have to let yourself believe that.'

'Hmm. That's the sticking point,' said Abbey. 'Not everyone thinks so.'

'Why shouldn't the old man look after you and your mom?' demanded Solí. 'He walked away from his responsibilities before. Just because you're adults now doesn't mean he should forget about them.'

'I never thought of it in those terms before, but you have a point,' said Abbey.

'You get in there and fight for your rights, girl,' Solí told her. 'I understand why your mom is putting her share back in the pot, but you should enjoy the feeling of being rich.'

'I'm not rich yet,' said Abbey. 'I'm still not sure I'll ever be. But it's a nice dream.'

It was more than a dream, Pete told her the following day when she called him. It was her right. And she and Ellen were being incredibly generous in giving back half of what had been left to them.

'I thought your mom might give it to you,' Pete said, and Abbey told him that in practice that was what would happen, but then she'd sign it over to the Fitzpatricks in whatever way the legal people thought best. Pete remarked that he would have started negotiations with a much lower offer, and Abbey told him that it wasn't a negotiation process, at which Pete guffawed and said that life was all about negotiation but that he was very happy for her.

It was nice for Pete to be happy for her instead of worried about her, thought Abbey. It was nice to see him smile.

She'd barely finished talking to Pete when her cell phone rang and she saw Ryan Gilligan's name on the display.

'Hello, Ryan,' she said.

'Hi, I got your email and your proposal,' said Ryan without preamble. 'I've got to tell you something first, though.'

'What?'

'Well, I spoke to Alex and we were about to put something to the Fitzpatricks, but before we did, we received an email ourselves. From Lisette and Zoey Fitzpatrick.'

'Oh?'

'They had a proposal to make too,' said Ryan. 'They've offered you and your mother a hundred thousand each.'

'They have?' Abbey was surprised. 'D'you think Donald and Gareth know about it? Does Suzanne?'

'I rather think this is an initiative from the Fitzpatrick wives.'

'But that's way worse than what we're suggesting,' said Abbey. 'I couldn't possibly buy the apartment with that.'

'Ah,' said Ryan. 'So that's what you plan to do with it.'

Abbey told him about Pete's purchase and how he wanted it for her.

'Why would Zoey and Lisette think we'd take such a small amount?' she asked, even as she acknowledged to herself that a few weeks earlier she would've jumped with joy at the thought of being offered that kind of money.

322

'I suppose they felt you might be OK with it,' said Ryan. 'You were so embarrassed about anything at all at the start.'

'I'm not embarrassed now,' she said, reminding herself that everything was relative. 'I've talked to my mom and she hasn't said that it'd be easier for a camel to get through the eye of a needle than for me to get into the kingdom of heaven if I accept it. Besides, we're still leaving a fair chunk to the rest of them. I think we're being very reasonable. Don't you?' she added anxiously.

'Yes, I do,' said Ryan. 'Alex will make your offer tomorrow and we'll take it from there.'

'OK,' said Abbey. 'Hopefully they'll say yes and everyone will be happy.'

'Total happiness,' said Ryan. 'The absolute aim of Celtic Legal.'

It was Alex Shannon who emailed the family with Ellen and Abbey's offer. He sent the same mail to all of them, advising that as Donald and Gareth currently intended to challenge Fred's bequests, there would be an inevitable delay before any funds could be released to them, but that if they accepted Abbey's proposal, he, Alex, would try to expedite things as soon as possible.

Suzanne, who a moment earlier had received a phone call from Jaime Roig telling her that a firm offer had been made by a rival consortium for the Mirador Hotel, picked up the phone and called Donald straight away. As far as she was concerned, Abbey and her mother were being very honourable and her brothers should accept the offer without any more fuss.

'I'm not happy,' said Donald.

'Why?'

'They're saying half the estate. But there's a lot of stuff in the house that we don't know about and that might be valuable.'

'So what? I'm sure you can come to an agreement about dividing that too. You hardly want anything for sentimental reasons, do you?'

'We need to get it all valued. To see exactly what's what.'

'Oh for crying out loud!' exclaimed Suzanne. 'Accept the damn offer so that we can get on with our lives.'

'It's a ploy,' said Donald. 'We can get more out of them. And, being honest, it's not more I want, it's everything.'

'Why?' demanded Suzanne. 'Why does it have to be all or nothing?'

'Because Dad shouldn't have done it in the first place,' said Donald. 'He usurped my position in the family and he's made fools out of everyone.'

'It doesn't bloody matter!'

'Yes,' said Donald. 'It does. *I'm* the eldest in this family. *I'm* his heir. He should have consulted *me*.'

'Get over yourself, Donald Fitzpatrick.' Suzanne could hardly contain her fury with her older brother. 'Who cares about that stuff? Nobody but you. Say yes to Abbey and put all this behind us.'

'I'm not agreeing,' Donald retorted. 'I don't see why I should and you can't make me.'

'But I need my share now!' cried Suzanne.

'You'll do better when we win this case. I promise.'

'Use your head!' Suzanne implored him. 'Dragging this through the courts as much to prove some kind of point as anything else is sheer madness – and will cost us a fortune anyway.'

'I don't care,' said Donald obstinately. 'I want what's ours and I don't want that madwoman acknowledged as part of our family. And that's final.'

Suzanne ended the call without another word, yearning for the time when you could bang the receiver on to its cradle with a satisfying thump to release your rage. Stabbing at a keypad button didn't allow the same release of energy. Her brother was such a dick, she thought, with his antiquated ideas of ancestry and inheritance. Not to mention commercially thick, because she knew she was right about the costs of any protracted legal action. She'd been under the impression that Donald needed that money because of his divorce, but he couldn't be that badly off if he was refusing to negotiate with Abbey Andersen. Gareth, however, was definitely in a financial hole. Everyone in Ireland who'd fancied themselves as a player in the property market had come a cropper. Suzanne had a certain amount of sympathy for her second brother, but his problems were of his own making. He'd never been a businessman, had scoffed at chasing profit in the past. It was a pity he'd been suckered in like so many others. Agreeing to the settlement was surely a way out for him.

She needed to get Gareth onside, make him talk to Donald and point out how stupid their older brother was being. She dialled the number.

It was Lisette who answered, sounding, to Suzanne's ears, tired and strained as she told her to hold on for a moment. Then Gareth came on the line. Suzanne asked if he was prepared to accept Ellen Connolly and Abbey Andersen's offer.

'I don't know,' said Gareth. 'There are other considerations.'

'Like what?'

'Well, they're trying to keep a lot. The house is worth at least a couple of million. Why should they get half of that sort of money?'

'Maybe it's not ideal,' said Suzanne. 'But the reality is that Dad made a decision and we have to live with it.'

'No we don't,' said Gareth. 'Don says—'

'Oh for God's sake, I've just been talking to Don. And he's an idiot!' retorted Suzanne.

'He's not,' said Gareth. 'He's been pretty successful, you know. And he was hard done by by Deirdre. She took him to the cleaners with a vengeance.'

'In which case, he hasn't shown himself to be great at negotiations in the past.'

'He thinks we can get everything,' said Gareth. 'The legal team he's putting together—'

'Excuse me? Legal team?' Suzanne was astounded. 'He doesn't need a legal team. Just advice.'

'Yes, but we need the best possible advice,' Gareth said.

325

'Give me patience!' Suzanne rolled her eyes in exasperation. 'Alex has already given us good advice. Don has his head up his arse, and from that position he's certainly not seeing anything clearly. Talk to him, Gar. Make him accept this damn offer. Then I can get my money and you'll get yours and we can all get on with our lives.'

'The problem is,' Gareth said, 'under their offer, I wouldn't even get half a million. And that isn't enough. There'll be taxes and—'

'Listen to yourself!' Suzanne interrupted him. 'Since when were you the sort of person who thought half a million wasn't a huge amount of money?'

'Since I became a property tycoon,' replied Gareth wryly.

'You're a teacher,' said Suzanne. 'You were never a property tycoon. Would you please stop thinking like that.'

'I might not be a tycoon, but I'm still up to my neck in property.'

'Oh Gar, everything will work out, honestly it will. But you need to get a sense of perspective on all this. So does Don.'

'I'll talk to him,' said Gareth. 'But I'm not sure it'll do any good.'

After he'd finished talking to Suzanne, Gareth went up to his den and started looking at French property sites again. The prices of houses in La Rochelle were marginally higher than they'd been the previous year. And the agent on the site he was looking at was actively seeking more properties. If they accepted Abbey's offer and also sold Papillon, they might conceivably break even. But if Donald was right and they won their challenge, then he might be able to hold on to their French home. Even though right now he hated anything to do with bricks and mortar. No matter how Lisette felt about it.

I don't know what to do. Lisette was messaging Zoey on Facebook. **Suzanne wants to accept the offer. Gareth is in two minds. My head hurts thinking about it.**

There's no way Don will accept half, typed Zoey. It's a matter of honour with him.

Half is better than nothing, responded Lisette.

I was hoping she might counter our own offer. Zoey's fingers flew over the keyboard. I thought she might come back with a counter of 250K, which would have been doable.

Don't you think this is?

What I think doesn't matter. It's what Don thinks that counts. Can't you work on him?

Perhaps if she'd come back and suggested 250K I might have been able to persuade him. But not half. He thinks it's way too much.

What if Deirdre had a word with him?

Are you mad? He hates the bitch.

She's not that bad.

Oh, please, typed Zoey. She feeds off him. And so do those leechy kids of his. He gives the girls money so that they'll like him, you know.

They love him because he's their father. Not because of money.

I'm not so sure about that, returned Zoey. You should hear their demands sometimes.

What are we going to do? Lisette could feel despair seeping through her fingers.

Let's meet. Zoey was typing quickly because she could hear Donald in the hallway outside their room and she didn't want him to see what she was doing. How about at Fred's. Tomorrow afternoon?

I've classes until 4 p.m. Does 5 work?

Perfect, typed Zoey. See you then.

Chapter 31

The exhibition hall that was holding the nail art competition that Abbey had entered was buzzing with excited participants and their models. The women wore their newly adorned nails with glamour and confidence and Abbey couldn't help thinking that she'd been far too conservative in the work she'd done. The theme for the competition was Seasons, and most of the other competitors had gone all out to make the nails of their models as bright and as colourful as possible. The girls in the 3D division had pulled out all the stops – Abbey had seen one of the models wearing nail extensions depicting branches on trees with tiny leaves dangling from the ends. It was amazing to look at, although obviously impractical on a day-to-day basis as the wearer wouldn't have been able to use her hands for anything. But still, she thought, the work was so brilliant it deserved a prize. Selina, who'd been surprised and pleased when Abbey told her she was entering the competition, had immediately offered to be her model, and now she was holding her carefully painted nails in front of her, showing them off to their best advantage even though Abbey wasn't at all hopeful that her depiction of the changing seasons across Selina's nails was good enough.

'I thought you'd have to be able to use your hands afterwards,' she remarked as another model with impossibly long nails walked by. 'Neither hers nor the Fall Tree set are at all practical.'

'It's art,' Selina pointed out. 'Art doesn't have to be practical.'

Abbey nodded, realising that the competition was about the skills you could use as a nail technician, not what your model could do afterwards. It's like high fashion, she thought. Bizarre but brilliant.

In the end another technician won the overall prize (she'd chosen spring as her theme, and her model's nails represented budding flowers), but Abbey did take the top prize in the art division, which meant a bear hug from Selina to go with her prize of product samples.

'The thing is,' Selina told her, 'if you start making a name for yourself, people might want you to endorse their products. You could even do a line of your own!'

Abbey could feel the salon owner's enthusiasm. And she was already thinking about how she could improve her designs and what she might do to make them stand out more. At the very least, she told herself later that night when she was curled up in front of the TV watching *CSI: LA*, she should do some 3D work as that seemed to get most of the attention. And she should come up with more art templates of her own. Old Masters, she thought suddenly. They'd be good. People would like to wear the *Mona Lisa* on their fingertips.

The following day Selina put up a huge poster in the window of the salon, advertising that the award-winning Abbey Andersen worked there and offering personal consultations with her. Abbey, who thought it was a bit OTT, was nevertheless astonished when the number of people making appointments for manicures and nail art doubled.

'You see,' said Selina. 'These things matter. I told you. Get yourself out there, girl. Put your name in lights.'

Abbey entered another competition a couple of weeks later. This time she was the overall winner for her 3D *Mona Lisa*, which everyone agreed was amazing. Selina put her trophies in the window and her client list grew again.

Claudia, who'd never come to the salon before, made an appointment to have her nails done before attending a business dinner with Pete. She brought a friend with her, a tall, stylish woman named Tina, who worked in a private investment company.

'Abbey is thinking of developing her own line of products,' Claudia told Tina. 'Might be a worthwhile investment for you.'

Abbey looked at Claudia, speechless. It was true that she'd mentioned it to Pete the last time they'd talked, but it was part of a casual conversation in which she'd said that when her money from Fred's estate finally came through (and obviously that was still a long way away), she might invest some of it in her own range of nail colours and art templates.

'There are plenty of products on the market already,' said Tina. 'Why would yours be any different?'

'Colours.' Abbey surprised herself by how quickly she answered. 'There's scope for creating a different type of palette and colours that give more special effects.'

'You think so?'

'Yes.' Now that she'd expressed aloud to a stranger what she'd been thinking about for the last couple of weeks, Abbey grew more animated. 'There are designs I'd love to do but the colour schemes aren't quite right.'

'Here's my card.' Tina handed it to her. 'Let's talk sometime.'

As they left, both delighted with their high-gloss finishes, Claudia turned to Abbey and kissed her on the cheek.

'I always knew you had talent,' she said. 'It's nice to see it blossom.'

Abbey was so astonished that she almost didn't notice the size of the tip that the two women had left her.

She had a fifteen-minute break at midday and so she popped out to buy a sandwich, still deep in thought about the potential for a business of her own. It seemed a huge step and one that she was ill-equipped to take, but now that the idea was taking

330

hold in her mind, she couldn't help giving it more and more space. It seemed to her that this was totally doing what Pete had said about developing her talents, and that Ellen would be proud of her too. Clearly Tina had thought that both she and her idea had potential or she wouldn't have passed over her card, and as for Claudia – Abbey had always felt Claudia simply tolerated her, but there had been real affection in the other woman's words. Abbey felt her heart beat faster as she thought more and more about it. Abbey's Art, she thought. Or Fab Fingers. Or – even better – Nailed!

She was smiling to herself, lost in her thoughts and not noticing the people around her, when she heard a familiar voice call her name. She looked up, startled, and saw Cobey Missen standing in front of her, wearing jeans, sneakers and a grey Giants fleece. His trademark Ray-Bans were pushed on to his head.

'How're you doing, Abbey?' he asked.

At first she couldn't speak. She realised that she was trembling. Shock, she told herself, at seeing him so unexpectedly. Anger at the way he'd left her. And . . . and – what? A sudden inexplicable desire for him to realise that he was still in love with her.

'What are you doing here?' she asked finally. 'I thought you were cruising the Caribbean or something.'

'I was,' he said. 'But I discovered it wasn't my kind of thing. The damn ship was too claustrophobic.'

'I suppose it's hard to walk out on someone when you're in the middle of the ocean together,' said Abbey tartly.

'Don't be like that, babes,' said Cobey. 'I'm sorry. You know I am.'

'You left without a word.' Her voice was clipped and angry. 'You borrowed money and you didn't pay me back. You owed rental even though I'd given it to you. You're a fraud, Cobey Missen.'

'Hey, I know. And I'm embarrassed about that.' There was contrition in both his eyes and his voice. 'I made a big mistake.'

'You could have told me,' said Abbey. 'I thought we were a couple. But we weren't.'

'I panicked,' Cobey said. 'I'll admit it. I was spending more than I was earning. The tour company was going through a slump and my wages were cut. I didn't want to tell you because I was ashamed.'

'I thought you loved me,' she said. 'I thought I loved you. People who love each other share things no matter what.'

'I could still love you and be ashamed to say anything,' protested Cobey. 'And that was the case. I needed to get away, clear my head, pay my debts.'

'So you signed up for a cruise?'

'I was working on the ship, not holidaying.' Cobey smiled ruefully at her and she felt her heart skip a beat. He'd always had a disarming smile. 'But it wasn't the great opportunity I thought it was going to be. It was damn hard work, let me tell you. Let me tell you,' he repeated, 'over a drink tonight.'

'I'm busy,' she said.

'Come on, Abbs. One little drink. I'll explain everything and maybe you can find it in your heart to forgive me.'

'No,' repeated Abbey, even though she was thinking that perhaps Ellen would like her to show forgiveness.

'One,' said Cobey again. 'I'll meet you at Cantina and buy you a cocktail.'

'I don't think . . .'

'Please,' he said. 'I want to apologise properly. I know I let you down. Hell, I let myself down.'

He looked so forlorn standing there in front of her that her resolve weakened. And she said yes.

In Dublin, the only topic of conversation was the challenge to Fred's will. Despite the fact that Lisette had urged Gareth to accept Abbey Andersen's offer (how much better do you want it to be? she'd demanded), Donald had persuaded him that he'd do better by contesting the will.

'You can't back out now,' he'd told his brother when Gareth suggested that perhaps Lisette was right and that they should take what they could get. 'It's not only about the money.'

'For Lisette it is,' said Gareth.

'Of course. Because she's not really family, is she? She married into the Fitzpatricks but she didn't grow up with us. She doesn't know what it was like to be a Fitzpatrick. Besides, she's French. She has different views.'

'She reckons that getting our hands on a definite amount now would be better than holding out for a potentially bigger sum in the future,' said Gareth. 'She's a very practical woman.'

'And I could agree with her if it wasn't that accepting the will means we also accept Dad's version of what happened with that Ita Dillon woman.'

'I think what happened was fairly clear,' said Gareth. 'She got pregnant. He abandoned her. She died. He felt guilty.'

'How could he even be sure the baby was his?' demanded Donald. 'She might have been a slapper sleeping with half the country, for all we know.'

'I doubt Dad would have left money to complete strangers unless he thought she'd told him the truth,' said Gareth. 'He must have believed it, otherwise he wouldn't have felt so guilty.'

'We're judging his actions then by the standards of today,' said Donald. 'So was he. He only did what anyone else would have done. He didn't need to beat himself up over it. I do understand a certain measure of guilt, but it was over fifty years ago. It pisses me off how everyone today is meant to apologise for things that happened in the past. We need to move on. Get over it.'

'You have a point.'

'Anyway, the biggest point is this. Ellen Connolly was never part of this family. She knows nothing about us. She didn't try to find out about us. She went off and became a nun. Allowing her and her daughter to have any part of our inheritance is an insult to what being a Fitzpatrick is all about.'

'So it's more about the family than the money?' Gareth looked at his brother in confusion.

'It's both. Money puts a value on everything. Being a Fitzpatrick is the most important thing. Giving this woman and her daughter half of everything – well, it's too much of an insult. Quite honestly, I believe that giving them anything at all is an insult to Mam.'

'I agree as far as Mam's memory is concerned,' said Gareth. 'Though financially—'

'I know both of us have financial reasons for wanting this over quickly,' Donald said. 'But we have to put them to one side while we work for what's right. It'll be worth it in the end, I promise you.'

'Yes, but—'

'Trust me,' Donald told his brother. 'I'm the eldest. I know what I'm doing.'

Gareth wanted to believe him. But he was still racked with doubts.

'I know what Donald's saying, but I don't think the courts will take the same view of the whole family thing. All they'll do is look at the money.' Zoey Fitzpatrick was sitting in Fred's kitchen with Lisette. The two of them had taken to meeting each other there on a regular basis and, much to their surprise, were enjoying the mutual moral support that talking about their situation gave. Neither of them mentioned the meetings to their husbands and naturally both kept secret the fact that they had dipped into Fred's secret cash hoard on a further two occasions. Of the original thirty thousand, ten now remained.

Lisette had managed to put her guilt behind her about taking the money. She'd used the first chunk to clear all of their outstanding utility bills, buy some new shoes for the children, get the boiler and her car serviced, pay off her credit card and have a facial at the local beauty salon, something that she'd once loved but had stopped doing since money had got tight. She'd also bought a few jars of her favourite Clarins products, which she'd been substituting with supermarket alternatives. No matter how much some people insisted that cheaper creams were equally effective, Lisette yearned for the luxury of the ones she'd grown to love.

She hadn't spent all of the cash, but knowing that it was safely tucked away in a pair of thick grey socks in the bottom drawer of her dresser gave her a sense of security. Fred's money had given her back a little piece of herself, she thought, and even though she still broke out in a rash of guilt every time she thought about taking it, she managed to push it to one side. Gareth had noticed that the bills had been paid, and she'd explained it by saying that she was giving extra grinds to students most afternoons. He was so relieved at seeing some of their outstanding debts disappear that he didn't question her any further, even though he should have known that she'd never have made enough giving private tuition to have paid off so many outstanding bills. This time his lack of financial savvy was working to her advantage. It was also fortunate that he wasn't the kind of man ever to notice what beauty products she used, because otherwise he'd definitely ask questions she wouldn't want to answer.

Zoey was using the money to keep herself in the style she was accustomed to without charging Donald's credit card. He'd noticed the apparent decrease in her spending and had thanked her for cutting back in what was a difficult time, although, he added, she could go on a total spree when they won the challenge. Zoey congratulated herself on how she'd used Fred's money to concentrate on visits to her hairdresser and the beauty salon rather than buying clothes. Clothes were important, but how you looked mattered even more, and Zoey knew that she would never compromise on that. Besides, whereas Donald expected her to look great all the time, he didn't notice every salon trip in the way he noticed new clothes or shoes.

'Disgruntled Deirdre was on the phone again,' she added as

she sipped her coffee (she'd bought ground beans for the cafetière on the basis that the instant muck in Fred's cupboard was undrinkable). 'She was banging on at Don about how she wanted her goddam money and that it was his fault that probate was delayed.'

'It *is* Donald's fault,' said Lisette. 'If it wasn't for him, I could make Gareth accept the offer from the Americans. Suzanne would be delighted that the will had finally gone to probate, and even though it's not enough for us, it would still help a lot. Are you sure you can't persuade him, Zoey?'

Zoey shook her head. 'He won't listen to me. It's a crusade as far as he's concerned. He feels he's been usurped as the head of the family, partly because Fred did this without talking to him first and partly because Abbey's mother is actually his older sister. Or half-sister, I suppose. Donald's always been the eldest. It really, really bothers him that she was born before him.'

'Well, his obsession is racking up more bills for the rest of us!' Lisette looked worried. 'I keep thinking of what you said. Fifty thousand a day when it gets to court. That's insane!' She took another biscuit from the pack. She was comfort eating whenever she was with Zoey, but she wasn't putting on any weight because at home she was unable to eat a thing. 'Why won't they make another offer to her?'

'I asked Don to do that,' said Zoey. 'But he said that there was no point. That he wasn't getting into horse-trading and that it was a matter of principle.'

'What's the point in having principles if we don't have any money at the end of it?'

'Don will work something out. He always does, no matter how bad it looks. You think he's down and out and then – boom! He comes up with something. Anyway, this whole thing – who's the eldest in the family, how they're all treated – well, it matters a lot to him.'

'Everyone in this family has their own agenda,' muttered Lisette.

'I thought that Fred dying might bring us all closer, but we're as far apart as ever.'

'It's brought you and me closer.' Zoey drained her coffee and rinsed the cup beneath the tap. 'C'mon. We have work to do.'

Lisette slid slowly off the stool. In addition to raiding Fred's cash, she and Zoey had decided that it was only right for them to take pieces of what had legitimately been left to them just in case things went badly in court and Abbey ended up with everything. They were choosing small items that wouldn't be missed. Lisette had already taken the silver snuff box and a small silver photo frame, while Zoey had chosen an emerald ring and matching earrings which she'd sold for a few hundred euros. Not that she'd needed the cash there and then; she'd just wanted to see what it was like to do it. Lisette hadn't sold the snuff box or the photo frame. She didn't think she'd get much for them in any event. They were both in the bottom drawer of her bedside locker. Like the money, it comforted her to know that they were there.

Standing in the crowded cocktail bar, a favourite haunt of theirs in the past, Abbey listened as Cobey explained again how his finances had spiralled out of control and how the savage pay cuts at the tour company had made things worse. He'd hoped, he said, to resolve everything without telling her, to get his own tour company up and running and to make a lot of money. But things hadn't worked out that way, and when the cruise ship opportunity came along, he'd jumped at it.

'I needed to get away for a bit and clear my head,' he told her.

'You should have said something to me. You took my money and then walked out!' She was still angry.

'I made a mistake. I'm sorry.'

'And now?' she asked. 'Where are you living now?'

'With Mike.'

'Right.'

'I called to the apartment,' he told her. 'I thought you might be still there.'

'How could I be? You were served with a notice to quit – which you didn't even tell me about.'

'I'm so, so sorry,' repeated Cobey. 'I never meant to put you in that position.'

But what did he think would happen when he walked out? she wondered. That the landlord would forget about the unpaid rent? Cobey knew better than that.

'I know I owe you money,' he said. 'I'll sort that out. But in the meantime . . .' He opened his wallet and took out some bills. 'Here's five hundred dollars.'

She hadn't been expecting that.

'I pay my debts,' said Cobey.

She didn't need his money now. Soon she'd have more than enough of her own.

'Take it,' said Cobey.

He owed her, though. And maybe he'd be insulted if she refused. So she took the money and put it into her purse.

'Good. That's done. We're back on a more equal footing. Let's talk about something else for a while.' Cobey looked at her hopefully.

She hadn't thought she'd ever speak to him again. Yet he was truly remorseful, he'd repaid her some money, and she couldn't help feeling sorry for him. Anyone could make a mistake. Besides, her mother's oft-spoken words about forgiveness and understanding were echoing in her head. If she couldn't forgive the man she'd once loved, then how could she possibly forgive other people? So she allowed him to buy her another five-spice margarita, which she drank while he told her stories about his life on the cruise ship and she felt her anger with him melt away. She'd forgotten how much he made her laugh. She'd forgotten how much she'd loved him.

'So what about you?' he asked as he ordered their fourth cocktail of the night. 'What have you been doing?'

Not drinking like this, she thought, her head woozy from alcohol and lack of food. I only ever drink this much when I'm with you.

'I heard,' he continued, 'that you'd been to Ireland.'

'Who told you that?' She drained her glass and put it on the bar counter.

'Someone saw it on your Facebook page,' he said vaguely. 'Something about tracing your roots.'

'Oh, that.'

'Or maybe it was on someone else's page,' said Cobey. 'Is it true that your grandmother left you a fortune?'

He must have seen the jokey comments, she thought. But she'd defriended him, hadn't she? Though maybe they still had a joint friend somewhere. Bloody privacy settings, she thought. I never get it right.

'Grandfather,' she told him. 'And not exactly.'

'But you were left something?'

'Mmm.' This wasn't a conversation she wanted to have. 'Maybe. It's a bit confusing at the moment.'

'Why?' asked Cobey.

'Oh, I was left a share in a house, but some of the family don't think I should have it, so there's a bit of a row going on.'

'Hopefully it'll all work out and you'll get what's yours,' said Cobey. 'A house in Ireland sounds great. Is it one of those cute little cottages?'

'No,' said Abbey. 'A proper house. But—'

'How much is it worth?' asked Cobey.

'I . . .'

'Sorry,' he said. 'None of my business. It would be nice for you to have something, that's all. You deserve good things, Abbey.'

People were saying that all the time. But it was strange to hear it from Cobey, after what he'd done. Now he was back again, she thought suddenly, and he'd heard about her inheritance. That was a coincidence. Wasn't it?

'I might not get anything at all,' she said.

'Let's hope you do.' Cobey handed her a freshly mixed margarita. 'But in the meantime – here's something else nice for you. Cheers.'

'I'm going to have a dreadful hangover in the morning,' she said. But she raised the glass all the same.

Chapter 32

Vanessa was horrified when she heard that Abbey had gone to a bar with Cobey.

'You what?' she exclaimed. She'd called around to Abbey's apartment and the two of them were sitting in the living room. Vanessa was drinking coffee. Abbey was trying to rehydrate after the cocktails with an isotonic drink. 'Are you nuts? Can I remind you that he cheated on you big time?'

'I think cheating *on* a person means seeing someone else. Cheating a person is different.'

'Now's not the time to be splitting hairs grammatically,' retorted Vanessa. 'Now's the time to cut that guy out of your life for ever.'

'He deserved a chance to explain. I wanted him to explain,' said Abbey.

'And after his explanation I hope you kicked his butt to the sidewalk.'

'I understood a bit more.'

'What's to understand?' Vanessa looked at her in horror. 'He's a cheat and a loser and you can't possibly be thinking of letting him into your life again.'

'I'm not letting him into my life. I'm—'

'Has he repaid you the money he owes you?' Vanessa interrupted her.

'He gave me five hundred dollars. He says he'll give me the rest as soon as he can.'

'You believe that?'

'I'll give him the benefit of the doubt.'

'Abbey! You're not your mom. You don't have to turn the other cheek on this one.'

'People do things they regret,' said Abbey. 'He's apologised and he's trying to make reparations.'

'He broke your heart.'

'I let my heart be broken,' said Abbey. 'That's a different situation altogether.'

'Have you heard anything from your Irish lawyer about the will?' asked Vanessa.

'What's that got to do with it?'

'Nothing,' said Vanessa. 'Only it seems strange to me that Cobey has turned up again when you might be rich.'

'That did cross my mind,' acknowledged Abbey. 'But it's rubbish. He didn't like the cruise ship, he came home, he apologised and he's trying to make things right.'

'Ever since you've come back from Ireland you've been in a much better place,' said Vanessa. 'You're doing so well with your career and with your life. Don't screw it up over a man.'

'Where I am in my life right now has nothing to do with Cobey Missen,' said Abbey. 'Nor has it anything to do with the Irish connection. I've focused more, is all.'

'Don't allow him to blur your focus then,' said Vanessa. 'Please, Abbey.'

'Stop nagging.' Abbey looked at her friend in irritation. 'Stop nagging and be happy that I'm OK with myself right now.'

Vanessa opened her mouth to protest. Then closed it again. There was no point in arguing with Abbey when she wore her grim and determined expression. All Vanessa could hope for was that her friend saw sense before she did something monumentally stupid.

Abbey went to Claudia and Pete's for Thanksgiving. Cobey had asked if she'd like to spend it with him, but even though she felt she should disentangle herself from the Carusos' lives, she wasn't ready to spend such an important day with Cobey yet. The previous year she'd visited Ellen at the monastery, but despite enjoying the ecumenical service, which was open to the local community on that day, she found it difficult to be one of many other visitors. Besides, there wasn't that much time available to spend on her own with Ellen.

She arrived with a bottle of Cabernet Sauvignon for Pete and an enormous bouquet of flowers for Claudia. She'd also brought a box of cupcakes for Joely and Grady, as well as a large bone tied with a red ribbon for Battle.

'Oh wow, this is amazing,' she said as she walked into the dining room and looked at the table, which Claudia had decorated in purple and gold.

'I did the stars,' said Joely proudly, showing her the confetti-sized purple and gold stars scattered around each place setting.

'You're amazing too,' said Abbey. 'And if your mom says it's OK, I'm going to paint your nails.'

'Can she, Mom?' Joely looked pleadingly at Claudia and then whooped in delight when her mother said yes. Abbey took the little girl into the children's den and varnished her nails in pink with silver glitter.

'Look at me!' cried Joely as they had a drink before dinner. 'I'm a princess.'

'You sure are, honey,' said Pete. 'Did you say thank you to Abbey?'

'Yes.' But Joely put her arms around her and kissed her again.

'Thanks for doing mine, too.' Claudia stretched her hands in front of her. Abbey had done them the previous day, but she hadn't realised that the purple and gold that Claudia had requested was to match her table decorations.

'You're welcome,' she said.

'Tina told me you did a wonderful job on hers for the event she was going to last week,' added Claudia. 'Something about her family tree?'

Abbey nodded. 'I adapted old photos of her parents and grand-parents,' she said. 'And on the other hand I did her husband's folk. It looked great.'

'You certainly seem to be incredibly busy lately,' said Pete. 'Sandra, from the office, said she has to wait two weeks for an appointment with you.'

'What can I say!' Abbey looked pleased. 'I'm much in demand.'

'Tina is very interested in you,' Claudia told her. 'I think that if you wanted to set up on your own, develop those nail colours, she'd be ready to listen.'

'Perhaps in the future,' said Abbey. 'I'm not quite ready yet. But I'm not ruling it out.'

'Hey, when Abbey gets her hands on the house in Ireland, she'll have plenty of her own money to invest,' said Pete.

'Not if I buy the apartment from you,' Abbey pointed out.

'We'll work something out,' Pete told her. 'Main thing is, you're on the up. Definitely.'

'You look fantastic too,' added Claudia. 'You've let your hair grow a bit and it suits you. Plus . . .' She looked critically at Abbey. 'There's something else. It's like you're taller . . . more . . . more . . .'

'More confident,' finished Pete. 'That's it, Abbey. You've lost that hangdog expression you usually have.'

'I don't usually have a hangdog expression,' protested Abbey.

'Not now,' agreed Claudia. 'But Pete's right. Before, you always seemed defensive. Now you're way more assertive. It suits you.'

Abbey knew that she wasn't half as assertive as Claudia appeared to think. She was still getting grief from both Solí and Vanessa over Cobey; she hadn't been able to convince them that she knew what she was doing with him and that she wouldn't have her heart broken again. When she was with Cobey – who she'd met with a few times since the cocktail night in Cantina – she'd let him set the agenda in deciding what to do and where to go, and she suddenly felt as though other people had more control over her than she did. Nevertheless, it was good to have someone in her life again, even if he was still at its periphery, no matter what Solí and Vanessa thought.

'Any new information on the will?' asked Pete when they were seated at the dining table and he was sharpening the carving knife.

'Ryan Gilligan rings me every week with an update,' said Abbey. 'But so far there's nothing to update me on.'

'I liked him,' said Pete. 'He's a good man.'

'Yes,' agreed Abbey. She smiled as she thought of Ryan. Their weekly conversations were always fun. He continued to call her his American cailín, while she'd taken to referring to him as her Irish buchaill. (She'd had problems with the pronunciation of the word, which he'd told her meant 'boy' in Irish, until he'd sent her an email with the phonetic spelling of boo-kill. But for some reason he still laughed – although kindly – at her accent.) 'What?' she added, realising that Pete was looking at her speculatively.

'Anything going on between you two?' asked Pete.

'Don't be silly,' she replied. 'He lives on the other side of the Atlantic.'

'Abbey's got a boyfriend!' cried Joely.

'Abbey doesn't have time for a boyfriend,' she told the little girl.

'Everyone has time for a boyfriend,' said Claudia. 'Just because you're doing well in the nail business doesn't mean you should cut men out of your life.'

'And just because you had a bad experience with one man doesn't mean you should tar us all with the same brush,' Pete told her.

'I'm over that,' said Abbey, still not mentioning that she was, if not officially dating, certainly seeing Cobey again.

'Good,' Pete said.

'That guy didn't deserve our Abbey,' Claudia declared. 'But he was a fool to let her go.'

The last time they'd met, Cobey had said the same thing to

her, but she hadn't been able to believe him. And if he'd been a fool to let her go, would she be a fool to take him back? Even though he'd apologised. Even though he was contrite. Even though she'd very nearly forgiven him.

Later that evening, as Claudia and Pete dozed in front of the movie they'd selected to watch on TV, and Grady and Joely both played video games, Abbey's phone rang.

'Hello,' said Ryan Gilligan when she answered it. 'How are things with you?'

'Good,' she said. 'I'm good, things are good – why are you calling? Is there anything new from the family?'

'Nothing worthwhile,' said Ryan. 'We've had a few letters from their solicitors but no offers from them, no signs that they're willing to negotiate.'

'Is it wrong of me to think that in saying we'd give them half we've been generous enough already?' asked Abbey. 'I mean – are they right? Are we being selfish? Should we give up everything?'

'Has your mom suggested you should?'

'No, it's not that. I haven't spoken to her since I visited her,' replied Abbey. 'But, you know, I can't help thinking that money for nothing is wrong.'

'You've definitely had a Catholic upbringing.' Ryan chuckled. 'Carrying all that guilt around because something nice has happened to you.'

'I'm not carrying guilt. Well, I guess maybe I am. Something nice happened to me but it came out of something awful, and the rest of the family are so upset.' She ran her fingers through her hair in distraction. 'I don't know what to think!'

'Think that Fred wanted to do right by his daughter,' suggested Ryan. 'That should make you feel OK.'

'Hmm. Maybe. So if you're not calling about the will – why are you?'

'Does there have to be a reason?' asked Ryan.

'Um, usually.'

'In that case, I'm ringing to wish you a happy Thanksgiving,' he told her.

'Thank you.'

'I know it's a big deal over there and that you give it the kind of attention we tend to give Christmas here. So I wanted to send the good wishes of everyone at Celtic Legal.'

'Thanks,' she said again.

'We're all thinking of you here in Dublin and hoping that things go well for you.'

'I wouldn't say all of you in Dublin are hoping that,' she said. 'I guess the Fitzpatricks are hoping quite the opposite.'

'Don't worry about the Fitzpatricks,' Ryan said. 'We're going to leave them for dust.'

'We are?'

'Absolutely,' he assured her.

'There's a part of me that wants to see Donald's face if that happens,' Abbey said. 'Although at the pace these things move – well, heaven knows when that will actually be.'

'True,' said Ryan. 'If we don't get an early hearing, I'll have to come up with another reason to bring you over to Ireland.'

'Why?'

'I miss you,' he said lightly

'Are you flirting with me?' she asked suddenly, realising that the tone of his voice was more playful than usual.

'Maybe a little,' he confessed.

'You're full of charm,' she told him. 'And I'm glad you're on my side. Because I'm sure you could be tough if you wanted.'

'Oh, and ruthless,' he assured her. 'As savagely ruthless as you needed me to be.'

'Maybe I won't need to see that part of you,' she said. 'Maybe we'll manage to settle all this before it gets that far.'

'Fingers crossed,' said Ryan. 'That's what we want too.'

'It was nice of you to call,' Abbey told him.

'You're welcome,' said Ryan. 'And don't forget, any time you need us – need me – we're here.'

'I'll keep that in mind,' she said, and wished him a good night.

She was still smiling to herself when her phone buzzed again. This time it was Cobey.

'I'm at Cantina,' he told her. 'You want to join me?'

'You know I'm with Pete and Claudia,' she said.

'Sure, but there's a great party going on and I'd love you to be here.'

'I can't,' she said.

'I was thinking that we could share a pitcher of margaritas.' He was persuasive. 'And then afterwards . . . perhaps back at your apartment . . . well, there were plenty of other things we liked to share.'

She hadn't invited him to the Torreblanca apartment yet. It was her place. Her refuge.

'Not tonight,' she said again.

'We're good together,' said Cobey softly. 'Remember how good?'

Of course she remembered. They'd clicked in the bedroom just as much as they'd clicked the first time their eyes had met. And she missed that closeness. But she was here with Pete and Claudia and their children. And she was part of their family. At least for this moment.

'Another time,' she promised. 'I'll call you.'

She slid her cell phone back into her bag.

Across the room, Pete opened one eye and looked at her. But she didn't notice. She was staring unseeingly at the television screen.

Chapter 33

After another meeting with Tierney and Gibson, the solicitors he'd engaged, Donald called a family conference, although the only family concerned were himself, Zoey, Gareth and Lisette. When Gareth told his wife that his brother wanted them all to get together, she suggested they drop round for dinner. She would cook for them, she said. It would be less expensive than eating out.

Gareth was taken aback at her suggestion – both because he hadn't been at all sure that she'd want to participate in any conversation about the will, and more especially because Lisette wasn't currently speaking to him. The row which had resulted in her freezing him out had happened when she discovered that he'd been in touch with the French agent about putting Papillon on the market. He tried to explain that it had been an exploratory move on his part to check out the process and the price that their holiday house might fetch, but Lisette had gone totally ballistic.

'I thought we agreed not to sell Papillon,' she yelled at him. 'I thought we'd agreed that it was also our home.'

'That's not what we decided at all,' Gareth told her. 'Be realistic, Lisette. The market in La Rochelle is good right now. No matter what happens with Dad's will, we need to offload property. If we get a good offer for Papillon, it makes perfect sense to sell.'

'We wouldn't have to if you'd accepted the offer made by Abbey Andersen.'

'Yes we would,' said Gareth. 'Even if we win the case, we'll have to sell something. Which has to be the house that people want to buy.'

'This is insane! I thought the whole idea of you supporting Donald in taking the case was so that we could keep Papillon. Now you're saying we'll sell it anyway!'

'But we won't be under pressure. Besides, Donald says—'

'Oh, if Donald says something, it must be right!' cried Lisette. 'Well that's not so. He's being stupid and so are you.'

'No he's not,' said Gareth. 'He's right. Dad shouldn't have done what he did. He undermined Donald and insulted the family.'

'And you are supporting him in this insane venture because he feels undermined!'

'I'm supporting him because he's right and because our solicitors think they can make a good case.'

'But you're talking about selling our home,' she wailed. 'You know how much I love it.'

'Look, if everything works out, we can buy another home in France. A bigger one. A better one.'

'You don't buy a 'ome. You buy a 'ouse.' Once again, Lisette's English was breaking down under pressure. 'Papillon is a 'ome. You should know that, Gareth. What you should be doing is telling Donald to get over 'is problems and settle with the Americans.'

'Why should they get anything?' asked Gareth. 'Why?'

'We 'ave gone over and over this,' said Lisette.

'Look, we're not doing as badly as we were before,' said Gareth. 'The extra money you've brought in from the grinds has made quite a difference. If we can hang on in for a bit longer, we might not have to sell Papillon. But if we do, it'll only be because we have a shot at something much bigger.'

Lisette stared at him wordlessly. She knew now why their foray into property speculation had gone so spectacularly wrong. Her husband hadn't a clue about finance. He still hadn't twigged that she couldn't possibly have earned all that money from giving grinds. He hadn't a clue about anything. She'd married a complete idiot who wanted to rob her of the one thing she really loved. Her home in La Rochelle.

'You will *not* do this,' she said tightly. 'I will stop you. I will go to Papillon myself and take the children with me.'

'What?' Gareth could hardly believe what she was saying.

'You 'eard me.' Her voice was trembling. 'I cannot let you sell Papillon.'

She'd stormed out of the room then, slamming the door behind her. And although later he'd told her that he wasn't going to do anything about Papillon yet, she'd turned away from him without speaking. Which was, more or less, how things had been ever since.

Donald and Zoey arrived within five minutes of the allotted time (Lisette was a stickler for punctuality, and the more cavalier attitude of the Irish towards timekeeping often infuriated her). Gareth poured them all a glass of red wine, while Donald sniffed appreciatively at the aromas coming from the kitchen.

'Coq au vin,' said Lisette.

'Smells delicious.' A nostalgic expression crossed Donald's face. 'My mum used to do casseroles when we were younger. No wine in them, of course, but they were full of flavour.'

'Good stewing meat is great for flavour.' Lisette spoke politely but without warmth. 'Unfortunately, not many people bother to learn how to cook properly.'

Donald shot a glance at Zoey. 'Like my wife.'

'Can't cook, won't cook,' said Zoey. 'That's what restaurants and pizza delivery are for.'

'But I told you before,' Lisette said to her. 'Good cooking is simple. Cheaper than eating out and a whole lot better for you than dial-a-pizza.'

'Lisette does lovely pizza,' said Gareth, relieved that his wife was prepared to be sociable but terrified that she'd lose her head again and start arguing with him in front of his brother and sister-in-law. Or have a stand-up row with Donald.

'I'll teach you if you like,' offered Lisette.

'Great idea,' said Donald.

'Perhaps,' said Zoey. She smiled at Lisette. 'Maybe not pizza. Maybe something tastier.'

'It would be my pleasure,' Lisette told her. 'Honestly.'

'It's nice to see you two getting on,' Donald remarked.

'We've found we have more in common than we thought,' Zoey said, and then winked at Lisette, who got up quickly and went into the kitchen to check on the food.

They didn't start talking about the will until after they'd finished the main course, which was when Donald told them that the solicitors were confident of getting a date to hear the case in the spring – much sooner than they'd originally expected.

'Which is excellent news,' he said. 'Because it means that we'll soon have what's rightfully ours. It's a disgrace that we can't even take keepsakes from the house.'

Lisette didn't dare look at Zoey, who was sitting directly opposite her.

'Paul Tierney is top-notch,' Donald continued. 'I'm extremely confident he'll get the judge to see the merit of our case.'

'I thought judges hated hearing cases,' said Zoey. 'I thought they wanted everyone to settle first.'

'There'll be no settlement.' Donald was firm. 'We want to rub the noses of Abbey Andersen and her mother right in it.'

'Why?' asked Lisette. Gareth shot her a worried glance.

'Because they've no right to be involved in anything to do with this family.'

'That's your opinion,' said Lisette.

'It's fact,' said Donald.

'You're wrong,' said Lisette. 'They have a right, no matter how much we disagree with it. But because you think your opinion is the most important of all, you are willing to put everything at risk.'

Donald's face darkened. 'I'm head of this family,' he said. 'And I'm fighting on behalf of all of us.'

352

'That's bullshit,' said Lisette. 'You're on some massive ego trip and—'

'Lisette.' Zoey looked at her sister-in-law. 'I know you don't agree with Donald, but he might be right.'

'Tierney thinks there are a couple of technical issues he can fight on,' Donald said. 'As well as the notion that Dad was barmy.'

'But he wasn't barmy,' objected Lisette.

'He damn well was. And if you're asked, that's what you'll say.'

'I will?'

'Yes. You can talk about how irrational he was. How he kept changing his mind about things. How he insisted on reaching into that cupboard, which was why he slipped and hurt his wrist.' Gareth thought it was time he spoke in support of his brother.

'I don't think spraining your wrist is a sign of insanity,' said Lisette.

'Don't be idiotic,' snapped Donald. 'You know what I mean.'

Lisette looked between her husband and his brother.

'What about the costs?' she asked.

'Manageable.'

'At fifty thousand a day?'

'What?' Gareth looked shocked. 'It can't be that much. Don, you said—'

'I have a deal with the solicitor,' said Donald. 'Trust me.'

'What if we lose?' asked Lisette.

'We won't lose.'

'But if—'

'For God's sake, Lisette!' Donald brought his fist down on the table and it juddered. 'Are you always this negative? It's no wonder my brother is stressed out.'

Lisette looked at Gareth. 'You have told your brother that you are stressed out because of me?'

'No. No, of course not. I'm stressed out because of everything!'

'But I am negative and this is worse for you?'

'I never—'

'But of course it is negative that I don't want to lose my home because of this . . . this desire to beat the Americans.'

'It's not a desire to beat them,' said Donald. 'It's a desire for what's right. To have it on record that I'm the head of the family.'

'That's not what the court will be deciding on,' said Lisette. 'It's about what Fred wanted. And he wanted, for reasons best known to him, to leave everything to those people and to hurt those who cared about him all his life. And it doesn't matter what you say, Donald, we could lose this case and you'll be 'ead of a broke family!'

'God Almighty!' Donald was about to continue when Zoey interrupted him.

'Lisette is being extreme, but she's stating a possibility,' she said. 'And perhaps we should think about accepting that offer, Don, or try to negotiate a bit more. We'd be doing it from a much stronger position now we know that they're prepared to give up half.'

'Didn't you hear a word I said?' demanded Donald. 'I. Am. Not. Negotiating. Negotiating implies that there's some kind of merit in her claim. There isn't.'

'Now who's barmy?' muttered Lisette.

'I'm doing my best for all of us,' said Donald.

'No you're not. You're blinded by some kind of feudal notion of how things should be. And you're going to destroy all of us in the process!' cried Lisette.

'I don't know how you live with this.' Donald turned to Gareth. 'She's the most obstinate, destructive person I've ever met in my life. She's a cloud of doom hovering over everything. No wonder you're stressed.'

'Thanks very much.' Lisette got up from the table. 'I didn't realise it was I who was the problem here.' She walked out of the room, banging the door behind her.

354

Zoey stood up too. 'I'll see if she's OK,' she said, and followed Lisette out of the room.

'Bloody women.' Gareth poured himself and his brother another glass of wine. 'They'd do your head in.'

'Lisette is afraid we'll lose Papillon. I tried to tell her that even if we accepted Abbey Andersen's offer, there was a chance we'd have to sell it, but she won't listen.'

'That's the thing,' said Don. 'We may as well go for broke; half just isn't enough.'

'It is for you, surely?' Gareth said. 'You're not crushed by debt like us.'

'I don't have a pile of houses to maintain,' agreed Donald. 'But I have Zoey. That woman goes through money like it's water. She could plough through the inheritance in a year without giving it a thought.'

Gareth shuddered. He dreaded to think what kind of state their finances would be in if Lisette was as profligate as his sister-in-law.

'Lisette's a cautious woman,' he said. 'Even when we were flipping the properties, she was always trying to do things conservatively. It's my fault we got into this mess.'

'All the same, she's the one who wants to keep the house in France.'

'She loves it. We both do.'

'I promise you,' said Donald, 'we will win this case and we will get our money. And you'll be able to keep your house in France and your head above water and Lisette will thank me at the end of it.'

'The truth is that she's brought in a lot of cash over the past few weeks giving extra tuition.' Gareth felt he had to point this out. 'The reason the pressure's still on is because all our bloody money goes on mortgages, though at least some of our arrears have been paid off. But Papillon – she's talking about leaving for France with the kids, Donald. I don't want her to do that.'

'Overdramatising,' remarked Donald. 'She's French, after all.'

'That doesn't mean—'

Donald interrupted his brother with a wave of his hand. 'Everything will be fine,' he said. 'Convince her of that. We'll come out laughing. You'll see.'

Gareth slumped back in his chair. He'd always supported his brother. But he wished he was convinced that he was doing the right thing.

'You OK?' asked Zoey as, in the kitchen, Lisette tore some paper towel from the roll and blew her nose. 'I'm sure Donald didn't mean to upset you.'

'Is that how people think?' Lisette sniffed. 'That I am pressurising Gareth all the time?'

'I don't think that,' said Zoey. 'I think you're amazing. You go out to work, run the house, look after the kids and did a great job with old Mr Fitzpatrick when he was alive. You're a wonderful wife and mother and he's damn lucky to have you.' She glanced around. 'Where are the kids tonight, by the way?'

'Having a sleepover with friends,' replied Lisette. 'As for the rest of it – I didn't do enough of a good job with Fred, did I? Otherwise he would've left it all to me.'

'And Donald would've gone apeshit again,' Zoey said. 'Jeez, Lisette, I want Fred's house as much as anyone, but money really is at the root of all evil, isn't it?'

'I'm so scared,' said Lisette. 'I keep thinking that not only will we lose Papillon but we'll lose Thorngrove too. And people will think that we are greedy, selfish people looking for Fred's money because we threw our own away.'

'You're not greedy or selfish.' Zoey put her arm around Lisette's shoulders. 'Donald has made up his mind. But even though he was never as tough as his dad, I trust him to know what he's doing.'

'You do?' Lisette looked at her doubtfully.

'He's ready for this fight,' Zoey assured her. 'I've never seen him so prepared.

'I don't want to fight,' said Lisette. 'I don't like fights when I don't know already who's going to win.'

'We will,' promised Zoey, as she handed Lisette another sheet of kitchen towel. 'Somehow.'

Suzanne had been extremely busy all day, and it wasn't until late in the evening, when she was sitting in her apartment, that she switched on her phone and saw a clatter of missed calls and emails. The calls were from Jaime Roig and Petra Summers. Jaime was telling her that the sale of the Mirador had fallen through and that it was on the market once again; Petra's calls were to say that she'd found some other investors who were interested in the hospitality industry and that if Suzanne could find an interesting project they might be willing to support her.

It was a sign, Suzanne thought. It had to be. She was destined to buy the Mirador. She would meet with Petra and the investors, and this time, she would be firmer in her negotiations with the bank. She would tell them that she was going to get a share of Furze Hill as well as her two hundred and fifty thousand, and she would find a way to convince them to lend her the money. So what if, in the end, Abbey Andersen and her mother walked away with her father's house? Suzanne was sure that once she had the loan money secured, she would be able to pay it back. Her original projections had been based on much higher borrowings anyway. It was only because the bankers had lost all their *cojones* that she was having to put anything into it herself.

She opened the photo gallery on her laptop and looked at the pictures she'd taken of the Mirador in all its faded glory. This was her hotel. The one she'd always dreamed of. It truly was. If only her stupid older brother would get over his obsession about their father's will, she could have her money and use it to persuade the banks that she was worth backing. She scrolled through her contacts and stopped at Donald's number. She was about to call him when she changed her mind.

Everything she'd had or done before, she'd done without anything from her father. She didn't need his money for this either. The owners of the Mirador wanted to sell. She had potential investors. She could do this on her own. And this time no damn bank was going to stop her.

Chapter 34

Abbey had planned to pick Ellen up from the airport, but her mother had insisted on making her own way to the apartment.

'I'm not helpless, you know,' she'd said over the phone from the monastery. 'I've plenty of experience of getting from Point A to Point B without getting lost.'

'I know,' said Abbey. 'But it's ten years since you've had to try.'

'My navigational skills haven't disappeared,' her mother reminded her. 'I'm still a capable person.'

Which Abbey knew she was, of course. But she couldn't help being concerned about her mother's venture into the outside world. A world which – no matter what Ellen might think – had changed dramatically during her time at the monastery.

Abbey had been surprised, but pleased, when the prioress had agreed that Sister Benita needed to go to Ireland to assist with family matters. When Ryan Gilligan had called with the news that a date for the court hearing had been set for the end of January, and that it was imperative Ellen be available to be there, Abbey had wondered how on earth that would happen. She knew that some of the nuns left the monastery from time to time to attend religious conferences or events, but this was very different. In the end, however, the prioress had been very understanding about Sister Benita's situation. But now that Ellen was on her own, Abbey wondered how easy it would be for her. They'd chosen to fly from San Francisco rather than San Diego because it was cheaper, but she was thinking it might have been better to have chosen her mother's local airport instead and not put her through the stress of travelling alone.

There was a ring at the bell and Abbey turned away from the window to answer it.

'It's me,' said Ellen.

'Mom! I was looking out for you but I didn't see you.' Abbey buzzed open the door. 'Come on up.'

A few moments later Ellen, dressed in a navy raincoat over the beige habit of the monastery, was stepping into the apartment. She hugged Abbey, then looked around her curiously.

'You were right,' she said. 'It's not the same at all.'

'Yes,' agreed Abbey. 'But it still feels warm and cosy and comfortable.'

Ellen looked pensive. 'I like it, but it doesn't trigger any memories. I thought it would.'

'Me too,' admitted Abbey. 'Even though Pete said it had been remodelled, I still imagined myself here just as it was.'

'Things change,' said Ellen. 'Nothing can be as it was before.'

'I guess not.' Abbey took her mother's coat and hung it in a small cupboard. 'D'you want to see your room?'

'Is that changed too?'

'They split the bedrooms so that they're both the same size,' explained Abbey. 'There isn't one big one and one tiny one any more.' She ushered her mother along the narrow corridor to the room. 'Here you go.'

'Lovely,' said Ellen as she looked at the neatly made bed with its pale blue quilt and the cream walls hung with a variety of paintings of Alcatraz. 'Yours?' She nodded at the paintings.

'Old ones.'

'Nice, though.'

'Thanks. I was going to say I'd let you get on and unpack, but as we're leaving in the morning, I reckon it's probably not worth your while.'

'No,' said Ellen. 'I don't have much to unpack anyway.'

The two of them stood in the room together without speaking. Then Abbey, without thinking about it, put her arms around her mother and hugged her. And Ellen hugged her in return.

Although Pete had offered to drive them to the airport, Abbey told him that they'd be better off getting a cab.

'It's a big thing for Mom to be outside the monastery,' she said. 'I think meeting you would be a bit overwhelming, and I don't need her to be overwhelmed in advance of meeting the Fitzpatricks.'

'Whatever you think,' said Pete. 'You look after yourself, you hear? And don't take any crap from anyone.'

'If the judge hands down crap, I think we have to take it,' Abbey told him.

'He won't.' Pete was certain. 'Your case is strong and they're fools for going after you like this.'

'Perhaps.'

'It is,' said Pete. 'Let your lawyer friend fight for what's yours.'

'Will do,' Abbey promised.

'Good luck, honey.'

His words were in her ears as she and Ellen walked through the terminal building. Ellen was wearing the coffee-coloured skirt with a fresh white blouse, flat brown shoes and the navy coat again. Abbey, who'd looked at the weather forecast for Dublin the previous evening, was concerned.

'There's snow,' she told Ellen. 'I'm not sure how much walking about we'll have to do, but I think you'll need something more than those shoes and that coat. Perhaps a couple of fleeces and some boots?'

'I have to wear my habit,' protested Ellen.

'Mom, your habit might be fine in the middle of the desert, but not in snow,' Abbey pointed out. 'I'm sure Sister Inez won't want you to catch pneumonia.'

'I'll be fine,' said Ellen, but Abbey was insistent, and after much nagging, Ellen caved in and bought a pair of fur-lined boots, a couple of warm jumpers (she refused to buy a fleece) and a knitted black skirt.

When she emerged from the dressing room, Abbey asked her how she'd got on and Ellen confessed that the black skirt had been a bit more figure-hugging than she'd expected and that for a moment she'd felt like Ellen Connolly again, and not Sister Benita. But, she added, the jumpers (one black and one cream) were long enough to cover her body and bulky enough to deal with her dilemma of suddenly looking fashionable. 'My stipend wasn't intended for clothes shopping,' she added as she paid for them at the till.

'Think of it as learning about the outside world again,' Abbey told her. 'Besides, you can give them all to the deserving poor when we're back.'

Ellen looked amused. 'I guess I can.'

'Will you change before we get to Dublin?' asked Abbey.

'Why? Are you ashamed of me like this?'

'Not at all,' replied Abbey, who was herself wearing skinny jeans tucked into her boots, and the Aran jumper she'd bought on her trip to Ireland topped with a fake-fur gilet. 'I'm afraid of you freezing your buns off.'

Ellen relented after they changed planes at JFK, and when she emerged from the ladies', Abbey looked at her in amazement.

'Oh my God,' she said. 'You're Mom again.'

'Don't be silly.' Ellen tried to be dismissive. 'I'm wearing a black skirt and jumper.'

'I know . . .' Abbey didn't know what to say. But she realised that Ellen was embarrassed at suddenly looking good, and so she started walking towards their gate, trying to hide her shock.

When they emerged into the arrivals hall at Dublin airport the following morning, Ryan Gilligan didn't recognise Sister Benita as anyone other than another of the travellers disembarking from the transatlantic flight. And then he saw Abbey.

'You look great,' he said as he kissed her briefly on one cheek. 'It's good to see you again.'

'You too. This is my mom.'

'The famous Ellen Connolly.' He extended his hand and she shook it. 'I wondered if we'd ever get to meet. It's a real pleasure.'

'Sadly the circumstances aren't exactly ideal,' said Ellen.

'Probably not,' agreed Ryan. 'But I think they're good for us. We have Judge Halligan for our case, and he's a very no-nonsense sort of guy. This way.' He led Ellen and Abbey towards the car park. 'I know you asked for somewhere a little less expensive for this trip, Abbey, but the Harbour Hotel was doing a brilliant low-season offer. Even with travelling expenses in and out of the city, it's a great deal.'

'Whatever you think.' Abbey shivered. The temperature was significantly lower than it had been in San Francisco, and there was a thin covering of snow on the pavement.

'This is nothing,' Ryan said when she commented on it. 'The last few years we've had heavy snowfalls and alpine-cold weather. At least the streets are clear, which means we can get around. Anyhow, you're well wrapped up for it in your geansaí.'

'G . . . g . . . geansaí?' she said through chattering teeth.

'Jumper.'

'Right.'

'You'll be grand,' he said.

She would always associate that phrase with him, she thought. Comforting, reassuring and motivational all at once. She'd be grand. Well, she'd be more than that after she got her hands on Fred Fitzpatrick's house. She'd be rich.

'I know you're probably tired, but I've organised a meeting with Alex for later this afternoon,' Ryan said as he opened the car door. 'It's to give you an idea of what'll happen tomorrow when we start.'

'You said this case could last three or four days.' Ellen got into the back seat, followed by Abbey, who'd hesitated for a moment, thinking that both of them sitting in the rear of the car made Ryan seem like a cab driver.

'That's what we reckon.'

'I'm terrible about legal matters, but why would it take so long?' she asked.

'Submissions by both sides. Cross-examination – the judge will want to ask about Mr Fitzpatrick's state of mind. We have two doctors appearing on our behalf too, who'll testify that there wasn't a bother on him, other than his distress at the Magdalene laundry stories.'

'That poor girl.' Ellen adjusted her seat belt. 'So terrible for her then, and the fallout is still happening now.'

'That poor girl was your mother,' said Abbey.

'I know,' said Ellen. 'I've been praying for her.'

'It might be better to pray for the people who are still alive and giving us grief,' remarked Abbey.

'I pray for them too,' said Ellen.

Abbey shot her an exasperated look. Ellen's face was serene.

'I hear you've been doing really well since I last saw you, Abbey,' said Ryan as he glanced at them in the rear-view mirror. 'Winning prizes and everything, Alex told me.'

'What prizes?' Ellen looked at her enquiringly, and Abbey told her about the nail art competitions.

'I've been picked to go to the Nailympics in London later this year,' she said. 'It's very exciting.'

'Yet you don't paint your own nails,' remarked her mother.

'Nail art is for the big occasion,' said Abbey. 'But you're wrong about my nails, Mom. They're varnished in nude.'

'Oh.'

'And the great result of the competitions is that I've never been busier. I could work twenty-four-seven if I wanted to. My client list has nearly doubled since November. Which, although a good thing, is a bit awkward right now, with having to take time out for this hearing. Plus, there's a friend of Claudia's who's interested in helping me set up on my own.'

'That sounds promising.' Ryan glanced in the mirror again. 'Does it interest you?'

'Perhaps,' said Abbey. 'I could let her invest in my business, or maybe I'll use the money we get from the sale of Mr Fitzpatrick's house instead.'

'I thought you were going to use that to buy the apartment,' said Ellen.

'I haven't decided.' Abbey sounded impatient. 'I don't know what I want to do yet, Mom. But the money gives me choices.'

'I see.' Ellen closed her eyes and clasped her hands together. Abbey wondered if she was praying. The previous night her mother had gone into her bedroom for over an hour to pray. And this morning, as the plane neared Ireland, she'd taken a string of rosary beads from her bag, an action that had made some of the people in the surrounding seats look at her with a certain amount of anxiety. Abbey wasn't sure if they thought she was some kind of religious terrorist about to blow them all to hell with the beads, or that her prayers were because she lacked confidence in the ability of the pilot to land them safely on the runway.

'Where are we going to have the meeting?' asked Abbey.

'In Mr Fitzpatrick's house,' Ryan told her. 'It's important that your mother sees it.'

'Will you be asking me to speak at this . . . trial . . . hearing . . . whatever you call it?' Ellen opened her eyes again.

'Possibly,' said Ryan. 'The key point they're making is that Mr Fitzpatrick wouldn't have left anything to you if he'd known that you were a nun. Alex may want you to answer some questions and prove that just because you're a nun doesn't mean you're a homicidal maniac.'

Ellen raised an eyebrow.

'They're making out that as far as Fred was concerned, all nuns had murderous intent.'

'Oh, but that's plain silly,' said Ellen.

'I know,' said Ryan. 'But they'll be saying that Dilly died at the hands of nuns.'

'Do we know that for certain?' asked Ellen.

'That's another point against the Fitzpatricks,' Ryan replied. 'She died shortly after giving birth. The fact that the baby came early may or may not have had anything to do with her treatment at the convent. It's not entirely clear from the available records. But it's certainly true that bad things happened in those places.'

'So tragic,' murmured Ellen.

Abbey reached out and squeezed her mother's hand. Ellen looked at her in surprise, but then smiled at her. Abbey continued to hold her hand. It was all very well talking about the past and the things that had happened, but the reality was that those things had happened to Ellen's mother. And she'd died after giving birth to Ellen herself. No matter how spiritual Ellen might be, or how she managed to rationalise everything in her world, the knowledge was surely painful.

Clara, the hotel receptionist, welcomed Abbey as an old friend and was equally effusive in her greeting of Ellen. She brought them up to a cosy bedroom with elegant furniture and an open fire burning in the grate, then unlocked the interconnecting door between it and an identical room. She told them that she hoped they had everything they needed and wished them a very pleasant stay.

'I'm not sure you'll be going for walks along the pier this time, Abbey,' she added. 'The wind chill has it a few degrees below freezing at the moment. Do please tell me if you need the heat turned up higher in either room.'

'It's perfect the way it is,' Ellen said. 'I love real flames.'

'It's natural gas,' said Clara apologetically. 'But it looks cosy.'

'It's grand.' Abbey was pleased with the opportunity to use her favourite Irish expression.

'Excellent.' Clara beamed at them and then left them alone.

'D'you like it?' Abbey asked her mother.

'The room? It's lovely.'

'No. Ireland.'

'First impressions are good,' replied Ellen.

'Everyone is super-friendly,' Abbey said. 'Well, except for the Fitzpatricks.'

'You can't blame them.'

'I'm not at all surprised they were ticked off,' acknowledged Abbey. 'I'm sure I'd be too if some stranger turned up and claimed my inheritance – not that I would ever have had an inheritance to claim. We tried to do the right thing – everyone said our offer was more than generous – but they didn't even come back with another proposal. Anyway . . .' She made a face. 'Donald and Gareth were rude and horrible about you, so they don't deserve it.'

'That's a bit harsh.' Ellen's own words were gentle

'So were they. In fact they were downright nasty and aggressive.'

'I'm sure they were stressed out at the time.'

'They've had plenty of opportunity to destress since,' said Abbey. 'Besides, they got money from their father before, which is more than Suzanne did.'

'You liked her?'

'Yes. I did.'

'And you think she should have got more?'

'Yes.'

'So are you planning to give something extra to her?'

Abbey sat on the deep windowsill and stared out across the bay. 'She was looking for an investment in a hotel project she was interested in. I don't know if she still is or not, but I'd be prepared to look at that.'

'To make money out of her?'

'No. To invest.'

'Which is sort of the same thing.'

'What are you trying to say, Mom? That we're still doing the wrong thing? You said the offer we made was fair.'

'And it was,' said Ellen. 'But sometimes people are too damaged to see fairness.'

'Does that mean we should back off? Simply because they aren't thinking clearly?'

'No. The problem, as I see it, isn't in what Mr Fitzpatrick . . .'

'Your father,' Abbey reminded her.

'Indeed. The problem isn't in what he's done. It's in how people are reacting to it. How it's making them feel.'

'At first I was shocked, but right now I'm feeling quite good about it,' said Abbey.

Ellen smiled. 'The prioress was pleased for you too,' she said.

'She was?' Abbey was startled.

'Of course. Like me, she wants you to be happy and comfortable.'

Abbey had never thought that the nuns would discuss their families, and said so.

'But why wouldn't we?' asked Ellen. 'We talk about a whole range of things. We don't sit around chanting prayers all day, you know. Besides, you're the only daughter that any of us has. We all take an interest in your well-being.'

'Wow.' Abbey was still taken aback.

'Anyway, we agree that when you're living in a material world, you certainly need some material goods to get by. There's no point in pretending that you can live a monastic life in San Francisco.'

Abbey couldn't help smiling.

'So we want you to be all right. We also want the Fitzpatricks to be all right. To be happy and content.'

'Right now, those two wishes seem to be totally incompatible,' observed Abbey.

'Hopefully not,' Ellen said. 'All the sisters are praying now.

Please God it will work out in the end and everyone gets what's right for them.'

'Getting money for nothing never seems exactly right,' said Abbey after she'd absorbed the knowledge that she seemed to be an honorary daughter to the nuns. 'But other people do. They win lotteries or get big payouts for other reasons. Why should I feel guilty? Why should you? Especially why should you? You were his daughter. Her daughter. And you were abandoned.'

'My parents didn't abandon me,' said Ellen gently. 'They chose me.'

Abbey got up from the windowsill. 'Sometimes it's exhausting knowing you,' she said. Then she went into the adjoining room and closed the door behind her.

Ryan collected them at the hotel an hour later. Both Abbey and Ellen had freshened up and made themselves some coffee in Ellen's room, so they were feeling somewhat more alert by the time they got into the car again.

'I kept falling asleep when I came here before.' Abbey hadn't spoken much to her mother in the past hour. When she'd tapped softly on the door between the rooms and opened it again, Ellen had been kneeling at the window, praying. She hadn't moved until Abbey had offered her the coffee, which they'd drunk in silence.

'It was probably the heat as much as anything back then,' Ryan said cheerfully. 'It was our hottest Indian summer ever, remember?'

'Sure do,' said Abbey.

'In as much as that wasn't entirely typical weather, neither is this.'

Lazy flakes of snow had begun to drift from the purple and grey sky to form a thin white carpet on the road ahead of them.

'But you said it's snowed before,' said Ellen. 'More than this.'

'Indeed it has. Though we're never properly geared up for it,' Ryan told her. 'It always seems to come as a surprise and causes total chaos. Fortunately, this isn't forecast to stay.'

369

'Hopefully not,' said Abbey. 'Otherwise getting up and down this hill might be difficult.'

'Fantastic views,' commented Ellen as they climbed higher.

'Best in Dublin,' said Ryan. 'That's why property here gets premium prices.'

Ellen glanced at Abbey. But she was gazing out of the car window, across the bay.

'Here we are.' Ryan pulled up outside Fred's house. 'Looks like Alex isn't here yet. Don't worry, by the way, the heat has been set to come on for a few hours every day. We don't want the house to fall victim to the weather.' He opened the pedestrian gate and led the way up the steps, warning them to be careful as they might be slippy.

'This is impressive,' said Ellen as Ryan took more keys from his pocket and selected one to open the door.

'It was awesome in the summer,' Abbey told her. 'All the flowers were out and the garden was magnificent. A bit unruly, maybe, but that only added to its charm.'

'Here we go.' Ryan opened the front door and they stepped inside. The first thing Abbey noticed was that the house seemed neater.

'As you know, Lisette has been taking care of things,' said Ryan. 'She comes every week.'

'She's doing a good job,' said Abbey.

'She's very thorough,' agreed Ryan as they walked through into the living room, which, Abbey thought, was a million times fresher-looking than on her previous visit.

'Anyone for tea?' Ryan looked at them enquiringly.

'We've just had coffee,' said Abbey.

'Yes, but the Irish make tea for every social occasion.' Ryan grinned at her.

'OK then.' She followed him into the kitchen, which had also been transformed by Lisette's cleaning. After a moment, Ellen joined them. She continued through the kitchen, towards Fred's office, while Abbey stayed with Ryan.

'Your mam is lovely,' he whispered to her. 'Not at all how I imagined her.'

'How did you imagine her?'

'I thought she'd look more . . . more homely,' he said. 'Or maybe more severe. Certainly more religious. But she's quite normal, isn't she? And I like that skirt and jumper combo she has going on. Not at all like the habit I imagined.'

Abbey chuckled and told him about their cold-weather shopping in San Francisco International.

'Good thinking,' said Ryan. 'We'd hate her to catch her death. Sorry,' he added. 'Possibly a bad phrase to use.'

Just as he was bringing the tea into the living room, where Ellen was now sitting, Alex arrived. He was carrying a briefcase stuffed with papers. He greeted Ellen warmly, like Ryan telling her he was pleased to finally meet her, and then started talking about Fred's will and how he, as the executor, was defending it.

'So it's your job to say that Mr Fitzpatrick was entitled to do what he liked with his money,' said Ellen.

'Exactly,' Alex told her. 'He really and truly wanted you to have something. It was extremely important to him. Those were his wishes and my job is to ensure that they are carried out. I have to admit I was shocked when Donald Fitzpatrick turned down your offer. I can't believe his solicitors allowed him to! Not that we can prevent anyone rejecting an offer, but I can't see them getting anything better.'

'Why do you think Mr Fitzpatrick felt it was important that I – we – have the house?' asked Ellen. 'It seems such a big thing.'

'Truthfully, I don't know,' replied Alex. 'However, I'm aware that he was concerned there'd be a row between his sons over the property. That one would want to buy the other out and that neither could afford to do so and it would end up messily. I think he thought this was a good solution.'

'I suppose anything we think about it is only conjecture,' said Ellen.

'Yes. I can only say what he told me. So,' Alex continued, 'let's get talking about tomorrow and how things might pan out.'

He took more papers from his case. And at that moment, they heard the sound of the front door being opened.

Chapter 35

Although Lisette finished classes early on Monday afternoons, she usually had a few sessions of private tuition afterwards. But today, tense and agitated about the upcoming hearing, she'd cancelled the grinds in favour of calling in to Furze Hill. Who knew when she'd next be able to sit in the kitchen she'd spent so much time cleaning and tidying that it was now a peaceful haven overlooking the sea? If – despite what Donald still insisted – the judge found against them, the house would no longer be theirs.

Not that she wanted it now anyway. Whereas once she'd dreamed about living there, it had become a symbol of the growing division between her and her husband. They hardly spoke these days, their opposing views on Fred's divisive legacy too far apart to bridge. Gareth spent most of his time in his den. Lisette presumed he was looking at French property sites. When he wasn't at the computer, he was talking to Don in a low, urgent voice. Don had found out about Lisette and Zoey's offer to the Americans. When Zoey told her, she said that he'd been angry with her at first, but then admitted that if Abbey and her mother had accepted, he probably would've agreed to it despite his principles, if only to get them out of their hair. But Abbey's own offer was too far away from anything reasonable, and besides, it wasn't about the money in the end, it was about the right to be a Fitzpatrick.

Gareth hadn't said anything at all to Lisette about the offer at first. In fact neither of them was talking much. They seemed to have completely lost their ability to hold a conversation. All they did was snap at each other. The last time they'd spoken about the will, she'd said that Don was behaving like a child in wanting all or nothing, and that Gareth was too weak to stand up to him. Gareth's jaw had tightened at that, and he'd retorted that he was supporting Don because they needed to stick together about this, not go off half-cocked like she and Zoey had done. She was relieved that he'd finally acknowledged it, but had yelled at him that at least she wasn't pissing their frugal resources away on a pipe dream. And then she'd added something about pissing the children's inheritance away too, and that all he was trying to prove was that he was as good as Don, but the truth was that when it came to business neither of them were, because they weren't cut-throat like his father and they should stop trying to pretend that they knew what they were doing because they didn't.

'I know exactly what I'm doing,' Gareth had responded. 'I'm trying to save our family's future, while all you want to do is hand it on a plate to someone else.'

That argument had ended with her storming upstairs and going to bed, thankful that their shouting hadn't woken the children. She'd lain there, barely containing her rage, until she'd heard Gareth come upstairs too. But he hadn't joined her in the bedroom; he'd slept in the guest room, where he'd stayed ever since.

Lisette couldn't quite believe that her marriage was falling apart at the seams. She'd always been proud of how she and Gareth had resolved things in the past, how they'd always managed to stick to their self-imposed rule of never going to sleep angry. Not that there had been many instances of it anyway. They were a good team. They believed in the same things. They shared the same values. Or at least they had. Because it was all very different now.

When she walked into the living room and saw Alex, Ryan, Abbey and the woman she realised must be Ellen Connolly (although she didn't look anything like the nun she'd imagined), Lisette stood still in shock. Although she'd noticed cars parked on

374

the street outside, it hadn't occurred to her that anyone would be at the house. The sight of them there, sitting on Fred's sofa, drinking tea from Fred's cups, was like a blow to the stomach.

'Lisette.' Alex stood up and extended his hand. 'How are you?'

She shook it automatically even as a part of her brain registered that this was something else that would annoy Gareth.

'I'm well.' Her reply was automatic too, no matter how she felt.

Abbey looked at her with concern. The last time she'd seen Lisette, she'd thought that Gareth's wife was as coolly elegant as she'd imagined all Frenchwomen to be. She'd looked quietly chic in her black dress, high heels and neatly styled white-grey hair. Today she was wearing jeans, trainers and the sort of fleece that Ellen had rejected. And even though there was still a certain elegance about her, her face was drawn and there were black circles beneath her eyes.

'Would you like some tea?' asked Alex.

'I . . . what are you doing here?' Lisette looked confused.

'Having a meeting,' Alex told her. 'But you're welcome to sit with us for a while. Did you come to tidy the house? It hardly needs it.'

'I . . .' Lisette didn't know what to say.

Ryan Gilligan got up, went to the kitchen and returned with another cup. He filled it with tea and offered it to Lisette.

'We've given you a shock.' Ellen spoke gently. 'I'm sorry.'

Lisette took a mouthful of hot tea (that bloody Lyons blend, she thought involuntarily; I should've thrown it in the bin). 'Are you . . .' She didn't finish the sentence, but stared at Ellen.

'I'm Sister Benita,' said Ellen. 'I'm Fred's daughter.'

Abbey looked at her mother. It was the first time Ellen had called herself Fred's daughter, and the words took her breath away. Because quite suddenly it was real. Quite suddenly she actually believed it. Fred Fitzpatrick, the man who'd died before her very eyes, was indeed Ellen's father, was indeed her own grandfather.

And because of that, they were connected to people like Lisette and her husband, and Zoey and Gareth and Suzanne. They were part of their family.

'You're not what I expected.' Lisette put the cup on the coffee table.

'I'm sure I would've been more like you expected if I hadn't had to buy some cold-weather clothes,' said Ellen.

'Maybe that's it.' Lisette continued to stare at her. 'You look – you look like Suzanne.'

And that was it, thought Abbey. That was what had shocked her when Ellen had first changed into the skirt and jumper. She didn't look like herself any more. She was an older version of Suzanne.

'I haven't yet met Suzanne,' said Ellen. 'I hope I will. But I'm glad to meet you.'

Ryan, Alex and Abbey were watching the two women. Lisette didn't speak. But then her mobile, loud and shrill, broke the silence that had descended on the room.

'I'm just outside the house.'

Lisette listened as Zoey told her she'd been driving past and seen her car outside.

'What are you doing there without me? Not raiding the safe, I hope!' Zoey was joking. She knew Lisette wouldn't dream of it. They were partners in crime when it came to lifting things from Furze Hill. 'Let me in, will you?'

Lisette looked at the people in front of her and told them Zoey was outside.

'Excellent,' said Ellen. 'I get to meet someone else.'

'I don't know if . . .' Alex looked doubtful.

'Let her in,' said Ellen.

Lisette got up and answered the door. They could hear her whispered words before she returned to the living room with Zoey.

Abbey looked at Zoey with interest. Unlike Lisette, she was as pretty and as up-to-the-minute as she remembered, wearing a pair of wool trousers and a fur-trimmed wool coat over wedge boots. A matching fur-trimmed hat was perched on her luxuriant brunette curls.

'Well, this is a turn-up,' she said when she stood in front of them. 'Staking an early claim, are you?'

'Hello,' said Ellen. 'I'm Sister Benita. It's good to meet you.'

'You're the reason for all the trouble,' said Zoey. 'You're the mad nun in the monastery. You don't look mad, but I suppose appearances can be deceiving.'

'I guess that's why one should never go on appearances,' said Ellen equably.

'Tea?' asked Alex.

'You have some nerve,' said Zoey, as she removed her hat and coat and draped them over a chair. 'Bringing them here. Using this place like your own.'

'And you've come here because . . .?' There was a touch of frost in Alex's normally urbane voice.

'I saw Lisette's car outside. I thought she was cleaning. I was going to help.'

Everyone looked at Zoey's immaculate, stylish trousers and the silk blouse that had been revealed when she'd taken off her coat. Zoey realised that she wasn't exactly dressed for cleaning.

'I chat to her while she's working,' she clarified.

'How good of you,' said Alex. 'You come here a lot, do you?'

'We had to,' said Zoey. 'You can see that Lizzie's done a great job on the house. It was a tip before.'

'That was thoughtful,' said Ellen.

'You can't be a nun.' Zoey was shaking her head. 'You're too . . . too . . . you're normal. Which,' she said abruptly, 'isn't good for us.' She looked at Lisette. 'That's their strategy. Make her look as though she isn't a nun at all. Make her look like Suzanne.'

Lisette stared at her and then at Ellen. And then she started to cry.

'There's no need to be upset.' Ellen stood up and moved towards Lisette. 'There's nothing to cry about.'

But Lisette's shoulders continued to shake with the ferocity of the tears that were now spilling down her cheeks. Alex and Ryan looked uncomfortable, while Abbey watched as her mother put her arm around the other woman and gently drew her towards her. Zoey, meanwhile, continued to stare at Ellen, as though unconvinced she was a real person.

'*Je suis désolée.*' Lisette finally moved away from Ellen. 'I am sorry. I didn't mean to . . .' She took the tissue that Ellen handed her and wiped her eyes. 'This is silly of me.'

'You're upset,' said Ellen. 'Everyone gets upset. There's nothing silly about it.'

'What's silly is *why* she's upset,' said Zoey. 'Why she has to be. Why I have to be. You're supposed to be a nun. You're supposed to embrace poverty. But you're grabbing our inheritance from under our noses. You and your daughter. You have a plan, haven't you, to take it all and leave us without a thing.'

'Hardly without a thing,' said Alex. 'Sister Benita and her daughter made a more than generous offer, which you turned down. As you already know, Mr Fitzpatrick made previous provision for his sons as well as the money and goods he left this time. In this current will he also made provision for his daughters. And his grandchildren.'

'I wasn't married to Donald back then!' cried Zoey. 'I didn't see any of it. Disgruntled Deirdre got her mitts on everything.'

'Disgruntled Deirdre?' Ellen was confused.

'His ex-wife. Though I suppose that's another thing that counts against him as far as you're concerned. I'm his second wife. He's divorced. You lot don't believe in divorce, do you? You think men and women should stick together even when they're utterly miserable. He didn't meet me until after that bitch Deirdre had cheated on him. Then she took him to the cleaners, the skanky cow.'

Ryan stifled a grin at Zoey's words. Abbey hid her own smile behind her hand. Alex said nothing.

'There is clearly a lot of emotion going on here,' said Ellen as she sat down again, having given Lisette another comforting hug. 'Perhaps you'd better explain it all from your point of view.'

So Zoey, with occasional input from Lisette, told Ellen about the impact that Fred's decision had had on the two brothers: Don's rage at being usurped as the eldest, Gareth's view that he had to support him, their anger about what their father had done and their belief – certainly in Gareth's case – that Fred's legacy would have eased his money worries.

'Then you guys sail in here without a care in the world and take what's rightfully ours, and that, you know, is plain wrong!' said Zoey.

'But as we said, they made an extremely generous offer, which you turned down,' said Alex.

'Why should anything go to them?' demanded Zoey. 'Half will probably get hoovered up by the convent, sorry, monastery and the rest – well, little Miss Butter-Wouldn't-Melt-in-My-Mouth there will be able to live a life that she damn well shouldn't be accustomed to.'

'And why shouldn't she?' asked Ryan. 'What makes you more entitled to it than her?'

'Stop!' Ellen held up her hand. 'Stop with all this bitterness and anger and self-justification. Can't you see that it's poisoning your souls?'

'Easy to say!' Zoey couldn't contain her rage. 'Easy to say when the poisoning of yours has been greatly eased by what the old man has left you.'

'Zoey.' Lisette put her hand on her sister-in-law's arm. 'Sister Benita is right. We are . . . This is wrong. All of it. Everything we've said and done.'

'We're not wrong.' There was a warning tone in Zoey's voice. 'We've only ever done what we thought was fair.'

Ryan looked at her curiously, but Ellen was speaking again.

'I think we should pray,' she said.

'For crying out loud!' Zoey was infuriated. 'Now she's playing the God card.'

But everyone fell silent as Ellen bent her head and began to speak. 'Oh Lord, fill our hearts with Your love. Help us to understand Your will.'

Fred's will, more likely, thought Abbey, as she peeped at the others from beneath her lowered lashes. Her eyes locked with Zoey's, which were as amused as her own. That surprised Abbey. She'd thought that Zoey was hard and tough, but all at once she realised that although the other girl's words might have been angry, they were fearful too. And concerned. For herself, she wondered, or for her husband? The man who'd been cheated and who'd lost everything.

Money should make things easier, she thought. But somehow, for everyone in the Fitzpatrick family, it had led to some very difficult choices.

Chapter 36

The snow was falling more heavily by the time Abbey and Ellen returned to the hotel. They went into the lounge and sat beside another gas fire, although this one was much bigger than the one in their room. Ellen warmed her hands in front of it while Abbey stared into the blue and yellow flames. When one of the hotel staff asked if they'd like anything to eat or drink, they both declined.

'I couldn't possibly ingest any more tea,' said Ellen. 'I'm not used to it at weird hours of the day.'

Abbey thought her mother sounded tired. She was tired herself, and all the information that Ryan had given her was making her head spin. He'd kept up a conversation on the way back to the hotel, telling them that they'd meet with the barrister before going into the court the next day and that nothing either Lisette or Zoey had to say would make any difference – not that they'd be likely to get a chance to speak anyway. The truth was, Ryan said, that most cases ended up being more legal argument than anything else. And it was always possible that the Fitzpatricks would suddenly realise they were wasting their time and withdraw it. Which would be good for Alex, Ryan added, who was annoyed at having his professional integrity called into question.

'Why does he think it's being called into question?' asked Ellen, and Ryan replied that challenging the will insinuated that Alex had given wrong advice to Fred when he'd turned up with his home-written document.

'So it's important for him to be seen to win?' asked Ellen.

'Yes,' said Ryan.

'And important for the two Fitzpatrick brothers to be seen to win too,' she mused.

'If it was only about the money, they would have accepted your offer,' Ryan pointed out. 'It was a seriously good deal. Clearly position in the family is very important to Donald, and the discovery that he's not his father's eldest child seems to have left him feeling disrespected in some way.'

'That's mental,' said Abbey. 'His position in the family won't come to much if we win and get everything! He'll be in a worse situation.'

'Sometimes people don't think clearly under pressure,' said Ryan.

Ellen had nodded at his words and then retreated into a contemplative silence that Abbey hadn't wanted to break. As she'd got out of the car, Ryan had squeezed her hand and told her not to worry, that everything would work out fine.

'Grand?' she murmured, and he'd squeezed her hand again and said yes, grand.

But, she thought, as she turned up the flames of the gas fire, legal battles never turned out to be grand, even if the decision went your way. Pete had told her that before, and Pete was always right.

Her phone rang, startling her.

'Babes?'

'Hi, Cobey.' She lowered her voice. 'What's up?'

'Nothing,' he said. 'I thought I'd call, see how things were going for you.'

The last time they'd met, the night before Ellen had arrived in San Francisco, she'd told him about going to Ireland to sort out the situation regarding Fred's will. She'd tried to keep it all low-key, but somehow she'd ended up telling him more than she'd meant to about the Fitzpatricks, the house and the money. He'd been determined that she should fight for what was hers. He'd told her that she was lucky that the Fitzpatricks hadn't accepted the offer of half, because in the end, when the judgment was handed down and she got everything, she'd be much better off. And it was right, Cobey added, that her mother was handing over her share to Abbey; nuns didn't need money, but single girls living in the city did. He had then proceeded to tell her how best she should spend it. He wasn't so keen on the idea of her buying the apartment (who wants to be tied down to a single place? he'd asked); he thought she should take time out and travel the world. Live a little, he'd said, enjoy the good things in life.

Abbey had listened to Cobey itemising the things that money could buy and wondered if, at the end of his shopping list, there'd be anything left. Then he'd added that they could rent a nice place overlooking the bay – better than the apartment they'd previously shared and better than the one she was now living in. When she'd told him that she liked where she lived, he'd remarked that it wasn't a rich girl's apartment and she was going to be rich. She owed it to herself, Cobey told her, to get somewhere great. And then he'd mentioned a downtown block with amazing views towards the ocean which would suit her perfectly. And him too, he'd added, because it was an easy commute to the office where he hoped to start work.

Abbey hadn't missed the fact that he was continually talking as though the two of them were going to live together on her return from Ireland, but she didn't say anything. Now, despite Cobey asking her questions about the legal process, she didn't say very much either.

'I'm looking forward to you coming home,' he said. 'I miss you.'

'I miss you too.' She said the words automatically. 'I have to go now,' she added. 'I'll talk to you later.'

She ended the call and stared into the fire. It seemed as though she and Cobey were a couple again, and she wasn't entirely sure how that had happened. She'd forgiven him for walking out on her because, as her mother would point out, it was important to forgive, and Cobey had got himself into a pressurised situation. But she hadn't planned on being his girlfriend again. She wasn't quite sure that was who she wanted to be.

'Anything you want to talk about?' Ellen asked.

She'd almost forgotten her mother was still in the room. Ellen was so damned quiet and self-effacing these days that she seemed to melt into her surroundings.

'Not really,' said Abbey.

'OK.' Ellen settled back into her chair and opened a well-thumbed copy of the bible.

'You must know the story by now,' remarked Abbey.

Ellen looked up at her. 'Every good book deserves to be read more than once.'

'I guess.'

'And you get something new out of it every time,' Ellen said. 'Let not your hearts be troubled, neither let them be afraid. John 14:27.'

'You think my heart is troubled?' asked Abbey.

'Well, everyone's heart is troubled at some point,' said Ellen. 'And this is a troubling time.'

'It shouldn't be,' Abbey said. 'I'm going to have money. And I like that idea, Mom. It makes me feel confident and good about myself.'

Ellen gazed at her thoughtfully. 'Why do you need money to feel confident and good about yourself?' she asked. 'Haven't you been doing well lately? Isn't that what you've been telling me? That your nail business is going from strength to strength? That you've won competitions and you're going to this Nail Olympics thing?'

'Nailympics,' corrected Abbey. 'Yes, but all those things happened to me after I heard about Fred Fitzpatrick's will. After I realised that I could be rich.'

'So the people who judged the nail art knew about the will?' Ellen looked at her enquiringly.

'Well, no, but—'

'And all those extra clients you told me about came to you because you'll have money?'

'Mom . . .'

'And you're only good at what you do because of the actions of a man you hardly knew?'

Abbey shook her head slowly.

'It's not that simple.'

'This person, a man I'm thinking, who you miss – does he need you to have money?'

Abbey looked at Ellen, a shocked expression on her face.

'Why would you say that?'

'I'm trying to find out why it matters to you.'

'Money matters to everyone. Except you and the rest of the nuns, because you're looked after in the monastery. You don't have to care about things like the rest of us.'

Ellen said nothing.

'Oh!' Abbey suddenly despaired of her mother. 'Even when you're not talking, you're managing to melt my head!' She stood up. 'I'm going up to my room. I don't want to talk any more.'

She'd been sitting there on her own for about twenty minutes when her phone rang again. She looked at it warily, deciding that if it was Cobey she wasn't going to answer. But it was Ryan Gilligan's name she saw on the display.

'I thought I'd check that you're OK,' he said. 'The scene in the house earlier was a bit upsetting.'

'I'm . . . I'm grand,' she said.

'You don't sound grand, you sound glum.'

'I've been having existential conversations with my mother,' she told him, and he chuckled.

'She's an interesting woman,' he said.

'That's one way of putting it,' said Abbey.

'She's very calm.' Ryan disregarded the slight edge to Abbey's voice. 'When she looks at you, it's like she's peering into your soul.'

'You think?'

'That's how I felt,' he said. 'She made me feel a bit superficial, to be honest.'

'She does that to me all the time.' Abbey's tone was dry.

'I wondered . . .'

'Yes?'

'Would you like to meet me?' he asked. 'For a drink, a glass of wine, something like that?'

Talking to Ryan was easier than talking to her mom. Or talking to Cobey Missen. She needed to be with someone easy. And hell, she could do with some alcohol to take the edge off her feelings.

'I'd love to,' she said.

'Excellent. I'm outside the hotel now.'

'You are?'

'After I dropped you there, I went back to the office with Alex. Then I decided to return here. Just in case.'

'Give me five minutes,' said Abbey.

She looked at herself in the mirror, rubbed some blusher on her too-pale cheeks, then ran her brush through her hair and spritzed herself with Benefit B Spot. She pulled on her jacket and walked downstairs. Her mother was still sitting in the lounge in front of the fire, her eyes closed. Abbey thought that perhaps she'd fallen asleep. She didn't go over to her, but instead asked Clara to tell her that she'd be back later.

Ryan was standing in the reception area waiting for her. He smiled and took her by the arm, telling her they were going to walk as far as the Bloody Stream, a pub near the railway station. The falling snow deadened the sound of their footsteps, and Ryan kept a tight hold of her as they walked along the white streets.

'I can't believe I'm walking on snow,' said Abbey. 'Every so often we get a blast of Canadian air on the West Coast and there's all sorts of snowy predictions, but it hasn't happened yet.'

'You've never had snow?' He was incredulous.

'Not enough to make a snowball.' Abbey bent down and scooped some up in her hand. 'Jeez, it's cold, though.'

'Snow usually is,' remarked Ryan with good humour.

They went inside the pub, which was heaving with people, most of whom were hoping that the cold snap wouldn't last.

'We're not properly set up for it,' explained Ryan as he placed a glass of red wine in front of Abbey. 'It's something that's better in the anticipation than the reality.'

'Maybe tomorrow will be like that.' Abbey shivered suddenly. 'I thought it would be exciting. But now . . .' Her voice trailed off and she gazed into her glass.

'It'll be fine,' said Ryan. 'It's not like a criminal trial or anything.'

'No, but it's messing with people's heads, isn't it?' said Abbey. 'And Zoey and Lisette . . .'

'. . . shouldn't have been at the house today,' said Ryan.

'They were very upset, though. Lisette looks awful.'

'Not your problem.'

'Do she and Gareth need the money that badly? Has this property thing completely flattened them?'

'If it has, it's only because Gareth overextended himself during the property boom trying to make a quick buck,' said Ryan.

'And Donald? It seems so strange that he'd jeopardise everything just because he feels insulted.'

'People do the strangest things,' said Ryan. 'I can't tell you the number of times they've taken impossible cases only to prove a point. Lots of clients say that they want to stand up in court and prove that their adversary was wrong about something. It's an expensive therapy, especially if you lose.'

'Sure is.'

'Let's not talk about tomorrow. Tell me about yourself instead. Do you like being San Francisco's hottest nail technician?'

'I'm a nail artist now,' she corrected him with a smile. 'I've changed my business cards to reflect that. It's been going well.

My *Mona Lisa* design is a big favourite. Though last month it was my holiday Christmas tree that was asked for most.'

'I'm glad it's working out for you,' said Ryan.

'So am I,' she said. 'I said to my mom that it had all come right since hearing about the will. I think she's horrified at the thought that money might be behind my success.'

'The money is great, but you haven't actually got your hands on it yet,' said Ryan. 'It's your talent that's making you successful, Abbey.'

'That's what Mom was trying to make me believe.'

'Well, yes. Because it's true.'

She stared at him. 'I thought it was her being . . . well . . . being a nun.'

'Abbey Andersen! How can you be so unsure of yourself? Of your own worth?' Ryan spoke firmly. 'You're a smart, talented woman.'

'Oh, I don't think—'

'Stop with the false modesty,' he said. 'Of course you're smart, and your art is amazing. I hung that sketch of me you did at Alcatraz on my wall in the office. Everyone who sees it thinks it's great.'

She was pleased that he'd liked it enough to hang it up, but she reminded him that it was merely a quick drawing, and nothing special.

'It is to me,' said Ryan. 'As for your nail art – I'm sure that's equally good. So, you know, accept that you've talent, for heaven's sake.'

Abbey looked thoughtful. 'I don't try to be particularly modest,' she said. 'But I don't see myself as a proper artist.'

'You are,' said Ryan. 'You've got to believe that.'

He put his arm around her and hugged her. Abbey allowed herself to relax into his hold. It was comforting. And more than that, it felt right. But after a moment she sat up straight again.

'You're right,' she said. 'All the things I've achieved . . . everything since last year . . . its been my own doing, hasn't it?'

'Without a doubt.'

'Except for the apartment.'

'The apartment you're thinking of buying with Mr Fitzpatrick's money?'

She told him about Pete's involvement.

'Sounds nice,' said Ryan. 'Though you don't have to buy it, do you? You can rent from him. I bet he'd sign a long lease for you.'

'I guess he would.'

'Irish people are very hung up on property,' said Ryan. 'We like to own it. It's a historical thing, but it was part of our downfall a few years ago – why Gareth and Lisette got themselves into trouble too. I rent my place. It means that I can move on more easily. To places that mean a lot. To people who mean a lot too.'

She looked at him uncertainly, and he hugged her again.

'All I'm saying is that you don't have to tie yourself down for Pete. He's definitely a nice man, but, you know, he's not your father, Abbey, and he doesn't control your life. You do.'

'You and my mom both,' she said. 'Telling me I'm a talented person. Telling me not to tie myself down or do things for other people. Are you conspiring together?'

'Not intentionally,' Ryan assured her. 'All I want, Abbey Andersen, is for you to be happy.' He leaned forward and kissed her softly on the forehead. 'Because every Irish cailín deserves to be happy.'

'Thank you.'

He was very different to Cobey, she thought. He was kind and gentle and caring in a way she'd never experienced before. Of course that was probably just because she was his client – his about-to-be-wealthy client. All the niceness could be a sham. Maybe he was horrible to the people closest to him.

Her eyes met his and he looked at her unwaveringly. If he was a fake, she thought, he was a damn good fake. She didn't want him to be a fake. She wanted to believe that he meant it when he said that all he wanted was for her to be happy. Because right now, with his arm resting on her shoulders, she was.

Neither Lisette nor Zoey had told their respective husbands about meeting Ellen and Abbey at Furze Hill. Lisette and Gareth were still hardly speaking. Donald was too busy reading legal documents to notice his wife.

You n me are so f*cked, Zoey instant-messaged Lisette. *The legal eagles were very suspicious of us being at the house.*

You don't think they know about the safe, do you?

Nah. But still. Not good.

Aargh.

Oh well, fingers xxed.

I was hoping the nun would be a wizened old crone. But quelle surprise!

A bit of a shocker all right. Maybe she'll be in her habit tomorrow.

I wouldn't bet on it. They want her to look normal.

She looks quite hot in the all-black outfit. Who would've thought?

Hot but kindly. Unfortunately.

D'you think there's a chance of them coming in with another offer?

It's too late for that. It's all or nothing in this war. And if – when – we lose, I don't know what will happen with me and Gar.

Why?

It's all gone wrong between us.

Don't say that. You're a strong couple.

We were. Not now.

Bloody hell. Zoey's fingers thumped the keypad. *Fred Fitzpatrick didn't know what he was doing when he made that will. It would've been far better if he'd died without writing one at all.*

Chapter 37

Although it had continued to snow lightly during the night, the roads were passable and Ryan Gilligan collected Abbey and Ellen on time from the hotel the following morning.

'Will we need to give evidence, d'you think?' Abbey asked.

'Not today. But Alex wants you to be there.'

'Will all the Fitzpatricks be there too?'

'I don't know,' replied Ryan. 'I wouldn't have expected Gareth and Lisette to show up, because they're both teachers and have limited time off during school hours, but I heard on the radio this morning that a number of schools are closed because of the weather, so it's quite possible.'

'Is it too cold to go to school?' Ellen shivered as she got into the car.

'No,' said Ryan. 'But every time we have snow, some schools report heating problems or frozen pipes which force them to close.'

'There was a snow day for schools in San Diego last year,' said Ellen as she rubbed her hands together. 'The snow was high up in the mountains but the kids were really excited.'

'I like snow, but not if I have to travel in it.' Ryan turned up the heating. 'Hopefully it won't disrupt things in court today.'

'That would be awful,' said Abbey. 'After me and Mom coming over and everything . . .'

'I'm sure it'll be grand,' said Ryan as he pulled gently away from the kerb. 'We'll get this show on the road, don't you worry.'

* * *

391

There was snow on the domed roof of the court building, which overlooked the river Liffey. Abbey, Ellen and Ryan stood outside for a moment. Abbey felt light-headed. It was hard to believe that somehow she was caught up in the legal system of another country. And although she hadn't committed a crime, she couldn't help feeling guilty as she walked up the steps leading into the building.

'It's sort of . . . overwhelming.' She realised that she was whispering as she looked at the barristers wearing gowns and wigs hurrying past, bundles of files and folders in their arms.

'It can be intimidating all right,' agreed Ryan. 'But you don't have to worry, Abbey.'

'I'm not worried,' she lied. 'I . . .' She didn't want to be here, she realised. She didn't want to be disputing Fred's will in front of a judge. She didn't want any part of it.

'Hello, everyone.' Alex walked up and joined them. 'We're in Court Three. Judge Halligan. Sensible, reasonable man.'

'No last-minute sensible, reasonable offers from the Fitzpatricks?' asked Ryan.

Alex shook his head. 'The judge will be aghast that we haven't come to an agreement. The courts aren't the place to try to prove a point.'

'I guess it's that old adage about an eye for an eye leaving everybody blind,' said Ellen.

'Did the Bible say that too?' Abbey looked surprised.

'Martin Luther King Junior,' replied Ellen. 'He had a point. He also said the time was always right to do the right thing.'

'We *are* doing the right thing,' said Abbey. 'Aren't we?'

They went into the courtroom. Donald, Gareth, Lisette and Zoey were already there, along with their legal team. It all seemed very formal and serious to Abbey, who'd expected something more relaxed. It wasn't a murder trial, after all!

The judge spoke but Abbey couldn't understand a word he'd said. His accent was broad and quite unlike Ryan's, and she whispered to him that she was lost about what was going on.

'Judge Halligan's from Kerry,' he whispered. 'Even I don't understand his accent sometimes. But he's sharp as a tack.'

The judge was asking the Fitzpatricks' legal team to outline their case. Their barrister got up and started to speak. It wasn't a polished speech like Abbey was used to hearing on TV legal dramas. The barrister stopped and started, hummed and faltered a few times.

'He sounds like he doesn't know what he's talking about,' she murmured to Ryan. 'That's good.'

'It's legalese,' Ryan told her. 'He doesn't have to convince a jury, only the judge. And they all get off on the jargon, you know.'

Abbey listened carefully as the barrister continued to speak. He was talking about Mr Fitzpatrick and his children and how much of a family man he had been. She didn't know if she believed a word of it or not, but what was certainly true was that he had been a father to Donald, Gareth and Suzanne. But not to Ellen. Because Ellen had been handed over to the Connollys and he'd been happy to see the back of her.

She looked across at the Fitzpatricks. Lisette was a pale imitation of the woman she'd been before, stick thin in the dark trouser suit she was wearing. Donald and Gareth looked grim. Zoey was, as always, groomed to within an inch of her life, but Abbey could see that there was worry in her eyes. She has nothing to worry about, thought Abbey. She has a husband who'll look after her. None of them have anything to worry about. I shouldn't start feeling sorry for them. That's what they want.

After what seemed like an age, while the barristers argued back and forth, the judge called for a recess. Ryan took them to a nearby café for something to eat, but Abbey couldn't swallow.

'Are you all right?' asked her mother.

'I . . . it's different to what I expected,' she said. 'Seeing them there. Listening to what the legal people are saying. Knowing that he's talking about us when he says "defendants" . . . It all seems surreal.'

'That's the law for you.' Ryan was upbeat and cheerful.

'But it's people's lives!' cried Abbey. 'Ours. Theirs.'

'Well, today we care more about yours than theirs,' Ryan told her.

She stirred the bowl of soup in front of her and didn't say anything at all.

When they came back to the courthouse, she made her way to the ladies' room. She needed to be on her own for a bit. Her mind was in a whirl as she tried to process what had gone on that morning and decide whether it had been good for them or not. Ryan thought so, but Ryan was one of the most positive people she'd ever met. She reminded herself that this wasn't a life-or-death issue for them, that they wouldn't be any worse off if they lost, that Fred's legacy was a bonus, a windfall. That getting the house was winning the jackpot. And that he'd wanted them to hit it.

The door to the ladies' opened and Lisette walked in. She stopped short at the sight of Abbey, who could see that the other woman's eyes were tired and red-rimmed.

'I was just leaving,' Abbey said.

Lisette stepped aside and stumbled. Abbey reached out to steady her.

'Are you all right?'

'How can I be all right?' asked Lisette. 'I should be teaching children French poetry, but I'm here instead.'

Abbey didn't know what to say.

'Would you settle?' Lisette's words were urgent. 'If they said they'd accept the offer you made before, would you agree to it again now?'

'Why would they even consider it?'

'I want them to stop all this,' Lisette said. 'I begged Gareth last night. But Donald is so determined and he's dragging Gar along with him.'

'I know,' said Abbey.

'It's do or die for him,' said Lisette. 'Crazy stuff. I don't know what he's said to make Gareth support him. Money never motivated him before. This isn't him, you know.'

'Today it seems that it is,' said Abbey.

Lisette looked at her angrily for a moment, then, almost instantly, the anger, along with the urgency and despair of earlier, left her. 'I didn't want Fred to die,' she said. 'We got on well together and I liked him, even though he could be difficult. But I suppose I thought he'd look after us. Stupid, really. Why should he?'

'I'm sorry,' said Abbey.

'What have you to be sorry about.' Lisette sounded defeated. 'Fred had his reasons for leaving you the house. All I wish is that he'd thought about what he was doing to the rest of us first.'

Abbey looked at her. Lisette's eyes were clouded and the lines etched on her face were deeper than she remembered.

'What has it done to you?' she asked. 'You personally, I mean.'

'Besides wreck my marriage?' Lisette's laugh was entirely humourless. 'Besides turn me into a . . .' She broke off. She didn't think it would be a good idea to confess to having taken money and silver from the house. Not while the case was going on.

'Why has it wrecked your marriage?' asked Abbey.

'I told you. It's turned Gareth into a different person. Me too. And neither of us likes who we've become. Neither of us knows who the other person is any more.'

'But you're still together,' said Abbey.

'Who knows for how long.' Lisette sighed deeply. 'Even if we win. Even if we get everything, I don't think we can ever go back to the way we were before. I saw a side of him that I didn't like. And maybe he saw the same in me.'

Abbey said nothing.

'We shouldn't have been depending on Fred to get us out of the mess we got ourselves into,' continued Lisette. 'Donald shouldn't have had massive expectations either. His self-worth shouldn't be tied up in being the eldest. That's what upsets him most. That there was a child before him.'

'Even if you win the case, that won't change,' said Abbey. 'My mom will still exist.'

'I know. And if we lose, he'll be worse. Heaven knows what it'll to do him and Zoey.' Lisette paused. 'If we lose, Gareth will be devastated. We'll have spent money we don't have . . .' She stifled a sob. 'And all for what?'

Abbey didn't know what to say. She left Lisette repairing her make-up in the ladies', but she didn't go back into the courtroom herself. She was still standing in the entrance lobby when Ellen came to see where she was.

'Why should I feel bad?' asked Abbey after telling her of her encounter with Lisette. 'I'm not responsible for the problems in her marriage and I'm certainly not responsible for how Donald feels. And she agrees that Mr Fitzpatrick was entitled to do what he liked with his money.'

'That's true,' said Ellen.

'So why do I feel so sorry for her? Why do I care what happens to them? And why do I feel like I'm some greedy, grasping bitch for wanting what the old man left me?'

'It's perfectly natural to feel concern for them,' said Ellen. 'And I know that you're not greedy or grasping – or a bitch.'

'I'm not?'

'You were never a greedy person.'

'Do you think we're doing the wrong thing?' Abbey's faced was pinched. 'Do you think Mr Fitzpatrick did the wrong thing?'

'Those are two very different questions,' said Ellen.

Abbey looked at her mother. Ellen's face was as serene as always, her blue eyes calm and understanding.

'He wanted to make things right for Dilly,' Abbey said. 'He wanted to make it up to you.'

'I know.'

'It's all about you,' said Abbey. 'How he felt.'

'No. It's all about him.'

'Oh stop!' Abbey's shout was louder than she realised and startled even herself. 'Stop,' she said again, more quietly but with greater force. 'Stop being so damn nice and reasonable and non-judgemental about everything, and for once in your life tell me how you goddam feel!'

'How I feel doesn't matter,' said Ellen.

'It does to me!' cried Abbey. 'It matters a lot. I want to know how you feel about everything. About Mr Fitzpatrick. About the money. About Dilly. About me.'

'I love you,' said Ellen.

'How could you possibly love me when you left me?' Suddenly the words that Abbey had never been able to say before poured from her. 'You left me for something that I could never compete against. For a religion. For God. For a whole different life.'

'It wasn't a competition.'

'Yes it was,' said Abbey. 'And I lost. I lost you.'

'Of course you didn't,' said Ellen. 'I'm always here. With you. Whenever you need me.'

'No you're not,' said Abbey. 'You're there for other people. For the sisters. For those who come on retreats. For those who ask you to pray for them. But not for me.'

'I pray for you.'

'Oh, please.' Abbey was disdainful. 'What good has that ever done for me? Has it stopped me from doing stupid things or falling for the wrong person or . . . anything!'

'I can't protect you from life,' said Ellen. 'No matter where I might be or what I might be doing, you'll follow your own heart and make your own mistakes. But I can pray that you learn and grow from the experience and—'

'Dammit, Mom!' cried Abbey. 'Stop praying for me to be a good person and just . . . just . . .' She broke off, fighting against the tears that were brimming in her eyes.

Ellen looked at her daughter, a stricken expression on her face. And then she reached out and drew Abbey to her, holding her close and running her fingers through her hair as she'd done when Abbey had been a small girl.

'I'm sorry,' she whispered. 'I'm sorry.'

Abbey leant against Ellen's chest, feeling the thump of her mother's heart. The movement of her fingers through her hair soothed her as it had always soothed her in the past. She stayed immobile for almost a minute and then she lifted her head.

'I'm the one who should be sorry,' she said as she took a tissue from her bag and blew her nose. 'Letting you down like this.'

'You're not letting me down,' said Ellen. 'You've never let me down. It was me who—'

'Please, Mom.' Abbey gulped. 'You're the good person here. You're the nun.'

'I'm as flawed as anyone,' said Ellen. 'And isn't that what they want to prove in that courtroom? That everyone is flawed.'

'I think they want to prove that you're even more flawed *because* you're a nun.' Abbey's smile was watery.

'Maybe I am,' said Ellen.

'You're not,' Abbey told her.

'As a mother, I'm very flawed.' Ellen sighed. 'And for that, I truly am sorry, Abbey.'

'Oh, like I've said before, you could've turned out much worse.' This time Abbey's smile was a little stronger.

'I love you,' said Ellen. 'You do know that, don't you? Just because I have this . . . this other relationship doesn't mean I ever stopped loving you.'

'I thought I should come first,' admitted Abbey.

'I understand.'

'But what you have – it's very different, isn't it?'

'I can't explain,' said Ellen. 'I wish I could.'

'You don't have to,' Abbey told her.

'I feel I should. But I don't know how.'

'I guess . . . I guess you have to concentrate on what you're good at,' said Abbey. 'On the praying. Maybe I need it no matter what I say.'

'I always pray for good things to happen to you,' Ellen told her. 'I always will.'

'And this thing now?' Abbey wiped her eyes. 'What have you prayed about for this?'

'That we – you and I – make the right choice,' said Ellen.

'Oh Mom.' Abbey looked at her resignedly. 'We already know what that choice has to be.'

When they returned to the courtroom, Abbey sat down beside Ryan and took a deep breath.

'We've changed our minds,' she whispered. 'We don't want anything at all.'

'What?' He looked at her in shock and then glanced around the courtroom.

'We can't do it,' she said. 'I never should've let it get to this.'

'Abbey,' he said, his voice low and urgent. 'This is what Mr Fitzpatrick wanted.'

'He wanted to let me and Mom know that he was sorry,' whispered Abbey. 'She knows that.'

Ryan turned his gaze to Ellen, who was sitting impassively beside her daughter.

'What did you say to her?' he asked. 'Why are you doing this?'

'I didn't say anything,' said Ellen. 'This is Abbey's choice to make.'

Ryan looked at her sceptically.

'Oh hell.' Abbey sighed. 'I've never believed in this inheritance, Ryan, you know that. I've always struggled with the idea, but for a while I thought I deserved it. I thought it was the greatest thing that had ever happened to me.'

'You do deserve it,' said Ryan. 'You both do.'

'No,' Abbey said. 'We don't. We haven't lost out by not being part of Mr Fitzpatrick's family. We've been our own family.'

'Abbey . . . you're talking about a lot of money.'

'I know.'

'Are you sure it's not that you're finding all this . . .' he gestured at the courtroom, 'a bit overpowering?'

'It's overpowering all right. But that's not it, Ryan. The truth is that Mr Fitzpatrick should've left everything to his close family, not us.'

'Ellen is his daughter,' said Ryan.

'His natural daughter, yes,' agreed Ellen. 'But I'll always really be the daughter of John and Mamie Connolly and the mother of Abbey Andersen. And my close family, besides Abbey, is now the community in Los Montesinos.'

Ryan stared at her for a moment, then turned to Abbey. 'I know that your mam has spiritual reasons for her decision. But what about you?'

'Mom already said that she was giving her half to me,' said Abbey. 'That's why we made the offer; it was giving her money back. But he should never have left anything to me in the first place. I don't need anything from him to be fine with who I am and how I've been brought up.'

'Abbey – he wanted to do this.'

'He was wrong,' said Abbey.

Ryan sighed, then nodded slowly. 'I'll need to work out with Alex the best way of approaching this.'

'I don't want to let Alex down,' said Abbey. 'You told me that it was important to him not to be seen as having given wrong advice to Mr Fitzpatrick. I like Alex. I think he's a good man. I don't want him to lose face.'

'We need to talk,' said Ryan. 'Me and Alex, and then we need to talk with the other solicitors and barristers. We have to ask the judge for some time.'

'OK.' Abbey still felt sick. She knew she was doing the right thing, but she realised it was causing a lot of trouble. She closed her eyes. And then she felt a hand squeeze hers and she opened them again.

'Everything will be all right,' said Ellen. 'I promise.'

'I hope so,' said Abbey. 'Because right now I feel like I've messed up again.'

* * *

There was shocked jubilation in the small room where Donald, Gareth, Zoey and Lisette had been informed of Abbey's decision by their legal advisers.

'I told you!' Donald was triumphant, a wide smile on his face and his chest puffed out. 'They knew they didn't have a case.'

'They had a very good case.' Donald's barrister was astounded. 'Courts rarely overturn wills. I could see that Halligan was sceptical about us.'

'But the judge would've realised that the Americans were nothing more than money-grabbers,' said Gareth.

'I don't think so,' said Paul Tierney. 'As you know, Donald, I advised against—'

'And see what that would've done!' Donald was scornful. 'You legal people are so concerned with the law that you don't understand justice.'

'You might be right about that,' said the barrister. 'But I'm astonished all the same.'

'You see!' cried Donald as the legal team left the room. 'I'm the eldest and I look after you all. I knew what I was doing. I always did. So now, Lisette Fitzpatrick, with all your doom and gloom – who's the daddy? Who?'

'Don!' Zoey punched him gently in the ribs. 'Get a grip.'

'Sorry.' For a moment, Don looked embarrassed. But then he did a quick jig. He couldn't help it. His position as head of the family had been vindicated beyond a shadow of a doubt, and now he wanted to celebrate.

Although there was paperwork and agreements to sign, the final outcome was that the house and contents were now part of Fred's estate and, according to their barrister, who'd rejoined them after some discussion with Alex's, would be divided between Fred's three children, Donald, Gareth and Suzanne.

'It has to be that way?' asked Donald. 'Because originally we thought it would be just me and Gareth.'

'Once the house becomes part of the estate, yes,' said his barrister. 'Abbey Andersen is also still entitled to the five thousand euros that your father left her.'

'You're not going to dispute that too, are you?' Lisette's voice was anxious.

Donald hesitated.

'Don!' Zoey looked at him sternly.

'No, no,' he said. 'All I'm thinking now is that Suzanne should be pleased with me despite opposing me. She's done better than she would have otherwise.'

'It's not about who does well and who doesn't,' Zoey told him.

'Huh?' He looked at her in astonishment. 'That's exactly what it's about.'

'We're in a lot better position than we were a few days ago.' Lisette had shed at least ten years since the agreement. 'Maybe it's not as perfect as you would have liked, Don, but it's a damn sight better than seeing Abbey and her mother walk away with it.'

'We'll get started on the paperwork,' said Paul. 'But that's the end of it. Congratulations, everybody.'

'Thanks,' said Donald. 'I knew we had right on our side.'

'It's a surprise to me,' Paul rubbed the back of his neck, 'that even in the law, justice sometimes happens.'

Donald and Gareth insisted on going to the nearby Morrison Hotel and ordering a bottle of champagne.

'Not only have we got everything we wanted, but we've also saved on a chunk of legal fees,' said Donald as he poured the alcohol into their glasses. 'And I know you were doubtful, ladies, but we took the right approach.'

'My hero,' said Zoey, and took a sip of champagne.

'I'd love to know why they suddenly changed their minds.' Gareth sounded as though he still couldn't believe it. 'Did they find out something? Do they know something? Is there a catch?'

Lisette and Zoey exchanged suddenly worried glances. Was there a catch? they wondered. Had Abbey and Ellen discovered that they'd raided the safe? Did they have some other plan that nobody knew about? A plan that would scupper everything?

'We have to talk to them,' said Lisette urgently while Donald and Gareth congratulated each other again. 'You and me both.'

'I guess so.'

'We won't say anything to the boys.'

'Too right,' agreed Zoey. 'This is just between us.'

In the time they'd been in court, the temperature had risen and the morning's snow had turned to slush. It meant that the return drive to Howth was quicker than the journey into the city had been.

'Is Alex mad at us?' asked Abbey.

'He'll get over it.' Ryan told her. 'Gives him time to focus on other cases.'

'I'm sorry,' said Abbey. 'I'm sorry that I left it till the last minute to do what was right.'

'It would've been just as right for you to take what had been left to you,' said Ryan.

'Somehow it never felt that way.'

'But Fred Fitzpatrick wanted to look after you,' protested Ryan.

'He wanted to look after his family.' Ellen spoke for the first time since they'd got into the car. 'And the truth is that we're not his family. We're people who are related to him by blood. Family is more than that.'

'He wanted to make it up to that woman, though, didn't he? Dilly.'

'Giving money to me and Abbey couldn't change what happened to her. More important was that he thought about her in the end. Regretted how things had turned out, respected her.'

'I wonder what she was like,' Abbey said. 'Seems to me that you must be more her than him, Mom.'

'Seems to me that I'm more of a Connolly than a Fitzpatrick,' said Ellen.

'You believe in nurture not nature, so.' Ryan stopped the car outside the hotel.

'Yes,' said Ellen. 'I realise that I might have genetic links to the Fitzpatricks. But I'll always be Ellen Connolly.'

'I thought you were Sister Benita now,' observed Abbey. 'I thought you'd left Ellen Connolly behind.'

'I can never leave a part of myself behind,' said Ellen. 'Nobody can. Everything that's happened to us makes up who we are today. That's as true of a nun as a pop diva.'

'You know many pop divas?' asked Abbey.

'A very famous one does occasional retreats at Los Montesinos,' replied Ellen.

'No?' Abbey's eyes widened. 'Who?'

'I can't tell you that,' said Ellen. 'But you'd be surprised.'

'Mom! That's so not fair! Give me a clue.'

Ellen smiled. 'No. But not everyone is exactly how they appear to the outside world either.'

'Lady Gaga? Katy Perry? What about Madonna?' Abbey looked at her hopefully.

'My lips are sealed,' said Ellen. And she winked at them as she got out of the car.

Because they'd thought that the court hearing would last a few days, Ellen and Abbey were booked into the Harbour Hotel until the end of the week. Ryan told them that they needn't worry about the bill, it would be looked after by the estate.

'Are you sure?' asked Abbey.

'Definitely,' he assured her. 'And don't feel bad about that, for heaven's sake.'

'I don't. To be honest,' she added, 'I feel like a weight has been lifted off my shoulders.'

'You're freaky.' But he sounded amused. 'If I'd handed over a valuable property for nothing, I'd be feeling a bit hard done by.'

'I guess I'm my mother's daughter after all,' Abbey said. 'Unfortunately.'

'Or maybe fortunately,' he said. 'You did an incredibly generous thing today.'

'Thanks.'

'Perhaps we'll meet again before you go back to the States?'

'I sure hope so.'

'Great.' He kissed her on the cheek. 'I'll be in touch. Meantime, I'd better get back to the office. Things to do.'

'Goodbye,' said Ellen. 'It was nice meeting you.'

'You too,' he said. 'You've changed my ideas of what nuns are like.'

'Only because you saw me out of my environment,' Ellen told him. 'I can look incredibly stereotypical when I choose.'

She and Abbey went into the hotel lounge and sat in front of the fire again.

'I'm proud of you,' she told Abbey. 'It wasn't about money, and you knew that all the time.'

'Pete won't agree,' said Abbey. 'And Claudia will go ballistic.'

'Oh?'

'Even though she accepts me as part of Pete's life, I'm a constant reminder that he had a relationship with you,' said Abbey. 'Maybe she's afraid that one day he'll leave me an inheritance too. Wow, I don't even want to think that might happen!'

'Pete knows better,' said Ellen.

'I hope so. But there's still the apartment to deal with.' Abbey grimaced. 'I'm not looking forward to broaching that with him.'

'I'm sure it'll work out. Things do, for Pete.'

'Except with you,' Abbey told her.

Ellen looked rueful. 'I'm sorry about that,' she said. 'He's a good man. But he's happy now, isn't he?'

'Yes,' said Abbey. 'He is.'

'So he's found his place and the right woman, and I'm glad for him. Now I only have to worry about you.'

'Do you worry about me?'

'All the time,' said Ellen.

'Seriously?'

'Perhaps worry is the wrong word,' conceded Ellen. 'But you're always top of my prayer list.'

'What do you pray for me?' asked Abbey.

'That you fulfil your potential and that you find happiness.'

'Like – happiness with a man?'

'Only if that's what you want,' said Ellen. 'Love is wonderful but you shouldn't ever define yourself by a man.'

'I told you – Ryan Gilligan isn't in my life,' said Abbey. 'He's a nice guy and everything, but—'

'I was thinking of the man you spoke to on the phone,' said Ellen. 'The one you miss.'

'Oh. Cobey.'

'Is he not the man who walked out on you?' Ellen's voice had lost its usual serenity.

'Yes.'

'And he's back?'

'Not . . . not as such. And possibly not at all now.'

Even as she spoke, her phone vibrated and she saw a text message from him.

How's it goin'? he asked. *You a millionairess yet?*

He was only interested in the money. She knew that. He'd turned up after he'd heard about it and he talked about it constantly. What it would buy, what they could do with it, where they could go . . . and she'd let him because she'd liked . . . well, she knew it now, she'd liked being the one in control. For as long as she was a potential source of cash, she had Cobey Missen exactly where she wanted him. And she'd liked that. Only it wasn't healthy, and it certainly wasn't a relationship.

It's going OK, she typed. *But I won't ever be a millionairess. Because I've just signed everything away.*

She knew that he'd call to see if she was telling the truth, so she turned off her phone and put it in her bag.

'Well?' asked Ellen.

Abbey grinned suddenly. 'Very well! It's cool, Mom. I know what I want and it's certainly not Cobey Missen. I know what I don't want too. And I'll get there in my own way.'

'Excellent,' said Ellen. 'I'm sorry I won't be there to watch over you.'

'Don't be,' said Abbey. 'A nun's gotta do what a nun's gotta do.'

'I love my life at the monastery,' said Ellen.

'I know.'

'But the last few days have been exhilarating.'

'Mom!' Abbey stared at her. 'You wouldn't think of leaving, would you?'

'I . . .' Ellen turned her gaze towards the flames of the fire. 'I don't think so. But I've been wondering . . . if my reasons for joining were the right ones. If I was trying to escape . . .'

'Escape what?'

'Sometimes day-to-day life is hard to take,' said Ellen. 'You know that already, don't you? You think you're doing it right but you still make mistakes. It's nice to have a community to help take the strain.'

'Weren't you happy before?' asked Abbey.

'It's not that,' said Ellen. 'I didn't quite feel like I fitted properly. I should have. I liked what I did and I had you – it should have been enough. On one level it was. But on another . . . I don't want you to think you're not enough for me, Abbey. It's just that there was another part of my life that I had to explore.'

'I understand.'

'Ever since you came to see me with the news about the inheritance, I've been halfway back in my old life. I'm remembering why it was fun.'

'What would you do if you didn't make your final profession? If you left?' Abbey couldn't believe what Ellen was saying.

'I'm nowhere near thinking that,' said Ellen. 'All I'm doing is . . . asking questions. Re-evaluating. Like you did.'

'Seems like we've all had to do a lot of re-evaluating,' said Abbey. 'You, me and the Fitzpatricks.'

'Hopefully we'll all come to the right conclusions, too,' said Ellen.

'I'll have to do some more when we get back to the States,' Abbey told her. 'Especially when it comes to the apartment.'

'Perhaps Pete will give you a long-term let.'

'Perhaps. Though I'm not sure I could afford what that might be. He hasn't charged me anything till now. He said I could repay him out of the house sale money, and I'm not looking forward to telling him there won't be any.'

'He'll get over it.'

'Poor Pete,' said Abbey. 'First you, now me. Both of us letting him down.'

'I'll pray for him,' said Ellen.

'You'll be exhausted with so much praying to do,' remarked Abbey.

'I never get tired of praying,' said Ellen. 'Honestly.'

As she'd already known, Pete was horrified when Abbey rang him and told him what they'd done.

'I'm sorry about the apartment,' she said. 'But I've been googling real estate in the area and it's doing pretty well, so hopefully it's a good investment for you.'

'I bought it as a good investment for *you*,' protested Pete. 'Something sensible to do with your inheritance. I thought you were OK with all of it. I should never have let you go to Ireland with only your mother in tow. I might have guessed she'd be a bad influence on you.'

'It was nothing to do with Mom,' said Abbey. 'It was me. And

Pete, you can tell Claudia not to worry. Just because I won't be buying the apartment doesn't mean I'll be looking to bunk up in your house again.'

'She's not worried about that,' said Pete. 'She only wants you to be all right.'

Perhaps that was true. Perhaps all that Claudia wanted was for Abbey to be less dependent on Pete in the future. Abbey had thought the money would make that the case, but even now, knowing that she was in the exact same financial situation as before, she believed that their relationship had changed anyway. Pete would always be there for her, but she wouldn't need to depend on him quite so much. Because she'd grown accustomed to thinking more for herself and living with the consequences, whether it was to do with her career or her personal life.

'And you're right about the real estate prices,' added Pete. 'Another apartment in the block recently sold for more than I paid for yours.'

'That's good news, isn't it?' she said.

'Yes, but I wanted you to make the money,' Pete replied. 'And I wanted you to have a nice place to live.'

'I'm sure I'll find somewhere.'

'I'd like it if you rented from me,' Pete told her. 'I'll do a good deal for you and—'

'We'll talk when I get back,' she told him. 'I might not be able to afford it, and I don't want special treatment, Pete. I'll find somewhere, even if I have to share. Don't worry about me.'

'I've never heard you talk like this before,' he said. 'You're way more decisive than usual.'

'I feel decisive,' she said. 'I feel – oh, I dunno Pete, I guess I'm happy, is all.'

'They say money doesn't buy happiness,' remarked Pete.

'Maybe giving it to someone else does,' she joked.

'I'll take your word for it,' he said, but he sounded happy himself.

Then she called Cobey. If Pete had been horrified, Cobey was furious.

'We could have done so much!' he cried. 'You're some crazy woman, Abbey Andersen.'

'I guess you'll be heading back to the cruise liner,' she said. 'Now that I'm not worth anything any more.'

'I came back because I missed you,' said Cobey.

Perhaps that was true. Or perhaps he really believed it. But Abbey knew that he didn't miss her enough to want to be with her without the money. She hadn't wanted to believe that at first. But today she was facing up to things. And facing up to the fact that Cobey – fun though he was to be with – was something of a fair-weather boyfriend was something that she should've done before now.

'You still owe me money,' she reminded him. 'If you want to keep in touch with me, you can put it into my bank account. If you don't – well . . .'

'You're a hard-hearted woman,' said Cobey.

'And you're a freeloader,' she told him. 'We were good for a while but I'm not in the business of having someone break my heart on a regular basis.'

'I didn't break your heart,' said Cobey.

'You did,' Abbey said. 'But now that it's mended, I want to keep it that way.'

Both Solí and Vanessa were disappointed that she'd given up the money, but they both agreed that that disappointment was balanced out by the fact that she'd also dumped Cobey Missen.

'I'd rather you were poor but happy than rich and living with that ass-wipe,' said Vanessa.

'He wasn't a total ass-wipe,' protested Abbey. 'He was a bit of a fool, is all. Hey, and I'm not poor,' she added. 'I've nearly doubled my earnings in the salon the last few months. I'm doing OK.'

'And there's the possibility of your own business,' added Vanessa.

410

'Which I'm seriously thinking about,' said Abbey. 'Everything will work out. I know it will.'

'I know it will too,' said Vanessa. 'And I can't wait to see you again. So get yourself back here double-quick, Miss Andersen, and we'll have a girlie night.'

'I aim to be home soon,' Abbey said. 'And I'll call you the minute I am.'

The following day, as the weather turned even milder, Abbey and Ellen went into the city centre. Abbey took Ellen to Christ Church, which she'd seen before but knew her mother would love, and then they went to Dublin's other cathedral, St Patrick's, after which Abbey declared herself cathedraled out and spiritually sated, so they went for something to eat before returning to the hotel.

'You'll be sick of the sight of me before the week is out,' said Ellen.

'We used to be together all the time,' Abbey reminded her. 'It's nice for me to be with you now, though I'm sure you're used to much more time on your own.'

'Not entirely,' Ellen said. 'I live in a community. We do a lot of things together.'

'That's different.'

'Yes, it is,' agreed Ellen. 'Anyway, what I really meant was that if you want to spend some time with that man of yours, that's fine by me.'

'If you mean Ryan, he's not my man,' said Abbey. 'He can't possibly be. We live on different continents.'

'I'm not suggesting that you marry him,' Ellen pointed out. 'Just that you spend time with him, if that's what you want to do.'

'If he calls, I'll see him. If he doesn't, I won't.'

'Have fun while you can, Abbey,' said Ellen. 'Enjoy life and whatever it throws at you. You only get one shot at it.'

Abbey was about to reply when the phone in the room rang

411

and Clara told her that there was someone at reception looking for her.

'Who?' asked Abbey.

'Suzanne Fitzpatrick,' said Clara.

'Tell her I'll – we'll be right down.'

It was entirely coincidental that both Suzanne and Ellen were dressed in similar skirts and jumpers, but it made the likeness between them even more obvious. The two women looked at each other with startled eyes, then embraced.

'Well, no chance of you not being Dad's daughter,' said Suzanne. 'And I'm delighted to think that I might age as well as you.'

Ellen smiled. 'It's good to meet you.'

'I had to come.' Suzanne turned to Abbey and hugged her too. 'When Donald phoned me and told me – well, I couldn't not. Especially because the sale of the Mirador to the other group fell through and Petra and I have put a new consortium together ourselves and we have enough to buy it. But the money I get when we sell the house . . . it will help dramatically, Abbey. So thank you. Thank you very much.'

'You're welcome.'

'But it's more than thank you.' Suzanne looked anxious. 'I wanted to be sure. Because, yes, the money will mean a lot to me, but what about you?'

'Hey,' Abbey said. 'I'm a nun's daughter. We do the whole simple living thing.'

'Maybe.' Suzanne's eyes flickered between them. 'But you're giving up so much, both of you.'

'You can't give up what you never had,' said Abbey.

'Hmm, well, Donald was positively ecstatic on the phone. A bit too full of himself. Called it a great victory for natural justice and reminded me that he'd been right all along to fight you.'

'Maybe he was,' said Abbey. 'After all, this way, you get what you deserve. And you do deserve it, Suzanne. I know how hard you work.'

'Thanks,' said Suzanne. 'I'll have to work even harder when I own the Mirador. But I'm so looking forward to it. Of course it still has to all happen,' she added. 'But I'm feeling very positive. Fingers crossed.'

'I'll say a prayer,' promised Ellen.

'I'm sure family prayers are better than any other sort,' said Suzanne. 'And I want to get to know you,' she added. 'I realise that you live this cloistered life, but I've never had a sister before.'

'Half-sister,' said Abbey.

'I don't care. Sister, half-sister, quarter-sister . . .'

'Sister Benita,' added Ellen. 'That's what I'm known as.'

'What would you like me to call you?' asked Suzanne. 'Benita? Ellen?'

'I don't know.' Ellen considered for a moment. 'I think – outside the monastery – Ellen is who I am.'

'Fine by me,' said Suzanne. 'Can we get together later tonight and have a chat?'

'That'll be fun,' said Ellen. And she meant it.

Suzanne's visit literally was a flying one, because she was going back to Spain the following evening, but although the three of them had agreed to meet for lunch the next day, Abbey cried off, because she'd developed a migraine.

'Are you sure you'll be OK?' asked Ellen as she pulled on her boots.

'Of course,' replied Abbey, who'd taken some pills. 'It's only from all the tension. Go have fun with her.'

'I know she said it was nice to have a sister figure in her life, but it's sort of nice for me too,' admitted Ellen.

'I'm glad you think so,' said Abbey. 'And I like Suzanne a lot. Tell her I will, very definitely, come to Spain when she opens her hotel.'

413

She rested her head on the cool, crisp pillowcase and closed her eyes, allowing her mind to go blank. But as her headache started to ease, various thoughts returned. Mostly about the future. She wouldn't be returning to California as a rich person. She wouldn't be buying the apartment from Pete – perhaps she wouldn't even be able to live there any more. But she would be coming home knowing that she'd done the right thing. And that she was closer to Ellen than at any time since she'd made her decision to join the monastery. She understood her mother more and respected her view. And even though she might not have found riches in Ireland, she'd found people. She doubted she'd ever be close to Donald and Gareth, or their wives, but it was nice to know that they were there. And there was also Suzanne, who was smart and kind and who wanted her to spread her wings and use her talents, just like Pete did. She would do that, she thought. She would do her best. There was nothing more anyone could ask of her.

Her head had improved enough so that she was sitting in the window, sketching with the hotel pencil on a sheet of hotel paper when the phone rang and Clara told her that there was someone else at reception to see her.

Who now? wondered Abbey, and was surprised when Clara added that it was Zoey Fitzpatrick. She went into the bathroom and dabbed concealer on the dark circles under her eyes, swirled some warm blusher on her pale cheeks and went downstairs.

Donald's wife looked amazing in an on-trend black coat with leopardskin boots and a matching hat. She greeted Abbey with a wide smile (which took her totally by surprise), then said that she and Lisette wanted to have a private chat with her and could she meet them later at Fred's house.

'What on earth do you want to talk about?' asked Abbey.

'This and that,' replied Zoey, who still couldn't tell whether or not Abbey knew they'd taken stuff from the house. 'But we think it's important. Lisette's at work today, so can you be there at five o'clock?'

Abbey was intrigued. What could Zoey's this and that possibly be? She thought that perhaps meeting the two Fitzpatrick wives was something that Ryan would advise against, but her natural curiosity overcame her caution and she agreed to be at Furze Hill at the appointed hour.

Ellen returned to the hotel with Suzanne just as Abbey was leaving. She told them that her headache had gone and then explained about Zoey's request.

'Interesting,' said Suzanne. 'I wouldn't trust that pair as far as I could throw them.'

'There's nothing for me to have to trust them about now,' said Abbey. 'I thought they'd be glad never to have to see me again.'

'Perhaps they want to thank you,' Ellen suggested.

'I didn't get the feeling that thanks were on their agenda,' Abbey said.

'D'you want me to come with you?' asked her mother.

'No thanks,' said Abbey. 'I'll deal with this on my own. Unless you want to come,' she added. 'Unless you don't want to be left here on your own?'

'I've lagged behind in my prayers,' Ellen said. 'This is a good opportunity for me to catch up.'

As far as Abbey could tell, her mother spent a lot of her free time praying, and she found it hard to imagine that she could possibly have fallen behind in her conversations with God. She said goodbye to Ellen and promised Suzanne, who was waiting for a cab to take her to the airport, that she'd let her know how things went with the Fitzpatrick wives. Then she got into the taxi that she'd already ordered herself.

It was the first time she'd been to Furze Hill in twilight and the first time she'd seen the lights of the city circling the bay with their beads of yellow from Fred's magnificent lounge.

'It's lovely,' she said to Lisette and Zoey, who, having escorted her into the house, were watching her. 'I bet it's going to be a wrench selling this place.'

'Hmm, well, that may yet lead to other arguments.' Zoey made a face. 'Donald doesn't want to sell it at all, but we don't have the money to buy Lisette and Suzanne out, so I don't know where it'll all end.'

'Oh, not more legal battles, I hope.' Abbey looked horrified.

'I hope not too,' said Lisette. 'I can't help feeling we've got ourselves into a "be careful what you wish for" scenario. Now that our husbands have got what they want – what they were entitled to – we're hoping to persuade them to be sensible.'

'Arguing the case wasn't sensible,' said Abbey. 'But it worked out for them in the end. Maybe they're the sort of people who fall on their feet.'

'It doesn't normally feel like that,' said Lisette ruefully. 'Certainly not over the last few years.'

'Why did you cave in?' Zoey asked Abbey. 'All the advice was that you'd win the case, you know.'

'It seemed the right thing to do.' Abbey repeated the words she'd said so many times, words that nobody other than her mother appeared to understand.

'There isn't anything more, is there?' asked Zoey. 'You're not planning on . . . on any other actions?'

'Like what?' asked Abbey.

'Oh God, we'd better come clean. Not that it matters,' Zoey added hastily. 'You gave up everything he left you, which was the house and the contents, and so it doesn't exactly matter any more, but still . . .'

'Still what?'

Lisette was the one who told her about the safe and the money. And the pieces of silver and jewellery that they'd taken.

'We were under pressure,' she said. 'We were afraid we'd lose everything.'

'And the silver and jewellery were ours anyway,' Zoey added. 'We were taking it early, that's all.'

'But we were wrong to take the cash,' said Lisette. 'It could've been yours and that means that we were sort of stealing.'

'Why are you still worried now that it actually is yours?' said Abbey.

'But it wasn't then,' said Lisette. 'We thought that maybe you were going to sue us or something. That you'd take your revenge on the whole family by labelling us as criminals.'

'Wow.' Abbey's eyes widened. 'You think I'm a much more devious person than I am. I'd never have thought of that!'

'You're very annoying, you know,' said Zoey. 'You and your mother. All sweet and nice and understanding.'

'But I do understand,' said Abbey. 'I would've been hopping mad too if someone had come from nowhere to grab my inheritance.'

'Yeah, but I bet you wouldn't have fought tooth and nail for it.'

'Maybe under different circumstances I would. Or maybe it was the saintly influence of my mom.'

'She's certainly not what I expected,' said Lisette.

'Me neither,' agreed Zoey.

'She's never been what anyone expects,' Abbey told them. 'Not even in the days before she was a nun.' She told them a little about their travels in Latin America, and the two women listened, asking questions about the places she'd been and the people she'd met .

'You've had an exciting life,' said Lisette.

'Everyone else's life sounds far more exciting than your own,' Abbey told her. 'At least, that's what I always think. It wasn't that exciting when I was living it and it certainly hasn't been that exciting the last few years. All I've done is hang out in San Francisco, go to work and have a few crappy relationships.'

'We all have those,' said Zoey.

'But Zoey has proved that it can come right in the end,' added Lisette.

Zoey made a face at her. 'I still have another one to deal with,' she said.

'What?' Lisette stared at her. 'There's someone else? Who?'

'It's not another man,' said Zoey. 'But the way Donald felt about Abbey and her mom is the way I've felt about Disgruntled Deirdre and his daughters. Thing is, I didn't like his attitude. I thought he was being unreasonable, even though I understood where he was coming from. It made me think that maybe I've been a bit unreasonable about Deirdre and the girls too. So I thought that perhaps I could try a bit harder with them.'

'Zoey!' Lisette looked surprised. 'That's a big change.'

'I know. And I'm not guaranteeing I'll end up liking the first Mrs Fitzpatrick. Or those annoying girls. But maybe I can tolerate them a little more.'

'Donald will be pleased, though,' said Lisette.

'I know. And I want to do it for him as much as anything,' Zoey said. 'One day I hope to have kids of my own. I don't want bad feeling between everyone.'

'I'm glad if something good came out of all the trauma,' said Abbey. 'And my mom would be pleased to think that your lives changed for the better.'

'Your own life probably would've changed a lot more for the better if you'd got this place,' Zoey observed. 'You could've sold it and bagged a nice sum of money for yourself and done whatever you wanted.'

'I don't think the money is what changes things,' Abbey said. 'I think you have to change yourself. Which maybe I've done a bit over the last few months too. Just like the rest of you.'

'Will you come back to Ireland?'

'Perhaps.'

'Will you call us if you do?'

'If you want me to.'

'It might be nice,' said Lisette. 'You . . . you're family, after all.'

Abbey looked pleased. 'A little bit family,' she amended.

'You did the right thing for us,' said Lisette. 'That makes you as much a part of this family as anyone, and, you know, I can't

418

help feeling that we're still treating you badly when you've been so good to us.'

'Please don't worry about me,' said Abbey. 'I was fine before I knew about all of you and I'll be fine when I go back to the States. I don't want to be part of any further discussions you have about Mr Fitzpatrick's legacy and I truly don't want anything from you.'

'Well, look, don't you think—'

Abbey stopped her. 'I have everything I need.'

'Even if you're not interested in money – and we got you so wrong about that – we wanted to give you this anyway,' said Zoey. She reached behind the sofa. 'We thought maybe it would remind you of Fred and of Ireland.'

'Oh!' Abbey couldn't help smiling. It was the painting from Fred's office. The one she'd noticed when she'd been trying to save his life. The one of the rock in the sea. 'It's lovely,' she said. 'Thank you.'

'It's only a token gesture,' said Lisette. 'The boys don't know we're giving you anything. They're still a bit raw about the whole thing. But . . .'

'Thanks,' said Abbey again.

'And here's a card from us. With our contact information,' said Zoey. 'We're both on Facebook too, so if you want to friend us, we'd be delighted.'

'OK.' Abbey was touched.

'And now, if you like, we'll drop you back to your hotel,' said Lisette.

'Grand,' said Abbey, enjoying the fact that she could use the word again.

They left the house together.

She didn't look back.

Chapter 38

Ryan and Ellen were sitting together in Ellen's now regular place beside the fire when Abbey walked into the hotel. He stood up and greeted her with a quick kiss to the cheek.

'How's your headache?' he asked.

'Gone.'

'When your mam told me you were meeting Lisette and Zoey, I worried that it might come back worse than ever.'

'Thankfully not.' She told both of them about the Fitzpatrick women's confession and showed them the painting.

'They shouldn't have taken anything from the house!' Ryan was shocked.

'It doesn't matter now,' said Abbey. 'In the end, they were only taking their own stuff.'

'It could've – should've – been yours,' objected Ryan.

'But it isn't,' said Abbey. 'And now I have a nice painting.'

Ryan shook his head. 'I'm glad all our clients aren't like you and Ellen,' he said. 'We'd be destroyed by goodness.'

'Please stop telling me I'm good!' cried Abbey. 'I'm so not. All I am is someone who's looking forward to getting back to her own life.'

'Won't you miss us?' asked Ryan.

She smiled. 'I'll miss you for sure.'

'You will?' He looked intently at her.

'Of course.'

'Would you two like to be alone?' asked Ellen as they continued to look at each other without speaking.

'No. No. It's OK,' said Abbey.

'Ryan was saying to me that he'd promised to take you to dinner but that he hadn't managed it before today,' said Ellen. 'As I've already had lunch with Suzanne, I'll be fine here with my prayer book if you two want to eat together.'

'You've been praying all afternoon,' Abbey said.

'You can never have too much prayer,' said Ellen.

'I did come here to see if you wanted to have dinner with me,' Ryan confessed to Abbey. 'Even if things didn't work out the way Alex and I expected, I felt it would be good to have a celebratory meal together. After all, we didn't actually lose the case.'

'That'd be lovely,' she said. 'Let me go freshen up first.'

She went up to the room and changed into a sapphire-blue wraparound dress which enhanced her bust and flattered her waist. It was one of her favourite dresses, and she'd packed it for whatever celebration she'd been sure they'd have when the judge ruled in their favour and awarded her and Ellen the ownership of Furze Hill. Was I out of my mind, she asked herself, to give in without a fight? To be going home with nothing when I could have gone home with everything? Did Mom's presence here influence me somehow?

She spritzed her throat and her wrists with perfume and went downstairs again. Ryan and Ellen were still chatting companionably beside the fire.

'You look sensational,' said Ryan as she approached them.

'Thank you.' Sensational was pushing it, she added, but she was glad that he liked the dress.

'I don't think it is.' There was a tone of wonder in Ellen's voice. 'I never realised before what a lovely daughter I have.'

'Genetics,' said Ryan. 'She takes after you.'

Ellen, laughing, told him he was a charmer, and he said that he did his best, and then he took Abbey by the arm and led her outside.

'There's a lovely seafood restaurant not too far from here,' he said. 'We can walk if you don't mind.'

'Sounds good to me.'

They strolled along the pavement in silence, but it was an easy silence, she thought, and she didn't feel the need to fill it with chatter. Even when they got to the restaurant, she was happy to look at the menu and choose what she wanted to eat without much conversation. It wasn't until they'd both been served starters that Ryan started to talk about the Fitzpatricks again.

'Don't,' said Abbey. 'I've put that behind me. I hope they get what they want out of the house – although going on what Lisette and Zoey told me, that might not be plain sailing either. However, it's their problem, not mine, so let's stop talking about them. Tell me about you instead. Any more missing persons cases?'

'Nothing so exciting,' he said. 'I'm working on a boring old corporate case now.' He explained the background to her, and she listened to him, entranced as always by his accent, loving the softness of it, wondering if Irish girls thought their men sounded sexy every time they opened their mouths. Probably not, she reasoned. It's a grass being always greener thing again, isn't it? Anything and anyone different always seemed better, more intriguing. She wondered what Cobey was doing now, if he'd already moved on to someone with greater prospects than her, someone prettier and richer and able to give him the kind of life he wanted. Poor girl, she thought suddenly. Whoever she might be, Abbey felt sorry for her.

'Why do I get the idea that you'd rather be somewhere else?' asked Ryan.

'I'm so sorry.' She put down her knife and fork. 'I'm putting everything that's happened into context.'

'And where in that context do I fit?' he asked.

'You're one of the nicest people I've ever met,' she told him. 'With the hottest accent in the world.'

'Jeez, and there I thought I had you spellbound by my witty conversation.'

'That too,' she said with a grin.

'I'll miss you when you go back,' said Ryan. 'You were one of the best clients I ever had.'

'Maybe not the most profitable.'

'It wasn't about the money,' said Ryan.

'For a case that they wanted to be all about the money, the two of us are hopeless!' Abbey sat back, an amused expression on her face. 'I was thinking earlier that I got more out of it than money, in the end. I got to know the female Fitzpatricks, and I think we might stay in touch. That definitely wouldn't have happened if me and Mom had taken the house.'

'You think it was worth it?' he asked. 'To be friends with people who – well, Lisette and Zoey had their eye on Fred's stuff for a long time.'

'They expected to get it and I won't blame them for that,' she said. 'Anyway, Mom and Suzanne kinda clicked, which was nice. Plus she's invited me back to Spain, and she'll visit the States later in the year. She worked in San Francisco for a while, you know. Just think – I might even have bumped into her in the street and not known who she was. I do feel like she's family to me. Which was definitely worth it, because I didn't have anyone before.'

'I think she would've been quite happy for you to have the house.'

'Perhaps. But Donald and Gareth wouldn't and that would've widened the split between them. It's not right that the three of them should resent each other. Anyhow, Gareth and Lisette's marriage is under huge stress, and if they'd lost the case I think it would have been a hammer blow for them. As it is . . . well, I have my fingers crossed. If everyone comes out intact, it's definitely been worth it.'

'You care that much?'

'I think I do,' she said.

'You're amazing,' said Ryan.

'Don't say that – with your accent I believe every single thing you say.'

He laughed. 'So what's next for you, Abbey Andersen?'

'Well, you know about my burgeoning nail artist career, and hopefully I'll make a success of that. But I plan to do other things too. As well as travelling more, I want to get back into painting again. I know I'll never be world famous, but that's not important. It makes me happy.' She told him of her idea to paint snow-covered Californian landmarks and he nodded his approval.

'I'd like to keep in touch with you too,' he said. 'I mean, I know it's difficult for it to become anything more than it is now, with the distance between us and everything. But if we can stay friends . . . I'd like that.'

'Me too,' said Abbey. 'Besides, maybe you'll be sent to the States again sometime.'

'Sadly, I doubt it. You were my coolest ever assignment.'

'Perhaps you can come on vacation. Visit me.'

'Definitely. I'd like to trek down to Los Montesinos one day. See where your mom lives.'

'I'm sure she'd like that too. Anyway, it's easy to stay friends no matter where you are in the world these days.'

'Which is a really good thing,' he said. 'Now that I've found an American cailín, I'm in no rush to let her go.'

He took them to the airport the next morning and he kissed Abbey goodbye, another gentle meeting of their lips, in full view of Ellen.

'You like him?' she said when they were sitting in the lounge.

'Sure I do. But we're only talking about being friends. Anything else is expecting too much.' Nevertheless, Abbey was reliving the kiss, thinking that she'd felt more from the pressure of Ryan's lips than she ever had with Cobey, and wondering how soon it would be before she saw him again.

'I'll pray,' said Ellen, which made Abbey give her an extra hard hug.

She hugged her extra hard the following day too, when Ellen, now dressed again in her coffee-coloured skirt and white blouse, checked in for her San Diego flight.

'It was great having you back,' Abbey told her.

'It was good to be back.' Ellen sighed. 'I know now why they make us go through so much before making our vows. And why we rarely leave the monastery. It's hard to say goodbye to the people you love. Especially knowing that you won't see them or talk to them for a long time.'

'But you love the sisters,' said Abbey. 'And you have this thing going with God . . .'

Ellen smiled. 'I know. But it's not the same as loving your own daughter. The last few days were full-on, though. We couldn't live like that all the time.'

'No, we couldn't,' agreed Abbey. 'All the same – if you ever want to leave . . . not that I'm trying to influence you at all . . .'

'I'll ask for guidance,' said Ellen. 'That I do the right thing for the right reason. Like you did.'

'Oh, you prayed for that to happen, did you?'

'Not a bit,' said Ellen. 'Only that you'd be comfortable with the choices you made. Which I hope you are.'

'Yes, I am,' said Abbey. 'And I want you to be too. So if prayer means you come up with something new – we can work that out. I can't help sensing, though, that you'll feel like you're at home again when you get back to Los Montesinos.'

'I like that you're not trying to pressure me one way or the other,' said Ellen.

'Nobody could pressure you, Mom,' said Abbey. 'Same as nobody pressured me either. We're strong women, both of us.'

They hugged again. And then Ellen picked up her bag and walked through the gate to board her flight home.

Chapter 39

A couple of weeks later, Solí and Vanessa came to Abbey's apartment for a nail-care evening. Her friends brought food and wine and she did their nails in return. It was the first opportunity she'd had to fill them in fully on the details of her visit to Ireland.

'So, bottom line is you got nothing out of it, but you don't care because your career as a nail technician – or should I say artist – is romping along, you've more than doubled your earnings over the last month, you won another prize in a competition, and you've got a great rental on the apartment from Pete,' said Vanessa as she looked at her vibrant red nails, each now adorned with a tiny diamanté stone. 'I applaud your generosity, but, quite frankly, I think you're off your head. You should have stuffed them for whatever you could.'

'And I'm not sure that your bonus long-distance relationship with the hunky lawyer is adequate compensation,' added Solí, whose own nail art was a funky design in green and gold.

'Oh, look, I still ask myself from time to time if I did the right thing,' admitted Abbey. 'But deep down I think I did. Besides, it's nice to have some sort of family in the background, no matter how far away they are. I'm keeping in touch with them and I'll be visiting Suzanne before she opens her hotel to give advice on the nail bar. I'm looking at some exclusive designs for her.'

'So all's well that ends well,' said Vanessa. 'Except that you're not a millionairess and you could have been.'

'Which would have been nice,' agreed Abbey. 'But I'm doing so much better than I was, and that's worth more to me than anything.'

'Was it totally weird?' asked Solí. 'Going into court. Seeing all those judges and stuff in wigs – I mean, wigs!'

'They're not obligatory,' said Abbey. 'The judge in our court didn't have one. Not that I can remember much about it, because I was in a complete spin at the time. But you're right, that whole part of it was weird. Other parts, like spending time with my mom, weren't.'

'She's still at the monastery?'

'Yes,' replied Abbey. 'Despite her minor wobble, I think she'll stay there. Going to Ireland took her out of her comfort zone, but I honestly think that Los Montesinos is home for her.'

'You always swore that you'd had enough travelling, and yet you ended up flitting across the Atlantic twice and you intend to do it again – both to visit Suzanne and to go to the Nailympics,' Vanessa pointed out. 'So she could change too.'

'Possibly.' Abbey grinned. 'I'm not holding out for that, though. Anyway, right now I'm happy with my lot. At least I will be after you pour me another of those excellent mojitos.'

'Coming right up,' said Vanessa.

The three girls clinked their glasses together. Vanessa started to tell the other two about her new boss at the bank (all talk, no action), while Solí reminded them that they had to come to the exhibition of landscapes that the gallery was putting on soon, and which included three of Solí's own works.

'Of course we're coming,' said Abbey. 'I think it's great that they're finally recognising your talent.'

'One day we'll include paintings by you,' said Solí. 'You need to build up a body of work.'

'I'll never be as good as you, but I've been experimenting.' Abbey crossed the room and brought back a canvas to show her friend. '*Snow on Alcatraz.*'

'Oh Abbey, it's amazing!' Solí looked at the almost monochrome painting, in which Abbey had depicted high drifts of snow against the starkness of the prison building. 'It's really unusual.'

'I got the idea in Dublin,' Abbey explained. 'I want to pick out Californian landmarks and paint them in the snow.'

'Maybe this will be your exhibition.'

'Maybe. Maybe not,' said Abbey. 'I can always try selling some down at the Pier, see how it goes.'

'Well, show them to me when you've got them done. Although you should put them on your walls. They're still remarkably bare.' Solí looked around the apartment.

'I know. I know. I keep meaning to do some more home decorating, but I guess I was a bit reticent about it until the whole Irish situation was resolved. And the situation with Pete, too.'

'He's OK with letting this place to you?' asked Vanessa.

'Yes, it's all worked out perfectly. He has other properties in town, you know, so it's all being looked after by the rental company now. Which I'm happy about. Keeps it on a business footing, although to be fair to Pete, he's giving me a slam-dunk deal on the rental, even though I told him I didn't want any favours.'

'He's a great guy,' said Vanessa.

'I'm lucky to have him in my life,' agreed Abbey. She turned slightly. 'What are you doing, Solí?'

Her friend was looking through the other paintings that Abbey had left in the corner of the room.

'Oh, checking on your old work too. But this isn't one of yours, is it?' She held up the painting that Lisette and Zoey had given her. Abbey had taken it out of the rather ornate and old-fashioned gilt frame it had been in because it would have been far too much trouble to bring it home that way. So now it was loose among the rest of her paintings.

'God, no.' She explained the gift from the Fitzpatrick women. 'I took it because they were clearly so guilty about having raided his safe that they needed me to accept something.'

'It was in his office?' Solí was studying it as she spoke.

'It's odd that they picked it for me,' said Abbey. 'The wall was completely covered in photos and prints and paintings. But that one caught my eye when I was giving him CPR. I kept looking at it, telling Fred to be strong like the rock. And I felt comforted by it too. I like the way the sunlight hits the stone. Reminds me of Alcatraz. Made me feel at home.'

'Did they say anything about it?' asked Solí.

'Like what?' By now, Abbey detected an undercurrent in her friend's voice.

'Where he got it?'

'No.'

'It's just . . .' Solí's eyes were narrowed as she looked even more closely at it. 'It's not in the greatest condition, I guess. But you know we studied Irish art in college?'

'Hey, one class,' Abbey reminded her. 'And the only painter I remember was Francis Bacon, because we used to have similar ones in the Geary Street gallery. Probably half the reason I stopped working there – they used to freak me out so much.'

'Not the sort of thing you want hanging at the end of your bed,' agreed Solí. 'This is different. Not a Bacon, sadly, because they go for millions these days.'

'D'you recognise the painter?' asked Abbey.

'I think so,' replied Solí. 'I think this was painted by Jack Yeats.'

Abbey frowned. 'Jack Yeats? *The* Jack Yeats? The brother of that Irish poet?'

'W. B. Yeats was the poet, Jack was the painter,' Solí reminded her. 'Look at the brushwork here. And here. And . . .' she grinned as she indicated the corner of the painting, 'there is, of course, the signature.'

Abbey examined the painting. 'I didn't recognise it as a Yeats on the wall,' she said doubtfully. 'But then, I probably wouldn't. D'you really think it's him?'

'It could be,' said Solí. 'Certainly worth checking out.'

'Is it valuable?' asked Vanessa.

'That depends,' replied Solí. 'Some of his paintings have sold for forty or fifty thousand.'

'Seriously?' Abbey was impressed.

'But one of them went for over a million.'

Abbey and Vanessa stared at her.

'It was a much bigger painting, and in the height of a craze, so . . .' Solí shrugged. 'I wouldn't get my hopes up, but you might still get a reasonable five-figure sum for this, Abbey. Maybe even a bit more if it's a good day.'

'Oh my God!' Vanessa looked at Abbey, her eyes sparkling with excitement. 'You could be rich after all.'

Abbey continued to stare at the painting, at the sea and the rock that had reminded her of home. She didn't say a word. There were none to express the tangled emotions that were running through her.

She called Lisette and asked if there had been a special reason why she and Zoey had chosen that particular painting to give her.

'No,' Lisette had replied. 'It was one he liked and so we thought it would be a bit more meaningful for you. He said that his father had been given it instead of payment by a friend of his back in the nineteen thirties. His father was a farmhand, from Sligo,' Lisette added.

'Was he given any more?' asked Abbey.

'I don't know,' replied Lisette. 'We're going through Fred's things now.'

'Well go through them carefully,' Abbey told her. 'Because this painting might be valuable, and perhaps there are others.'

Lisette and Zoey immediately engaged an expert to look at Fred's pictures, but there were no more Yeatses among them, although he reckoned that some of the paintings by lesser-known artists could fetch a few thousand euros.

'I guess you might feel a bit sore about giving me this one,' said Abbey, when Lisette rang her with the news.

'To be truthful, Donald and Gareth were furious when they found out,' confessed Lisette. 'But Abbey, you gave us back so much, you deserve it. They'll come round eventually, I hope.'

'Are things still difficult between you and Gareth?' asked Abbey.

'It's hard for everybody,' replied Lisette. 'Donald is trying to put a deal together so that he can buy the house. He wants it and so does Zoey. But it all depends on him selling his own and – well, Gareth and I need our money quickly, so there are still some obstacles to overcome. On the plus side, Zoey went shopping with Karen and Sorcha the other day and nearly melted Donald's credit card. But he was so pleased that they'd been out together that he didn't say a word. Gar and I seem to be getting back on track with each other again, too. He's actually . . . he's a bit ashamed of how manic he was about everything, which is why I'm pretty sure he's not going to want to pursue the issue of the painting. So hopefully we can work things out in the end. And at least we're not being pressurised by Suzanne. She emailed me the other day. She thinks the hotel will be open ahead of schedule.'

'I know, she emailed me too,' said Abbey. 'And I'm sure everything will work out for you guys.'

'Funny thing – I've talked to Suzanne more in the last few weeks than in all the years I've been married to Gareth. She's good fun, has a different perspective to the boys. It's refreshing. Zoey and I have become really firm friends too, which I never would've thought.'

'Perhaps one day we can all get together again,' said Abbey. 'In Fred's house. With everything sorted.'

'I'm afraid that could be a few years away yet,' said Lisette. 'At least as far as Don and Gar are concerned. But it would be nice if the female members of the family could meet up again. Maybe your mother could come too?'

Abbey wasn't sure. She hadn't spoken to Ellen since she'd returned to Los Montesinos, and although she knew that her mother hadn't yet made her final profession, she couldn't help

431

feeling that she had settled back quite happily into the community of sisters. But for the first time in her life, she didn't resent it. She wanted Ellen to be happy and content no matter where she was. Because the truth was that she was happy and content herself. Suddenly her life seemed to be moving along on an even keel. She was enjoying her work, her social life was good, and she didn't have the nagging feeling that there was something missing any more. Cobey Missen had gone to LA, hoping to take part in a reality TV show. He hadn't tried to reach her before he left and Abbey was relieved that he'd gone. Although if he'd hung round a little longer, she thought, the whole thing might have started again, because he'd have found out about the painting, and knowing him, he'd have been ready to advise her on how to maximise her cut from that too.

Part of Abbey wanted to keep Fred's painting, but the idea of having something of potential value in her apartment worried her. Besides, a painting by a famous artist needed to be kept in a more controlled environment, with a steady temperature, to maintain it in good condition. Admittedly Fred's study hadn't been ideal, but Abbey felt it had been better than anything she could provide. So in the end, she decided that selling it was the best thing to do. She had to admit that her motives weren't entirely down to the fact that she wanted what was best for the painting. The idea of a tidy five-figure sum was an appealing one too.

She'd been to lots of auctions, particularly when she'd worked part time at the gallery, but she'd never been a seller at one before. Not a run-of-the-mill seller either – at today's auction, taking place in New York, the main interest was the painting titled *Sligo Rock* by Jack Yeats. As she sat in her seat and waited for it to come under the hammer, she read the catalogue description over and over again.

Sligo Rock, *painted in or around 1930, is loosely impressionist while conveying an enduring strength. It is a signature work by a much-loved Irish artist.*

Pete had pointed to the words 'signature work' and murmured that they should add another few thousand dollars to the price. 'I was so mad at you when you passed up that house,' he said. 'And I'm still mad because there's no way this painting can make up for it. But at least you struck lucky with it. At least they didn't give you one of the photos of the old cars.'

'I'll ask for one to replace this,' Abbey murmured. 'I need to have something to remember my grandfather by.'

'Perhaps you can buy yourself a nice piece of jewellery,' suggested Pete. 'You'd remember him every time you wore it.'

'There's a thought,' said Abbey. 'Most of my jewellery is from handicraft stalls. I've never had an expensive piece before.'

'Of course the Yeats mightn't even reach the reserve,' Pete warned her as they listened to Lot 45, a small painting by a little-known painter, sell for five thousand dollars. 'These things are unpredictable.'

The auction house had set the reserve at fifty thousand. As far as she was concerned, fifty thousand dollars was a windfall for a painting that she hadn't expected to be worth more than a senti-mental value, but she knew that Pete would be devastated if it didn't make more than that. Given the fact that she'd disappointed him over the house and left him as the owner of the apartment, she didn't want him to feel gutted over the Yeats, even if he was being over-optimistic.

'Hello, Abbey.'

She looked around in astonishment, and a wide beam broke out on her face. Sliding into the empty seat on her right was Ryan Gilligan.

'What on earth are you doing here?' she asked.

'I wanted to surprise you,' he said. 'That's why I didn't say I was coming over. But the flight was late and I came straight from the airport. I thought I'd miss the auction.'

'We're up next,' she said. 'I'm terrified.'

'Don't be.' He took her hand in his. 'Like you said to me a hundred times, it's only money.'

It was evident that many people in the room had been waiting for the appearance of *Sligo Rock*. And it was evident, too, that the painter was more skilled than the others that had come before him. There was a vibrancy and a strength in the work that had been absent in all of the others. Abbey's fingers tightened around Ryan's. On her other side, Pete took her left hand in his. The three of them sat joined together as the auctioneer began to speak.

The opening bid was below the reserve price, and Abbey felt a stab of disappointment. It wasn't entirely for the money, she realised; it was because she wanted other people, people who could afford it, to like *Sligo Rock* as much as she did. She wanted them to want it. She wanted to think that it would go to someone who cared.

And then the bids began to creep up. They reached the reserve and went higher. And higher again. And then the auctioneer said 'a hundred thousand dollars' and Abbey held her breath. This was it. Pete's secretly hoped-for price.

'One hundred and twenty.'

She was startled as she became aware that the bids were continuing.

'One hundred and fifty.'

She realised that she was squeezing both Pete and Ryan's hands ever more tightly.

'Two hundred thousand dollars.'

Abbey gasped. So did Pete, but that was because she'd grasped his hand so tightly she'd almost broken it.

'Two hundred and ten.'

There was a buzz around the room now.

'Two hundred and twenty-five.'

'Two hundred and fifty.'

Abbey was hearing the numbers but hardly able to comprehend them.

'Three hundred thousand dollars.'

It was slowing down now. She was almost relieved. Three

hundred thousand dollars was more than she'd ever dreamed of. She remembered looking at the painting as she'd willed Fred's heart to start beating again, urging him to be strong.

'Three hundred and twenty. Fifty. Seventy.'

Abbey blinked rapidly. She looked at the monitor on the wall to check that she was hearing correctly. The figures were displayed in red.

'Four hundred thousand dollars.'

Now it was Pete who was squeezing her hand, and she realised that she was forgetting to breathe again. She inhaled slowly, through her nose.

'Four hundred and twenty. Thirty. Forty. Fifty. Four hundred and fifty thousand dollars. All done?'

That had to be it, surely, thought Abbey. There was no way anyone would pay more for her painting, no matter how beautiful.

'Five hundred thousand dollars.'

There was an excited hum around the auction room. The auctioneer looked to left and right. But this time there were no further bids.

'Sold,' he said. 'For five hundred thousand dollars to the telephone bidder.'

There was a round of applause, and Abbey realised that tears were streaming down her cheeks.

'Congratulations!' whispered Ryan.

'Tremendous!' whooped Pete. 'This is celebration time.'

As they left the room, Abbey said that she wanted to go outside for a moment.

'Are you OK?' asked Ryan.

'I'm good,' she said. 'I just need a minute to myself.'

She walked out of the door and stood in a shaft of cool sunshine. She realised that she was shaking. A few months ago she'd been broke, dumped and uncertain of her future. Now she was worth half a million dollars, was working on paintings of her own and was constantly in demand as a nail artist. She'd lost the house and yet Fred's legacy had worked out for her after all.

She turned as she heard footsteps approaching her.

'Sure you're all right?' asked Ryan.

And she had Ryan too, she realised. However that might work out in the future, he was here with her now.

'Yes. It was all a bit . . . a bit overwhelming for a moment.'

'I know.' He smiled at her.

'Thanks for everything,' she said.

'You're welcome.' He put his arm around her. 'You need to come back inside now. There's papers and stuff to go through, and Pete wants to make sure you sign on the dotted line.'

She texted Lisette, Zoey and Suzanne with the news of the sale price, because they had all asked to be told. Each one of them sent back a congratulatory text. And she knew they meant it.

Pete had arranged a celebration meal at Delmonico's and invited Ryan to come along too. Abbey, thrilled to be in an iconic restaurant, ordered steak without first checking the price on the menu as she once would have done, and as she knew she'd do again when she came back to earth. Pete called for champagne and she told him that she could get used to the millionaire lifestyle, so maybe it was a good thing that the painting hadn't gone over the half-million mark as Pete had secretly hoped it might.

'It was still an outstanding bid,' said Ryan.

'Just think, though,' said Pete. 'If you'd stuck to your guns, you would've got the house *and* the painting.'

'In that case I might never have found out the true worth of the painting,' Abbey pointed out. 'And now that I know the bidder is donating it to a gallery, I'm even more pleased. This way it's out there in the art world and hopefully it'll be appreciated.'

'I think you did exactly the right thing,' Ryan said. 'You acted with your heart and not your head.'

'You're kidding me, right?' Pete looked at him. 'You're a lawyer and you're saying that?'

'I'll be drummed out of the profession,' agreed Ryan. 'But as Abbey is an artist in everything she does, I think it's right she acts with her heart.'

'She always did.' Pete turned to her. 'And I love her for it.'

'I love her for it too,' said Ryan, which caused Pete to whistle nonchalantly as he looked at both of them.

'And I love both of you,' said Abbey. 'Now pour me some more of that champagne, Pete. Tonight I'm being Cinderella and I don't want my feet to touch the ground.'

At nine o'clock, Pete said that he had to return to the hotel. He had some business matters to take care of, he told them, and he wanted to call Claudia.

'Give her my love,' said Abbey. 'And tell her thanks.'

'What for?' asked Pete.

'For being there,' Abbey said. 'Even though sometimes she mightn't have wanted to be.'

'All she ever wanted, and all I wanted too, was for you to be able to stand on your own two feet,' he said.

'And now I am,' said Abbey.

'And you've other people to support you.'

'Oh, Pete.' Abbey stood up and hugged him. 'You'll always be my biggest, my best support. Always.'

'Take care, honey,' he said. 'And take care of her,' he added to Ryan.

'He's a good man,' said Ryan as Pete left the restaurant.

'Most people *are* good.' Abbey sat down again. 'Most people want to do the right thing by each other. Only sometimes we don't know how.'

'And you do?'

'I have an excellent teacher in my mom. But I don't always get it right and I'm not some kind of saint.' Her eyes twinkled. 'Tell you something, if you come back to my hotel, I'll show you just how unsaintly I can be.'

'Abbey Andersen!' Ryan looked at her in mock horror. 'I'm just a poor guy from Ireland. Which, I'll remind you, is the island of saints and scholars. I'm not sure I could cope with you being unsaintly.'

'I bet my bottom dollar you could,' said Abbey.

'Are we now in a proper long-distance relationship?' asked Ryan. 'Because that's going to be tough.'

'I've been through tough,' Abbey told him. 'And I don't mind what sort of relationship we have in the future. Because for tonight – tonight it's grand.'

She leaned across the table and kissed him. And as he led her back to the hotel later, she knew that whatever else happened between them was going to be absolutely grand too.

Chapter 40

Tipperary, Ireland: 55 years ago

Dilly could hear the cries of her newborn baby. More than anything she wanted to get out of bed and comfort her. But she was too sore to move. Every bone in her body ached. Every part of her body hurt. She remembered the sting of the leather belt as it crossed her shoulders. She remembered the jolting pain as she slipped and fell on the tiled floor. She remembered the sudden tearing sensation in her stomach and the terror she felt as she knew that her baby was coming. She remembered blood. She remembered being half dragged, half carried to the infirmary.

There had been urgent whispers, commands, arguments. To her. At her. About her. That part was a blur. She didn't remember if she'd answered. If she'd said anything at all. But she remembered hearing her baby cry. And she recognised that cry now.

She tried to move, and the pain shot through her again. She groaned softly. She had to get up. She had to. She swung her legs over the side of the bed and her feet touched the cold tiles of the floor. She walked slowly and unsteadily out of her room and across the narrow corridor. The cries of her baby were louder now.

'Mother of God, child, what are you doing!'

The nun was like a black shadow emerging from the walls of the building. She hurried over to where Dilly was crouched by the crib, her fingers pressed hard against the side of it.

'She was crying,' she said. 'She needed me.'

'You're in no fit state to be out of bed,' said the nun. 'I'll look after the baby.'

'No,' said Dilly. 'She's mine.'

'I know that.' The nun's voice was soft, far gentler than Dilly was used to. It surprised her. 'I know she's yours.'

'I have to take care of her,' said Dilly. 'I love her.'

'Of course you do,' said the nun. 'But right now you need to get back into bed. You've lost a lot of blood, you know. You're very weak.'

'I have to be strong,' said Dilly. 'For my baby. I have to look out for her. I have to care for her.'

She closed her eyes as a wave of dizziness engulfed her.

'The best you can do for her now is to get back into bed,' said the nun gently.

'I won't leave her.' Dilly could feel the tears in her eyes. 'She needs me. She's my daughter.'

'I'll bring her to you. Come on, now, Ita. Come on.'

She didn't believe the nun. She never believed them. But she was powerless to do anything about it. Her eyes blurred and she moaned softly. Then she felt the nun's arms around her, gently lifting her and supporting her so that she could walk back to the infirmary. She felt secure in her hold, unthreatened and unafraid. She hadn't realised that there were nuns like her. Not here.

'Now,' said the nun. 'Back into bed with you.'

She was being so kind, thought Dilly. It was nice to have kind ones.

Her head was spinning and her vision blurred again. It was hard to stay focused, hard to stay alert. But she had to be alert because the nun was bringing her baby. She wanted to see her baby. To tell her how much she loved her.

'Here you are.'

She felt the warmth of her daughter against her chest and looked down at her. She blinked rapidly until she could see the baby's creamy skin, her tuft of hair and her startlingly blue eyes.

'Oh,' said Dilly. 'She's beautiful.'

'Of course she is. She takes after you.' The nun looked at both of them. Dilly saw that her eyes were blue too. Not as beautiful as her daughter's eyes. But blue. And compassionate.

'You're not Sister Anthony,' she said, realising for the first time that this nun was younger than the one that all the girls feared.

'No,' she said. 'I'm only here for a few days. I'm Sister Benita.'

'Benita,' whispered Dilly. 'That's a nice name.'

She closed her eyes, still holding the baby.

Sister Benita kissed her gently on the forehead.

'You're a good mother,' she said. 'I'll keep you and your child in my prayers.'

Two weeks later, Sister Benita cradled the baby girl gently in her arms as she walked into the visitors' room. The couple sitting on the hard wooden chairs looked up eagerly, hope in their eyes.

'Mr and Mrs Connolly,' said Sister Benita. 'This is your daughter. Take good care of her. She was loved very much indeed. She deserves all the love you can give.'

'Oh.' Mamie Connolly took the baby and kissed her softly on the cheek. 'Oh, Ellen. It's so good to have you at last. Come on, it's time to bring you home.'

EUROPEAN UNION LAW
Third Edition

Alina Kaczorowska

Routledge
Taylor & Francis Group

LONDON AND NEW YORK

Third edition published 2013
by Routledge
2 Park Square, Milton Park, Abingdon, Oxon OX14 4RN

Simultaneously published in the USA and Canada
by Routledge
711 Third Avenue, New York, NY 10017

Routledge is an imprint of the Taylor & Francis Group, an informa business

© 2013 Alina Kaczorowska

First edition published by Routledge-Cavendish 2009
Second edition published by Routledge 2011

British Library Cataloguing in Publication Data
A catalogue record for this book is available from the British Library

Library of Congress Cataloging in Publication Data
Kaczorowska, Alina.
European Union law / Alina Kaczorowska.
   p. cm.
ISBN-13: 978-0-415-44797-3 (pbk)
ISBN-10: 0-415-44797-6 (pbk)
1. Law—European Union countries.   2. European Union.   I. Title.
KJE947.K333 2008
341.242'2—dc22   2008004117

ISBN: 978-0-415-69597-8 (hbk)
ISBN: 978-0-415-69598-5 (pbk)
ISBN: 978-0-203-59786-6 (ebk)

Typeset in Times New Roman
by RefineCatch Ltd, Bungay, Suffolk

Printed and bound by CPI Group (UK) Ltd, Croydon, CR0 4YY